About the Authors

...dy has been a bookworm since she was a ...When she isn't writing Kate enjoys reading, ...live music, ballet and the gym. She lives with ...sband, student children and their spaniel in ...h, England. You can contact her via her website: ...atehardy.com

...e Mortimer was born in England, the youngest of ...children. She began writing in 1978, and has now ...n over one hundred and seventy books for Mills ...oon. Carole has six sons, Matthew, Joshua, Timothy, ...el, David and Peter. She says, 'I'm happily married ...r senior; we're best friends as well as lovers, which ...bably the best recipe for a successful relationship. ...ve in a lovely part of England.'

...ed with a poor sense of direction and a propensity ...ad, **Annie Claydon** spent much of her childhood ...n books. A degree in English Literature followed ...career in computing didn't lead directly to her ...ect job—writing romance for Mills & Boon—but ...has no regrets in taking the scenic route. She lives ...ondon: a city where getting lost can be a joy.

With Love From

COLLECTION

With Love From London

KATE HARDY

CAROLE MORTIMER

ANNIE CLAYDON

Paper from
responsible sources

FSC

FSC C007454

This book is produced from independently certified FSC™ paper
to ensure responsible forest management.

For more information visit: www.harpercollins.co.uk/green

Printed and bound in Spain
by CPI, Barcelona

MILLS & BOON

First Published in Great Britain 2020
By Mills & Boon, an imprint of HarperCollins*Publishers*
1 London Bridge Street, London, SE1 9GF

WITH LOVE FROM LONDON © 2020 Harlequin Books S.A.

Falling for the Secret Millionaire © 2016 Pamela Brooks
At the Ruthless Billionaire's Command © 2017 Carole Mortimer
Doctor on Her Doorstep © 2012 Annie Claydon

ISBN: 978-0-263-28160-6

™

MIX

FALLING FOR THE SECRET MILLIONAIRE

KATE HARDY

For my friend Sherry Lane, with love (and thanks for not minding me sneaking research stuff into our trips out with the girls!) xxx

CHAPTER ONE

'ARE YOU ALL RIGHT, Miss Thomas?' the lawyer asked.

'Fine, thank you,' Nicole fibbed. She was still trying to get her head round the news. The grandfather she'd never met—the man who'd thrown her mother out on the street when he'd discovered that she was pregnant with Nicole and the father had no intention of marrying her— had died and left Nicole a cinema in his will.

A run-down cinema, from the sounds of it; the solicitor had told her that the place had been closed for the last five years. But, instead of leaving the place to benefit a charity or someone in the family he was still speaking to, Brian Thomas had left the cinema to her: to the grandchild he'd rejected before she'd even been born.

Why?

Guilt, because he knew he'd behaved badly and should've been much more supportive to his only daughter? But, if he'd wanted to make amends, surely he would've left the cinema to Nicole's mother? Or was this his way to try to drive a wedge between Susan and Nicole?

Nicole shook herself. Clearly she'd been working in banking for too long, to be this cynical about a stranger's motivations.

'It's actually not that far from where you live,' the solicitor continued. 'It's in Surrey Quays.'

Suddenly Nicole knew exactly what and where the cinema was. 'You mean the old Electric Palace on Mortimer Gardens?'

'You know it?' He looked surprised.

'I walk past it every day on my way to work,' she said. In the three years she'd been living in Surrey Quays, she'd always thought the old cinema a gorgeous building, and it was a shame that the place was neglected and boarded up. She hadn't had a clue that the cinema had any connection with her at all. Though there was a local history thread in the Surrey Quays forum—the local community website she'd joined when she'd first moved to her flat in Docklands—which included several posts about the Electric Palace's past. Someone had suggested setting up a volunteer group to get the cinema back up and running again, except nobody knew who owned it.

Nicole had the answer to that now. She was the new owner of the Electric Palace. And it was the last thing she'd ever expected.

'So you know what you're taking on, then,' the solicitor said brightly.

Taking on? She hadn't even decided whether to accept the bequest yet, let alone what she was going to do with it.

'Or,' the solicitor continued, 'if you don't want to take it on, there is another option. A local development company has been in touch with us, expressing interest in buying the site, should you wish to sell. It's a fair offer.'

'I need a little time to think this through before I make any decisions,' Nicole said.

'Of course, Miss Thomas. That's very sensible.'

Nicole smiled politely, though she itched to remind the solicitor that she was twenty-eight years old, not eight.

She wasn't a naive schoolgirl, either: she'd worked her way up from the bottom rung of the ladder to become a manager in an investment bank. Sensible was her default setting. Was it not obvious from her tailored business suit and low-heeled shoes, and in the way she wore her hair pinned back for work?

'Now, the keys.' He handed her a bunch of ancient-looking keys. 'We will of course need time to alter the deeds, should you decide to keep it. Otherwise we can handle the conveyancing of the property, should you decide to sell to the developer or to someone else. We'll wait for your instructions.'

'Thank you,' Nicole said, sliding the keys into her handbag. She still couldn't quite believe she owned the Electric Palace.

'Thank you for coming in to see us,' the solicitor continued. 'We'll be in touch with the paperwork.'

She nodded. 'Thank you. I'll call you if there's anything I'm unsure about when I get it.'

'Good, good.' He gave her another of those avuncular smiles.

As soon as Nicole had left the office, she grabbed her phone from her bag and called her mother—the one person she really needed to talk to about the bequest. But the call went straight through to Susan's voicemail. Then again, at this time of day her mother would be in a meeting or with one of her probationers. Nicole's best friend Jessie, an English teacher, was knee-deep in exam revision sessions with her students, so she wouldn't be free to talk to Nicole about the situation until the end of the day. And Nicole definitely didn't want to discuss this with anyone from work; she knew they'd all tell her to sell the place to the company who wanted to buy it, for the highest price she could get, and to keep the money.

Her head was spinning. Maybe she would sell the cinema—after all, what did she know about running a cinema, let alone one that hadn't been in operation for the last five years and looked as if it needed an awful lot of work doing to it before it could open its doors again? But, if she did sell the Electric Palace, she had no intention of keeping the money. As far as she was concerned, any money from Brian Thomas ought to go to his daughter, not skip a generation. Susan Thomas had spent years struggling as a single mother, working three jobs to pay the rent when Nicole was tiny. If the developer really was offering a fair price, it could give Susan the money to pay off her mortgage, go on a good holiday and buy a new car. Though Nicole knew she'd have to work hard to convince her mother that she deserved the money; plus Susan might be even more loath to accept anything from her father on the grounds that it was way too late.

Or Nicole could refuse the bequest on principle. Brian Thomas had never been part of her life or shown any interest in her. Why should she be interested in his money now?

She sighed. What she really needed right now was some decent caffeine and the space to talk this through with someone. There was only one person other than her mother and Jessie whose advice she trusted. Would he be around? She found the nearest coffee shop, ordered her usual double espresso, then settled down at a quiet table and flicked into the messaging program on her phone. Clarence was probably busy, but then again if she'd caught him on his lunch break he might have time to talk.

In the six months since they'd first met on the Surrey Quays forum, they'd become close and they talked online every day. They'd never actually met in person;

and, right from the first time he'd sent her a private message, they'd agreed that they wouldn't share personal details that identified them, so they'd stuck to their forum names of Georgygirl and Clarence. She had no idea what he even looked like—she could have passed him in the street at any time during the three years she'd been living at Surrey Quays. In some ways it was a kind of coded, secret relationship, but at the same time Nicole felt that Clarence knew the real her. Not the corporate ghost who spent way too many hours in the office, or the much-loved daughter and best friend who was always nagged about working too hard, but the *real* Nicole. He knew the one who wondered about the universe and dreamed of the stars. Late at night, she'd told him things she'd never told anyone else, even her mother or Jessie.

Maybe Clarence could help her work out the right thing to do.

She typed a message and mentally crossed her fingers as she sent it.

Hey, Clarence, you around?

Gabriel Hunter closed his father's office door behind him and walked down the corridor as if he didn't have a care in the world.

What he really wanted to do was to beat his fists against the walls in sheer frustration. When, when, *when* was he going to stop paying for his teenage mistake?

OK, so it had been an awful lot worse than the usual teenage mistakes—he'd crashed his car into a shop front one night on the way home from a party and done a lot of damage. But nobody had been physically hurt and he'd learned his lesson immediately. He'd stopped going round with the crowd who'd thought it would be fun to spike his drink when he was their designated driver. He'd knuckled down to his studies instead of spending most of his time partying, and at the end of his final exams he'd got one of the highest Firsts the university had ever awarded. Since then, he'd proved his worth over and over again in the family business. Time after time he'd bitten his tongue so he didn't get into a row with his father. He'd toed the party line. Done what was expected of him, constantly repented for his sins to atone in his father's eyes.

And his father still didn't trust him. All Gabriel ever saw in his father's eyes was 'I saved you from yourself'. Was Evan Hunter only capable of seeing his son as the stupid teenager who got in with a bad crowd? Would he ever see Gabriel for who he was now, all these years later? Would he ever respect his son?

Days like today, Gabriel felt as if he couldn't breathe. Maybe it was time to give up trying to change his family's view of him and to walk away. To take a different direction in his career—though, right at that moment, Gabriel didn't have a clue what that would be, either. He'd spent the last seven years since graduation working hard in the family business and making sure he knew every single detail of Hunter Hotels Ltd. He'd tried so hard to do the right thing. The reckless teenager he'd once been was well and truly squashed—which he knew was a good thing, but part of him wondered what would have happened if he hadn't had the crash. Would he have grown out of the recklessness but kept his freedom? Would he have felt as if he was really worth something, not having to pay over and over for past mistakes? Would he be settled down now, maybe with a family of his own?

All the women he'd dated over the last five years saw him as Gabriel-the-hotel-chain-heir, the rich guy who could show them a good time and splash his cash about, and he hated that superficiality. Yet the less superficial, nicer women were wary of him, because his reputation got in the way; everyone knew that Gabriel Hunter was a former wild child and was now a ruthless company man, so he'd never commit emotionally and there was no point in dating him because there wasn't a future in the relationship. And his family all saw him as Gabe-who-made-the-big-mistake.

How ironic that the only person who really saw him for himself was a stranger. Someone whose real name he didn't even know, let alone what she did or what she looked like, because they'd been careful not to exchange those kinds of details. But over the last six months he'd grown close to Georgygirl from the Surrey Quays forum.

Which made it even more ironic that he'd only joined the website because he was following his father's request to keep an eye out for local disgruntled residents who might oppose the new Hunter Hotel they were developing from a run-down former spice warehouse in Surrey Quays, and charm them into seeing things the Hunter way. Gabriel had discovered that he liked the anonymity of an online persona—he could actually meet people and get to know them, the way he couldn't in real life. The people on the forum didn't know he was Gabriel Hunter, so they had no preconceptions and they accepted him for who he was.

He'd found himself posting on a lot of the same topics as someone called Georgygirl. The more he'd read her posts, the more he'd realised that she was on his wavelength. They'd flirted a bit—because an internet forum was a pretty safe place to flirt—and he hadn't been able to resist contacting her in a private message. Then they'd started chatting to each other away from the forum. They'd agreed to stick to the forum rules of not sharing personal details that would identify themselves, so Gabriel had no idea of Georgygirl's real name or her personal situation; but in their late-night private chats he felt that he could talk to her about anything and everything. Be his real self. Just as he was pretty sure that she was her real self with him.

Right now, it was practically lunchtime. Maybe Georgygirl would be around? He hoped so, because talking to her would make him feel human again. Right now he really needed a dose of her teasing sarcasm to jolt him out of his dark mood.

He informed his PA that he was unavailable for the next hour, then headed out to Surrey Quays. He ordered a double espresso in his favourite café, then grabbed his phone and flicked into the direct messaging section of the Surrey Quays forum.

And then he saw the message waiting for him.

Hey, Clarence, you around?

It was timed fifteen minutes ago. Just about when he'd walked out of that meeting and wanted to punch a wall. Hopefully she hadn't given up waiting for him and was still there. He smiled.

Yeah. I'm here, he typed back.

He sipped his coffee while he waited for her to respond. Just as he thought it was too late and she'd already gone, a message from her popped up on his screen.

Hello, there. How's your day?

I've had better, he admitted. You?

Weird.

Why?

Then he remembered she'd told him that she'd had a letter out of the blue from a solicitor she'd never heard of, asking her to make an appointment because they needed to discuss something with her.

What happened at the solicitor's?

I've been left something in a will.

That's good, isn't it?

Unless it was a really odd bequest, or one with strings.

It's property.

Ah. It was beginning to sound as if there were strings attached. And Gabriel knew without Georgygirl having to tell him that she was upset about it.

Don't tell me—it's a desert island or a ruined castle, but you have to live there for a year all on your own with a massive nest of scary spiders before you can inherit?

Not quite. But thank you for making me laugh.

Meaning that right now she wanted to cry?

What's so bad about it? Is it a total wreck that needs gutting, or it has a roof that eats money?

There was a long pause.

It needs work, but that isn't the bad thing. The bequest is from my grandfather.

Now he understood. The problem wasn't with what she'd been left: it was who'd left it to her that was the sticking point.

How can I accept anything from someone who let my mother down so badly?

She'd confided the situation to him a couple of months ago, when they'd been talking online late at night and drinking wine together—about how her mother had accidentally fallen pregnant, and when her parents had found out that her boyfriend was married, even though her mother hadn't had a clue that he wasn't single when they'd started dating, they had thrown her out on the street instead of supporting her.

Gabriel chafed every day about his own situation, but he knew that his family had always been there for him and had his best interests at heart, even if his father was a control freak who couldn't move on from the past. Georgygirl's story had made him appreciate that for the first time in a long while.

Maybe, he typed back carefully, this is his way of apologising. Even if it is from the grave.

More like trying to buy his way into my good books? Apart from the fact that I can't be bought, he's left it way too late. He let my mum struggle when she was really vulnerable. This feels like thirty pieces of silver. Accepting the bequest means I accept what he—and my grandmother—did. And I *don't*. At all.

He could understand that.

Is your grandmother still alive? Maybe you could go and see her. Explain how you feel. And maybe she can apologise on his behalf as well as her own.

I don't know. But, even if she is alive, I can't see her apologising. What kind of mother chucks her pregnant daughter into the street, Clarence? OK, so they were angry and hurt and shocked at the time—I can understand that. But my mum didn't know that my dad was married or she would never have dated him, much less anything else. And they've had twenty-nine years to get over it. As far as I know, they've never so much as seen a photo of me, let alone cuddled me as a baby or sent me a single birthday card.

And that had to hurt, being rejected by your family when they didn't even know you.

It's their loss, he typed. But maybe they didn't know how to get in touch with your mother.

Surely all you have to do is look up someone in the electoral roll, or even use a private detective if you can't be bothered to do it yourself?

That's not what I meant, Georgy. It's not the finding her that would've been hard—it's breaking the ice and knowing what to say. Sometimes pride gets in the way.

Ironic, because he knew he was guilty of that, too. Not knowing how to challenge his father—because how could you challenge someone when you were always in the wrong?

Maybe. But why leave the property to *me* and not to my mum? It doesn't make sense.

Pride again? **Gabriel** suggested. And maybe he thought it would be easier to approach you.

From the grave?

Could be Y-chromosome logic?

That earned him a smiley face.

Georgy, you really need to talk to your mum about it.

I would. Except her phone is switched to voicemail.

Shame.

I know this is crazy, she added, but you were the one I really wanted to talk to about this. You see things so clearly.

It was the first genuine compliment he'd had in a long time—and it was one he really appreciated.

Thank you. Glad I can be here for you. That's what friends are for.

And they were friends. Even though they'd never met, he felt their relationship was more real and more honest than the ones in his real-life world—where ironically he couldn't be his real self.

I'm sorry for whining.

You're not whining. You've just been left something by the last person you expected to leave you anything. Of course you're going to wonder why. And if it is an apology, you're right that it's too little, too late. He should've patched up the row years ago and been proud of your mum for raising a bright daughter who's also a decent human being.

Careful, Clarence, she warned. I might not be able to get through the door of the coffee shop when I leave, my head's so swollen.

Coffee shop? Even though he knew it was ridiculous—this wasn't the only coffee shop in Surrey Quays, and he had no idea where she worked so she could be anywhere in London right now—Gabriel found himself pausing and glancing round the room, just in case she was there.

But everyone in the room was either sitting in a group, chatting animatedly, or looked like a businessman catching up with admin work.

There was always the chance that Georgygirl was a man, but he didn't think so. He didn't think she was a bored, middle-aged housewife posing as a younger woman, either. And she'd just let slip that her newly pregnant mother had been thrown out twenty-nine years ago, which would make her around twenty-eight. His own age.

I might not be able to get through the door of the coffee shop, my head's so swollen.

Ha. This was the teasing, quick-witted Georgygirl that had attracted him in the first place. He smiled.

We need deflationary measures, then. OK. You need a haircut and your roots are showing. And there's a massive spot on your nose. It's like the red spot on Mars. You can see it from outer space.

Jupiter's the one with the red spot, she corrected. But I get the point. Head now normal size. Thank you.

Good.

And he just bet she knew he'd deliberately mixed up his planets. He paused.

Seriously, though—maybe you could sell the property and split the money with your mum.

It still feels like thirty pieces of silver. I was thinking about giving her all of it. Except I'll have to persuade her because she'll say he left it to me.

Or maybe it isn't an apology—maybe it's a rescue.

Rescue? How do you work that out? she asked.

You hate your job.

She'd told him that a while back—and, being in a similar situation, he'd sympathised.

If you split the money from selling the property with your mum, would it be enough to tide you over for a six-month sabbatical? That might give you enough time and space to find out what you really want to do. OK, so your grandfather wasn't there when your mum needed him— but right now it looks to me as if he's given you something that you need at exactly the right time. A chance for independence, even if it's only for a little while.

I never thought of it like that. You could be right.

It is what it is. You could always look at it as a belated apology, which is better than none at all. He wasn't there when he should've been, but he's come good now.

Hmm. It isn't residential property he left me.

It's a business?

Yes. And it hasn't been in operation for a while.

A run-down business, then. Which would take money and time to get it back in working order—the building might need work, and the stock or the fixtures might be well out of date. So he'd been right in the first place and the bequest had come with strings.

Could you get the business back up and running?

Though it would help if he knew what kind of business it actually was. But asking would be breaking the terms of their friendship—because then she'd be sharing personal details.

In theory, I could. Though I don't have any experience in the service or entertainment industry.

He did. He'd grown up in it.
That's my area, he said.
He was taking a tiny risk, telling her something per-

sonal—but she had no reason to connect Clarence with Hunter Hotels.

My advice, for what it's worth—an MBA and working for a very successful hotel chain, though he could hardly tell her that without her working out exactly who he was—is that staff are the key. Look at what your competitors are doing and offer your clients something different. Keep a close eye on your costs and income, and get advice from a business start-up specialist. Apply for all the grants you can.

It was solid advice. And Nicole knew that Clarence would be the perfect person to brainstorm ideas with, if she decided to keep the Electric Palace. She was half tempted to tell him everything—but then they'd be sharing details of their real and professional lives, which was against their agreement. He'd already told her too much by letting it slip that he worked in the service or entertainment industry. And she'd as good as told him her age. This was getting risky; it wasn't part of their agreement. Time to back off and change the subject.

Thank you, she typed. But enough about me. You said you'd had a bad day. What happened?

A pointless row. It's just one of those days when I feel like walking out and sending off my CV to half a dozen recruitment agencies. Except it's the family business and I know it's my duty to stay.

Because he was still trying to make up for the big mistake he'd made when he was a teenager? He'd told her the bare details one night, how he was the disgraced son in the family, and that he was never sure he'd ever be able to change their perception of him.

Clarence, maybe you need to talk to your dad or whoever runs the show in your family business about the
situation and say it's time for you all to move on. You're
not the same person now as you were when you were
younger. Everyone makes mistakes—and you can't
spend the rest of your life making up for it. That's not
reasonable.

Maybe.

Clarence must feel as trapped as she did, Nicole
thought. Feeling that there was no way out. He'd helped
her think outside the box and see her grandfather's bequest another way: that it could be her escape route.
Maybe she could do the same for him.

Could you recruit someone to replace you?

There was a long silence, and Nicole thought maybe
she'd gone too far.

Nice idea, Georgy, but it's not going to happen.

OK. What about changing your role in the business instead? Could you take it in a different direction, one
you enjoy more?

It's certainly worth thinking about.

Which was a polite brush-off. Just as well she hadn't
given in to the urge to suggest meeting for dinner to
talk about it.

Because that would've been stupid.

Apart from the fact that she wasn't interested in dating anyone ever again, for all she knew Clarence could be in a serious relationship. Living with someone, engaged, even married.

Even if he wasn't, supposing they met and she discovered that the real Clarence was nothing like the online one? Supposing they really didn't like each other in real life? She valued his friendship too much to risk losing it. If that made her a coward, so be it.

Changing his role in the business. Taking it in a different direction. Gabriel could just imagine the expression on his father's face if he suggested it. Shock, swiftly followed by, 'I saved your skin, so you toe the line and do what I say.'

It wasn't going to happen.

But he appreciated the fact that Georgygirl was trying to think about how to make his life better.

For one mad moment, he almost suggested she should bring details of the business she'd just inherited and meet him for dinner and they could brainstorm it properly. But he stopped himself. Apart from the fact that it was none of his business, supposing they met and he discovered that the real Georgygirl was nothing like the online one? Supposing they loathed each other in real life? He valued his time talking to her and he didn't want to risk losing her friendship.

Thanks for making me feel human again, he typed.

Me? I didn't do anything. And you gave me some really good advice.

That's what friends are for. And you did a lot, believe me. He paused. I'd better let you go. I'm due back in the office. Talk to you later?

I'm due back at the office, too. Talk to you tonight.

Good luck. Let me know how it goes with your mum.

Will do. Let me know how it goes with your family.

Sure.

Though he had no intention of doing that.

CHAPTER TWO

By THE TIME Nicole went to the restaurant to meet her mother that evening, she had a full dossier on the Electric Palace and its history, thanks to the Surrey Quays forum website. Brian Thomas had owned the cinema since the nineteen-fifties, and it had flourished in the next couple of decades; then it had floundered with the rise of multiplex cinemas and customers demanding something more sophisticated than an old, slightly shabby picture house. One article even described the place as a 'flea-pit'.

Then there were the photographs. It was odd, looking at pictures that people had posted from the nineteen-sixties and realising that the man behind the counter in the café was actually her grandfather, and at the time her mother would've been a toddler. Nicole could definitely see a resemblance to her mother in his face—and to herself. Which made the whole thing feel even more odd. This particular thread was about the history of some of the buildings in Surrey Quays, but it was turning out to be her personal history as well.

Susan hardly ever talked about her family, so Nicole didn't have a clue. Had the Thomas family always lived in Surrey Quays? Had her mother grown up around here? If so, why hadn't she said a word when Nicole had bought her flat, three years ago? Had Nicole spent all this time living only a couple of streets away from the grandparents who'd rejected her?

And how was Susan going to react to the news of the bequest? Would it upset her and bring back bad memories? The last thing Nicole wanted to do was to hurt her mother.

She'd just put the file back in her briefcase when Susan walked over to their table and greeted her with a kiss.

'Hello, darling. I got here as fast as I could. Though it must be serious for you not to be at work at *this* time of day.'

Half-past seven. When most normal people would've left the office hours ago. Nicole grimaced as her mother sat down opposite her. 'Mum. Please.' She really wasn't in the mood for another lecture about her working hours.

'I know, I know. Don't nag. But you do work too hard.' Susan frowned. 'What's happened, love?'

'You know I went to see that solicitor today?'

'Yes.'

'I've been left something in a will.' Nicole blew out a breath. 'I don't think I can accept it.'

'Why not?'

There was no way to say this tactfully. Even though she'd been trying out and discarding different phrases all day, she hadn't found the right words. So all she could do was to come straight out with it. 'Because it's the Electric Palace.'

Understanding dawned in Susan's expression. 'Ah. I did wonder if that would happen.'

Her mother already knew about it? Nicole stared at her in surprise. But how?

As if the questions were written all over her daughter's face, Susan said gently, 'He had to leave it to someone. You were the obvious choice.'

Nicole shook her head. 'How? Mum, I pass the Electric Palace every day on my way to work. I had no idea it was anything to do with us.'

'It isn't,' Susan said. 'It was Brian's. But I'm glad he's finally done the right thing and left it to you.'

'But you're his daughter, Mum. He should've left it to you, not to me.'

'I don't want it.' Susan lifted her chin. 'Brian made his choice years ago—he decided nearly thirty years ago that I wasn't his daughter and he is most definitely not my father. I don't need anything from him. What I own, I have nobody to thank for but myself. I worked for it. And that's the way I like it.'

Nicole reached over and squeezed her mother's hand. 'And you wonder where I get my stubborn streak?'

Susan gave her a wry smile. 'I guess.'

'I can't accept the bequest,' Nicole said again. 'I'm going to tell the solicitor to make the deeds over to you.'

'Darling, no. Brian left it to you, not to me.'

'But you're his daughter,' Nicole said again.

'And you're his granddaughter,' Susan countered.

Nicole shrugged. 'OK. Maybe I'll sell to the developer who wants it.'

'And you'll use the money to do something that makes you happy?'

It was the perfect answer. 'Yes,' Nicole said. 'Giving the money to you will make me very happy. You can pay off your mortgage and get a new car and go on holiday. It'd be enough for you to go and see the Northern Lights this winter, and I know that's top of your bucket list.'

'Absolutely not.' Susan folded her arms. 'You using that money to get out of that hell-hole you work in would make me much happier than if I spent a single penny on myself, believe me.'

Nicole sighed. 'It feels like blood money, Mum. How can I accept something from someone who behaved so badly to you?'

'Someone who knew he was in the wrong but was too stubborn to apologise. That's where we both get our stubborn streak,' Susan said. 'I think leaving the cinema to you is his way of saying sorry without actually having to use the five-letter word.'

'That's what Cl—' Realising what she was about to give away, Nicole stopped short.

'Cl—?' Susan tipped her head to one side. 'And who might this "Cl—" be?'

'A friend,' Nicole said grudgingly.

'A *male* friend?'

'Yes.' Given that they'd never met in real life, there was always the possibility that her internet friend was actually a woman trying on a male persona for size, but Nicole was pretty sure that Clarence was a man.

'That's good.' Susan looked approving. 'What's his name? Cliff? Clive?'

Uh-oh. Nicole could actually see the matchmaking gleam in her mother's eye. 'Mum, we're *just* friends.' She didn't want to admit that they'd never actually met and Clarence wasn't even his real name; she knew what conclusion her mother would draw. That Nicole was an utter coward. And there was a lot of truth in that: Nicole was definitely a coward when it came to relationships. She'd been burned badly enough last time to make her very wary indeed.

'You are allowed to date again, you know,' Susan said gently. 'Yes, you picked the wrong one last time—but don't let that put you off. Not all men are as spineless and as selfish as Jeff.'

It was easier to smile and say, 'Sure.' Though Nicole

had no intention of dating Clarence. Even if he was available, she didn't want to risk losing his friendship. Wanting to switch the subject away from the abject failure that was her love life, Nicole asked, 'So did you grow up in Surrey Quays, Mum?'

'Back when it was all warehouses and terraced houses, before they were turned into posh flats.' Susan nodded. 'We lived on Mortimer Gardens, a few doors down from the cinema. Those houses were knocked down years ago and the land was redeveloped.'

'Why didn't you say anything when I moved here?'

Susan shrugged. 'You were having a hard enough time. You seemed happy here and you didn't need my baggage weighing you down.'

'So all this time I was living just round the corner from my grandparents? I could've passed them every day in the street without knowing who they were.' The whole thing made her feel uncomfortable.

'Your grandmother died ten years ago,' Susan said. 'When they moved from Mortimer Gardens, they lived at the other end of Surrey Quays from you, so you probably wouldn't have seen Brian, either.'

Which made Nicole feel very slightly better. 'Did you ever work at the cinema?'

'When I was a teenager,' Susan said. 'I was an usherette at first, and then I worked in the ticket office and the café. I filled in and helped with whatever needed doing, really.'

'So you would probably have ended up running the place if you hadn't had me?' Guilt flooded through Nicole. How much her mother had lost in keeping her.

'Having you,' Susan said firmly, 'is the best thing that ever happened to me. The moment I first held you in my arms, I felt this massive rush of love for you and that's never changed. You've brought me more joy over the years than anyone or anything else. And I don't have a single regret about it. I never have and I never will.'

Nicole blinked back the sudden tears. 'I love you, Mum. And I don't mean to bring back bad memories.'

'I love you, too, and you're not bringing back bad memories,' Susan said. 'Now, let's order dinner. And then we'll talk strategy and how you're going to deal with this.'

A plate of pasta and a glass of red wine definitely made Nicole feel more human.

'There's a lot about the cinema on the Surrey Quays website. There's a whole thread with loads of pictures.' Nicole flicked into her phone and showed a few of them to her mother.

'Obviously I was born in the mid-sixties so I don't remember it ever being called The Kursaal,' Susan said, 'but I do remember the place from the seventies on. There was this terrible orange and purple wallpaper in the foyer. You can see it there—just be thankful the photo's black and white.' She smiled. 'I remember queuing with my mum and my friends to see Disney films, and everyone being excited about *Grease*—we were all in love with John Travolta and wanted to look like Sandy and be one of the Pink Ladies. And I remember trying to sneak my friends into *Saturday Night Fever* when we were all too young to get in, and Brian spotting us and marching us into his office, where he yelled at us and said we could lose him his cinema licence.'

'So there were some good times?' Nicole asked.

'There are always good times, if you look for them,' Susan said.

'I remember you taking me to the cinema when I was little,' Nicole said. 'Never to the Electric Palace, though.'

'No, never to the Electric Palace,' Susan said quietly.

'I nearly did—but if Brian and Patsy weren't going to be swayed by the photographs I sent of you on every birthday and Christmas, they probably weren't going to be nice to you if they met you, and I wasn't going to risk them making you cry.'

'Mum, that's so sad.'

'Hey. You have the best godparents ever. And we've got each other. We didn't need them. We're doing just fine, kiddo. And life is too short not to be happy.' Susan put her arm around her.

'I'm fine with my life as it is,' Nicole said.

Susan's expression said very firmly, Like hell you are. But she said, 'You know, it doesn't have to be a cinema.'

'What doesn't?'

'The Electric Palace. It says here on that website that it was a ballroom and an ice rink when it was first built—and you could redevelop it for the twenty-first century.'

'What, turn it back into a ballroom and an ice rink?'

'No. When you were younger, you always liked craft stuff. You could turn it into a craft centre. It would do well around here—people wanting to chill out after work.' Susan gave her a level look. 'People like you who spend too many hours behind a corporate desk and need to do something to help them relax. Look how popular those adult colouring books are—and craft things are even better when they're part of a group thing.'

'A craft centre.' How many years was it since Nicole had painted anything, or sewn anything? She missed how much she enjoyed being creative, but she never had the time.

'And a café. Or maybe you could try making the old cinema a going concern,' Susan suggested. 'You're used to putting in long hours, but at least this time it'd be for you instead of giving up your whole life to a job you hate.'

Nicole almost said, 'That's what Clarence suggested,' but stopped herself in time. She didn't want her mother knowing that she'd shared that much with him. It would give Susan completely the wrong idea. Nicole wasn't romantically involved with Clarence and didn't intend to be. She wasn't going to be romantically involved with anyone, ever again.

'Think about it,' Susan said. 'Isn't it time you found something that made you happy?'

'I'm perfectly happy in my job,' Nicole lied.

'No, you're not. You hate it, but it makes you financially secure so you'll put up with it—and I know that's my fault because we were so poor when you were little.'

Nicole reached over the table and hugged her. 'Mum, I never felt deprived when I was growing up. You were working three jobs to keep the rent paid and put food on the table, but you always had time for me. Time to give me a cuddle and tell me stories and do a colouring book with me.'

'But you're worried about being poor again. That's why you stick it out.'

'Not so much poor as vulnerable,' Nicole corrected softly. 'My job gives me freedom from that because I don't have to worry if I'm going to be able to pay my mortgage at the end of the month—and that's a good thing. Having a good salary means I have choices. I'm not backed into a corner because of financial constraints.'

'But the hours you put in don't leave you time for anything else. You don't do anything for *you*—and maybe that's what the Electric Palace can do for you.'

Nicole doubted that very much, but wanted to avoid a row. 'Maybe.'

'Did the solicitor give you the keys?'

Nicole nodded. 'Shall we go and look at it, then have coffee and pudding back at my place?'

'Great idea,' Susan said.

The place was boarded up; all they could see of the building was the semi-circle on the top of the façade at the front and the pillars on either side of the front door. Nicole wasn't that surprised when the lights didn't work—the electricity supply had probably been switched off—but she kept a mini torch on her key-ring, and the beam was bright enough to show them the inside of the building.

Susan sniffed. 'Musty. But no damp, hopefully.'

'What's that other smell?' Nicole asked, noting the unpleasant acridness.

'I think it might be mice.'

Susan's suspicions were confirmed when they went into the auditorium and saw how many of the plush seats looked nibbled. Those that had escaped the mice's teeth were worn threadbare in places.

'I can see why that article called it a flea-pit,' Nicole said with a shudder. 'This is awful, Mum.'

'You just need the pest control people in for the mice, then do a bit of scrubbing,' Susan said.

But when they came out of the auditorium and back into the foyer, Nicole flashed the torch around and saw the stained glass. 'Oh, Mum, that's gorgeous. And the wood on the bar—it's pitted in places, but I bet a carpenter could sort that out. I can just see this bar restored to its Edwardian Art Deco glory.'

'Back in its earliest days?' Susan asked.

'Maybe. And look at this staircase.' Nicole shone the torch on the sweeping wrought-iron staircase that led up to the first floor. 'I can imagine movie stars sashaying down this in high heels and gorgeous dresses. Or glamorous ballroom dancers.'

'We never really used the upper floor. There was always a rope across the stairs,' Susan said.

'So what's upstairs?'

Susan shrugged. 'Brian's office was there. As for the rest of it… Storage space, I think.'

But when they went to look, they discovered that the large upstairs room had gorgeous parquet flooring, and a ceiling covered in carved Art Deco stars that stunned them both.

'I had no idea this was here,' Susan said. 'How beautiful.'

'This must've been the ballroom bit,' Nicole said. 'And I can imagine people dancing here during the Blitz, refusing to let the war get them down. Mum, this place is incredible.'

She'd never expected to fall in love with a building, especially one which came from a source that made her feel awkward and uncomfortable. But Nicole could see the Electric Palace as it could be if it was renovated— the cinema on the ground floor, with the top floor as a ballroom or maybe a place for local bands to play. Or she could even turn this room into a café-restaurant. A café with an area for doing crafts, perhaps like her mum suggested. Or an ice cream parlour, stocked with local artisan ice cream.

If she just sold the Electric Palace to a developer and collected the money, would the building be razed to the ground? Could all this be lost?

But she really couldn't let that happen. She wanted to bring the Electric Palace back to life, to make it part of the community again.

'It's going to be a lot of work to restore it,' she said.

Not to mention money: it would eat up all her savings and she would probably need a bank loan as well to tide her over until the business was up and running properly.

'But you're not afraid of hard work—and this time you'd be working for you,' Susan pointed out.

'On the Surrey Quays forum, quite a few people have said how they'd love the place to be restored so we had our own cinema locally,' Nicole said thoughtfully.

'So you wouldn't be doing it on your own,' Susan said. 'You already have a potential audience and people who'd be willing to spread the word. Some of them might volunteer to help you with the restoration or running the place—and you can count me in as well. I could even try and get some of my probationers interested. I bet they'd enjoy slapping a bit of paint on the walls.'

'Supposing I can't make a go of it? There's only one screen, maybe the possibility of two if I use the upstairs room,' Nicole said. 'Is that enough to draw the customers in and make the place pay?'

'If anyone can do it, you can,' Susan said.

'I have savings,' Nicole said thoughtfully. 'If the renovations cost more than what I have, I could get a loan.'

'I have savings, too. I'd be happy to use them here,' Susan added.

Nicole shook her head. 'This should be your heritage, Mum, not mine. And I don't want you to risk your savings on a business venture that might not make it.'

'We've already had this argument. You didn't win it earlier and you're not going to win it now,' Susan said crisply. 'The Electric Palace is yours. And it's your choice whether you want to sell it or whether you want to do something with it.'

Nicole looked at the sad, neglected old building and

knew exactly what she was going to do. 'I'll work out some figures, to see if it's viable.' Though she knew that it wasn't just about the figures. And if the figures didn't work, she'd find alternatives until they *did* work.

'And if it's viable?' Susan asked.

'I'll talk to my boss. If he'll give me a six-month sabbatical, it'd be long enough for me to see if I can make a go of this place.' Nicole shook her head. 'I can't quite believe I just said that. I've spent ten years working for the bank and I've worked my way up from the bottom.'

'And you hate it there—it suppresses the real Nicole and it's turned you into a corporate ghost.'

'Don't pull your punches, Mum,' Nicole said wryly.

Susan hugged her. 'I can love you to bits at the same time as telling you that you're making a massive mistake with your life, you know.'

'Because mums are good at multi-tasking?'

'You got it, kiddo.' Susan hugged her again. 'And I'm with you on this. Anything you need, from scrubbing floors to working a shift in the ticket office to making popcorn, I'm there—and, as I said, I have savings and I'm happy to invest them in this place.'

'You worked hard for that money.'

'And interest rates are so pathetic that my savings are earning me nothing. I'd rather that money was put to good use. Making my daughter's life better—and that would make me very happy indeed. You can't put a price on that.'

Nicole hugged her. 'Thanks, Mum. I love you. And you are so getting the best pudding in the world.'

'You mean, we have to stop by the supermarket on the way back to your flat because there's nothing in your fridge,' Susan said dryly.

Nicole grinned. 'You know me so well.'

* * *

Later that evening, when Susan had gone home, Nicole checked her phone. As she'd half expected, there was a message from Clarence. Did you talk to your mum?

Yes. Did you talk to your dad?

To her pleasure, he replied almost instantly.

No. There wasn't time.

Nicole was pretty sure that meant Clarence hadn't been able to face a row.

What did your mum say? he asked.

Even though she had a feeling that he was asking her partly to distract her from quizzing him about his own situation, it was still nice that he was interested.

We went to see the building.

And?

It's gorgeous but it needs work.

Then I'd recommend getting a full surveyor's report, so you can make sure any renovation quotes you get from builders are fair, accurate and complete.

Thanks. I hadn't thought of that.

I can recommend some people, if you want.

That'd be great. I'll take you up on that, if the figures stack up and I decide to go ahead with getting the business back up and running.

Although Nicole had told herself she'd only do it if the figures worked out, she knew it was a fib. She'd fallen in love with the building and for the first time in years she was excited at the idea of starting work on something. Clarence obviously lived in Surrey Quays, or he wouldn't be part of the forum; so he'd see the boards come down from the front of the Electric Palace or hear about the renovations from some other eagle-eyed person on the Surrey Quays website. She really ought to tell him before it started happening. After all, he was her friend. And he'd said that he had experience in the entertainment and service industry, so he might have some great ideas for getting the cinema up and running again. He'd already made her think about having a survey done, which wouldn't have occurred to her—she'd just intended to find three builders with good reputations and would pick the middle quote of the three.

But, even as she started to type her news, something held her back.

And she knew what it was. Jeff's betrayal had broken her trust. Although she felt she knew Clarence well, and he was the only person she'd even consider talking to about this apart from her mum and best friend, she found herself halting instead of typing a flurry of excited words about her plans.

Maybe it was better to wait to tell him about it until she'd got all her ducks in a row and knew exactly what she was doing.

What's stopping you going ahead? he asked.

I need to work out the figures first. See if it's viable.

So your mum said the same as I did—that it'll get you out of the job you hate?

Yes, she admitted.

Good—and you're listening to both of us?

I'm listening, she said. But it's still early days, Clarence. I don't want to talk about it too much right now—

She couldn't tell him that she didn't trust him. That would mean explaining about Jeff, and she still cringed when she thought about it. How she'd been blithely unaware of the real reason Jeff had asked her to live with him, until she'd overheard that conversation in the toilets. One of the women touching up her make-up by the mirror had said how her boyfriend was actually living with someone else right then but didn't love her—he was only living with the other woman because his boss wasn't prepared to give the promotion to someone who wasn't settled down, and he was going to leave her as soon as he got the promotion.

Nicole had winced in sympathy with the poor, deluded woman who thought everything was fine, and also wanted to point out to the woman bragging about her fickle lover that, if he was prepared to cheat on his live-in girlfriend with her, there was a very strong chance he'd do exactly the same thing to her with someone else at some point in the future.

The woman had continued, 'She's a right cold fish, Jeff says. A boring banker. But Jeff says he really, really loves me. He's even bought me an engagement ring—look.'

There were encouraging coos from her friends; but Nicole had found herself going cold. Jeff wasn't exactly a common name. Even if it were how many men called Jeff were living with a girlfriend who was a banker? Surely it couldn't be…? But when the woman had gone on to describe cheating, lying Jeff, Nicole had realised with devastating clarity that the poor, deluded woman she'd felt sorry for was none other than herself.

She shook herself. That was all baggage that she needed to jettison. And right now Clarence was waiting for her reply.

She continued typing.

In case I jinx it. The building's going to need a lot of work doing to it. I don't mean to be offensive and shut you out.

It is what it is, he said. No offence taken. And when you do want to talk about it, Georgy, I'm here.

I know, Clarence. And I appreciate it.

She appreciated the fact he kept things light in the rest of their conversation, too.

Goodnight, Georgy. Sweet dreams.

You, too, Clarence.

CHAPTER THREE

'IT'S A PIPE DREAM, Gabriel. You can't create something out of nothing. We're not going to be able to offer our guests exclusive parking.' Evan Hunter stared at his son. 'We should've got the land on the other side of the hotel.'

'It was a sealed bid auction, Dad. And we agreed what would be reasonable. Paying over the odds for the land would've wrecked our budget and the hotel might not have been viable any more.'

'And in the meantime there's an apartment block planned for where our car park should be,' Evan grumbled.

'Unless the new owner of the Electric Palace sells to us.'

Evan sighed. 'Nicole Thomas has already turned down every offer. She says she's going to restore the place.'

'It might not be worth her while,' Gabriel pointed out. 'She's a banker. She'll understand about gearing—and if the restoration costs are too high, she'll see the sense in selling.' He paused. 'To us.'

'You won't succeed, Gabriel. It's a waste of time.'

Maybe, Gabriel thought, this was his chance to prove his worth to his father once and for all. 'I'll talk to her.'

'Charm her into it?' Evan scoffed.

'Give her a dose of healthy realism,' Gabriel corrected.

'The place has been boarded up for five years. The paint-work outside is in bad condition. There are articles in the Surrey Quays forum from years back calling it a flea-pit, so my guess is that it's even worse inside. Add damp, mould and vermin damage—it's not going to be cheap to fix that kind of damage.'

'The Surrey Quays forum.' Evan's eyes narrowed. 'If she gets them behind her and starts a pressure group...'

'Dad. I'll handle it,' Gabriel said. 'We haven't had any objections to the hotel, have we?'

'I suppose not.'

Gabriel didn't bother waiting for his father to say he'd done a good job with the PR side. It wasn't Evan's style. 'I'll handle it,' he said again. 'Nicole Thomas is a hard-headed businesswoman. She'll see the sensible course is to sell the site to us. She gets to cash in her inheritance, and we get the space. Everybody wins.'

'Hmm.' Evan didn't look convinced.

So maybe this would be the tipping point. The thing that finally earned Gabriel his father's respect.

And then maybe he'd get his freedom.

The figures worked. So did the admin. Nicole had checked online and there was a huge list of permissions and licences she needed to apply for, but it was all doable. She just needed to make a master list, do some critical path analysis, and tackle the tasks in the right order. Just as she would on a normal day at her desk.

Once she'd talked to her boss and he'd agreed to let her take a sabbatical, she sat at her desk, working out how to break the news to her team.

But then Neil, her second-in-command, came in to her office. 'Are the rumours true?'

It looked as if the office grapevine had scooped her. 'What rumours?' she asked, playing for time.

'That you're taking six months off?'

'Yes.'

He looked her up and down, frowning. 'You don't *look* pregnant.'

Oh, honestly. Was the guy still stuck in the Dark Ages? 'That's because I'm not.'

'Then what? Have you got yourself a mail-order bride-groom on the internet—a rich Russian mafia guy who wants to be respectable?' He cackled, clearly pleased with himself at the barb.

She rolled her eyes, not rising to the bait. Neil liked to think of himself as the office wise-guy and he invari-ably made comments for a cheap laugh at other people's expense. She'd warned him about it before in his annual review, but he hadn't taken a blind bit of notice. 'You can tell everyone I'm not pregnant. I'm also not running off to Russia, thinking that I've bagged myself a millionaire bridegroom only to discover that it was all a big scam and I'm about to be sold into slavery.' She steepled her fingers and looked him straight in the eye. 'Are there any other rumours I need to clarify, or are we done?'

'Wow—I've never heard you…' He looked at her with something akin to respect. 'Sorry.'

She shrugged. 'Apology accepted.'

'So why are you taking six months off?'

'It's a business opportunity,' she said. 'Keep your fin-gers crossed that it works, because if it doesn't I'll be claiming my desk back in six months' time.'

From him, she meant, and clearly he recognised it be-cause his face went dull red. 'No offence meant.'

'Good,' she said, and clapped him on the shoulder. 'Little tip from me. For what's probably the six millionth time I've told you, Neil, try to lose the wisecracks. They make you look less professional and that'll stand in the way of you being promoted.'

'All right. Sorry.' He paused. 'Are you really going today?'

'Yes.'

'Without even having a leaving do?'

'I might be coming back if my plans don't work out,' she reminded him, 'so it would be a bit fake to have a leaving do. But I'll put some money behind the bar at the Mucky Duck—' the nearby pub that most of her team seemed to frequent after work '—if you're all that desperate to have a drink at my expense.'

'Hang on. You'll pay for your own sort-of leaving do and not turn up to it?'

That was the idea. She spread her hands. 'What's the problem?'

Neil shook his head. 'If it wasn't for the fact you're actually leaving, I'd think you'd be slaving behind your desk. You never join in with anything.'

'Because I don't fit in,' she said softly. 'So I'm not going to be the spectre at the feast. You can all enjoy a drink without worrying what to say in front of me.'

'None of us really knows you—all we know is that you work crazy hours,' Neil said.

Which was why nobody ever asked her about how her weekend was: they knew she would've spent a big chunk of Saturday at her desk.

'Do you even have a life outside the office?' Neil asked.

And this time there was no barb in his voice; Nicole squirmed inwardly when she realised that the odd note in his voice was pity. 'Ask me again in six months,' she said, 'because then I hope I might have.' And that was the nearest she'd get to admitting her work-life balance was all wrong.

'Well—good luck with your mysterious business opportunity,' he said.

'Thanks—and I'll make sure I leave my desk tidy for you.'

Neil took it as the dismissal she meant it to be; but, before she could clear her desk at the end of the day, her entire team filed into her office, headed by her boss.

'We thought you should have these,' he said, and presented her with a bottle of expensive champagne, a massive card which had been signed by everyone on their floor, and a huge bouquet of roses and lilies.

'We didn't really know what to get you,' Neil said, joining them at Nicole's desk, 'but the team had a whip-round.' He presented her with an envelope filled with money. 'Maybe this will help with your, um, business opportunity.'

Nicole was touched that they'd gone to this trouble. She hadn't expected anything—just that she'd slip away quietly while everyone else was at the bar across the road.

'Thanks. You'll be pleased to know it'll go to good use—I'll probably spend it on paint.'

Neil gaped at her. 'You're leaving us to be an artist?'

She laughed. 'No. I meant masonry paint. I've been left a cinema in a will. It's a bit run-down but I'm going to restore it and see if I can get it up and running properly.'

'A *cinema*? Then you,' Neil said, 'are coming across to the Mucky Duck with us right now, and you're going to tell us everything—and that's not a suggestion, Nicole, because we'll carry you over there if we have to.'

It was the first time Nicole had actually felt part of the team. How ironic that it had happened just as she was leaving them.

'OK,' she said, and let them sweep her across the road in the middle of a crowd.

The next day, Nicole was in the cinema with a clipboard and a pen, adding to her list of what she needed to do when her phone rang.

She glanced at the screen, half expecting that it would be her daily call from the lawyer at Hunter Hotels trying to persuade her to sell the Electric Palace, even though she'd told him every time that the cinema wasn't for sale. Not recognising the number on her screen, and assuming it was one of the calls she was waiting to be returned, she answered her phone. 'Yes?'

'Ms Thomas?'

'Yes.'

'It's Gabriel Hunter from Hunter Hotels.'

Clearly the lawyer had realised that she wasn't going to say yes to the monkey, so now it was the organ-grinder's turn to try and persuade her. She suppressed a sigh. 'Thank you for calling, Mr Hunter, but I believe I've made my position quite clear. The Electric Palace isn't for sale.'

'Indeed,' he said, 'but we have areas of mutual interest and I'd like to meet you to discuss them.'

In other words, he planned to charm her into selling? She put on her best bland voice. 'That's very nice of you to ask, but I'm afraid I'm really rather busy at the moment.'

'It won't take long. Are you at the cinema right now?'

'Yes.'

She regretted her answer the moment he asked, 'And you've been there since the crack of dawn?'

Had the Hunters got someone spying on her, or something? 'Not that it's any of your business, but yes.' There was a lot to do. And she thought at her best, first thing in the morning. It made sense to start early.

'I'd be the same,' he said, mollifying her only slightly. 'So I'd say you're about due for a coffee break. How about I meet you at the café on Challoner Road in half an hour?'

'Where you'll have a carnation in your buttonhole and be carrying a copy of the *Financial Times* so I can recognise you?' She couldn't help the snippy retort.

He laughed. 'No need. I'll be there first—and I'll recognise you.'

Hunter Hotels probably had a dossier on her, including a photograph and a list of everything from her route to work to her shoe size, she thought grimly. 'Thank you for the invitation, but there really isn't any point in us meeting. I'm not selling.'

'I'm not trying to pressure you to sell. As I said, I want to discuss mutual opportunities—and the coffee's on me.'

'I'm not dressed to go to a café. I'm covered in dust.'

'I'd be worried if you weren't, given the current condition of the cinema. And I'd be even more worried if you were walking around a run-down building wearing patent stilettos and a business suit.'

There was a note of humour in Gabriel Hunter's voice. Nicole hadn't expected that, and she quite liked it; at the same time, it left her feeling slightly off balance.

'But if you'd rather I brought the coffee to you, that's fine,' he said. 'Just let me know how you take your coffee.'

It was tempting, but at least if they met in a neutral place she could make an excuse to leave. If he turned up at the cinema, she might have to be rude in order to make him leave and let her get on with things. And, at the end of the day, Gabriel Hunter was working on the business next door to hers. They might have mutual customers.

So he probably had a point about mutual opportunities. Maybe they should talk.

'I'll see you at the café in half an hour,' she said.

She brushed herself down and then was cross with herself. It wasn't as if he was her client, and she wasn't still working at the bank. It didn't matter what she looked like or what he thought of her. And if he tried to push her into selling the Electric Palace, she'd give him very short shrift and come back to work on her lists.

So Nicole Thomas had agreed to meet him. That was a good start, Gabriel thought. He'd certainly got further with her than their company lawyer had.

He worked on his laptop with one eye on the door, waiting for her to turn up. Given that she'd worked in a bank and her photograph on their website made her look like a consummate professional, he'd bet that she'd walk through the door thirty seconds earlier than they'd agreed to meet. Efficiency was probably her middle name.

Almost on cue, the door opened. He recognised Nicole immediately; even though she was wearing old jeans and a T-shirt rather than a business suit, and no make-up whatsoever, her mid-brown hair was pulled back in exactly the same style as she'd worn it at the bank. Old habits clearly died hard.

She glanced around the café, obviously looking for him. For a moment, she looked vulnerable and Gabriel was shocked to feel a sudden surge of protectiveness. She worked for a bank and had worked her way up the management ladder, so she most definitely didn't need protecting; but there was something about her that drew him.

He was horrified to realise that he was attracted to her.

Talk about inappropriate. You didn't fall for your business rival. Ever. Besides, he didn't want to get involved with anyone. He was tired of dating women who had preconceived notions about him. All he wanted to do was talk to Nicole Thomas about mutual opportunities, point out all the many difficulties she was going to face in restoring the cinema, and then talk her into doing the sensible thing and selling the Electric Palace to him for a price fair to both of them.

Nicole looked round the café, trying to work out which of the men sitting on their own was Gabriel Hunter. Why on earth hadn't she looked him up on the internet first, so she would've known exactly who she was meeting here? Had she already slipped out of good business habits, just days after leaving the bank? At this rate, she'd make a complete mess of the cinema and she'd be forced to go back to her old job—and, worse still, have to admit that she'd failed in her bid for freedom.

Then the man in the corner lifted his hand and gave the tiniest wave.

He looked young—probably around her own age. There wasn't a hint of grey in his short dark hair, and his blue eyes were piercing.

If he was the head of Hunter Hotels when he was that young, then he was definitely the ruthless kind. She made a mental note to be polite but to stay on her guard.

His suit was expensively cut—the sort that had been hand-made by a good tailor, rather than bought off the peg—and she'd just bet if she looked under the table his shoes would be the same kind of quality. His shirt was well cut, too, and that understated tie was top of the range. He radiated money and style, looking more like a model advertising a super-expensive watch than a hotel magnate, and she felt totally scruffy and underdressed in her jeans and T-shirt. Right then she really missed the armour of her business suit.

He stood up as she reached his table and held out his hand. 'Thank you for coming, Ms Thomas.'

His handshake was firm and a little tingle ran down Nicole's spine at the touch of his skin against hers. How inappropriate was that? They were on opposite sides and she'd better remember that. Apart from the fact that she never wanted to get involved with anyone again, the fact Gabriel Hunter was her business rival meant he was totally out of the running as a potential date. Even if he was one of the nicest-looking men she'd ever met. Didn't they say that handsome is as handsome does?

'Mr Hunter,' she said coolly.

'Call me Gabriel.'

She had no intention of doing that—or of inviting him to call her by her own first name. They weren't friends; they were business rivals.

'How do you like your coffee?' he asked.

'Espresso, please.'

'Me, too.' He smiled at her, and her heart felt as if it had done a backflip.

'If you haven't been here before, I'd recommend the Guatemala blend.'

'Thank you. That would be lovely,' she said politely.

This was the kind of café that sold a dozen different types of coffee, from simple Americanos and cappuccinos through to pour-over-and-siphon coffee; and she noted from the chalk board above the counter that there were a dozen different blends to choose from, all with tasting notes, so this was the kind of place that was frequented by serious coffee drinkers. The kind of coffee bar she half had in mind for the Electric Palace, depending on whether she kept it as a cinema or turned it into a craft café.

But Gabriel Hunter unsettled her.

She wasn't used to reacting like that towards someone. She hadn't reacted to anyone like that since Jeff. Given her poor judgement when it came to relationships, she really didn't want to be attracted to Gabriel Hunter.

Focus, Nicole, she told herself sharply. Business. Work. Nothing else.

Gabriel came back to the table carrying two espressos, and set one cup and saucer in front of her before sitting down opposite her again.

She took a sip. 'You're right; this is excellent. Thank you.'

'Pleasure.' He inclined his head.

Enough pleasantries, she decided. This was business, so they might as well save some time and cut to the chase. 'So, what are these mutual interests you wanted to discuss?' she asked.

'Our businesses are next door to each other. And they're both works in progress,' he said, 'though obviously the hotel renovation is quite a bit further on than the cinema.'

'Are you thinking mutual customers?'

'And mutual parking.'

His eyes really were sharp, she thought. As if they saw everything.

'Are you really going to run the place as a cinema?' he asked.

She frowned. 'Why would I discuss my business strategy with a competitor?'

'True. But, if you are going to run it as a cinema, I'm not sure you'll manage to make it pay, and it's not going to be good for my business if the place next door to me is boarded up and looks derelict,' he said bluntly. 'Most people would choose to take the Tube into the West End and go to a multiplex to see the latest blockbuster. One screen doesn't give your customers a lot of choice, and you'll be competing directly with established businesses that can offer those customers an awful lot more.'

'That all depends on the programming.' She'd been researching that; and she needed to think about whether to show the blockbusters as they came out, or to develop the Electric Palace as an art-house cinema, or to have a diverse programme with certain kinds of movies showing on certain nights.

'With your background in banking—' well, of course he'd checked her out and would know that '—obviously you're more than capable of handling the figures and the finance,' he said. 'But the building needs a lot of work, and restoring something properly takes a lot of experience or at least knowing who to ask.'

'It's been boarded up for the last five years. How would you know the place needs a lot of work?' she asked.

'Because if you leave any building without any kind of maintenance for five years, there's going to be a problem,' he said matter-of-factly. 'Anything from damp caused by the tiniest leak in the roof that's built up unnoticed over the years, through to damage from mice or rats. None of it will be covered by insurance—assuming that there was any premises insurance in place at all while it was closed—because that kind of damage counts as a gradually operating cause.'

There was definitely insurance in place. That was the first thing she'd checked. But she also knew he had a point about uninsured damage. And she'd noticed that he was using legal terms as if he was very, very familiar with even the tiniest of small print. She'd need to be very careful how she dealt with him.

'And then there's the state of the wiring and the plumbing,' he continued. 'Even if the rats and mice have left it alone, the cabling's probably deteriorated with age, and do you even know when it was last rewired? For all you know, it could still be nineteen-fifties wiring and it'd need replacing completely to make it safe. Without safe wiring, you won't get public liability insurance or any of the business licences you need.'

Just when she thought he'd finished, he continued, 'And then there's lead piping. Unless your water pipes have been completely replaced since the nineteen-sixties, there's a good chance you'll have lead piping. You'll need to get that replaced—just as we're having to do, next door.'

She didn't have a clue when the wiring had last been done, or even how to check what its current state was like, or how to check the water pipes. 'That's precisely why I'm having a survey done,' she said, grateful that Clarence had suggested that to her. 'So then I'll know exactly what needs to be done and what to ask builders to quote for.'

'So where are your customers going to park?' he asked.

'The same place as they would at the multiplexes in town—there's no need to park, because they'll either walk here or take the Tube,' she countered. 'Where are yours going to park?'

Even though he was pretty impassive, there was the tiniest flicker in his eyes that gave him away. And then she realised. 'That's why you want to buy the Electric Palace,' she said. 'So you can raze it to the ground and turn the space into a car park.'

'It's one option.' He shrugged. 'But if the building is

in better condition than I think it is, it could also work as the hotel's restaurant or conference suite.'

She shook her head. 'It's not a restaurant. It's a purpose-built cinema.'

'But it's not a listed building. The use could be changed very easily.'

She stared at him. 'You've already checked that out?'

'As we do with any building we consider developing,' he said, not looking in the slightest bit abashed. 'If a building's listed, it means we'll have to meet strict criteria before we can make any alterations, and it also means extra site visits and inspections—all of which adds time to a project. And time is money.'

She blinked. 'Are you saying you rush things through?'

'No. Cutting corners means offering our clients a substandard experience, and we don't do that. Hunter Hotels is about high quality,' he said. 'What I mean is that if a building isn't listed, then we don't get the extra admin hassle when we renovate it and we don't have any enforced down-time while we wait for inspections.' He looked her straight in the eye. 'Then again, if the council were to decide your cinema ought to be listed...'

'Are you threatening me?'

'No, I'm pointing out that you need to get various licences. The council might look at your application and decide that a purpose-built Edwardian *kursaal* really ought to be on the Statutory List of Buildings of Special Architectural or Historical Interest. Especially as there aren't many of them left.'

His voice was bland, but she was pretty sure he was enjoying this. Gabriel Hunter was a corporate shark—and he'd just spotted a weakness and was playing on it. She narrowed her eyes at him. 'It feels as if you're threatening me.'

'Not at all. I'm just warning you to be prepared, because you clearly don't have any experience of dealing with premises—and, as your building's been boarded up for the last five years, there's a pretty good chance you have hidden damage that's going to take a lot of time and money to sort out. The longer it takes to get the building up and running, the longer it'll be before it starts to pay for itself, and the more likely it is that you'll run into other roadblocks.'

Gabriel Hunter was being perfectly polite and charming, but Nicole thought that he was definitely trying to worry her to the point where she'd think that the burden of restoring the cinema would be too heavy and it would be easier to sell the place. To him. 'The Electric Palace isn't for sale,' she repeated. 'So, unless you have some constructive suggestions—like offering my clients a special pre-movie dinner menu—then I really don't think we have anything more to talk about, Mr Hunter.'

'A special dinner menu is a possibility. And in return you could offer my clients a special deal on ticket prices.'

'You seriously think we could work together?' And yet she couldn't shake the suspicion that this was all a smokescreen. She knew that Hunter Hotels wanted her to sell. 'I've just refused to sell my cinema to you. Why would you want to work with me?'

'It is what it is,' he said.

She looked at him in surprise. 'Clarence says that all the time.' The words were out before she could stop them.

'Who's Clarence?' he asked.

She shook her head. 'Nobody you know.' Clarence had nothing in common with Gabriel Hunter, and it was extremely unlikely that they knew each other. Even if they did know each other, in real life, they were so different that they probably loathed each other.

* * *

Clarence.

It wasn't exactly a common name. Gabriel didn't know anyone else called Clarence, whether in real life or online.

Surely Nicole couldn't be…?

But, as he thought about it, the pieces fell rapidly into place. Georgygirl had just inherited a commercial building—a business she'd been mysterious about. He knew she hated her job, and was planning to take a sabbatical to see if she could turn the business around and make it work.

Nicole Thomas had just inherited the Electric Palace and, according to his sources, she was taking a sabbatical from the bank.

So was Nicole Thomas *Georgygirl*?

This was the first time he'd actually connected his online and real life, and as the penny dropped it left him reeling.

The girl he'd met online was warm and sweet and funny, whereas Nicole Thomas was cool and hard-headed. Georgygirl was his friend, whereas Nicole Thomas had made it very clear that not only were they not friends, they were on opposite sides.

The whole reason he'd resisted meeting Georgygirl was because he'd been afraid that they'd be different in real life, not meeting each other's expectations. And then he'd lose her friendship, a relationship he'd really come to value over the months.

It looked as if his fears had been right on the nail. Georgygirl was completely different in real life. They weren't compatible at all.

Nicole clearly hadn't worked out yet that he was Clarence. Even if she'd researched Hunter Hotels, she wouldn't have connected Clarence with Gabriel. He'd let it slip that he worked in the leisure industry, but that was such a broad category that it was unlikely she'd connect it with hotel development.

Given that they didn't like each other—he ignored that spark of attraction he'd felt, and that surge of protectiveness he'd felt towards her—maybe he could leverage the ruins of their friendship. He could keep pointing out the downsides of the building and the difficulties she was going to face; then he could offer her an easy option. One he hoped she'd take, and she'd sell the Electric Palace to him.

OK, so he'd lose Georgygirl's friendship completely. But he'd pretty much lost that anyway, hadn't he? Once she knew who he was, she'd turn away from him. He'd be naive to think it could be different and could ever lead to anything else.

'I guess you're right,' he said. 'We probably don't have mutual interests. I'll let you get on. Thank you for your time.'

'Thank you for the coffee,' she said.

He gave her the briefest of nods and walked out before his disappointment could betray him.

Later that evening, a message came in on Gabriel's screen.

Hey, Clarence. How was your day?

OK, I guess, he typed back, feeling slightly uneasy because he knew exactly who she was, while he was pretty sure she still didn't know the truth about him. How was yours?

Pretty grim. I met the guy who wants to buy my business.

Uh-oh. Clarence would be sympathetic; Gabriel wasn't so sure he wanted to hear what she had to say about him.

OK... he said, playing for time.

He's a corporate shark in a suit, she said.

Ouch. Well, it was his own fault. He should've told her face to face who he was when he'd had the chance. Now it was going to get messy. He'd limit the damage and tell her right now.

I had a meeting today too, he said. With someone I was expecting to be my enemy, but who turned out to be someone I've been friends with for a long time.

That's good, isn't it? she asked.

He wasn't so sure. But he was going to have to bite the bullet.

Nicole, I think we need to talk.

Nicole stared at her screen. She'd never, ever given Clarence her real name. So why was he using it now? How did he know who she was?

Then a seriously nasty thought hit her.

She dismissed it instantly. Of course Clarence couldn't be Gabriel Hunter. He just couldn't. Clarence was kind and sweet and funny.

But he knew her real name without her telling him. And there was no way he could have connected Georgy-girl with Nicole Thomas. They'd never shared real names or the kind of personal details that would link up. So the only logical explanation was that Clarence was Gabriel.

Are you trying to tell me *you're* the corporate shark? she typed, desperately wanting him to tell her that he wasn't.

But his reply was very clear.

I don't think of myself that way, but you clearly do. Yes. I'm Gabriel Hunter.

Clarence really was Gabriel Hunter?

She couldn't quite take it in.

And then she felt sick to her stomach. Yet again, she'd fallen for someone and he'd turned out to be using her. Jeff had only asked her to date him and then move in with him because he'd wanted promotion and his boss had a thing about only promoting young men if they were settled. And now Clarence had betrayed her in exactly the same way: he hadn't made friends with her because he liked her, but because he'd wanted to leverage their friendship and persuade her to sell the Electric Palace to Hunter Hotels.

What a stupid, naive fool she was.

How long have you known who I am? she demanded, wanting to know the worst so she could regroup.

I only realised today, he said. When you talked about Clarence. Then the pieces fitted together. You'd inherited a business and you were taking a sabbatical to see if you could make it work. So had Georgy.

But you didn't say a word to me at the café.

I might have got the wrong end of the stick. There might've been another Clarence.

Because it's *such* a common name? she asked waspishly.

OK. I wanted time to get my head round it, he said. Right then I didn't know what to say to you.

So how long have you known that the Electric Palace was mine?

We knew it belonged to Brian Thomas—we'd approached him several times over the last couple of years and he'd refused to sell. We didn't know who his heir was until his will was made public. Then we contacted you—and at that point I didn't know you were Georgy.

He really expected her to believe that?
But now it's out in the open, he continued.
And how.

There's something I'd like you to think about.

Against her better instincts, she asked, What?

You know that art café you talked to me about, a couple of months ago? If you sell the cinema, that'd give you the money to find the perfect place for it. To find a building you're not going to have to restore first. It'll save you so much time and hassle. It'd give you the space to follow your dreams straight away instead of having to wait while you rebuild someone else's.

Nicole stared at the screen in disbelief. He was picking up on the private dream she'd told him about in a completely different context and was using it to pressure her into selling?

You actually think you can use our former friendship to make me sell to you? she asked, not sure whether she was more hurt or disgusted. Oh, please. You're a corporate shark through and through. The Electric Palace isn't for sale—not now and not in the foreseeable future. Goodbye, Clarence.

She flicked out of the messaging programme and shut down her laptop before he could reply.

It was hard to get her head round this. Her friend Clarence was actually her business rival, Gabriel Hunter. Which meant he wasn't really her friend—otherwise why would he have tried to use their relationship to put pressure on her to sell?

And to think she'd told him things she'd never told anyone else. Trusted him.

Now she knew who he really was, her worst fears had come true. He wasn't the same online as he was in real life. In real life, she disliked him and everything he stood for.

She'd lost her friend.

And she'd lost the tiny bit of her remaining trust along with that friendship.

CHAPTER FOUR

GABRIEL'S MOOD THE next day wasn't improved by another run-in with his father—especially because this time he couldn't talk to Georgygirl about it and there was nobody to tease him out of his irritation.

He also couldn't share the bad pun that a friend emailed him and that he knew Georgy would've enjoyed. He thought about sending her a message, but she'd made it pretty clear that she didn't want to have anything to do with him. That 'Goodbye, Clarence' had sounded very final.

She didn't message him that evening, either.

Not that he was surprised. Nicole Thomas wasn't the kind of woman who backed down. She was a cool, hardheaded businesswoman.

By the following morning, Gabriel realised why his dark mood refused to lift. He *missed* Georgygirl. She'd made his life so much brighter, these last six months. It had felt good, knowing that there was someone out there who actually understood who he really was, at heart. And he was miserable without her.

Did she miss Clarence, too? he wondered.

OK, so Nicole had called him a corporate shark. Which he wasn't. Not really. He wasn't a pushover, but he was scrupulously fair in his business dealings. His real identity had clearly come as a shock to her. Hers had been a shock to him, too, but at least he'd had time to get his head round it before he'd talked to her, whereas he hadn't given her a chance to get used to the idea. Then she'd accused him of using their former friendship to make her sell the cinema to him, and he knew she had a point. He *had* tried to leverage their former friendship, thinking that it was all that was left.

But if she missed him as much as he missed her, and she could put aside who he was and see past that to his real self—the self he'd shared with her online—then maybe they could salvage something from this.

In any case, their businesses were next door to each other. It would be the neighbourly thing to do, to take her a coffee and see how she was getting on. The fact that he was attracted to her had nothing to do with it, he told himself. This was strictly business, and maybe also a chance to fix a relationship that he valued and he missed.

He dropped in to his favourite coffee shop—the one where he'd met Nicole the other day—picked up two espressos to go and two dark chocolate brownies, then headed for Mortimer Gardens.

The front door to the cinema was closed, but when he tried the handle it was unlocked. He opened it and went into the lobby. 'Hello?' he called.

Nicole came into the lobby from what he assumed was the foyer, carrying a clipboard. 'What are you doing here?' she asked.

'I brought you coffee.' He offered her the paper cup and one of the two paper bags.

She frowned. 'Why?'

'Because we're neighbours. You've been working hard and I thought maybe you could do with this.'

'Thank you,' she said coolly and politely, 'but there's really no need.'

He sighed. 'Nicole, I don't want to fight with you— and I could drink both espressos myself and eat both brownies, but that much caffeine and sugar in my system at once would turn me into a total nightmare. Take pity on my staff and share it with me.'

'I...'

He could see the doubt in her face, so he added, 'For Clarence and Georgy.'

She shook her head. 'Forget Georgy. She doesn't exist. Any more than Clarence does.'

'We do exist—we're real. And can you please just take the coffee and cake instead of being stubborn and stroppy? They don't come with strings attached.'

She stared at him. Just when he was about to give up and walk away, she gave the tiniest nod. 'I guess. Thank you.' She took the coffee and the brownie. 'Though actually I do feel beholden to you now.'

'There's no need. It's just coffee. As I said, no strings. I'm being neighbourly.'

'I guess I should be neighbourly, too, and invite you to sit down—' she gestured to his suit '—but you're really not dressed for this place.'

'Maybe.' He noticed that she was wearing jeans and another old T-shirt, teamed with canvas shoes; her hair was pulled back tightly into a bun. Out of habit from her banking days, or just to try and stop herself getting so dusty? Who was the real Nicole—the banker, or the girl who dreamed of the stars?

'I was just working through here.'

Gabriel followed her through into the foyer, where she'd set up a makeshift desk at one of the tables. She'd taken down the boarding on one of the windows to let some light in.

'Lighting not working?' he asked.

'The electricity supply's due to be reconnected some time today,' she said. 'I'm using a torch and this window until then.'

'And you have some spare fuses in case some of the circuits blow when the electricity's back on?'

She folded her arms and gave him a narrow-eyed look. 'I might be female, Mr Hunter, but I'm neither stupid nor helpless.'

He sighed. 'That wasn't what I was implying. You know I know you're not stupid or helpless. What I'm saying is that I have a couple of electricians next door if you run into problems, OK?'

'Since when does a hard-headed businessman offer help to the business next door?'

When it was owned by a friend, one whom he happened to know was doing this single-handedly. Not that he thought she'd accept that. And part of him thought that he was crazy. Why *would* he help her, when he wanted her to sell the place to him? He ought to be making life hard for her, not bringing her coffee and offering help from his staff.

Yet part of him wondered—was there a compromise? Could he forge a deal that would both please his father *and* help his friend? 'Damage limitation,' he said. 'If your place goes up in smoke, it's going to affect mine.' It was true. The fact that he couldn't quite separate Nicole from Georgygirl was irrelevant.

'Right.' She grabbed a cloth and rubbed the worst of the dust from one of the chairs. 'Since you're here, have a seat.'

'Thank you.' He sat down.

'So why are you really here?' she asked.

Because he missed her. But he didn't think she was ready to hear that. He wasn't sure he was ready to hear that, either. 'Being neighbourly. Just as you'd do if you were a lot further on in the restoration here and I'd just started up next door.'

'With the exception that I wouldn't be trying to buy your hotel so I could raze it to the ground to make a car park for my cinema,' she pointed out.

'I did say that was one option. There are others,' he said mildly. He just hadn't thought them all through yet. He wanted the land for car parking. Restoring the cinema instead and using it as part of the hotel was unlikely to be cost effective. To give himself some breathing space, he asked, 'Why did you call yourself Georgygirl on the forum?'

It was the last question Nicole had expected. She frowned. 'What's that got to do with the cinema?'

'Nothing. I'm just curious. Before I knew who you were, I assumed maybe your name was Georgina, or your surname was George. And then afterwards I thought of the film.'

'A film that's half a century old and has never been remade—and you loathe romcoms anyway.' Or, at least, Clarence did. She didn't know what Gabriel Hunter liked. How much of Clarence had been real?

'OK. So I looked it up on the internet. But the synopsis I read—well, it doesn't fit you. And neither does the song. You're not dowdy and any male with red blood would give you a second glance.'

'I wasn't fishing for compliments,' she said crisply. 'For the record, I'm not interested in flattery, either.'

'I was merely stating facts. Though there is one thing,'

he said. 'You're Nicole on the outside and Georgy on the inside.'

Two parts of the same person. Was it the same for him? Was the nice side of Gabriel Hunter—Clarence—real? But he'd lied to her. How could she trust him? Especially as she'd made that mistake before: putting her trust in the wrong man. She'd promised herself she'd never repeat that mistake again.

'So—why Georgygirl?' he asked again.

'It's not from that film. If you must know, it's George, as in Banks, because I'm—well, was—a banker, and girl because I'm female.'

'George Banks from *Mary Poppins*,' he said. 'I don't think you'd believe that feeding the birds is a waste—so I'm guessing that you never find the time to fly kites.'

'Clever.' And a little too close to the truth for her comfort. 'So why did you call yourself Clarence?'

'Because my name's Gabriel.'

She frowned. 'I'm not following you.'

'As in the angel,' he said.

She scoffed. 'You're no angel.'

'I don't pretend to be. I just happen to have the name of an angel.'

The Archangel Gabriel; and an angel called Clarence. *'It's a Wonderful Life.'* Her favourite film: the one she watched with her mother every Christmas Eve and wept over every time the townsfolk of Bedford Falls all came with their savings to help George Bailey. She shook her head. 'No. You should've called yourself Potter.'

'Harry?'

'Henry,' she corrected.

He grimaced. 'I know you think I'm a corporate shark, but I'd never cheat or steal like Henry Potter.' He looked her straight in the eye. 'For the record, that wasn't my teenage mistake, or have you already checked that out?'

'Once I found out who you really were, I looked you up,' she admitted. 'I saw what the papers said about you.'

'It is what it is.' He shrugged. 'So now you know the worst of me.'

'Yes. It's a hell of a teenage mistake, crashing your car into someone's shop.'

'While drunk. Don't forget that. And my father had enough money to hire a top-class lawyer who could get me off on a technicality. Which makes me the lowest of the low.' He suddenly looked really vulnerable. 'And you think I don't know that?'

She winced. Clarence had told her he regretted his teenage mistake bitterly. That he was still paying for his mistake over and over again. There was a lot more to this than the papers had reported, she was sure.

And she'd just been really, really mean to him. To the man who'd made her life that bit brighter over the last six months. How horrible did that make her?

Then again, Gabriel had tried to leverage their friendship to make her sell the cinema to him. Which made him as much of a user as Jeff. And that was something she found hard to forgive.

'Mr Hunter, we really have nothing to say to each other.'

'Georgy—Nicole,' he corrected himself, 'we've talked every night for months and I think that's real.'

'But your company wants to buy my cinema.'

'Yes.'

'It's not for sale. Not now, and not ever.'

'Message received and understood,' he said. 'Have you spoken to a surveyor yet?'

'No,' she admitted.

'I can give you some names.'

'I bet you can.'

He frowned. 'What's that supposed to mean?'

'A surveyor who'll tell me that there's so much wrong, the best thing I can do is raze it to the ground and sell you the site as a car park for your new hotel?' she asked waspishly.

'No. I'm really not like Henry Potter,' he said again. 'I was trying to be nice. To help you, because I have experience in the area and you don't.'

'Why would you help me when we're business rivals?'

'Because we don't have to be rivals,' he said. 'Maybe we can work together.'

'How?'

'What do you intend to do with the place?'

'You've already asked me that, and my answer's the same.' She looked at him. 'Would you tell a business rival what your strategy was?'

He sighed. 'Nicole, I'm not asking for rivalry reasons. I'm asking, are you going to run it as a cinema or are you going to use the space for something else? You once said if you could do anything you wanted, you'd open a café and have a space where people could do some kind of art.'

'It's a possibility,' she allowed. 'I need to sort out my costings first and work out the best use of the space.' And she really had to make this work. She didn't want to lose all her savings and her security—to risk being as vulnerable as her mother had been when Nicole was growing up, having no choices in what she did.

'If you want to set up an art café,' he said, 'maybe I can help you find better premises for it.'

'And sell you the cinema? We've already discussed this, and you can ask me again and again until you're blue in the face, but it's not happening. Whatever I do, it'll be done right here.'

'OK. Well, as a Surrey Quays resident—'

'You mean you actually live here?' she broke in. 'You didn't just join the forum to listen out for people protesting against your development so you could charm them out of it?'

He winced. 'That was one of the reasons I joined the forum initially, I admit.'

So she'd been right and their whole relationship had been based on a lie. Just as it had with Jeff. Would she never learn?

'But I do live in Surrey Quays,' he said, and named one of the most prestigious developments on the edge of the river. 'I moved there eighteen months ago. And I'm curious about the cinema now I'm here. It's been boarded up ever since I've lived in the area.'

'You seriously expect me to give you a guided tour?'

'Would you give Clarence a tour?' he asked.

Yes. Without a shadow of a doubt. She blew out a breath. 'You're not Clarence.'

'But I am,' he said softly. 'I know things about you that you haven't told anyone else—just as you know things about me. We're friends.'

Was that true? Could she trust him?

Part of her wanted to believe that her friendship with Clarence wasn't a castle built on sand; part of her wanted to run as fast as she could in the opposite direction.

Hope had a brief tussle with common sense—and won. 'All right. I'll show you round. But it'll have to be by torchlight,' she warned.

'Cinemas are supposed to be dark,' he said with a smile.

She wished he hadn't smiled like that. It gave her

goose-bumps. Gabriel Hunter had a seriously beautiful mouth, and his eyes were the colour of cornflowers.

And why was she mooning over him? Ridiculous. She needed to get a grip. Right now. 'This is the foyer—well, obviously,' she said gruffly, and shone the torch round.

He gave an audible intake of breath. 'The glass, Nicole—it's beautiful. Art Deco. It deserves to be show-cased.'

The same thing she'd noticed. Warmth flared through her, and she had to damp it down. This was her business rival Gabriel Hunter, not her friend Clarence, she reminded herself.

'The cinema itself is through here.'

He sniffed as she ushered him through to the auditorium, then pulled a face. 'I'm afraid you've got a mouse problem. That's a pretty distinctive smell.'

'They've chomped the seats a lot, too.' She shone a torch onto one of the worst bits to show him.

'There are people who can restore that. I know some good upholst—' He stopped. 'Sorry. I'll shut up. You're perfectly capable of researching your own contractors.'

She brought him back out into the foyer. 'From what you said the other day, you know that this place was originally an Edwardian *kursaal* or leisure centre. The downstairs was originally a skating rink and the upstairs was the Electric Cinema.'

'Does that mean you have a projection room upstairs as well as down?' he asked.

'I'm still mapping the place out and working my way through all the junk, but I think so—because in the nineteen-thirties it was changed to a ballroom upstairs and a picture house downstairs.'

'So is upstairs still the ballroom?'

Upstairs was the bit that she hoped would make him

change his mind about ever asking her to sell again. Because surely, working for a company which renovated old buildings and redeveloped them into hotels, he must have some appreciation of architecture? Clarence would love it, she knew; but how much of Clarence had been designed simply to charm her and how much of Clarence was really Gabriel? That was what she hadn't worked out yet. And until she did she wasn't prepared to give him the benefit of the doubt.

'The stairs,' she said, gesturing towards them.

'That's beautiful, too. Look at that railing. I can imagine women sweeping down that staircase in floaty dresses after waltzing the night away.'

Just as she'd thought when she'd seen the staircase. And there was no way that Gabriel could've known she'd thought that, because she hadn't told him. So was his response pure Clarence, and that meant Clarence was the real part of him, after all?

'And this room at the top,' she said as they walked up the stairs, 'was used by Brian as a store-room, or so Mum says.'

'Is your mum OK?' he asked.

She frowned. 'OK about what?'

'This place. It must have memories for her. And, in the circumstances...' His voice faded.

'She's fine. But thank you for asking.'

'I wasn't being polite, and I wasn't asking for leverage purposes, either,' he said softly. 'I was asking as your friend, Nicole.'

Gabriel wasn't her friend, though.

Saying nothing, she opened the door to the upper room and handed him the torch. 'See what you think.'

He shone the torch on the flooring first. 'That looks like parquet flooring—cleaned up, that will be stunning.'

He bent down to take a closer look. 'Just look at the inlay—Nicole, this is gorgeous.'

But it wasn't the really stunning bit of the room. She still couldn't understand why her grandfather had wasted it by using the room as storage space.

'Look up,' she said.

Gabriel shone the torch upwards and she actually heard his intake of breath. 'Is that plasterwork or is it pressed tin?' he asked.

'I assume it's plasterwork. I didn't even know ceilings could be made of anything else. Well, except maybe wood?'

'Do you have a ladder?' he asked.

'It doesn't tend to be something that a banker would use in their everyday job, so no,' she said dryly.

'I'll bring one over from next door later this afternoon, so we can take a closer look,' he said.

We? she wondered. It was *her* cinema, not his. But at least he seemed to appreciate the ceiling.

'Do you still want to raze the place to the ground, then?' she asked.

'No,' he admitted. 'If that ceiling's tin, which I think it might be, that's quite rare in England and it'll probably get this building listed. Look at those Art Deco stars— they're absolutely amazing.'

He'd already told her that if a building was listed it meant extra work and delays. 'You mean, that ceiling will get the building listed if someone drops the council an anonymous letter telling them about it?' she asked sharply.

'If you mean me or anyone at Hunter's, no. That's not how I operate. But I've got experience in this sort of thing, Nicole. I can help you. We're not on opposite sides.'

'It feels like it.'

'We've been friends for a while. We probably know more about each other than most of our non-online friends know about us.'

'But do we really?' she asked. 'How do we know it wasn't all an act?'

'It wasn't on my part,' he said, 'and I'm pretty sure it wasn't on yours.' He held her gaze. 'Have dinner with me tonight.'

No. Common sense meant that she should say no.

But the expression in his eyes wasn't one of triumph or guile. She couldn't quite read it.

'Why do you want to have dinner with me?' she asked.

Gabriel couldn't blame her for being suspicious. He *had* been trying to buy her cinema, planning to turn it into a car park for his hotel. But now he'd seen the building and its potential he was looking at the whole thing in a different light. Maybe there was a way to compromise. OK, so he wouldn't get the parking, but he might get something even better. Something that would benefit them both.

'Because then we can talk. Properly.' He sighed. 'Look, you know my background's in the service and entertainment industry. I've worked with several renovations, bringing a building kicking and screaming back to life and then into the modern age. I've got a lot of knowledge that could help you, and a lot of contacts that would be useful for you.'

'And what's in it for you?'

She was so prickly with him now. And he wanted their old easy-going relationship back. 'Does something have to be in it for me?'

'You have a reputation as a very hard-headed businessman. I can accept that you'd maybe do charity work, because that would double up as good PR for Hunter Hotels, but I'm not a charity.' She looked at him again. 'So why would you help me for nothing?'

'Because,' he said softly, 'I live in Surrey Quays and this building is part of my community. Plus Georgy-girl's my friend and I'd like to help her make her dreams come true.'

'And there's really nothing in it for you? At all?'

Maybe this was the time for honesty. And she was right in that there was some self-interest. 'Do you remember suggesting to me that I ought to take the family business in a different direction—that I should do something that really interests me, something that gives me a challenge?'

'Yes.'

'Maybe this would be my challenge.'

'And that's it? To help someone you think is your friend and to give yourself an intellectual challenge?'

And to give him some freedom. But he wasn't quite ready to admit how stifled he felt. Not to Nicole. Georgy was a different matter; but right now Nicole wasn't Georgy and she didn't trust him. 'That's it,' he said. 'Have dinner with me tonight and we can discuss it properly.'

Nicole intended to say no, but the words that came out of her mouth were different. 'Only on condition we go halves on the bill tonight—and I owe you for the coffee and brownie.'

'You can buy me coffee later in the week,' he said. 'I'll be around next door.'

'You're trying to tell me you're the boy next door, now?'

He shrugged. 'My business is next to yours and I have a Y chromosome, so I guess that's the same thing.'

She shook her head. 'It's a million miles away, Mr Hunter, and you know it.'

He didn't argue with her; instead, he said, 'I'll book somewhere for dinner. I already know we both like Italian food. I'll pick you up at, what, seven?'

'I suppose you've already looked up my address,' she said, feeling slightly nettled.

'On the electoral roll, yes.' He paused. 'It would be useful to have each other's phone number in case one of us is delayed.'

'True.' And in the meantime she might be able to think up a good excuse not to meet him, and could text him said good excuse. She grabbed her phone from her pocket. 'Tell me your number, then I'll text you so you'll have mine.'

It only took a matter of seconds to sort that out.

'Thank you for showing me round,' he said. 'I'll see you later.'

'OK.'

But she couldn't stop thinking about him all afternoon. Was she doing the right thing, going to dinner with him? Could they work together? Or was she just setting herself up for yet another fall and it'd be better to call it off?

Halfway through the afternoon there was a knock on the front door, and she heard Gabriel call, 'Hello? Nicole, are you here?'

She was about to ask what he thought he was doing when she realised that he'd changed into jeans and an old T-shirt—making him look much more approachable than his shark-in-a-suit persona—and he was carrying a ladder.

'Why the ladder?' she asked.

'Remember I said I'd bring one over? I thought we could take a closer look at your ceiling,' he said.

'Don't you need to be somewhere?'

He smiled. 'I don't have to account for every minute of my time. Anyway, I promised you a ladder. Given that you've already said a ladder isn't part of your everyday equipment—whereas it *is* part of mine—I'll carry the ladder and you do the torch?'

'No need for a torch. The electricity's back on now.'

'The fuses are OK?'

'So far, yes, but obviously I'll need to get the wiring checked out properly.'

This time he didn't offer help from his team next door; part of her was relieved that he'd got the message, but part of her was disappointed that he'd given up on her so quickly. Which was ridiculous and contrary. She didn't want to be beholden to Gabriel Hunter for anything. But she missed her friend Clarence.

'Let's go take a look at that ceiling,' he said instead.

In the old ballroom, he rested the ladder against the wall.

'So you're going to hold the ladder steady for me?' she asked.

'Do you know what to look for?' he checked.

'No, but it's my ceiling.' And she wanted to be the first one to look at it.

He grinned, as if guessing exactly what was going through her mind. 'Yes, ma'am. OK. You go up first and take a look.' He took the camera from round his neck and handed it to her. 'And photographs, if you want.'

She recognised the make of the camera as seriously expensive. 'You're trusting me with this?'

'Yes. Why wouldn't I?'

He clearly wasn't as suspicious and mean-minded as she was, which made her feel a twinge of guilt. 'Thanks,' she said. She put the camera strap round her neck so it'd leave her hands free, then climbed up the ladder. Close up, she still didn't have a clue whether she was looking at plasterwork or tin. But she duly took photographs and went back down the ladder.

Gabriel reviewed her photographs on the rear screen of the camera.

'So can you tell whether it's tin or plasterwork from the photographs?' she asked.

He shook his head. 'Would you mind if I went up and had a look?'

'Go ahead. I'll hold the ladder steady.'

As he climbed the ladder, Nicole noticed how nice his backside looked encased in faded denim. And how inappropriate was that? She damped down the unexpected flickers of desire and concentrated on holding the ladder steady.

'It's definitely pressed tin,' Gabriel said when he came back down. 'It was very popular in early twentieth-century America because it was an affordable alternative to plasterwork, plus it was lightweight and fireproof. So I guess that's why it was used here, to keep the ceiling fireproof. The tin sheets were pressed with a die to make patterned panels, then painted white to make them look as if it was plasterwork. Though, if that's still the original paint up there, it's likely to be lead, so you need to be careful and get a specialist in to restore the panels.'

'It sounds as if you've come across this before.'

He nodded. 'There was a tin ceiling and tin wainscoting in a hotel we renovated three or four years ago. Basically you need to strip off the old paint to get rid of the lead—for health and safety reasons—then put on a protective base coat, patch up any damage and repaint it.' He paused. 'Usually the panels were painted white, but there seem to be some traces of gold on the stars.'

She looked up at the ceiling. 'I can imagine this painted dark blue, with gold stars.'

'Especially with that floor, this would really work as a ballroom—and ballroom dancing is definitely on trend. There are even fitness classes based on ballroom dance moves. You could take the *kursaal* back to its roots but bring it into this century at the same time.'

He was talking a lot of sense. Putting things into words that she'd already started to think about. 'It's a possibility.' She continued staring at the ceiling. 'There are all kinds of styles around the cinema, everything from Edwardian through to slightly shabby nineteen-seventies. It's a mess, and it'd be sensible to take it back to one point in time. And, with features like this, it'd make sense to restore the building back to how it was when it was a ballroom and cinema. It's a shame there won't be any colour pictures to give me any idea what the original decorative schemes looked like, though. There definitely isn't any paperwork giving any details.'

'Actually, there might be colour photos,' he said, and grabbed his phone. After a few seconds' browsing, he handed the phone to her so she could see for herself. 'Just as I thought. According to this website, colour photos exist from as far back as the middle of the eighteen hundreds.'

'But weren't they coloured by hand, back then—so they were colourised rather than actually being printed in colour?' Nicole pointed out.

'Look, you can see the three different print overlay colours at the edge of this one.' He pored over the screen with her. 'But it also says the process was time-consuming.'

'And expensive, so it'd be reserved for really big news stories—unless I guess someone was really wealthy and did it as a hobby. Though would they have taken a picture of the building?'

'There might be something in the local archive office,' he said. 'Photos or sketches that people haven't seen for a century.'

They looked at each other, and Nicole thought, he's as excited by this as I am. But was this Clarence standing next to her or Gabriel? She couldn't be sure. And, until she was sure, she didn't dare trust him. 'Maybe,' she said carefully.

He'd clearly picked up her wariness, because he said, 'It is as it is. I'd better let you get on. See you at seven.'

'OK.'

Though when Nicole got home it occurred to her that he hadn't told her where they were going, and she didn't have a clue whether she was supposed to dress up or dress down.

She thought about it in the shower while she was washing her hair. If she wore jeans, she'd feel uncomfortable in a posh restaurant—and would he take her somewhere posh to try to impress her? But if she dressed up, she'd feel totally out of place in a more casual bistro.

Little black dress, she decided. Something she would feel comfortable in no matter the situation. And high heels, so he'd know she wasn't intimidated by him.

Bring it on, she thought.

Bring it on.

CHAPTER FIVE

GABRIEL PARKED OUTSIDE Nicole's flat. Nerves fluttered in his stomach, which was absolutely ridiculous, and completely out of character. This wasn't a real date; it was discussing mutual business interests. There was no reason why he should be feeling like this.

Yet this was Nicole. Georgygirl.

And that made things that little bit more complicated.

He and Nicole were on opposite sides. Rivals. And yet Georgy was his friend. The girl he'd got to know over the last six months and really liked. The one person who saw him for who he really was.

How ironic that, now they'd met in real life, she didn't see him at all. She saw Gabriel Hunter, the ruthless businessman: not Clarence, her friend.

He shook himself. It was pointless brooding. Things were as they were. All he could do was make the best out of it and try to salvage a few things from this mess. Maybe he could reach a better understanding with her, in business if nothing else.

Nicole lived in a quieter part of Surrey Quays, in what he recognised as a former industrial complex that had been turned into four-storey apartment blocks. The brickwork was a mellow sand colour; one side had floor-to-ceiling windows and the three upper storeys had a wrought iron balcony. There were trees and raised planted beds in the square, and the whole thing was pretty and peaceful—exactly the kind of place where he'd expected Georgy to live.

He pressed the button to her intercom.

'I'm on my way,' she said.

Economical with words, as usual, he thought with a smile.

But he was blown away when she walked out of the doors to the apartment block. She was wearing a simple black shift dress, with high-heeled black court shoes and no jewellery. Her hair was still pulled back from her face, but this time it was in a sophisticated updo that reminded him of Audrey Hepburn.

'You look amazing,' he said, before he could stop himself.

She inclined her head. 'Thank you.'

And now he felt like he was on his first date all over again. Which was stupid, because as a teenager he'd been overconfident and reckless, never worrying about what people thought of him. He took a deep breath. 'It's only a short drive from here.'

'Short enough to make it more sensible to walk? I can change my shoes.'

'We'll drive,' he said.

He half expected her to make an acerbic comment about his car—a sleek convertible—but she climbed into the passenger seat and said nothing. It wasn't exactly an easy silence between them, but he had no idea what to say, so he concentrated on driving. And she did nothing to dispel the awkwardness between them, either.

Was this a mistake?

Or was she as confused by this whole thing as he was?

Once he'd parked and they were out of the car, he gestured to the narrowboat moored at the quay. 'The food at this place is excellent,' he said.

She read the sign out loud. 'La Chiatta.'

'Italian for "the barge",' he translated.

'Effective.' But then she looked at the narrowboat and the ramp which led from the quay to the deck. The tide was low, so the angle of the ramp was particularly steep. From the expression on her face, Nicole clearly realised she wouldn't be able to walk down that ramp in high heels. Although clothing was something they'd never really talked about in their late-night conversations, Gabriel had the strongest feeling that Nicole almost never wore high heels and had only worn them tonight to prove a point.

'We have two choices,' he said. 'We can go somewhere else that doesn't have a ramp.'

'But you've booked here, yes? It's not fair to the restaurant if we just don't turn up.'

He shrugged. 'I'll pay them a cancellation fee so they don't lose out.'

'What's the second choice?'

Something that would probably get him into trouble, but he couldn't stop himself. 'This,' he said, and picked her up.

'Gabriel!'

It was the first time she'd used his given name and he rather liked it.

But maybe picking her up had been a mistake. Not because she was too heavy, but because she was so close that he could feel the warmth of her skin and smell the soft floral scent of her perfume, and it made him want to kiss her.

That was so inappropriate, it was untrue.

'Hold on tight,' he said, and carried her down the ramp before setting her on her feet again.

'I don't believe you just did that,' she said, sounding shocked.

Clearly tonight she was seeing him as Gabriel the corporate shark, not Clarence. 'No, it was a solution to a problem. By the time we've finished dinner the tide will have changed and you'll be able to walk up the ramp relatively easily.'

She gestured towards the ramp, where a man and a woman were gingerly making their way down together. 'He's not carrying her.'

'Probably because she's wearing flat shoes. No way could you have walked down that ramp in *those* without falling over.' He gestured to her shoes.

'You could've warned me.'

'I didn't even think about it,' he admitted.

'Or I could have taken off my shoes just now.'

'And ended up standing on a sharp stone or something and hurting yourself? My way was simpler, and it's done now so there's no point in arguing about it.'

'If you say, "It is what it is",' she warned, 'I might just punch you.'

He laughed. 'Think about it. It's true. Come and have dinner, Nicole. Have you been here before?'

'No.'

'The pasta is amazing.'

She didn't looked particularly mollified, but she thanked him politely for opening the door for her and walked inside.

This was supposed to be a business discussion, Nicole thought, so why did it feel like a date?

And she still couldn't quite get over what Gabriel had

just done on the ramp. Even Jeff, back in the days when she was still in ignorant bliss of his affair and trusted him, wouldn't have done something like that.

What was worse was that she'd liked being close to Gabriel—close enough to feel the warmth of his skin and smell the citrusy scent of whatever shower gel he used.

And, just before he'd set her back down on her feet, she'd actually wondered what it would be like if he kissed her.

She needed to get this out of her head right now. They weren't friends and they weren't dating; this was strictly business.

Once the waitress had brought their menus and she'd ordered a glass of red wine—noting that Gabriel was sticking to soft drinks—she looked at him. 'Is there anything in particular you recommend?'

'The honeycomb cannelloni is pretty good, and their ciabatta bread is amazing.'

'Sounds good.' At least their tastes meshed when it came to food. He hadn't lied to her about that, then.

Once the waitress had taken their order, he leaned back in his chair. 'Thank you for agreeing to meet me tonight, Nicole.'

'As you say, it's business and neither of us has time to waste. We might as well eat while we discuss things, and save a bit of time.'

She really hoped that it didn't show in her voice how much she was having to fight that spark of attraction. She was absolutely *not* going to let herself wonder what it would be like to run her fingers through his hair, or how the muscles of his back would feel beneath her fingertips.

To distract herself, she asked, 'So what really happened?'

He looked puzzled. 'When?'

'Your teenage incident.'

* * *

Gabriel really hadn't expected her to bring that up. Where was she going with this? Was it to distract him and make him agree to a business deal that, in a saner moment, he would never even have considered? Or maybe he was just being cynical because he'd spent too long in a ruthless business world. Maybe she really did want to know. He shrugged. 'You said you'd read up about it, so you already know the details.'

'I know what was reported, which isn't necessarily the same thing.'

That surprised him, too. She was more perceptive than he'd expected. Then again, how could he tell her the truth? It felt like bleating. And at the end of the day he was the one who'd done something wrong. He shrugged again. 'I was nineteen years old, from a wealthy and privileged background and full of testosterone. My whole crowd was identikit. I guess we all thought we were invincible.'

'I don't buy it,' she said.

'Why not?'

'It was your car, right?'

'Yes,' he admitted.

'Even full of testosterone, I don't think you would've been stupid enough to get behind the steering wheel of a car if you'd been drinking.' She gestured to his glass of mineral water. 'And I notice you're not even having one glass of wine now—which I assume is because you're driving.'

It warmed him. Even if Nicole did see him as her business rival, someone she shouldn't even like, she was being fair to him. And she'd picked up on the thing that the newspapers hadn't. 'It is. I wouldn't put anyone at risk like that.'

'So what really happened?'

He shook his head. 'It doesn't matter now. I was the one behind the wheel with alcohol in my bloodstream, I was the one who crashed into the shop, and I was the one whose father's expensive lawyer got me off on a technicality. It was my fault.'

'You didn't actually know you'd been drinking, did you?'

He knew she was perceptive, but that really shocked him. 'What makes you say that?' he asked carefully.

'Because,' she said, 'even given that you might've had a lot of growing up to do back then, there's a massive difference between high spirits and stupidity, and you're not stupid. Not with the highest First your university had ever awarded and an MBA from the best business school in the country.'

'So you really did do some digging on me.' He wasn't sure if he was more impressed or discomfited.

'Just as you did on me,' she pointed out, 'so get off your high horse and answer the question.'

'You're right. I didn't know I'd been drinking,' he said. 'I assume there was vodka in my orange juice— something I wouldn't have tasted.'

'So the people who spiked your drink got away with it.'

'I got away with it, too,' he reminded her. 'On a technicality.'

'Maybe Gabriel did,' she said. 'But I know a different side to you.'

She was actually recognising who he was? Gabriel was stunned into silence.

'You've stuck out a job you don't enjoy, out of loyalty,' she continued, 'because your dad sorted out the mess you made, so you didn't have a criminal record and could finish your law degree. And I think Clarence would've done something more. At the very least, Clarence would've gone to see the shop owners and apologised.'

He squirmed. Now he really understood why she'd made it up the ranks so swiftly at the bank, despite not having a degree. She was the most clear-sighted person he'd ever met. 'Do we have to talk about this?' Because he could see where this was going, and it made him antsy.

'If we're really going to work together in any way, shape or form,' she said, 'I need to know who you are. Are you the heir to Hunter Hotels, who dates a different woman every week?'

'Strictly speaking, I haven't dated at all for the last six months.' Since he'd first started talking to her online. Which hadn't actually occurred to him until now. Was that why he hadn't dated? Because part of him was already involved with her?

'Or are you really my friend Clarence?' she asked.

'It's not that black and white,' he said. Part of him was Gabriel, the heir to Hunter Hotels, desperate to make up for his past mistakes and yet feeling stifled. And part of him was Clarence, a man who actually connected with people around him. If the crash hadn't happened, what would his life have been like? He wouldn't have had to spend so much time biting his tongue and reminding himself to be grateful. Maybe he could've been Clarence all the time. 'I could ask you the same. Are you Nicole Thomas, the workaholic banker, or are you Georgygirl, who dreams of the stars?' He paused. 'And you've got the stars, right on the ceiling of your cinema.'

'Maybe I'm a bit of both,' she said.

'And so,' he said, 'am I.'

'So what did you do?'

He sighed. 'You're not going to let this go, are you?

Nicole, it's not public knowledge and I want it to stay that way.'

'Who else knows?'

'Two others.'

'Not your father?'

'No,' he admitted. Evan Hunter had decreed that everything was done and dusted. The shopkeeper had been paid off, Gabriel didn't have a criminal record and, although Evan hadn't said it in so many words, Gabriel would be paying for that mistake for the rest of his life. He certainly had, to date. And he felt as if he'd never earn his father's respect.

'The shopkeeper, then,' Nicole said. 'And his wife.'

She was good, he thought. Incisive. Good at reading people and situations. 'I'm saying nothing until I know this stays with you,' he said.

'Do you trust me?'

'Do you trust me?' he countered.

She sighed. 'We're back to the online-or-real-life thing. Two different people.'

'Are we? Because I'd trust Georgygirl and I think you'd trust Clarence.'

She spread her hands. 'OK. It's your decision.'

If he told her, it would give her leverage.

If he didn't, it would tell her that he didn't trust her and she couldn't trust him.

He thought about it. Was it a risk worth taking? Strategically, it meant giving a little now to gain a lot in the future.

'Obviously my father paid for the damage to the shop,' he said. 'But you can't solve everything with money.'

'So what did you do?' Her voice was very soft. Gentle. Not judgemental. And that made it easier to tell her.

'I went to see the Khans,' he said. 'With a big bouquet

of flowers and a genuine apology. And I said that money alone wasn't enough to repay the damage I'd done, so until the end of my degree I'd work weekends in their shop, unpaid, doing whatever needed doing.'

'Stocking shelves?'

'Sometimes. And sorting out the newspapers for the delivery boys—which meant getting there at five in the morning. And don't forget sweeping the floor and cleaning out the fridges.'

She raised her eyebrows. 'It must've killed your partying, having to be at work for five in the morning at weekends.'

'The crash kind of did that anyway,' he said. 'It was my wake-up call.'

She looked straight at him. 'You weren't just a shopboy, were you?'

'I was at first,' he said. 'It was six months before the Khans started to believe that I wasn't just a posh boy slumming it, but eventually I became their friend.' He smiled. 'I used to eat with them on Sundays after my shift in the shop. Meera taught me how to make a seriously good biryani, and Vijay taught me as much as my father did about business management and having to understand your own business right from the bottom up. Though in return when I did my MBA I helped them streamline a few processes and negotiate better terms with their suppliers.'

'Do you still see them?'

'Not as often nowadays, but yes. Their kids are teenagers now; they were very small when the crash happened. Sanjay, their eldest, is off to university next year, and I've given him the lecture about partying and getting in with the wrong crowd.' As well as sponsoring the boy through the three years of his degree, but Nicole didn't need to know that.

When the food arrived, she tasted her cannelloni and looked thoughtful.

'Is it OK?' he asked.

'More than OK. You were right about the food, just as you were right about the coffee on Challoner Road.' She paused. 'What you did for the Khans...that's what I'd expect Clarence to do.'

'Clarence wouldn't have been stupid enough to go round with the over-privileged crowd in the first place,' he pointed out.

'You're human. We all make mistakes.'

Which revealed that she had a weakness, too. That she'd made a life-changing mistake. One that maybe held her back as much as his did him. 'What was yours?' he asked softly.

She shook her head. 'It's not important.'

'I told you mine. Fair's fair.'

She looked away. 'Let's just say I put my trust in the wrong person.'

'And you think I'm going to let you down, the same way?'

She spread her hands. 'Gabriel Hunter, known for being a ruthless businessman—is it any wonder I think his offer of help with the cinema comes with strings?'

'Or you could see it as Clarence,' he countered, 'who really needs a new challenge, and a way to take the family business in a different direction.'

'OK. Just supposing the Electric Palace was yours... what would you do?'

'Bring the building back to life, and then get it listed so nobody can ever try to raze it to the ground and turn it into a car park,' he said promptly. 'In that order.'

She smiled. 'Right. But seriously?'

'You've got two main rooms, both with projectors, yes?'

'Yes?'

'Do you know the capacity of the rooms?'

'There are three hundred and fifty seats in the lower room.'

'The upper room's smaller. We'd need to measure it properly, but I'd guess we could fit seventy-five to a hundred.' He looked thoughtful. 'I really like your idea of taking the Electric Palace back to how it was when it was first built. You've got the ceiling upstairs, the parquet flooring and the amazing glass in the foyer. We need to look in the archives and ask on the Surrey Quays forum to see if anyone's got any old newspapers or magazines, or anything that has pictures or sketches or a detailed description of how it was.'

'But originally it was a cinema and ice rink,' she reminded him.

'I don't think an ice rink would bring in enough footfall or spend,' he said. 'The next incarnation would work better—the cinema and the ballroom. But keep the Art Deco glass. That's too stunning to lose.'

'You really want to turn the upstairs room back into the ballroom?'

'No. I think it'd work better as a multi-purpose room,' he said. 'If you didn't have fixed seats, you could use it as a cinema; but you could also use it as a ballroom and a conference venue.'

'Conference venue?' she asked.

He knew he was probably speaking too soon, but it was the perfect solution. A way to work together, so he could help his friend *and* impress his father. 'Conference venue,' he confirmed. 'The chairs you use for the cinema—they could be placed around the edge of the dance floor on ballroom nights, and they could be moved easily into whatever configuration you need for a conference, whether it was horseshoe or theatre-style. And if you use tables that fit together, they'd also work as occasional tables for the cinema and ballroom nights.' He warmed to his theme. 'Or for any club that wants to hire the room—you could still do the craft stuff. Offer people crafternoon tea.'

'Crafternoon tea?' She looked mystified.

'A session of craft—whether it's sewing or painting or pottery—followed by afternoon tea. Hence crafternoon tea,' he explained.

'That's the most terrible pun I've ever heard,' she said. 'Maybe. But would anyone really hire that room for a conference? I can't see it.'

'You have a hotel next door,' he said. 'Which would hire the room as a main conference suite, and there could be breakout rooms for the conference next door.'

'What about refreshments and meals for the conference delegates?'

'Depends on your staff and facilities. That's when we'd work together,' he said. 'We'd have to sort out costings and come up with something that was fair to both of us. I'm thinking out loud, here, but maybe you'd do the coffee and a buffet lunch, and I'd do the evening sit-down meal, because my kitchen has a bigger capacity than yours.'

'Right,' she said.

'And then there's downstairs,' he said, ignoring the fact that she didn't seem enthusiastic—once he'd worked out the costings and she could see it would benefit both of them, she'd come round. 'We have the main cinema. We can restore the seats. As I said, I know specialist upholsterers who can do that.'

'The seats are old and uncomfortable. The multiplexes offer VIP seating. Maybe that's the sort of thing I should put in.'

He shook his head. 'We can't compete with the multiplexes, not with one full-time and one part-time screen. They have twenty or more screens and can offer staggered film times. We can't.'

'So maybe we need to offer something different.'

He wondered if she realised that she was using the word 'we'. Though he wasn't going to call her on it, and risk her backing away again. 'Such as?'

'When I was looking at what my competitors offer, I saw an idea I really liked—a place that had comfortable sofas instead of traditional cinema seating, and little tables where people could put their drinks or food,' she said.

'Like having the best night in, except you've gone out for it?' he asked. 'So you've got all the comfort and convenience of home, but professional quality sound and vision—actually, that would work really well.'

'And when the ushers take you to your seat, they also offer to take your order for food and drink. Which they bring to you and put on the little table.'

'I like that. A lot. But serving alcohol and hot food means getting a licence,' he said, 'and we'd have to think about what we offer on the menu.'

'We could have cinema-themed food,' she said. 'But it has to be easy to eat. Pizza, burgers, hot dogs and chicken.'

'Would that replace traditional cinema snacks?'

'No. Not everyone would want a meal. I think we need to include the traditional stuff, too—popcorn, nachos, bags of chocolates. And tubs of ice cream from a local supplier.'

Her eyes were shining. He'd just bet his were the same. Brainstorming ideas with her was the most enjoyment he'd had from anything work-related in a long, long time. And he had a feeling it was the same for her.

'You know what this is like?' he asked.

'What?'

'Talking to you online. But better, because it's face to face.'

Then he wished he hadn't said anything when she looked wary again.

'Excuse me,' she said. 'I need the Ladies'.'

'The toilets are that way.' He indicated in the direction behind her.

'Thanks.'

On her way to the toilets, Nicole stopped by the till and handed over her credit card. 'Mr Hunter's table,' she said. 'The bill's mine. Please make sure that you charge everything to me.'

'Of course, madam,' the waiter said.

She smiled. 'Thanks.' It would save any argument over the bill later. And, given that Gabriel had already bought her two coffees and a brownie, she felt in his debt. This would even things out a little.

You know what this is like? Talking to you online. But better. His words echoed in her head.

He was right.

And she really didn't know what to do about it, which was why she'd been a coward and escaped to the toilets.

Tonight, Gabriel wasn't the corporate shark-in-a-suit; he was wearing a casual shirt and chinos that made him far more approachable. He'd attracted admiring glances from every single female in the restaurant—and it wasn't surprising. Gabriel Hunter was absolutely gorgeous.

But.

They were still on opposite sides. They shouldn't be wanting to have anything to do with each other, let alone help each other. And could she trust him? Or would he let her down as badly as Jeff had?

She still didn't have an answer by the time she returned to their table. And she was quiet all through pudding.

And when he discovered that she'd already paid the bill, he looked seriously fed up. 'Dinner was my idea, Nicole. I was going to pay.'

'And I told you, the deal was that we went halves.'

'So why did you pay for the whole lot?'

'Because you bought me two coffees and a brownie, and I don't like being in anyone's debt. I pay my way.'

'Now I'm in your debt.'

She smiled. 'That suits me.'

'It doesn't suit me. And we haven't really finished our conversation.'

Excitement fluttered in her stomach. So what was he going to suggest now? Another business meeting over dinner? Coffee at his place?

'We kind of have,' she said. 'You've agreed that the Electric Palace should be restored, and you know it's not for sale.'

'But,' he said, 'we haven't agreed terms for conference hire, or whether you're going to use my kitchen facilities to save having to build your own.'

'That assumes I'm going to develop the cinema the way you see it. I have my own ideas.' At the end of the day, this was *her* business. She'd spent ten years marching to someone else's tune, and she wasn't about to let Gabriel take over—even if he did have more experience than she did.

'I think we need another meeting,' he said.

He looked all cool and calm and controlled. And Nicole really wanted to see him ruffled.

But maybe that was the red wine talking. Even though she'd stuck to her limit of no more than one glass. Cool, calm and controlled would be better for both of them.

'I don't have my diary on me,' she said.

His expression very clearly said he didn't believe a word of it, but he spread his hands. 'Text me some times and dates.'

So now the ball was in her court?

She could turn him down.

Or they could explore this. See where the business was going.

See where they were going.

She damped down the little flicker of hope. She couldn't trust him that far. Jeff had destroyed her ability to trust.

'I'll text you,' she said. Because that gave her wriggle room. A chance to say no when she'd had time to think about it on her own. Gabriel was charming and persuasive; Jeff had been charming and persuasive, too, and following his ideas had got her badly burned. Who was to say that this wouldn't be the same?

'Good.'

The ramp was much more manageable now the tide had turned, and this time Gabriel didn't sweep her off her feet. Nicole wasn't sure whether she was more relieved or disappointed. And he didn't suggest coffee at his place; she wasn't quite ready to offer him coffee at hers. So he merely saw her to the door of her apartment block—brushing off her protests that she was perfectly capable of seeing herself home from the car park with a blunt, 'It's basic good manners.'

And he didn't try to kiss her goodnight, not even with a peck on the cheek.

Which was a good thing, she told herself. They didn't have that kind of relationship. Besides, she wasn't good at relationships. Hadn't Jeff's mistress said that Nicole was a cold fish? So looking for anything else from this would be a huge mistake. It would be better to keep things strictly business. And, even better than that, to keep her distance from him completely.

CHAPTER SIX

'HELLO? IS ANYONE THERE?'

Nicole went in search of the voice, to discover a man standing in the entrance to the cinema, holding a metal box of tools.

'Are you Nicole Thomas?' he asked.

'Yes,' she said.

'I'm Kyle. The boss wants me to do a quick check on your wiring.'

'Boss?' Did he mean Gabriel? But she hadn't asked Gabriel for help—and this felt a bit as if he was trying to take over.

She thought quickly to find a polite way to refuse, and it clearly showed on her face because Kyle said, 'The boss said you'd tell me thank you but you don't need any help, and he says to tell you he wants me to check your wiring's OK to make sure this place doesn't burn down and set his hotel on fire.'

It was a comment that Gabriel had made before. It wasn't something she could counter easily, and this would either reassure her or be an early warning of difficulties to come. Plus it wasn't Kyle's fault that Gabriel made her antsy. She smiled at him. 'OK. Thank you. Can I offer you a coffee? I'm sorry, I don't have any milk or sugar.'

'You're all right. I just had my tea break next door.'

'Right. Um, I guess I need to show you where the fuse box is, to start with?'

'That, and I'll check a few of the sockets to be on the safe side.'

She showed him where the fuse box was, and left him to get on with it.

He came to find her when he'd finished. 'There's good news and bad,' he said.

'Tell me the bad, first,' she said.

'You've got a bit of mouse damage to some of the cabling around the fuse box, because it was an area they could get to.'

'Will it take long to fix?'

He shook his head. 'And the good news is the wiring's been redone at some point in the last thirty years. You haven't got any aluminium cable, lead-sheathed cable or the old black cables with a rubber sheath which would mean it was really old and could burn the place down. I would recommend getting a full system check, though, when you get that little bit of cabling replaced.'

'Thank you. That's good to know. I appreciate your help.'

'No worries.' He sketched a salute and left.

Nicole made a mental note to call in to the hotel later that afternoon with a tin of chocolate biscuits to say thanks. Though she knew who she really needed to thank. Strictly speaking, it was interference, but she knew Gabriel had only done it to help—and he'd dressed it in a way that meant she could accept it. She grabbed her phone and called him. 'Thank you for sending over your electrician.'

'Pleasure. So you didn't send him away with a flea in his ear?' Gabriel asked.

'You kind of pre-empted me on that.'

'Ah, the "I don't want you to set my hotel on fire" thing. And it's true. Total self-interest on my part.' He laughed. 'So how is the wiring?'

'Apparently there's a bit of mouse damage so I'll need to replace some of the cabling, but the good news is that it's modern cable so I'm not looking at a total rewire.'

'That's great. Have you sorted out a surveyor yet?'

'I have three names.' Though she knew she was working quite a way out of her experience zone. Although she wanted to keep her independence and sort out everything herself, was that really the right thing for her business? It would be sensible to ask for advice from someone who knew that area—like Gabriel—instead of being too proud and then making a mistake that could jeopardise the cinema. Asking for help would be pragmatic, not weak. Suggesting they got together to talk about it wasn't the same as suggesting a date. And it wasn't just an excuse to see him. It really wasn't, she told herself firmly. She wasn't going to let her attraction to him derail the cinema restoration project. She cleared her throat. 'I was wondering if maybe I could buy you a coffee and run the names by you.'

'Strictly speaking, I'm the one beholden to you and ought to be the one buying the coffee. You paid for dinner last night,' he reminded her.

'You paid for coffee twice. I still owe you coffee twice.'

'In which case I owe you dinner. When are you free?'

Help. That felt much more like a date. And she wasn't ready. 'Let's focus on the coffee,' she said. 'When are you at the hotel next?'

'About half-past two this afternoon.'

'The perfect time for a coffee break. See you then.'

And it was as easy as that. She knew how he liked his

coffee. She also knew he had a weakness for chocolate brownies, as long as it was dark chocolate. So, at twenty-nine minutes past two, Nicole walked in to the building site next door with two espressos, two brownies and a tin of chocolate biscuits, and asked the first person she saw to point her in the direction of Gabriel Hunter.

He was in a room which was clearly earmarked as a future office, and he was on the phone when she arrived; he lifted his hand in acknowledgement, and she waited in the corridor until he'd finished the call, to give him some privacy.

'Good to see you, Nicole,' he said.

Was that Clarence talking, or Gabriel the shark-in-a-suit? 'Coffee and a brownie,' she said, handing them over. 'And these biscuits are for Kyle, your electrician. To say thank you for checking out my wiring.'

'I'll make sure he gets them. And thank you for the coffee. Having a good day?' he asked, smiling at her.

That definitely sounded more like Clarence speaking. And the way he smiled made her stomach flip. With a real effort, Nicole forced herself to focus on business. 'Yes. How about you?'

He shrugged. 'It is as it is.'

His eyes really were beautiful. So was his mouth. It would be so very, very easy to reach out and trace his lower lip with her fingertip...

And it would also be insane. To distract herself, Nicole muttered, 'As I said, I've got to the stage where I need a surveyor and quotes from builders.'

'Obviously you know to add at least ten per cent to any quote, because with a renovation job you're always going to come across something you don't expect that will need fixing,' he said. 'And to allow extra time for unexpected delays as well. Even if you've had a survey done first, you're bound to come across something that will affect your schedule.'

'If the building is structurally sound, then I want the cinema up and running in eight weeks.'

'Eight weeks?' He looked shocked. 'Isn't that a bit fast?'

'It's the start of the school holidays,' she said. 'And it's always good to have a goal to work towards rather than being vague about things. That way you can plan and actually accomplish something instead of delivering nothing but hot air.'

'True.' He blew out a breath. 'But eight weeks is a big ask. Even if the place is structurally sound, it needs complete redecoration, you've got to sort out the fixtures and fittings, and there's no way you'll be able to do anything at all with the upstairs room until the ceiling's been sorted, not with that lead paint.' He frowned. 'I was thinking, that's probably why your grandfather used it as a storage room.'

'Because it would be too expensive to fix it, or it would take too much time?'

'Either or both,' he said. 'Just bear in mind you might not be able to have the whole building up and running at once. You might have to scale back to something more doable—say, start with the downstairs screen and kiosk refreshments only.'

Which would mean a lower income. And Nicole needed the place to make a decent profit, because she knew now that she really didn't want to go back to the bank. She wasn't afraid of hard work or long hours; she'd do whatever it took to make a go of the Electric Palace. But now she wanted to put the hours in for herself, not for a corporation that barely knew her name. 'I'm opening in eight weeks,' she said stubbornly.

'Where's your list of surveyors?' he asked.

'Here.' She flicked into the notes app on her phone and handed it to him.

He looked through the list. 'The first one's good, the second will cancel on you half a dozen times because he always overbooks himself, and the third is fine. I always like to get three quotes, so do you want the name of the guy I use, to replace the one who won't make it?'

'I'm eating humble pie already, aren't I?' she pointed out.

'Strictly speaking, you're eating a dark chocolate brownie,' he said, 'which you paid for. So no.' He sighed. 'OK. Would you have let Clarence help?'

She nodded.

'Say it out loud,' he said.

She would've done the same and made him admit it aloud, too. She gave in. 'Yes. I would've accepted help from Clarence.'

'Well, then. I thought we agreed at dinner that we're not on opposite sides?'

'We didn't really agree anything.'

'Hmm.' He added a set of contact details to her list and handed the phone back. 'I'd say from your old job that you'd be good at summing people up. Talk to all of them and go with the one your instinct tells you is right for the job.'

He wasn't pushing his guy first? So maybe he really was fair, rather than ruthless. Maybe she could trust him. 'Thank you,' she said.

'Pleasure.' He paused. 'What about builders?'

'I was going to ask the surveyor for recommendations.'

'That's a good idea.' He looked her straight in the eye. 'Though, again, I can give you contact details if you'd like them. I know you don't want to feel as if you owe me anything, but a recommendation from someone you know is worth a dozen testimonials from people you don't.'

'True.'

'And I wouldn't give you the name of someone who was unreliable or slapdash. Because that would affect my reputation,' he said.

She believed him. At least, on a business footing. Any other trust was out of her ability, right now.

'While you're here, do you want to see round the place?' he asked.

'You're going to give me a tour of the hotel?'

'Fair's fair—I made you give me a tour of the cinema,' he pointed out.

She smiled. 'That would be nice.'

The walls were made of the same mellow honey-coloured brick as her flat. She noticed that the ceilings of the rooms were all high.

'So this was an industrial complex before?' she asked.

'It was a spice warehouse,' he said, 'so we're naming all the function rooms accordingly. Cinnamon, coriander, caraway...'

'Sticking to the Cs?'

He laughed. 'I was thinking about maybe using a different letter on each floor. And I'm toying with "The Spice House" as our hotel name.'

'That might get you mixed up with a culinary supplier or an Indian restaurant,' she said.

'I'm still thinking about it,' he said.

'So this is a business hotel?'

One without the exclusive parking they'd planned originally. Instead, next door would be the cinema. And if Nicole would agree to keep the upper room as a flexible space and not just a fixed second screen, maybe there was a way they could work together. Something for the leisure side and not just the conference stuff she'd resisted earlier. Something that also might make his father finally see that Gabriel had vision and could be trusted with the future direction of the business.

'Business and leisure, mixed,' he said. 'We'll have a hundred and twenty-five bedrooms—that's twenty-five per floor on the top five floors—plus conference facilities on the first floor. We'll have meeting rooms with all the communications and connections our clients need, and a breakout area for networking or receptions. I want to be able to offer my clients everything from training and team-building events through to seminars and product launches. That's on the business side. On the leisure side, we can offer wedding receptions. I'm getting a licence so we can hold civil ceremonies here, too.' He paused. 'Though I've been thinking. Maybe you should be the one to get the wedding licence.'

'Me?' She looked surprised. 'You think people would want to get married in a cinema?'

'They'd want to get married in your upstairs room, especially if you're going to do the ceiling the way you described it to me,' he said. 'And that sweeping stair-case would look amazing in wedding photos. The bride and groom, with the train of the bride's dress spread out over the stairs, or all the guests lined up on the stairs and leaning on that wrought iron banister—which would look great painted gold to match the stars on the ceiling.'

'So they'd have the wedding at the cinema, then go next door to you for the reception?'

'For the meal, yes. And then the upper room could turn back into a ballroom, if you wanted, with the bar next door or a temporary bar set up from the hotel if that's easier. Between us, we'd be able to offer a complete wedding package. The hotel has a honeymoon suite with a modern four-poster, and a health club and spa so we can offer beauty treatments. The morning of the wedding, we could do hair and make-up for the bride, attendants and anyone else in the wedding party. And maybe we could have a special movie screening, the next morning—something for the kids in the wedding party, perhaps?'

Working together.

Could it really be that easy?

'It's a possibility,' she said. 'But I want to think about it before I make any decision.'

'Fair enough.'

'So what else is in your health club and spa, apart from a hairdresser and beautician?'

'A heated pool, a gym with optional personal training packages, a sauna, steam room and whirlpool bath.' He ticked them off on his fingers. 'It's open to non-residents, like our restaurant.'

'And, being The Spice House, you'll specialise in spicy food?'

'Not necessarily, though we might have themed specials.' He smiled. 'The food will be locally sourced as far as possible, with seasonal menus. So far, it's all pretty standard stuff and I'd like to be able to offer our clients something a bit different, too, but I need to sit down and think about it.'

'If you want to brainstorm,' she said, 'and you want to bounce ideas off—well, your neighbour…' The words were out before she could stop them.

'I'd like that,' he said. 'We came up with some good

stuff between us about the cinema. And we've barely scratched the surface there.'

Georgygirl and Clarence. Their old friendship, which was in abeyance right now while she got her head round the fact that her friend was actually her business rival.

Could they transfer that friendship to a working relationship?

It would mean trusting him.

Baby steps, she reminded herself. She just needed to spend a little more time with him. Work out if he really was the same in real life as he'd been privately with her online.

He showed her round the rest of the hotel, then introduced her to his site manager. 'If anything crops up next door,' he said, 'come and see Ray.'

'If I don't know the answer myself,' Ray said, 'I'll know someone who does and can help sort it out for you.'

'Thank you,' she said, shaking Ray's hand and liking how his handshake was firm without being overbearing.

Gabriel walked her to the door. 'Well, good luck with the surveyors and what have you. Let me know how you get on.'

'I will.'

For a moment, she thought he was going to lean forward and kiss her, and her heart actually skipped a beat.

But instead he held out his hand to shake hers.

Her skin tingled where he touched her. And she didn't dare look him in the eye, because she didn't want him to know what kind of effect he had on her. Besides, hadn't Jeff's mistress called her a cold fish? And Gabriel had dated a lot of women. Beautiful women. Passionate women. Way, way out of her league. Her confidence sank that little bit more.

'See you later,' she muttered, and fled.

* * *

When Nicole spoke to the surveyors, she found that Gabriel had been right on the money. The first one was booked up for the next few weeks, the second agreed to drop round that afternoon but then texted her half an hour later to cancel, the third could make it the following week, and the guy that Gabriel had recommended was able to see her first thing the next morning. Better still, he promised to have the report ready by the end of business that day.

It suited her timescale, but Nicole had the distinct feeling that Gabriel had called in a favour or two on her behalf. She couldn't exactly ask the surveyor if that was the case, and she felt it'd be mean-spirited to ask Gabriel himself—it would sound accusatory rather than grateful.

But there was something she could do.

She texted him.

Hey. You busy tomorrow night?

Why?

She really hoped this sounded casual.

Thought I could buy you dinner.

Absolutely not. I still owe you dinner.

But this is dinner with strings.

Ah. Dinner with strings?

She backed off.

OK. Sorry I asked.

* * *

Gabriel looked at the text and sighed. He hadn't meant to sound snippy at all. He'd been teasing her. That was the thing about texting: you couldn't pick up the tone.

He flicked into his contacts screen and called her. 'What are the strings, Nicole?'

'Builder names,' she said.

'You don't have to buy me dinner for that.'

'Yes, I do.'

Was this Nicole's way of saying she wanted to spend time with him but without admitting it? he wondered. But he knew he was just as bad. He wanted to spend time with her, too, but didn't want to admit it to her. 'Dinner would be fine. What time?'

'Seven? I thought maybe we could go to the pizza place just down from the café in Challoner Road. Meet you there?'

'Fine. Want a lift?'

'I'll meet you there,' she repeated.

Nicole and her over-developed sense of independence, he thought with an inward sigh. 'OK. See you at seven.'

She was already there waiting for him when he walked into the pizzeria at precisely one minute to seven, the next evening. She was wearing a pretty, summery dress and he was tempted to tell her how nice she looked, but he didn't want to make her back away. Instead, he asked, 'How did the survey go?'

'Remarkably quickly. Considering that normally people are booked up for at least a week in advance, and it takes several days to do a survey report, it's amazing that your guy not only managed to fit me in this morning,' she said, 'he also emailed me the report at the close of business this afternoon.'

Oh. So she'd picked up the fact that he'd called in a

favour. Well, of course she would. She was bright. 'Remarkable,' he said coolly.

'*Incredibly* remarkable,' she said, 'which is why I'm buying you dinner to say thank you for whatever favours you called in on my behalf. And I've already given the waiter my card, so you can't—'

He laughed, and she stopped. 'What?'

'You're such a control freak,' he said.

'No, I'm not.' She folded her arms in the classic defensive posture. 'I just don't want to—'

'—be beholden to me,' he finished. 'Is that what your ex did?'

She flushed. 'I don't know what you're talking about.'

Something had made her super-independent, and he had a feeling that there was a man involved. A man who'd broken her trust so she didn't date any more? 'Everything came with strings?' he asked softly.

'No. I just pay my own way, that's all. Right now, I feel I owe you. And I'm not comfortable owing you.'

'Friends don't owe each other for helping,' he said gently. Perhaps it was mean of him, using insider knowledge of her family and closest friends, but how else was he going to make Nicole understand that this was OK? 'Do you insist on going halves with your mum or Jessie? Or work a strict rotation on whose turn it is to buy coffee?'

'No,' she admitted. 'And how do you know about Jessie? Is your dossier that big?'

'No. You told me about your best friend when we were talking late one night, Georgy,' he reminded her. 'And I happen to have a good memory.'

She sighed. 'I guess. Can we go back to talking about surveyors?'

'Because it's safe?'

She gave him a speaking look. 'We ought to look at the menu. They'll be over in a minute to take our order.'

Was she running scared because this felt like a date? Or was the wariness specific to him? He decided to let her off the hook. For now. 'We don't need to look at the menu. I already know you're going to order a margherita with an avocado and rocket salad,' he said instead.

She looked at him. 'And you'll pick a quattro formaggi with a tomato and basil salad.'

He could swear she'd just been about to call him 'Clarence'.

And this was what he'd fantasised about when he'd messaged her over the last few months. Going on a date just like this, where they'd talk about anything and everything and knew each other so well that they could finish each other's sentences.

Except this wasn't a date. She'd called it dinner with strings. Because she felt beholden to him. And he didn't quite know how to sort this out.

'Dough balls first?' he suggested.

'Definitely.' She looked at him. 'This is weird.'

'What is?'

'We know each other. And at the same time we don't.'

'More do than don't,' he said. But he could tell that something was holding her back. Someone, he guessed, who'd hurt her. Was that why she found it hard to trust him? The one topic they'd always shied away from was relationships. He'd stopped dating because he only seemed to attract the kind of women who wanted someone else to fund a flashy lifestyle for them, and he was tired of the superficiality. Though he knew without having to ask that Nicole wouldn't discuss whatever was holding her back. He'd just have to persuade her to tell him. Little by little.

The waiter came to take their order, breaking that little bit of awkwardness.

And then Nicole went back into business mode. 'Builders,' she said, and handed him her phone.

He looked at her list. 'They're all fine,' he said. 'It's a matter of when they can fit you in. If you get stuck, I can give you some more names.'

'Thank you.'

'So how was the survey?' he asked. 'Is there much structural stuff to do?'

'A small amount of rewiring, a damp patch that needs further investigation, a bit of work to the windows, doing what you already said to the upstairs room ceiling, and then the rest of it's cosmetic.'

'Even if you can get a builder to start straight away,' he said, 'it's still going to take a fair bit of time to do all the cosmetic stuff. If you renovate the seats in the auditorium, it'll take a while; and if you rip them out completely and replace them with the sofas you were talking about, you'll have work to do on the flooring. And there's the cost to think about. Doing something in a shorter time-scale means paying overtime or getting in extra staff— all of which costs and it'll blow your budget.'

She raised her eyebrows. 'You're telling an ex-banker to keep an eye on the budget?'

He smiled. 'I know that's ironic—but you've fallen in love with the building, and there's a danger that could blind you to the cost.'

'I guess.'

'It is—'

'—what it is,' she finished with a wry smile.

The waiter brought the dough balls and the garlic butter to dip them into, and they focused on that for a moment—but then Gabriel's fingers brushed against Nicole's when they both reached for a dough ball at the same time.

It felt like an electric shock.

He hadn't been this aware of anyone in a long, long time. And he really didn't know what to do about it. If he pushed too hard, she'd back away. If he played it cool, she'd think he wasn't interested.

This felt like being eighteen again, totally unsure of himself—and Gabriel was used to knowing what he was doing and what his next move would be.

The only safe topic of conversation was the cinema. And even that was a minefield, because she'd backed off every time he'd suggested working together.

'There is one way to get a bigger workforce without massive costs,' he said.

She frowned. 'How?'

'Remember that group on the Surrey Quays forum who said they wanted the cinema up and running again? I bet they'd offer to help.'

She shook her head. Her mother had suggested the same thing, but it felt wrong. 'I can't ask people to work for me for nothing.'

'You can if it's a community thing,' he said. 'They're interested in the building. So let them be involved in the restoration. If they don't have the expertise themselves, they'll probably know someone who does. And any retired French polisher would take a look at that countertop in your foyer and itch to get his or her hands on it.'

'Nice save, with the "or her",' she said dryly.

'I'm not sexist. Being good at your job has nothing to do with your gender,' he pointed out.

'It still feels wrong to ask people to work for free.'

'What about if you give them a public acknowledgement? You could have a plaque on the wall in the foyer with the names of everyone who's been involved.'

'I like that idea,' she said slowly. 'And they're my target audience, so it makes sense to talk to them about what I'm doing—to see whether they'd be prepared to support it and see a movie at the Electric Palace rather than going into the West End.'

'You want their views on the programming, you mean?' he asked.

She nodded. 'If I show any of say the top three block-busters, I'll have to pay the film distributors at least half the box office receipts,' she said. 'And I'll be compet-ing with the multiplexes—which we both know I can't do effectively.'

'So what's the alternative? Art-house or local film-makers? Because that'd mean a smaller potential audi-ence.'

'I need to find the right mix of commercial films, re-gional and art-house,' she said. 'Maybe I need to run it as a cinema club.'

'That might limit your audience, though,' he said. 'You could always put some polls up on the Surrey Quays website to see what kind of thing people want to see and when. And think about a loyalty scheme. Buy ten tickets and get a free coffee, that sort of thing.'

'It's a thought.'

He could tell she was backing off again, so he kept the conversation light for the rest of their meal.

'Thank you for dinner,' he said. 'Can I walk you home?'

'I live in the opposite direction to you,' she reminded him.

He shrugged. 'The walk will do me good.'

'Then, put that way, OK.'

His hand brushed against hers on the way back to her

flat, and he had to suppress the urge to curl his fingers round hers. They weren't dating.

And it was even harder to stop himself kissing her goodnight. Her mouth looked so soft, so sweet. He itched to find out how her mouth would feel against his.

But this wasn't appropriate. If he did what he really wanted to do, she'd run a mile. He took a step back. 'Well. Goodnight. And thank you again for dinner.'

'Thank you for the advice and the brainstorming,' she said, equally politely.

'Any time.' He smiled, and turned away before he did anything stupid. She still wasn't having those late-night conversations with him like they used to have. And until they'd got that easiness back, he needed to keep his distance.

The more he got to know her, the more he wanted to know her. He *liked* her. But she clearly didn't feel the same way about him.

It is what it is, he reminded himself.

Even though he really wanted to change things.

CHAPTER SEVEN

ONLY ONE OF the builders on Nicole's list could actually come to look at the cinema within the next couple of days. One was too busy to come at all and the third couldn't make it for another month. She'd already cleared out as much junk as she could from the cinema so, until she'd seen the builder's quote and agreed the terms of business, Nicole knew she couldn't do much more at the cinema. All the paperwork was up to date, too, and she was simply waiting on replies. To keep herself busy instead of fretting about the downtime, she headed for the archives.

There were newspaper reports of the opening of the Kursaal in 1911, but to her disappointment there were no photographs. There was a brief description of the outside of the building, including the arch outside which apparently had Art Deco sun rays in the brickwork, but nothing about the ceiling of stars. She carefully typed out the relevant paragraphs—the font size was too small to be easily read on a photograph—and was about to give up looking when the archivist came to see her.

'You might like to have a look through this,' she said, handing Nicole a thick album. 'They're postcards of the area, from around the early nineteen hundreds. There might be something in there.'

'Thank you,' Nicole said. 'If there is, can I take a photograph on my phone?'

'As long as you don't use flash. And if I can think of any other sources which might contain something about the cinema, I'll bring them over,' the archivist said.

Halfway through the postcard album, Nicole found a postcard of the Electric Palace; she knew that, in common with other similarly named buildings, its name had changed after the First World War, to make it sound less German. Clearly by then someone had painted the outside of the building white, because the sun rays on the arch had been covered over, as they were now.

She photographed the postcard carefully, then slipped the postcard from the little corners keeping it in place so she could read the back. The frank on the stamp told her that the card had been posted in 1934. To her delight, the inscription referred to the writer spending the previous night dancing in the ballroom—and also to seeing the film *It Happened One Night*, the previous week.

Clarence would be pleased to know there was a reference to Frank Capra, she thought as she carefully photographed the inscription.

Gabriel, she corrected herself.

And that was the problem. She really wanted to share this with Gabriel. Yet she already knew how rubbish her judgement was in men. Getting close to Gabriel Hunter would be a huge mistake.

Then again, the man she was getting to know was a decent man. Maybe he wouldn't let her down. Or maybe he would. So it would be sensible to keep it strictly business between them. Even though she was beginning to want a lot more than that.

On Saturday night, Nicole was sitting on her own in her flat. Usually by now on a Saturday she'd be talking to

Clarence online, but she hadn't messaged him since she'd found out who he really was. She hadn't spent much time on the Surrey Quays website, either; it had felt awkward. Nobody had sent her a direct message, so clearly she hadn't been missed.

Nobody had been in touch from the bank, either, to see how things were going. It had been stupid to think that the last leaving drink had been a kind of new beginning; she was most definitely out of sight and out of mind. Her best friend was away for the weekend and so was her mother, which left her pretty much on her own.

She flicked through a few channels on the television. There was nothing on that she wanted to watch. Maybe she ought to analyse her competitors and start researching cinema programming, but right at that moment she felt lonely and miserable and wished she had someone to share it with. Which was weak, feeble and totally pathetic, she told herself.

Though she might as well admit it: she missed Clarence.

Did Gabriel miss Georgygirl? she wondered.

And now she was being *really* feeble. 'Get over it, Nicole,' she told herself crossly.

She spent a while looking up the programming in various other small cinemas, to give herself a few ideas, and then her phone rang. She glanced at the screen: Gabriel. So he'd been thinking of her? Pleasure flooded through her.

Though it was probably a business call. Which was how it ought to be, and she should respond accordingly. *Sensibly.* She answered the phone. 'Good evening, Gabriel,' she said coolly.

'Good evening, Nicole. Are you busy tomorrow?' he asked.

'It's Sunday tomorrow,' she prevaricated, not wanting to admit to him that her social life was a complete desert.

'I know. But, if you're free, I'd like to take you on a research trip tomorrow.'

'Research trip?' Was this his way of asking her out without making it sound like a date? Her heart skipped a beat.

'To see a ceiling.'

Oh. So he really did mean just business. She did her best to suppress the disappointment. 'Where?'

'Norfolk.'

'Isn't that a couple of hours' drive away?'

'This particular bit is about two and a half hours away,' he said. 'I'll pick you up at nine tomorrow morning. Wear shorts, or jeans you can roll up to your knees, and flat shoes you can take off easily. Oh, and a hat.'

'What sort of hat?'

'Whatever keeps the sun off.'

'Why? And why do I need to take my shoes off?'

'You'll see when you get there.' And then, annoyingly, he rang off before she could ask anything else.

Shorts, a hat and flat shoes.

What did that have to do with a ceiling?

She was none the wiser when Gabriel rang the intercom to her flat, the next morning.

'I'm on my way down,' she said.

'You look nice,' he said, smiling at her when she opened the main door to the flats. 'That's the first time I've ever seen your hair loose.'

To her horror, Nicole could feel herself blushing at the compliment. Oh, for pity's sake. She was twenty-eight, not fifteen. 'Thanks,' she mumbled. It didn't help that he was wearing faded denims and a T-shirt and he looked really *touchable*. Her fingertips actually tingled with the urge to reach out and see how soft the denim was.

And then he reached out and twirled the end of her hair round his fingers. Just briefly. 'Like silk,' he said.

She couldn't look him in the eye. She didn't want him to know that she felt as if her knees had just turned to sand. 'So what's this ceiling?' she asked.

'Tin. Like the cinema. Except restored.'

'And you know about it because…?'

'I've seen it before,' he said, and ushered her over to his car. 'This is why I said you need a hat, by the way.'

'Show-off,' she said as he put the roof of his convertible down.

He spread his hands. 'There aren't that many days in an English spring or summer when you can enjoy having the roof down. This is one of them. Got your hat?'

She grabbed the baseball cap from her bag and jammed it onto her head. 'Happy?'

'Happy. You can drive, if you want,' he said, surprising her.

She blinked. 'You'd actually trust me to drive this?'

'It's insured,' he said, 'and I know where we're going, so I can direct you.'

'I don't have a car,' she said. 'I use public transport most of the time. The only time I drive is if there's a team thing at work and I have a pool car. That doesn't happen very often.'

'But you have a licence and you can drive.' He handed her the car keys. 'Here. Knock yourself out.'

'Why?'

'Because it'll distract you and stop you asking me questions,' he said. 'And also because I think you might enjoy it. This car's a lot of fun to drive.'

He trusted her.

Maybe she needed to do the same for him.

'Thank you,' she said.

Gabriel's directions were perfect—given clearly and in plenty of time—and Nicole discovered that he was right. His car really was fun to drive. And it was the perfect day for driving a convertible, with the sun out and the lightest of breezes. Once they were on the motorway heading north-east from London, Gabriel switched the radio to a station playing retro nineties music, and she found herself singing along with him.

She couldn't remember the last time she'd enjoyed herself so much.

'Want to pull into the next lay-by and swap over?' he asked. 'Then you can just enjoy the scenery instead of concentrating on directions and worrying that you're going to take the wrong exit off a roundabout.'

'OK.'

They drove along the coast road, and she discovered that he was right; it really was gorgeous scenery.

'They found that famous hoard of Iron Age gold torcs near here, at Snettisham,' he said.

'Is that where we're going?'

'No.'

Annoyingly, he wouldn't tell her any more until he pulled in to a hotel car park.

'The Staithe Hotel,' she said, reading the sign. 'Would this place have the ceiling we're coming to see?'

'It would indeed.'

'Staithe?'

'It's an Old English word meaning "riverbank" or "landing stage",' he said. 'You see it mainly nowadays in place names in east and north-east England—the bits that were under Danelaw.'

Clearly he'd done his research. Years ago, maybe there

had been some kind of wharf here. 'Are we dressed suitably for a visit?' she asked doubtfully. 'It looks quite posh.'

'We're fine.'

Then she twigged. 'It's *yours*, isn't it?'

'The first hotel I worked on by myself,' he confirmed. 'It was pretty run-down and Dad wasn't entirely sure I was doing the right thing, when I bid for it at the auction, but I really liked the place. And the views are stunning.'

When they went in, the receptionist greeted them warmly. 'Have you booked a table?' she asked.

'No, but I'd like to see the manager—he's expecting me,' Gabriel said.

'Just a moment, sir,' the receptionist said, and disappeared into the room behind the reception desk.

The manager came out and smiled when he saw them. 'Gabriel, it's good to see you.' He shook Gabriel's hand warmly.

'You, too. Pete, this is my friend Nicole Thomas,' Gabriel said.

Friend. The word made her feel warm inside. Were they friends, now?

'Nicole, this is Pete Baines, my manager here.'

'Pleased to meet you, Mr Baines.' She shook his hand.

'Call me Pete,' the manager said. 'Any friend of Gabriel's is a friend of mine.'

'Nicole is renovating the cinema next door to the place I'm working on at the moment,' Gabriel explained, 'and her ceiling has a lot in common with the one in your restaurant.'

'I get you,' Pete said. 'Come with me, Nicole.' He ushered her into the restaurant.

The ceiling looked like elaborate plasterwork, as did the wainscoting around the fireplace.

'Believe it or not, that's tin, not carving or plaster,' Pete said. 'It's just painted to look that way. Obviously Gabriel knows a lot more than I do on that front—I just run the place and boss everyone about.'

'And very well, too. Pete, I know you're normally booked out weeks ahead,' Gabriel said.

'But you want me to squeeze you in for lunch?' Pete finished, smiling. 'I'm sure we can do something.'

'Any chance of a table on the terrace, outside?' Gabriel asked.

'Sure. I'll leave you to take a closer look at the ceiling. Can I get you both a drink?'

'Sparkling mineral water for me, please,' Nicole said.

'Make that two,' Gabriel added.

'I can't believe this isn't plasterwork,' Nicole said, looking at the ceiling and wainscoting.

'It's tin. The place was originally built in Victorian times by a local businessman. His son remodelled it to make the room look more Tudor and added the tin wainscoting and ceiling.' He flicked into his phone. 'This is what it looked like before the restoration.'

She looked at the photographs. 'It looks a mess, there—but you can't see any of the damage here.' She gestured to the wainscoting in front of her.

'I can let you have the restoration guy's name, if you'd like it. And, by the way, as you paid at La Chiatta, I'm buying lunch here. No arguments,' he said. 'Otherwise you'll just have to starve.'

'Noted,' she said. 'And thank you.'

When they sat out on the terrace and she'd read the menu, she looked at Gabriel. 'This menu's amazing. Is all the food locally sourced?' she asked.

'Yes. The locals love us, and we've had some good write-ups in the national papers as well—Pete gets foodies coming all the way from London to stay for the weekend. The chef's great and we're hoping to get a Michelin star in the next round,' Gabriel said.

'What do you recommend?'

'Start from the puddings and work backwards,' he said.

She looked at the dessert menu and smiled. 'I think I know what I'm having.'

'White chocolate and raspberry bread and butter pudding?' he asked.

At her nod, he grinned. 'Me, too.'

'Crab salad for mains, then,' she said.

'Share some sweet potato fries?' he suggested.

This felt much more like a date than the other times they'd eaten together—even though they'd officially come on a research trip to look at the tin ceiling.

The view from the terrace was really pretty across the salt marshes and then to the sea. 'I can't believe how far the sand stretches,' she said.

'That's why I said wear shoes you can take off and jeans you can roll up,' he said. 'We're going for a walk on the beach after lunch to work off the calories from the pudding, and to blow the cobwebs out.'

'I can't actually remember the last time I went to the beach,' she said.

'Me, neither. I really love this part of the coast. When the tide's out you can walk for miles across the sand, and you've got the seal colony just down the road at Blakeney.'

'You fell in love with Norfolk when you worked on the hotel, didn't you?' she asked.

'I very nearly ended up moving here,' he said, 'but London suits me better.'

'So is that your big dream? Living by the sea?'

'I love the sea, but I'm happy where I am,' he said.

She enjoyed the food, which was beautifully presented and tasted even better than it looked. Though her fingers brushed against his a couple of times when they shared the sweet potato fries, and her skin tingled where he'd touched her.

To distract herself, she said, 'There was something I wanted to show you yesterday. I found something in the archives.' She found the photographs she'd taken and handed her phone to him.

He looked at the front of the postcard, zoomed in on the script, and smiled. 'Well, how about that—a photograph of someone who danced there and saw a Capra film.'

'I thought of you,' she said. 'With the Capra stuff.'

'What a fantastic find.'

'There was a newspaper article, too.' She took the phone back to find her notes for him. 'The print's so tiny that a photograph wouldn't have helped, so I took notes. The outside of the building wasn't originally all white, and there's a sun ray on that semi-circle. Do you think I could get that back?'

'You need to talk to the builder—it depends on the condition of the brickwork underneath. But it's a possibility.' He gave her another of those knee-melting smiles. 'This is amazing. A real connection to the past. Thanks for sharing this with me.'

She almost told him that he was the one person she'd really wanted to share it with; but she knew he saw this as just business, so she'd be sensible and keep it light between them. 'I did look to see if there was a photograph of the warehouse in that scrapbook, but I'm afraid there wasn't anything.'

'I doubt there would be postcards of the warehouse.'

He shrugged. 'People didn't really pay that much attention to industrial buildings, except for things like train stations and museums.'

Once they'd said goodbye to Pete, Gabriel drove a little way down the road to the car park.

'Good—the tide's out,' he said.

'How do you know?'

'Because the car park's dry—I learned that one the hard way,' he said with a grin, 'though fortunately not in this car.'

Once they'd parked, he took a bag from the boot of the car.

'What's that?'

'Something we need to do, Georgy.'

Obviously he wasn't going to tell her until he was ready, so she let it go. She took her shoes off at the edge of the beach, as did he. As she walked along with her shoes in one hand, her other hand brushed against his a couple of times, and every single nerve-end was aware of him. With a partner, she thought, this place would be so romantic. But Gabriel wasn't her partner. Romance wasn't in the equation, not with Gabriel and not with anyone else.

'Is that a wreck out there?' she asked.

'Yes. It's not a good idea to walk out to it, though, as when the tide changes it comes in really quickly. And it comes in far enough to flood the road to the car park.' He stopped. 'Here will do nicely.'

'For what?'

'This.' He took a kite from the bag.

She burst out laughing. Now she understood why he'd called her Georgy again. 'I've never flown a kite before,' she reminded him.

'It's been a while for me,' he admitted. 'But this is the perfect place to start.'

'The wind's blowing my hair into my eyes. I need to tie my hair back,' she said, flustered. The idea of intense businessman Gabriel Hunter being carefree was something she found it hard to get her head around. She wasn't the carefree sort, either. But she was a different person when she was with him—Georgygirl. Just as she had a feeling that he was different when he was with her.

He waited while she put an elastic hairband in her hair, then handed her the kite. 'Stand with your back to the wind, hold the kite up, let out the line a little, and it will lift. Then you pull on the line so it climbs.'

She couldn't get the hang of it and the kite nosedived into the sand again and again. 'I'd better let you have this back before I wreck it,' she said eventually.

'No. Try it like this,' he said, and stood behind her with his hands over hers, guiding her so that the kite actually went up into the air, this time. He felt warm and strong, and Nicole couldn't help leaning back into him.

He tensed for a moment; then he wrapped one arm round her waist, holding her close to him.

Neither of them said a word, just concentrated on flying the kite; but Nicole was so aware of Gabriel's cheek pressed against hers, the warmth of his skin and the tiny prickle of new stubble. She could feel his heart beating against her back, firm and steady, and she was sure he could probably feel her own heart racing. Taking a risk, she laid her arm over his, curling her hand round his elbow.

They stood there for what felt like for ever, just holding each other close.

Then he slowly wound the kite in and dropped it on the sand, and twisted her round to face him.

'Nicole,' he said, and his eyes were very bright.

She couldn't help looking at his mouth.

And then he dipped his head and brushed his mouth against hers. So soft, so sweet, so gentle.

It felt as if someone had lit touch-paper inside her.

She slid her arms round his neck, drawing him closer, and let him deepen the kiss. Then she closed her eyes and completely lost herself in the way he made her feel, the warmth of his mouth moving against hers, the way he was holding her.

And then he broke the kiss.

'Nicole.' His voice was huskier, deeper. 'I'm sorry. I shouldn't have done that.'

'Neither should I.' What an idiot she'd been. Had she learned nothing from Jeff? She was a cold fish, useless at relationships.

'I... Maybe we need to get back to London,' he said.

She seized on the excuse gratefully. 'Yes. I have a lot to do for the cinema and I'm sure you're busy, too.'

No. He wasn't. He could delegate every single thing that he had on his desk for the next month and spend all his time with her.

That was what he wanted to do.

But that kiss had been a mistake. She'd backed away from him. He'd taken it too far, too fast and he knew he needed to let her regroup. He'd let himself be carried away by the fun of kite-flying. Acted on impulse. Blown it.

They walked back to the car, and he was careful this time not to let his hand brush against hers. And he kept the roof up in the car on the way back.

'No wind in your hair this time?' she asked.

He shrugged. 'It is what it is.'

'Why do you always say that?'

'It's something Vijay taught me. If you're in a situation and you can't change it, you need to accept that and make the best of it. Don't waste your energy in trying to change something that you can't change; focus instead on what you can do.'

'It's a good philosophy.'

He smiled. 'I would say it's very Zen—except he's a Hindu, not a Buddhist.'

Nicole had a feeling that Gabriel had been very lonely when he grew up and the Khans had been the first ones to make him really feel part of the family; whereas she'd always grown up knowing she was loved, by her mother and her godparents and the rest of her mother's friends. It didn't matter that she didn't have a big family by blood, or that her father had been a liar and a cheat, or that her grandparents were estranged.

She wondered how she'd moved from that to her place at the bank, where she'd never really been part of the team and had only really felt accepted on her very last day there.

It is what it is.

She couldn't change the past: but she could change her future.

So, when Gabriel parked outside her flat, she turned to face him. 'Would you like to come in for coffee?'

'Coffee?' Gabriel stared at her. 'Is that a good idea?'

'You're not a predator, Gabriel.'

'Thank you for that.' So maybe she'd forgiven him for that kiss?

'Come and have coffee,' she said.

'OK. That'd be nice.' He followed her upstairs to her

first-floor flat. The front door opened into a small lobby with five doors leading off. 'Storage cupboard, bathroom, kitchen, living room, bedroom,' she said, indicating the doors in turn. 'Do go and sit down.'

The walls in her living room were painted a pale primrose-yellow, and the floors were polished wood with a blue patterned rug in the centre. French doors at the far end of the room led onto a small balcony, and just in front of them was a glass-topped bistro table with two chairs. He was half surprised not to see a desk in the room, but assumed that was probably in her bedroom—not that he was going to ask. There were a couple of fairly anonymous framed prints on the walls, and on the mantelpiece there were a couple of framed photographs. The older woman with Nicole looked so much like her that Gabriel realised straight away she had to be Nicole's mother; the younger woman in the other photograph was wearing a bridal dress and Nicole appeared to be wearing a bridesmaid's outfit, so he assumed this was her best friend Jessie.

Looking at the photos felt a bit like spying; and he felt too awkward to sit on the sofa. In the end, he went through to the kitchen—which was as tidy and neat as her living room.

'Can I help?' he asked.

'No, you're fine. Do you want a sandwich or anything?'

He shook his head. What he really wanted was to be back on that beach with her in his arms, kissing him back. But that was a subject that could really blow up in his face. He needed to take this carefully. 'Thanks, but just coffee will do me.'

'Here.' She handed him a mug, and ushered him back into the living room. She took her laptop from a drawer and said, 'I was going to put a note on the Surrey Quays website tonight. As you're part of it, too, I thought maybe we could do this together.'

Was she suggesting that he told everyone who he was? He looked warily at her. 'I kind of like my anonymity there.'

'So be Clarence. You don't have to tell them you're Gabriel.'

'Are you going to out yourself?' he asked.

'I kind of have to, given that I've inherited the Electric Palace—but I think everyone's going to respond to me as Georgygirl. Nobody knows Nicole the banker.'

But was she Nicole, Georgy, or a mixture of the two? And could she drop the protective shell of being the hard-headed banker and become the woman he thought she really was? Because, with her, he found that he was the man he wanted to be. Not the one who kept his tongue bitten and seethed in silent frustration when he kept failing to earn his father's respect: the man who thought outside the box and saw the world in full colour.

She put her mug on the coffee table, signed into the Surrey Quays forum, and started to type.

'I guess "Electric Palace—news" is probably the best subject line to use,' she said.

'Probably,' he agreed.

She typed rapidly, then passed the laptop to him so he could see the screen properly. 'Do you think this will do?'

Sorry I've been AWOL for a bit. I've been getting my head round the fact that I'm the new owner of the Electric Palace—it was left to me in a will. It needs a bit of work, but my boss has given me a six-month sabbatical and I'm going to use it to see if I can get it up and running again.

I'm planning to start showing films in a couple of months—a mix of blockbusters, classics and art-house films, and maybe showcase the work of new local film-makers. I have a few ideas about what to do with the upper room—the old ballroom—and I really want it to be used as part of the community. If anyone's looking for a regular room for a dance class or teaching craft work or that sort of thing, give me a yell. And if anyone has photographs I can borrow to enlarge for the walls, I'd be really grateful.

Cheers, Georgygirl x

'So you're not going to ask for help restoring the place?' he asked.

She shook her head. 'That feels kind of greedy and rude.'

'There's a saying, shy bairns get naught,' he reminded her.

'And there's another saying, nobody likes pushy people. If people offer to help, that's a different thing.' She looked him straight in the eye. 'Someone fairly wise keeps telling me "it is what it is".'

'I guess.' He smiled. 'So what now?'

'We wait and see if anyone replies.'

'And you and me?' The question had to be asked. They couldn't keep pretending.

She sucked in a breath. 'I don't know. I've got a business to set up. I don't have time for a relationship. The same goes for you.'

'What if I think it's worth making time?'

She sighed. 'I'm not very good at relationships.'

'Neither am I.'

'So we ought to be sensible. Anyway, we're business rivals, so we're both off limits to each other.'

'Not so much rivals as working together. Collaborating. The wedding stuff, for starters,' he reminded her.

'We haven't agreed that.'

'I know, but it's a win for both of us, Nicole. We both get what we want. And it doesn't matter whose idea it was in the first place. It works.'

'Maybe.'

But this time there was no coolness in her voice—she sounded unsure, but he didn't think it was because she didn't trust his judgement. It felt more as if she had no confidence in herself. Hadn't she just said she wasn't good at relationships?

'You kissed me back on the beach,' he said softly. 'I think that means something.'

She flushed. 'Temporary loss of sanity. That's what kite-flying does to you.'

'We're not flying kites now. And we're back in London.' He raised an eyebrow. 'What would you do if I kissed you again?'

'Panic,' she said.

She'd been straight with him. He couldn't ask for more than that. 'Thank you for being honest.' But he needed to be sure about this. 'Is it me, or is it all men?'

'I…' She shook her head. 'I'm just not good at relationships.'

He took her hand. 'He must have really hurt you.'

'He never hit me.'

'There's more than one way to hurt someone. It could be with words, or it could be by ignoring them, or it could be by undermining their self-esteem and constantly wanting to make them into someone they're not.'

'Leave it. Please.' Her eyes shimmered, and she blinked back the tears.

'I can't promise I won't hurt you, Nicole. But I can

promise I'll try my very best not to hurt you. If I do, it definitely won't be deliberate.' He lifted her hand up to his mouth and kissed the back of her hand. 'I have no idea where this thing between us is going. And I'm not very good at relationships. But I like the way I feel when I'm with you.' He owed her some honesty, too. 'I didn't want to meet Georgygirl in case she wasn't the same in real life as she was online. I didn't want to be disappointed.'

She looked away. 'Uh-huh.'

Was that what her ex had said to her? That she disappointed him? 'When I met you, I thought you were this hard-headed businesswoman, cold and snooty.'

She still didn't meet his eyes or say a word.

'But,' he said softly, 'then I got to know you a bit better. And in real life you're the woman I've been talking to online, late at night. You're clever and you're funny and you sparkle. That's who you really are.'

This time, she looked at him. 'So are you the man I've been talking to? The one who's full of sensible advice, who makes me laugh and who seems to understand who I am?'

'I think so. Because I've been more myself with you than I've been with anyone. For years and years,' he said.

'This is a risk.'

'You took risks all the time at the bank. You're taking a risk now on the Electric Palace.'

'Those were all calculated risks,' she pointed out. 'This isn't something I can calculate.'

'Me, neither. But I like you, Nicole. I like you a lot. And I think if we're both brave we might just have the chance to have something really special.'

'I'm not sure how brave I am,' she admitted.

'It's harder to be brave on your own. But you're not on your own, Nicole. We're in this together.'

* * *

Could she believe him?

Could she trust him—and trust that he wouldn't let her down like Jeff had?

She thought about it.

Gabriel could've taken advantage of her in business. But he hadn't. He'd been scrupulously fair. Pushy, yes, but his ideas really did work for both of them.

He'd also completely fried her common sense with that kiss on the beach.

And she'd been honest about her life right now. She was going to be crazily busy with the cinema. She didn't have time for a relationship. It was the same for him, getting the hotel next door up and running.

But they could make the time.

'OK. We'll see how it goes. No promises, and we try not to hurt each other,' she said.

'Works for me.'

She looked at him. 'So does that mean you're going to kiss me now?'

'Nope.'

Had she got this wrong? Didn't he want a relationship with her after all? Confused, she stared at him.

'You're going to kiss me,' he said. 'And then I'm going to kiss you back.'

Could it really be that easy?

She's a cold fish.

Nicole shoved the thought away. She didn't feel like a cold fish with Gabriel. He made her blood heat.

Slowly, hoping that she was going to get this right, she leaned over and touched her mouth to the corner of his.

He made a small murmur of approval, and she grew braver, nibbling at his lower lip.

Then he wrapped his arms round her and opened his mouth, kissing her back.

And Nicole felt as if something had cracked in the region of her heart.

She wasn't sure how long they stayed there, just kissing, but eventually Gabriel stroked her face. 'Much as I'd like to scoop you up right now and carry you to your bed, I don't have any condoms on me.'

She felt her face flame. 'Neither do I.'

'I've dated a lot,' he said, 'but for the record I'm actually quite picky about who I sleep with. And it's not usually on a first date, either.'

'Is today our first date?'

'Maybe. Maybe not.' He stole another kiss. 'Can I see you tomorrow?'

'You work next door to me. The chances are we'll see each other.'

'Not work. After,' he corrected.

'A proper date?'

'Give me a while to think up something to impress you.'

'Clarence,' she pointed out, 'wouldn't try to impress me. He'd just be himself.'

'And if I tried to impress Georgy, she would probably be so sarcastic with me that I'd have a permanent hole in my self-esteem.' He stole another kiss. 'See what we feel like after work? Drink, dinner, or just a walk along the waterfront?'

'Sounds good to me.'

'Tomorrow,' he said. 'I'm going now while I still have a few shreds of common sense left.'

'OK. And thank you for today. For the kite and the ceiling and…everything.'

'I liked the kite. I haven't done that in years. Maybe we

could do that again—say on Parliament Hill.' He kissed her one last time. 'See you tomorrow, Nicole.'

'See you tomorrow, Gabriel.' She saw him out.

Later that evening her phone pinged with a text from him.

Sweet dreams.

They would be, she thought. Because they'd be of him.

CHAPTER EIGHT

THE NEXT MORNING, Nicole came out of the shower to find a text from Gabriel on her phone.

Good morning :) x

She smiled and called him back. 'Don't tell me you're at work already.'

'No. I hit the gym first; it clears my head for the day. I'm walking to the hotel now. What are you doing today?'

'Talking to a builder.'

'Want some back-up?' he asked.

'Thanks for the offer, but I'm fine.'

'OK. But let me look at the quote—and the contract, when you get to that stage,' he said.

Her old suspicions started to rise, but quickly deflated when he added, 'I write contracts like this all the time, so it'll take me all of ten minutes to look over them. And my rates are good—I'll work for coffee and a brownie. Maybe a kiss.'

His candour disarmed her. 'OK. Thanks. Though I saw contracts all the time in my old job, too, you know,' she pointed out.

'I know, but you were more interested in cash-flow

and gearing than anything else,' he said. 'I bet you can analyse a balance sheet in half the time that I do.'

'Says Mr MBA.'

'Yeah, well. Has anyone replied to your post, yet?'

'I don't know. Hang on a sec.' She switched on her laptop and flicked in to the site. 'Oh, my God.'

'Is everything OK?' He sounded concerned.

'There's... Gabriel, take a look for yourself. There are loads and loads and loads of replies. I can't believe this.' She scrolled through them. 'So many names I recognise, and they all want to be part of it. Some people are offering me photographs. A few want to come and have a look round, in exchange for putting a bit of paint on the walls. I've got someone who used to be a projectionist, and offers from people who want to be ushers, and there's a couple of people who say they can't manage going up a ladder or holding a paintbrush because their arthritis is too bad but they'll come and make tea for the task team and do fetching and carrying and stuff.' Tears pricked her eyes. 'I don't know if I'm more humbled or thrilled.'

'I'm not surprised you've had that kind of reaction,' he said.

'Why?'

'Because people like you,' he said. 'Your posts are always thoughtful and considered, and people respect you.'

People actually liked her? Nicole couldn't quite get her head round that. In real life, she'd tended to keep part of herself back, particularly since Jeff's betrayal; but online, behind her screen name, she'd been more who she really was.

Would they all change their minds about her when they met her? Gabriel hadn't. But the doubts still flickered through her.

'I think,' he said, 'I take it back about it being a big

ask to be open in July. I think you're going to do it, Nicole, because you've got the whole community behind you. Including me.'

'Thank you.'

'Good luck with your builder. Call me if you need back-up.'

'I will.' She had no intention of doing so, but she appreciated the offer. 'Talk to you later.'

She went onto the forum to type in a reply.

I'm overwhelmed by everyone's kindness. Thank you so much. I'm going to be at the cinema most of the time, so do drop in and say hello if you're passing. I've got power and lights working now, so I can make you a cup of tea. And thank you again—all of you.

At five to eight, Patrick, Nicole's potential builder, arrived at the cinema. She made him a cup of tea and showed him round, explaining what she wanted to do with each room.

'That roof is stunning,' he said when he was at the top of the ladder in the upper room. 'Tin. That's not very common—but I know a guy who specialises in this stuff. The bad news is that he's booked up for months in advance, so you might have to leave the upstairs for a while until he can fit us in. Until you get rid of that lead paint, you're going to fall foul of regulations if you open it to the public.'

Just as Gabriel had warned her. 'I thought you might say that,' she said. 'The plan is, I want to use this room as a multi-purpose place—I'll have a proper screen so we can have a cinema, but also I want flexible staging so I can use it for a band and as a dance hall, or as a conference hall, or hire the room out to clubs or craft teachers.'

'Sounds good. What about the downstairs? With that mouse problem…'

'I've had the pest people out already and they've been back to check—they tell me that the mice are gone now,' she said, 'so it's just a matter of fixing the damage they've already done. But I'm not going to restore the seats quite as they are.' She explained about the sofas and tables.

'That sounds great. It'll be nice to see this place looking like she did back in the old days—or even better.'

It sounded, she thought, as if Patrick had fallen as much in love with the building as she had.

'You'll need a French polisher to sort out the bar, and there's a bit of damage to the glasswork that needs sorting out.'

'But it's all fixable,' she said. 'There is one other thing. I want it up and running in eight weeks.'

Patrick blew out a breath. 'You definitely won't get the upstairs done for then. Even downstairs might be pushing it—there isn't that much structural stuff, apart from the flooring once we've taken the old seats out, but there's an awful lot of cosmetic stuff.'

'I've, um, had offers of help from people who want to see the cinema restored,' Nicole said. 'If you have a site manager in charge, can they come and help?'

'Do any of them have experience?'

She grimaced. 'Um. Pass.'

'As I said, a lot of it is cosmetic. The more hands you have on deck, more chance you have of getting it done in your timeframe—as long as they do what the site manager asks and don't think they know better, it'll be fine,' Patrick said. 'So this is going to be a bit of a community project, then?'

'It looks like it.'

'They're the ones that make this kind of job feel really

worthwhile,' he said. 'OK. I'll go and work out a schedule of works and give you a quote.'

'I hate to be pushy,' Nicole said, 'but when are you likely to be able to get back to me? This week, next week?'

'Given that you want it done yesterday—I'll try to get it to you for close of business today,' Patrick said.

She could've kissed him. 'Thank you.'

'No problem. And thanks for the tea.'

'Pleasure.'

When he'd gone, she went next door to see Gabriel.

'How did it go?' he asked.

She beamed. 'Patrick's a really nice guy and he loves the building. He's giving me a quote later today—and he's fine about everyone coming to help.'

'Sounds good.'

'I know I'm supposed to get three quotes, but I think I'd work well with him.'

'It's not always about the money. It's about quality and gut feel, too.' He gave her a hug. 'I still want to see that quote and the contract, though. Have you thought any more about furniture? The average retailer isn't going to be able to deliver you the best part of two hundred sofas in the next six weeks—they won't have enough stock. You'll need a specialist commercial furnisher.'

'I'm getting pretty used to eating humble pie around you,' she said. 'So if that was an offer of a contact name, then yes, please.'

'Better than that. If I introduce you, you'll get the same terms that Hunter Hotels do—which will reduce your costs,' Gabriel said.

'Is this how you normally do business, getting special deals for neighbours?'

'No. And it's not because you're my girlfriend, either.

If we do the weddings and conferences, together, then if you use my suppliers I know your quality's going to be the same as mine. This is total self-interest.'

She didn't believe a word of it, but it made it a little easier to accept his help. 'It's really happening, isn't it?'

'Yes, it's really happening.' He kissed her. 'This is going to be amazing.'

Nicole spent the rest of the day finalising her lists for what needed to be done next, including applying for a wedding licence. Several people from the Surrey Quays forum dropped in to see her, some bringing photographs that she could borrow to have enlarged, framed and put on the walls in the reception area. She ran out of mugs and had to go next door to borrow some more mugs and coffee, to the amusement of Gabriel's team.

'So if you inherited this place from Brian...would your mum be Susan?' Ella Jones asked.

'Yes.'

'I always liked her—she was a lovely girl,' Ella said. 'Brian wasn't the easiest man. I always thought he was too hard on Susan.'

'He was but it was his loss, because my mum's amazing,' Nicole said.

'And so are you,' Ella's husband Stephen said. 'Most people would've thrown their hands up in the air at the state of this place and sold up. I bet him next door wanted this,' Stephen added, jerking his thumb in the direction of Gabriel's hotel, 'because the space would make a good car park for the hotel.'

'Gabriel Hunter's actually been really nice,' Nicole said. And if they knew he was Clarence... But it wasn't her place to out him. 'He's been very supportive. He's got a real eye for architecture and he sees the potential of this building, so he's working with me.'

'But that company—it just guts buildings and turns them into soulless hotel blocks,' Ella said.

'No, they don't. I've seen what he's doing next door and he's trying to keep as much of the character of the building as he can in the reception area, restaurant, bar, and conference rooms.'

Gabriel overheard the last bit of the conversation as he walked into the cinema foyer. And it warmed him that Nicole was defending him.

'If anyone here wants a tour next door, I'm happy to show you round,' he said. 'Oh, and since you pinched half my mugs, Nicole, I assumed you could do with some more supplies.' He handed her a two-litre carton of milk and a couple of boxes of muffins.

She smiled at him. 'I could indeed. Thanks, Gabriel.' She introduced him to everyone. 'They've lent me some wonderful postcards and photographs.'

'That's great,' he said. 'I'll go and put the kettle on and then take a look.'

Later that evening, he said to her, 'Thanks for supporting me when the Joneses seemed a bit anti. I thought you saw me as a shark-in-a-suit.'

'I know you better now. You don't compromise on quality and I think you'd be very tough on anyone who didn't meet your standards, but you're not a shark,' Nicole said. 'Oh, talking about being tough—Patrick emailed me the quote and contract. You said you wanted to look them over. How about I order us a Chinese takeaway while you do that?'

'Great,' he said. 'Let me have the surveyor's report as

well, so I can tie them up.' He went through the documents carefully.

'What do you think?' she asked when he'd finished.

'Not the cheapest, but it's a fair price and he's been thorough. It matches what the surveyor said. And you said you felt he'd work well with you. I'd say you're good to go with your instinct.'

Once she'd signed the contract and agreed the work plan, a new phase of Nicole's life started. She ended each day covered in paint and with aching muscles, but she was happier than she could ever remember. She'd got to know more people from the Surrey Quays forum in real life, and really felt part of the community.

And then there was Gabriel.

They were still taking things relatively slowly, but she was enjoying actually dating him—everything from a simple walk, to 'research' trips trying different local ice cream specialists, through to dinner out and even dancing. If anyone had told her even six months ago that she'd be this happy, she would never have believed them.

The one sticking point was that Patrick's predictions were right and the ceiling specialist was booked up for the next few months. Gabriel had tried his contacts, too, and nobody was available: so it looked as if the grand opening of the Electric Palace was going to be the cinema only and not the room with the amazing ceiling. Weddings and conferences were off limits, too, until the room was ready. And now she'd finally decided to work with him, she wanted it all to start *now*.

'When you want something done, you want it done now, don't you?' Gabriel asked when she'd expressed her disappointment.

'You're just as bad.'

'True.' He kissed her. 'Maybe the dates will change on another project and the specialist will be able to fit us in, but even so we can still use the upstairs foyer as the café, the downstairs bar, and the cinema itself.'

'It's going to be done at some point. I just have to be patient.' Nicole stroked his face. 'You know, I'm actually working longer hours than I was at the bank.'

'But the difference is that you love every second at the cinema.'

'I love seeing the changes in the place every day,' she said. 'And really feeling part of a team.'

'Part of the community,' he agreed. 'Me, too.' Other people had chipped in with information about the spice warehouse. 'And I've noticed that everyone's the same in real life as they are online. I wasn't expecting that.'

'And there's no snarkiness, nobody competing with each other—everyone's just getting on together and fixing things,' she said. 'I'm going to thank every single person by name on the opening night, as well as unveiling the board.'

'I'll supply the champagne to go with it,' he said.

She shook her head. 'You don't have to do that.'

'I know, but I want to. It's not every day your girlfriend manages to do something as amazing as this for the community.'

Nicole's mum and Jessie helped out at weekends and evenings, when they could. One evening, it was just the three of them working together, so Nicole ordered pizza when they stopped for a break.

'So when are you going to tell us?' Jessie asked.

'Tell you what?'

'About Gabriel,' Susan said.

'He's my neighbour, in business terms, and we have

mutual interests. It's made sense for us to work together,' Nicole said.

Jessie laughed. 'And you're telling us you haven't noticed how gorgeous he is?'

Nicole couldn't help it. She blushed.

'So how long has this been going on?' Susan asked.

'Um.' She'd been thoroughly busted.

'You might as well tell us now,' Jessie said. 'You know we're going to get it out of you.'

Nicole sighed and told them about how she'd met 'Clarence' on the Surrey Quays forum and he'd turned out to be Gabriel. 'So the man I thought was my enemy was actually my friend all along.'

'But you're more than friends?' Jessie asked.

'Yes.'

'He's a nice guy. Not like Jeff,' Susan said.

'Definitely not like Jeff.' Jessie hugged her. 'You seem happier, and I thought it was more than just the job. I'm glad. You deserve life to go right for you.'

At the end of a day when Nicole had spent close to fourteen hours painting—and her arm ached so much she barely had the strength to clean her brush—Gabriel called in to the cinema.

'I wondered what you felt like doing tonight.'

'I don't think I'm fit for much more than a hot bath and then crawling into my PJs,' she said.

'I was going to suggest cooking dinner for us.' He paused. 'You could have a bath at my place while I'm cooking—and I'll drive you home afterwards.'

This felt like the next step in their relationship, and Nicole wasn't sure if she was quite ready for that. Her doubts clearly showed in her expression, because Gabriel stole a kiss. 'That wasn't a clumsy pass, by the way. It was the offer of a hot bath and cooking for you because you look wiped out.'

'Thank you—I'd appreciate that. But I'm covered in paint.'

'I could collect stuff from your place first. Or I could cook at yours, if you don't mind me taking over your kitchen,' he suggested.

'You'd do that?'

'Sure—and then you can eat dinner in your PJs. Which is again not a come-on,' he said, 'because when you and I finally decide to take the next step I'd like you to be wide awake and enjoying yourself rather than thinking, oh, please hurry up and finish so I can go to sleep.'

She laughed. 'You,' she said, 'are a much nicer person than you like the world to think.'

'Well, hey. I don't want people to think I'm a push-over, or negotiating contracts and what have you would be very tedious.'

'You're still a good man, Gabriel.' And maybe this wasn't just business to him; maybe he really did like her, she thought. He'd talked about taking the next step. It meant another layer of trust: but from what she'd seen of him she thought she could trust him. He wouldn't let her down like Jeff had.

In the end he made a chicken biryani for her in her kitchen while she soaked in the bath. 'I would normally make my own naan bread rather than buying it ready-made from the supermarket,' he said, 'but I thought in the circumstances that you might not want your kitchen being cluttered up.'

'It still tastes amazing. I don't cook much,' she admitted.

'Lack of time or lack of inclination?' he asked.

'Both,' she said.

'I love cooking,' he said. 'It relaxes me.'

She smiled. 'Are you going to tell me you bake, as well?'

He raised an eyebrow. 'I wouldn't rate my chances against a professional but I make a reasonable Victoria sponge.'

'You're full of surprises,' she said.

'Is that a bad thing?' he asked.

'No, because they're nice surprises,' she said.

Which told him that she'd had a nasty surprise from her ex at some point. She still wouldn't open up to him, but Gabriel hoped she'd realise that he wouldn't hurt her—at least not intentionally.

Georgygirl had been important to him. But Nicole was something else. The way he felt when he was with her was like nothing he'd ever experienced before.

It couldn't be love—could it?

He'd never been properly in love in his life.

But he liked being with Nicole. With her, he could be truly himself. The problem was, could she trust him enough to be completely herself with him?

'Tonight,' Gabriel said, a week later, 'we're going to see the stars.'

'That's so sweet of you, but there isn't long until the cinema opens and all the dark sky spots are way up in Scotland or near the border.' She wrinkled her nose. 'I'd love to go with you, but I can't really take that much time off.'

'Actually, there are places in London,' he said, 'right in the city centre. And tonight's the night when Mars is at opposition.'

'The closest it gets to the earth and it's illuminated fully by the sun, so it's at its brightest—hang on, did you just say there are dark sky places in the middle of London?' she asked, surprised. 'Even with all the street lights?'

'There's an astronomy group that meets in the middle of one of the parks,' Gabriel said. 'I spoke to the guy who runs it and he says we can come along—they have an old observatory and we'll get a turn looking through the telescope. So we get to see the stars tonight—but we don't have to travel for hours, first.'

'Gabriel, that's such a lovely thing to do.' She kissed him. 'Thank you.'

'You've been working really hard. You deserve a little time out and I thought you'd enjoy this,' he said.

The observatory was exactly as she'd imagined it to be, with a rotating dome and an old brass telescope. Just as Gabriel had promised, they had the chance to look through the telescope and see some of the features of Mars—and the moon, too.

Nicole loved it, and she loved walking in the park hand in hand with Gabriel afterwards. 'I'm blown away that you've taken the effort to do this for me,' she said. Jeff had never indulged her love of the stars, saying it was a bit childish. 'I feel a bit guilty that I haven't done anything for you.'

'Actually, you have,' Gabriel said. 'You've made me feel better about myself than I have in years—and I have some idea now of what I want to do in the future.'

'Such as?'

'I need to work it out in my head,' he said, 'but you're the first person I'll talk to about it.'

She grimaced. 'Sorry. I was being nosey.'

'No, you're my partner and it's nice that you're interested. Some of the women I've dated have only been interested in the depth of my bank account.'

'I hope you don't think I'm one of those.'

'Given how much hard work it is to persuade you even to let me buy you dinner,' he said, 'I know you're not.'

'So why did you date them?'

'I guess I was looking for someone who understood me. The problem was, the nice girls were wary of me—either they'd heard I was a wild child as a student, or they saw me as this ruthless businessman in the same mould as my dad. And the others weren't interested in understanding me.'

'So you're a poor little rich boy?'

'Yes.' He batted his eyelashes at her. 'And I won't make a fuss if you decide to kiss me better.'

She laughed. 'That's the worst chat-up line I've ever heard.'

'It was pretty bad,' he admitted.

She smiled. 'I'll kiss you anyway.' And she did so. Lingeringly.

Over the next couple of weeks they grew closer, falling into a routine of having dinner together most nights, and then Gabriel would take Nicole home and they'd curl up on her sofa together, holding each other close and talking.

'So do I ever get to see the bat cave?' Nicole asked.

'Bat cave?' Gabriel asked, looking puzzled.

'You've been to my flat. Yours is clearly the bat cave—top secret.'

He laughed. 'Point taken. I'll make dinner there to-night.'

His flat was in a very modern development, with a balcony running along the length of the building, and all the rooms faced the river.

'Bathroom,' he said, gesturing to the various doors as

they stood in his small lobby, 'my bedroom and en-suite, main bathroom, living room, guest room.'

Like her flat, his had floor-to-ceiling windows, but his rooms were much bigger and so were the windows. Nicole adored the views.

The kitchen was just off the living room, and was about ten times the size of hers. It was clearly a cook's kitchen, with maple cupboards, worktops, and flooring. At the end of the living room, next to the kitchen, was his dining area; there was a large glass table with six comfortable-looking chairs. Three of the walls were painted cream, but the wall by the dining area was painted sky blue and held a massive painting of a stylised fish.

It looked like a show flat. And yet it also felt like home; the sofas looked comfortable, and she noticed he had the most up-to-date television.

'Home cinema?' she asked.

He nodded. 'But watching a film at home on your own isn't quite the same as going to the cinema with a group of friends. I think what you're doing to the Electric Palace is brilliant because you get the best of both worlds—all the comfort and all the social stuff as well.'

'I hope so.' The only thing Nicole couldn't see in the room was a desk. 'So you don't work at home?'

'The guest bedroom's my office,' he said. 'Though there is a sofa-bed in there if someone wants to stay over.'

He held her gaze for a moment. Would he ask her to stay over tonight? she wondered, and her heart skipped a beat.

She kept the conversation light while he cooked lemon chicken with new potatoes and she made the salad. But when they were lying on his sofa later that evening, he stroked her face. 'Stay with me tonight?'

She knew he didn't mean her to stay in the guest room. It meant spending the night in his bed. Skin to skin with him.

The next stage of their relationship.

Another layer of trust.

It was a risk. But the man she'd got to know over the last few weeks was definitely something special. Someone worth taking a risk for.

'I have a spare toothbrush,' he added.

She kissed him. 'Yes.'

And in answer he scooped her off the sofa and carried her to his bed.

A couple of days later, Nicole had some great news.

'My ceiling guy can fit us in,' Patrick said. 'The job he's working on has run into a bit of a legal wrangle, so he's got some spare time.'

'But doesn't he have a huge waiting list?' Nicole asked. 'Shouldn't he be seeing the next person on his list instead of queue-jumping me?'

'Probably,' Patrick said, 'but I've kept him up to date with what's happening here and he's seen the ceiling on your website. He says it's not a massive job—and also I think he fell in love with the stars and wants to be the one to work on it.'

'Got you,' Nicole said with a grin. 'Those stars really seem to do it for everyone.'

'I can't believe you've got all these people pitching in, too. I thought it was going to cost you an arm and a leg in overtime to get this done in your timeframe, but it's not.'

'No, but I do need to thank them. I'm going to have a board in the foyer with the names of everyone who's helped, and I'll unveil it on the opening night.'

'That's a nice idea.'

'I couldn't have done it without them,' Nicole said simply, 'so the very least they deserve is a public thank you.'

The person she most wanted to thank was Gabriel—for believing in her, and for being supportive. She just needed to work out how to do that.

'There is one thing,' Patrick said. 'Work on the ceiling means everything has to stop, because we can't do anything in that room until—'

'—the lead paint is gone,' she finished. 'Actually, that might fit in nicely.'

'Taking a holiday?'

'Sort of.'

She did some checking online, then called Gabriel. 'Is there any chance you can clear your diary for the next couple of days—preferably three?'

'Why?' he asked.

'That's on a need-to-know basis,' she said. 'I just need to know if it's possible.'

'Give me five minutes and I'll call you back.' He was as good as his word. 'OK, it's possible, but only if you tell me why.'

'It's a research trip. I could do with your views.' It wasn't strictly true, but she wanted to surprise him.

'All right. I take it that it's not in London, so do you need me to drive?'

'Nope. I'm borrowing a car. And I'll pick you up tomorrow at ten.'

It was a bright purple convertible Beetle, and Gabriel groaned when he saw it. 'You're going to tell me this is cinema-related because this is an update of Herbie, right?'

'I hadn't thought of that, but yes.' She grinned. 'Get in.'

'I thought you said my convertible was showing off?'

'Yeah, yeah.'

'So where are we going?'

'Road trip,' she said. 'Do you want to be Thelma or Louise?'

He groaned. 'This isn't going to end well.'

'Oh, it is. Trust me.'

She drove them down to Sussex, where she'd booked a couple of nights in an old fort overlooking the sea. She had a cool box in the back of the car filled with picnic food from a posh supermarket's chiller cabinet, and the weather forecast was good. This would be three days where they didn't have to worry about anything—they could just be together, relax and enjoy each other's company.

'Research?' Gabriel asked, eyeing the fort.

'Busted,' she said with a smile. 'I just wanted to take you away for a couple of days to say thanks for all you've done to help me.'

'It was pure self-interest. We have mutual business arrangements.'

'And I wanted to spend some time with you,' she said. 'Just you and me and the sea.'

'And an old fort—that's as awesome as it gets,' he said.

Three perfect days, where they explored the coast, ate at little country pubs and watched the sun setting over the sea. But best of all was waking up in his arms each morning.

Gabriel was everything Nicole wanted in a partner. He listened to her, he treated her as if her ideas mattered, he was kind and sweet and funny. And he could make her heart skip a beat with just one look.

The way she was starting to feel about him was like nothing else she'd ever known. She'd thought that she loved Jeff, but that paled into insignificance beside the way she felt about Gabriel.

But she couldn't shake the fear that it would all go wrong.

Everything had gone wrong when she'd moved in with Jeff. So, as long as they kept their separate flats and didn't say anything about how they felt, she thought, everything would be fine.

CHAPTER NINE

'I CAN'T BELIEVE how dim I am,' Gabriel said.

Nicole, curled up in bed beside him, just laughed. 'Dim is hardly the word to describe you. What brought that on?'

'The Electric Palace. We haven't looked in the film archives. And it's a *cinema*, for pity's sake. Moving pictures should've been the first place we looked.'

'Film archives? You mean, newsreels?'

'No. I was thinking of those Edwardian guys who went round the country taking films of everyday people,' he explained. 'They might have visited Surrey Quays.'

She looked at him. 'Actually, you're right, especially as your hotel was a spice warehouse—they specialised in factories, didn't they? So they're bound to have come to Docklands.'

Gabriel grabbed his phone and looked them up on the internet. 'Sagar Mitchell and James Kenyon. They made actuality films—everything from street scenes and transport through to sporting events, local industries and parades. The films used to be commissioned by travelling exhibitors, and were shown at town halls and fairgrounds.' He looked at her. 'And theatres.'

'If there aren't any films showing the warehouse or the theatre, we might still be able to find out if one of those films was shown at the Electric Palace—the Kursaal, as it was back then,' she said thoughtfully. 'That would be perfect for our opening night.'

'Have you decided what you want to show on the first night, yet?'

'I'd like one of the actuality films,' she said, 'and a classic film and a modern film, so we cover all the bases. Probably *It's A Wonderful Life*.'

'In July?' Gabriel looked surprised. 'It's a Christmas film.'

'It's brilliant at any time of year.' She punched his arm. 'Clarence, surely it'd get your vote?'

'Given your Surrey Quays forum name, what about *Mary Poppins*?' he suggested.

'We kind of did that on the beach in Norfolk,' she said.

'The first time I kissed you.' He kissed her lingeringly.

'You're an old romantic at heart,' she teased.

'Yeah.' He kissed her again.

'So, our classic film. Doesn't *Citizen Kane* top the list of the best films of all time?'

'Let's look up the list.' She did so, and grimaced. 'There are an awful lot on here I've never heard of, which is a bit pathetic for a cinema owner.'

'Let me have a look.' He glanced through them. 'I'm with you—haven't heard of most of these. And on opening night I think we need to have a broad appeal.'

'I did say I'd include some art-house evenings—I've been working on my scheduling—but I kind of want the film on the first night to be something I actually know. I'm standing by *It's a Wonderful Life*.'

'It's your show,' he said. 'And you're right. It's a good film.'

They snatched some time to visit the archives in the week. To Nicole's pleasure, there was footage of both the

Spice House and the Kursaal—and they were able to arrange to use it for the opening night. Better still, they had permission to take stills they could blow up and frame for their respective reception areas.

'Luck's definitely on our side,' Nicole said. 'I think this is going to work out.'

'I don't just think it,' Gabriel said, squeezing her hand. 'I *know* this is going to work out.'

Nicole was working on a section of wall when she heard a voice drawl, 'That's definitely not how you used to dress in the office.'

Recognising the voice, she turned round. 'Hey, Neil—nice to see you. You might like to know that wall over there is partly thanks to the office.'

'Glad to hear it—I'll tell the team.' He glanced round the foyer. 'This is really impressive, especially when you see those pictures on your website of what it looked like when you took over. So I take it you're not planning to come and claim your desk back?'

'I hope not.' She smiled at him. 'Are you enjoying the view from my desk?'

'Considering I don't have it, no.'

She stared at him in surprise. 'But you were a shoo-in to take over from me while I'm away and then permanently if I don't come back. What's happened?'

'We had a bit of a restructure and the boss headhunted this guy—and if you come back I think this guy will be *your* boss as well.' He sighed. 'I was never going to like him much anyway, because he got the job that I thought would be mine, but even without that...' He grimaced. 'I just don't like Jeff. He isn't a team player. I mean, OK, so you never came out with us on team nights out, but we all knew you had our backs in the office, whereas he'd sell us all down the river. He'd sell anything to make a profit.'

Jeff. She went cold. Surely not? 'Would that be Jeff Rumball?' she asked, trying to sound as casual as she could.

Neil looked surprised. 'Yeah—do you know him?'

'I haven't seen him for a while, but yes, I know him,' Nicole said. And the idea of failing to make the cinema a going concern and then having to go back to her old job, only to end up working for the man who'd betrayed her and left her self-esteem in tatters... Just no. It wasn't going to happen. 'My advice is to keep a low profile and to document everything. Copy things in to other people to be on the safe side, too,' she said.

'Got you.' Neil looked grim. 'We'd all rather you came back, you know.'

'Thanks for that,' she said with a smile, 'but I hope I'm going to make this place work.'

Although she chatted nicely with her former colleague and pretended to everyone else at the cinema that she was just fine, Neil's news left her feeling unsettled all day.

Jeff had used her to get ahead in his career. What was to say that Gabriel wasn't doing the same? Even though part of her knew she was being paranoid and completely ridiculous, she couldn't help the fears bubbling up—and Gabriel himself had admitted that he'd only joined the Surrey Quays forum at first to make sure he could head off any opposition to the development of the Spice House.

Eventually, sick of the thoughts whirling through her head, she left everyone working on plastering, painting, or woodwork, and walked to the café on Challoner Road to clear her head. She knew her mum was in meetings all day and Jessie was up to her eyes with her students in the middle of exam season, so she couldn't talk to them about Jeff.

Which left Gabriel.

Nicole had never actually told him about Jeff, but maybe this would be a way of laying that particular ghost to rest—and it would finally convince her that Gabriel was nothing like the man who'd let her down. She bought coffee and brownies, and headed for the Spice House.

But, as Nicole walked down the corridor to Gabriel's office, she could hear him talking. Clearly he was either in the middle of a meeting with someone or he was on the phone. What an idiot she was. She knew he was busy; she should have texted him first or called him to check when he might be free to see her for a quick chat.

She was about to turn away when she heard him say her name, almost like a question.

'Nicole? No, she's not going to give us any trouble, Dad.'

She went cold.

Jeff had used her to get on with his career. Right now, it sounded as if Gabriel was doing exactly the same. *She's not going to give us any trouble*—no, of course she wasn't, because he'd got her eating out of his hand. Over the last few months he'd grown close to her. He knew all her hopes and dreams; he'd made her feel that he supported her; and he'd made her feel that this thing between them was something special.

She'd thought he was different. After their rocky start, they'd learned to trust each other. They saw things the same way. They'd worked together to develop a conference package and a wedding package. She'd been so sure that she could trust him—with her heart as well as her business.

But that bit of conversation she'd just overhead made

it horribly clear that it had all been to keep her sweet and to make sure that, whatever he really had planned for the Spice House, she wasn't going to protest about it.

So she'd just made the same old mistake. Trusted a man who didn't love her at all and saw her as a way of getting what he wanted in business.

Sure, she could go in to his office now, all guns blazing. But it wouldn't change a thing. It wouldn't change the fact that she was stupid and trusting and naive. It wouldn't change the fact that Gabriel was a ruthless businessman who didn't let anything get in his way. So what was the point in making a fuss? It was over. Yelling at him wouldn't make her feel any better. Right now, she wanted to crawl into the nearest corner and lick her wounds—just as she had with Jeff.

She should never, ever have opened her heart like this. And she'd never, ever be stupid enough to open her heart to anyone again.

Feeling sick, she walked away, dumped the coffees and the brownies in the skip, and then sent Gabriel a text.

I can't do this any more. It's over.

Then she walked back in to the cinema and pretended that nothing was wrong. She was smiling on the outside, but on the inside she was purest ice.

She would never, ever let anyone take advantage of her like that again.

'Dad, I love you,' Gabriel said, 'but right at this moment you're driving me crazy. I know that you rescued me from the biggest mistake anyone could ever have made and I appreciate that. But it was nearly ten years ago now. I'm not the same person I was back then. And, if you can't see that, then maybe I'm in the wrong place.'

'What are you saying?' Evan demanded.

'Dad, do you really expect your hotel managers to run every single day-to-day decision past you, so your diary and your day is completely blocked up, or do you trust them to get on with the job you pay them to do and run the hotels?'

'Well, obviously I expect them to do the job I pay them to do,' Evan barked.

'Then let me do the same,' Gabriel said. 'You put me in charge of the Spice House, and I've got plans for the place. And yes, they do involve Nicole—we're doing some joint ventures with her, so we can offer something that little bit different to our clients, both business and leisure. And she's using our suppliers.'

Evan snorted in disgust. 'Using our name to get a discount.'

'Using our suppliers,' Gabriel pointed out, 'so her quality standards are the same as ours. It makes sense. And yes, she gets a discount. That way we both win, and more importantly we get to offer our customers what they want. Which means they'll stay loyal to us.'

'I suppose,' Evan said, sounding far from convinced.

Gabriel sighed. 'Look, I know I did wrong when I was nineteen. But I've spent years trying to make up for it. If you can't move past what I did and see that I'm a very different person now, then there isn't any point in me working for you. I'll step aside so you can employ the person you need to get the job done.'

'Are you resigning?' Evan asked in disbelief.

'I'm pretty close to it,' Gabriel said.

'But it's the family firm. You can't leave. What would you do? Set up in competition with me?'

'I'd work in a different sector,' Gabriel said. 'Which is actually what I'd rather talk to you about. I'd like to work with you. But it needs be on my terms now, Dad. I can't spend the rest of my life trying to do the impossible because it's making us both miserable, and Mum as well. This has to stop. Now.' His mobile phone beeped, and he glanced at the screen, intending to call whoever it was back later. But then he saw the message.

I can't do this any more. It's over.

It was from Nicole.

What? What did she mean, it was over? Had something happened at the cinema—had Patrick found something unfixable? Or did she mean *they* were over?

He didn't have a clue. As far as he knew, he hadn't done anything to hurt her. So what was going on?

'Dad, I have to go,' he said swiftly.

'Wha—?' Evan began.

'Later,' Gabriel said. 'I'll call you later, Dad. Something's come up and I need to deal with it right now.' And he put the phone down before his father could protest. This was something that was much more important than sorting out his career with his father. He had no idea what the problem was, but he needed to talk to Nicole and sort it out. *Now.*

He found her in the cinema, wielding a paintbrush. Outwardly, she was smiling, but Gabriel could see the tension in her shoulders.

'Can we have a word?' he asked.

'Why?' She looked wary.

'We need to talk.'

'I don't think so,' she said.

So she *did* mean they were over. Well, surely she didn't

think he was just going to accept that text message and roll over like a tame little lapdog? 'OK. We can do this in public, if you'd rather.'

Clearly recognising that he'd called her bluff, she shook her head. 'Come up to the office.'

He followed her upstairs, and she closed the door behind them.

'So what was that message about?' he asked.

'All deals are off,' she said, 'and I mean all of it—the conference stuff, the weddings, and us.'

'Why?'

'Because I heard you talking to your father, telling him that I wasn't going to give you any trouble.'

He frowned. 'You heard that?'

'I was coming to see you about something. I didn't realise you were on the phone and then I overheard you talking.'

'Well, it's a pity you didn't stay a bit longer and hear the rest of what I said,' he said, nettled. 'What did you think it meant?'

'That you were planning something I wouldn't like very much, but I wouldn't give you any trouble.' She gave him a cynical look. 'Because I'm your girlfriend, so of course I'll flutter my eyelashes and do everything you say. You *used* me, Gabriel.'

'Firstly,' Gabriel said, 'you only heard part of a conversation—and I have no idea how you've managed to leap to the most incredibly wrong conclusion from hearing one single sentence. And, secondly, I thought you knew me. Why on earth would you think I would use you?'

'Because my judgement in men is rubbish—and I've managed to pick yet another man who'd try to leverage our relationship for the sake of his career.'

'If anyone else had insulted me like that,' he said, 'I would be shredding them into little tiny bits right now. I've already worked out that your ex hurt you pretty badly and you won't talk about it, even to me—but now you get a choice. Either you tell me everything yourself, right now, or I'll go and talk to your mum and Jessie. And, because they love you, they will most definitely spill the beans to me.'

'So now you're throwing your weight about and threatening me?'

'No. I'm trying to find out why the hell you're acting as if you're totally deranged, and assigning motives to me that I wouldn't have in a million years,' he snapped. 'If you'd bothered to stay and overhear the rest of the conversation, Nicole, you would've heard me telling my father that we're working together on conferences and weddings, and everything's fine because we're using the same suppliers and we have the same attitudes towards our customers—and that if he can't move on from my past and see me as I am now, then maybe it's time for me to step aside and he finds the person he wants to run the show and I'll go and do something that makes me happy.'

Understanding dawned in her eyes. 'So you're not...?'

'No,' he said, 'I'm not planning to do anything underhand. That's not how I operate. I'm not planning to put sneaky clauses in our contract in such teensy, tiny print that you can't read them and then you'll be so far in debt to me that the only way out is to give me the cinema. I thought we were working together, Nicole. I thought we were friends. Lovers. I've been happier these last few weeks than I've ever been in my life—because I'm with you. So what the hell has gone wrong?'

She closed her eyes. 'I...'

'Tell me, Nicole, because I really can't see it for my-self. What have I done?'

'It's not you—it's me,' she said miserably.

'And that's the coward's way out. The way the guy dumps the girl without having to tell her what the real problem is. You're not a coward, Nicole. You're brave, you're tenacious, you make things work out—so tell me the truth.'

Nicole knew she didn't have any choice now. She'd let her fears get the better of her and she'd misjudged Gabriel so badly it was untrue. And she wouldn't blame him if he didn't want anything to do with her, ever again, after this.

'It's about Jeff,' she said. 'I'm ashamed of myself.'

He said nothing, clearly not letting her off the hook. Which was what she deserved, she knew. She took a deep breath. 'I didn't often go to parties when I started work. I was focused on studying for my professional exams and doing well at my job. I wanted to get on, to make some-thing of myself. But four years ago I gave in to someone nagging me in the office and I went to a party. And that's where I met Jeff. He was in banking, too—he worked for a different company, so I hadn't met him before. He was bright and sparkly, and I couldn't believe he could be interested in someone as boring and mousy as me. But we started dating.'

And what a fool she'd been.

'Go on,' Gabriel said. But his voice was gentler, this time. Not judging her.

Not that he needed to judge her. She'd already done that and found herself severely wanting.

'He asked me to move in with him. I loved him and I thought he loved me, so I said yes.'

'And that's when he changed?'

She shook her head. 'We moved in together and he was the same as he always was. He tended to go to parties without me, but that was fine.' She shrugged. 'I'm not really much of one for socialising. Outside work, I don't really know what to say to people.'

'You don't seem to have a problem talking to people at the cinema—and you definitely didn't seem to have a problem talking on the forum,' he pointed out.

'That's different.'

To her relief, he didn't call her on it. 'So what happened?'

'I can't even remember why, but I ended up going to this one party—and that's when I found out the truth about Jeff. I was in the toilet when this woman started talking to her friends about her boyfriend. I wasn't consciously trying to eavesdrop, but when you're in a toilet cubicle you can't really block people's words out.'

'True.'

'Anyway, this woman was saying that her boyfriend was living with someone else but didn't love her. She was a boring banker, and he was only living with her because there was going to be a promotion at work, and he knew his boss was going to give the job to someone who was settled down. The woman he was living with was the perfect banker's wife because she was a banker, too. Except the guy had bought the big diamond ring for her—for the mistress, not for the boring banker.' She grimaced. 'I felt so sorry for this poor woman who clearly thought her boyfriend loved her, but he was cheating on her and just using her to get on in his career. But then the woman in the toilets said his name. How many bankers are there called Jeff, who also happen to be living with a female banker?'

'Did you ask him about it?'

'Yes, because part of me was hoping that it was just

a horrible coincidence and there was some poor other woman out there being cheated on—not that I wanted to wish that on anyone, obviously. I just didn't want it to be true about me. But he admitted he was seeing her. He said that was the reason why he'd started dating me and the reason he'd asked me to move in, so his boss would think he was the right guy for the promotion.' She swallowed hard. 'Luckily I'd moved into his place rather than him moving into mine, so I packed my stuff and went to stay with Jessie until I could find a flat. That's when I moved here.' And she hadn't dated since.

Until Gabriel.

And she'd been so happy...but now she'd messed it up. Big time. Because she hadn't been able to trust him.

'Jeff sounds like the kind of selfish loser who needs to grow up, and I bet that promotion went to someone else,' Gabriel said.

'Actually, it didn't. He's very plausible. He got away with it. I have no idea what happened to his girlfriend, and I'm not interested in knowing.'

'So what does Jeff have to do with me?'

She bit her lip. 'You know I'm on a sabbatical?' At his nod, she continued, 'I thought my number two would take over from me in my absence, but it seems there's been a restructure in the office. Neil—my number two—came to tell me about it today. A new guy's been brought in over him and will probably be my new boss if I go back. And it's the worst coincidence in the world.'

'The new guy's Jeff?'

She nodded. 'I was coming to see you and—well, whine about it, I suppose. And then I heard what you said. And it just brought all my old doubts back. It made me think that I'd let myself be fooled all over again, by someone who was using me to get on in business.'

Gabriel took her hand. 'I'm sorry that you got blind-sided like that, but everyone makes mistakes. Just because you made a mistake trusting him, it doesn't mean that you can't trust anyone ever again.'

'I know that with my head,' she said miserably. 'But it's how I feel *here*.' She pressed one hand to her chest.

'I'm not using you to get on with business, Nicole. I never have.' He raked a hand through his hair. 'Actually I was going to talk to you tonight about the very first wedding in the Electric Palace and the Spice House. I thought it might be nice if it was ours.'

She stared at him. 'You were going to ask me to marry you?'

'You're everything I want in a partner. You make me laugh when I'm in a bad mood. You make my world a brighter place. I'm a better man when I'm with you. But...' He paused.

Yeah. She'd known there was a but. It was a million miles high.

'But?' She needed to face it.

'You need to think about it and decide if I'm what you want. If you can trust me. If you can see that I'm not like Jeff.' He gave her a sad look. 'I thought you saw me clearly, Nicole, that you were the one person in the world who knew me for exactly who I am. But you don't, do you? You're just like everyone else. You see what you want to see.' He dragged in a breath. 'Talk it over with your mum and Jessie, people you do actually trust. And come and find me when you're ready to talk. When you're ready to see me for who I am. And if you don't...' He shrugged. 'Well.'

And then he walked out of the office and closed the door quietly behind him.

CHAPTER TEN

IT WAS REALLY hard to wait and do nothing, but Gabriel knew that Nicole had to make this decision by herself. If she didn't, then at some point in the future she'd feel that he'd railroaded her into it, and it would all go pear-shaped.

Patience was a virtue and a business asset, he reminded himself. He had to stick to it. Even if it was driving him crazy.

The only way he could think of to distract himself was to bury himself in work. So he opened up a file on his computer and started outlining his proposal to take the business in a new direction. If his father wasn't prepared to let him do that, then Gabriel would leave Hunter Hotels and start up on his own. It was something he should probably have done years ago, but it was Nicole's belief in him that had helped him to take the final step and work out what he really wanted to do with his life. But did she believe in him enough to stay with him? Or had her ex destroyed her trust so thoroughly that she'd never be able to believe in anyone else?

He had no idea.

He just had to wait.

And hope.

* * *

Gabriel had walked away from her.

Nicole stared at the closed door.

Of course he'd walked away. She'd leapt to the wrong conclusions and hadn't even given him a chance to explain—she'd just thrown a hissy fit and told him it was over.

By text.

How awful was that?

He'd been the one who'd insisted on talking. He'd made her tell him about Jeff.

And he'd made it clear that she was the one letting her fears get in the way of a future. He'd said she was everything he wanted in a partner. That he wanted them to be the first people to get married in the cinema. But he hadn't tried to persuade her round to his way of thinking, or to make her feel bad about herself, the way Jeff had. He'd acknowledged that she'd been hurt in the past and she was afraid. And he'd said that she was the one who needed to think about it. To decide if he was what she wanted. If she could trust him. If she was ready to see him for who he really was.

He was giving her the choice.

And he'd advised her to talk it over with her mum and Jessie. He'd known this was something she couldn't do on her own, but he was clearly trying not to put pressure on her.

She grabbed her phone. Five minutes later, she'd arranged to meet her mother and Jessie in the park opposite Jessie's school, giving her enough time to nip home and change into clothes that weren't paint-stained and scrub her face.

Both her mum and Jessie greeted her with a hug. 'So what's happened?' Jessie asked.

Nicole explained about Neil's visit and her row with Gabriel. 'He told me to talk it over with people I trusted,' she said. 'Well, with you two.'

'So talk,' Susan said. 'How do you feel about him?'

Nicole thought about it. 'The world feels brighter when he's around.'

'Do you love him?' Jessie asked.

'Isn't that something I should say to him, first?' Nicole countered, panicking slightly.

'He told you to talk it over with us,' Susan pointed out, 'so no. Do you love him?'

Nicole took a deep breath. 'Yes.'

'And is it the same way you felt about Jeff?' Jessie asked.

Nicole shook her head. 'It's different. Gabriel sees me for who I am, not who he wants me to be. I don't worry about things when I'm with him.'

'You said he was a shark in a suit when you first met him,' Susan said thoughtfully.

'You've met him, so you know he isn't like that. He's been scrupulously fair. The problem's *me*.' She closed her eyes briefly. 'I'm too scared to trust in case I make a mistake again.'

'Everyone makes mistakes,' Jessie said.

'That's what Gabriel said. But what if I get it wrong with him?'

'OK—let's look at this the other way,' Susan said. 'Supposing you never saw him again. How would you feel?'

Like she did right now. 'There would be a massive hole in my life. He's not just my partner—he's my friend.'

'So the problem is down to Jeff—because he was a total jerk to you, you're worried that all men are like that, and if you let them close they'll all treat you like he did,' Jessie said.

'I guess,' Nicole said.

'Which means you're letting Jeff win,' Susan said briskly. 'Is that what you want?'

'Of course not—and anyway, I let Gabriel close to me.'

'And did he hurt you?' Jessie asked.

Nicole sighed. 'No. But I hurt him. I overreacted.'

'Just a tad,' Susan said dryly.

'I don't know how to fix this,' Nicole said miserably.

'Yes, you do,' Jessie said. 'Talk to him. Apologise. Tell him what you told us. Let him into your heart. And I mean really in, not just giving a little bit of ground.'

'Supposing…?' she began, then let her voice trail off. She knew she was finding excuses—because she was a coward and she couldn't believe that Gabriel felt the same way about her as she did about him.

'Supposing nothing,' Susan said. 'That's your only option, if you really want him in your life. Total honesty.'

'You're right,' she said finally. 'I need to apologise and tell him how I really feel about him.' And she'd have to make that leap of faith and trust that it wasn't too late.

Gabriel looked up when he heard the knock on his office door, hoping it was Nicole, and tried not to let the disappointment show on his face when he saw his father standing in the doorway.

'I didn't expect to see you,' he said.

Evan scowled. 'You said you'd call me back, and you didn't.'

The last thing Gabriel wanted right now was a fight. 'I'm sorry,' he said tiredly, and raked a hand through his hair. 'I got caught up in something.'

'I'm not criticising you,' Evan said, surprising him. 'I

was thinking I'd pushed you too far.' He looked Gabriel straight in the eye. 'We need to talk.'

'Yes, we do.' And this conversation had been a very long time coming. Gabriel paused. 'Do you want a coffee or something?'

'No.'

'OK. I'll tell Janey to hold my calls and I'm not interruptible for the time being.'

When Gabriel came back from seeing his PA, his father was staring out of the window. 'I see the cinema's nearly finished,' Evan remarked.

'Yes. It's a matter of restoring the sun ray on the half-moon outside and redoing the sign and that's it. It's pretty much done indoors, too.' He looked at his father. 'So what's this really about, Dad?'

'Sit down.'

Gabriel compromised by leaning against the edge of his desk.

'I owe you an apology.'

Now he knew why his father had told him to sit down—not to be bossy but to save him from falling over in shock. 'An apology?' He kept his voice very bland so he didn't start another row.

'What you said on the phone—you were right. Your mistake was nearly ten years ago and you're not the same person you were back then. You've grown up.'

'I'm glad you can see that now.'

Evan grimaced. 'I had you on speakerphone at the time. Your mother might have overheard some of what you said.'

Gabriel hid a smile. 'Mum nagged you into apologising?'

'Your mother doesn't nag. She just pointed a few things out to me. All the decisions you've made—some of them I wasn't so sure about at the time, but they've all come good. You have an astute business mind.'

Compliments from his father? Maybe he was dreaming. Surreptitiously, he pinched himself; it hurt, so he knew he really was awake.

'I saw that,' Evan said. 'Am I that much of a monster?'

'As a boss or as a father? And do you really have to ask?'

Evan sighed. 'I just worried about you, that if I wasn't on your case you might slip back into your old ways.'

'Maybe that was a possibility when I was twenty, but I'm not that far off thirty now—so it's not going to happen. I've grown up.'

'I guess I need to stop being a helicopter parent.'

'That,' Gabriel said, 'would be nice, but I guess it'd be hard to change a lifetime's habits.'

'Are you really going to leave the company?'

'Right now, I can't answer that,' Gabriel said. 'It might be better for both of us if I did. Then I can concentrate on being your son instead of having to prove myself to you over and over again at work.'

'You said about taking the business in a new direction. What did you have in mind?' Evan asked.

'We already have the hotels,' Gabriel said, 'for both business and leisure. The logical next step would be to offer holiday stays with a difference.'

'What sort of difference?'

'Quirky properties. Lighthouses, follies, water towers—places with heritage. Think somewhere like Lundy Island.'

'Old places that need restoring carefully?'

Gabriel nodded. 'That's what really interests me. I first started to feel that way when I did the Staithe Hotel, but working on this place and the cinema crystallised it for me.'

'Yes, I noticed you in a few of the photographs on the Electric Palace's website.'

Gabriel let that pass. 'This is what I really want to do. The way I want to take the company for the future. I like the research, looking up all the old documents and then trying to keep the heritage as intact as possible while making the building function well in modern terms. Fitting it all together.' He smiled. 'Hunters' Heritage Holidays. It's not the best title, but it'll do as a working one.'

'You've done a proposal with full costings?'

'Most of it's in my head at the moment,' Gabriel admitted, 'but I've made a start on typing it up.'

'You see things clearly,' Evan said. 'That's a good skill to have. I'd be very stupid to let that skill go elsewhere. And diversification is always a good business strategy.'

'So you'll consider it?'

'Make the case,' Evan said.

But this time Gabriel knew he'd only have to make the case once. He wouldn't have to prove it over and over again, the way he'd had to prove himself ever since university. 'Thanks, Dad. I won't let you down.'

'I know, son.' Evan paused. 'So do I get a guided tour of the cinema?'

'Not today,' Gabriel said. 'I have a few things to sort out with Nicole. But soon.'

Evan actually hugged him. 'Your mother wants you to come to dinner. Soon.'

'I'll call her later today,' Gabriel promised. With luck, by then Nicole would've had enough time to think about it—and with a little more luck he'd be able to take her home and introduce her to his family. As his equal.

After Evan left, Gabriel spent the afternoon working on his proposal. The longer it took Nicole to contact him, the more sure he was that she was going to call everything off.

Or maybe a watched phone never beeped with a text, in the same way that the proverbial watched pot never boiled.

He was called to deal with an issue over the spa and accidentally left his phone on his desk. He came back to find a text from Nicole.

I'm ready to talk. Can we meet in the park by the observatory at half-past five?

Please let this be a good sign, Gabriel thought, and texted her back.

Yes.

Nicole sat on the bench near the observatory, trying to look cool and calm and collected. Inside, she was panicking. Should she have planned some grand gesture to sweep Gabriel off his feet? Should she have spelled out 'sorry' in rose petals, or bought some posh chocolates with a letter piped on each one to spell out a message? Should she have organised a helicopter to whisk them away somewhere for a sumptuous picnic on a deserted beach, or—

And then all the words fell out of her head when she saw Gabriel walking up the path towards her.

He was still wearing a business suit, but he was wearing sunglasses in concession to the brightness of the afternoon. And his expression was absolutely unreadable.

He'd given her nothing to work on with his text reply, either. Just the single word 'yes'.

Help.

This could go so, so wrong.

'Hi.' He stood in front of the bench and gestured to it. 'May I?'

'Sure.' She took a deep breath. 'Gabriel. I'm sorry I hurt you.'

'Uh-huh.'

'I've been an idiot. A huge idiot. Because I was scared. I got spooked, and I should have trusted my instincts. I know you're not like Jeff. I know you're not a cheat or a liar. I know you have integrity.'

'Thank you.'

She still couldn't read his expression. Was he going to forgive her? Or had he, too, spent the time apart thinking about things and decided that she wasn't what he wanted after all?

All she could do now was be honest with him and tell him how she really felt.

'You've been there for me every step of the way. Firstly as Clarence and then as—well, once we realised who each other was in real life, and you made me see that you're not a shark in a suit. And ever since I first met you online, you've become important to me. Really important. I know I've behaved badly. And I'll understand if you don't want anything to do with me any more. But I think the Electric Palace and the Spice House have a lot to offer each other, and we've done so much work on our joint plans—it'd be a shame to abandon them.' She took a deep breath. 'But, most of all, Gabriel, I want you to forgive me and give me a chance to make it up to you. I have to be honest with you—I can't promise that I won't panic ever again. The hurt from what Jeff did went pretty deep. It shattered my confidence in me. I find it hard to believe that anyone can even like me for myself, let alone anything more. But I can promise you that, next time I have a wobble, I'll talk to you about it instead of over-reacting and doing something stupid.'

Still he said nothing.

'I love you, Gabriel,' she said quietly. 'And I don't know what to do about it. I can't turn it into a balance sheet or a schedule or a timetable. It's just there. All the time. I want to be with you. I know you've dated women who just saw you in terms of your bank account, but that's not how I see you. I don't need a huge rock on my finger or a mansion or a flashy car. I just want you. Gabriel Hunter, the man who loves the sea and the stars and very bad puns, who makes my heart beat faster every time he smiles, and who makes even a rough day better because he's *there*.'

'That's what you *really* want?' he asked.

She nodded. 'You told me to think about it, to talk it over with Mum and Jessie, and I have. You're what I want, Gabriel. You and only you. I trust you. And I see you for who you are—the man I want to spend the rest of my life with. If you'll have me. And you're right—it would be pretty cool if the first wedding at the Electric Palace and the Spice House was ours.'

He removed his sunglasses so she could actually see his eyes properly. 'Are you suggesting marriage?'

'Strictly speaking, you suggested it first,' she said. 'But a merger sounds good.'

'Hunter Hotels is my dad's business, not mine. We won't be going into this as equal partners,' he warned.

'Yes, we will. Because this isn't about money or property or business. It's about you and me. That's all that matters. I want to be with you, Gabriel. You make my world a better place and I'm miserable without you.'

'Same here,' he said, and finally he put his arms round

her. 'I love you, Nicole. I think I fell for you when I read that first message on the Surrey Quays forum. I was horrified when I met you and realised that my private friend was my business rival.'

'Except we're not rivals. We're on the same side.'

'Definitely.' He kissed her. 'So will you marry me?'

There was only one thing she could say. 'Yes.'

EPILOGUE

Three months later

GABRIEL, DRESSED IN top hat and tails, walked out of the honeymoon suite at the Spice House Hotel. The suite he'd be sharing with his bride, later tonight.

Everything was ready in the Coriander Suite—the tables were beautifully laid out and decorated for the wedding breakfast.

The Electric Palace was all decked out for a wedding, too. The old cinema was bright and gleaming, the bar in the downstairs foyer perfectly polished with trays of glasses waiting to be filled with champagne, and the Art Deco windows restored to their full splendour. On the walls were the plaque Nicole had unveiled on the opening night—thanking every single member of the Surrey Quays forum who'd helped to restore the cinema—along with framed enlargements of the Kursaal in its heyday and framed posters for *It's a Wonderful Life* and *Mary Poppins*.

There was a garland of ivory roses wound round the bars of the sweeping staircase to the upper floor, and when Gabriel glanced inside the upper room he could see that all the chairs were filled apart from the front row, which was reserved for his parents, Nicole's mother, and the bridesmaid.

The ceiling looked amazing. Just as Nicole had imagined it, the tin was painted dark blue and the stars were picked out in gold. There was an arch in front of the cinema screen, decorated with ivory roses and fairy lights.

All he needed now was to wait for his bride to arrive.

He glanced at his watch. He knew she wouldn't be late—that particular tradition was one that annoyed her hugely. But he was pretty sure she'd arrive exactly one minute early. Just because that was who she was.

The very first wedding in the Electric Palace and the Spice House.

Not because they were using their wedding as a trial run for their businesses, but because the buildings had brought them both together and there wasn't anywhere else in the world that would've been more perfect as their wedding venue.

And at precisely one minute to two the wedding march from Mendelssohn's *A Midsummer Night's Dream* began playing, and Gabriel turned round to watch his bride walking down the aisle towards him, on her mother's arm.

Her hair was up in the Audrey Hepburnesque style she'd worn the night he'd first taken her out to dinner, and the dress had a simple sweetheart neckline with a mermaid train that would look spectacular spread over the staircase. She looked stunning.

But most of all he noticed the expression in her eyes— the sheer, deep love for him. The same love he had for her.

'I love you,' he whispered as she came to stand beside him.

'I love you, too,' she whispered, and they joined hands, ready to join their lives together.

* * * * *

AT THE RUTHLESS
BILLIONAIRE'S
COMMAND

CAROLE MORTIMER

**With Many Thanks to all at Harlequin
Mills & Boon**

PROLOGUE

'WHAT'S *HE* DOING HERE?' Lia couldn't take her eyes off the man standing back slightly on the other side of the open grave where her father's coffin would soon be laid to rest.

'Who—? Oh, God, no...'

Lia ignored her friend's gasp of dismay as her feet seemed to move of their own volition, taking her towards the dark and dangerous man whose image had consumed her days and haunted her nightmares for the past two weeks.

'Lia—no!'

She was barely aware of shaking off Cathy's attempt to restrain her, her attention focused on only one thing. One man.

Gregorio de la Cruz.

Eldest of the three de la Cruz brothers, he was tall, at a couple of inches over six feet. His slightly overlong dark hair was obviously professionally styled. His complexion was olive-toned. And his face was as harshly handsome as that of a conquistador.

Lia knew he was also as cold and merciless as one.

He was the utterly ruthless, thirty-six-year-old billionaire CEO of the de la Cruz family's worldwide business empire. A business empire this man had carved out for himself and his two brothers over the past twelve years by sheer ruthless willpower alone.

And he was the man responsible for driving Lia's father to such a state of desperation that he'd suffered a fatal heart attack two weeks ago.

The man Lia now hated with every particle of her being.

'How dare you come here?'

Gregorio de la Cruz's head snapped up and he looked at Lia with hooded eyes as black and soulless as she knew his heart to be.

'Miss Fairbanks—'

'I asked how you *dare* show your face here?' she hissed, hands clenched so tightly at her sides she could feel the sting of her nails cutting into the flesh of her palms.

'This is not the time—'

His only slightly accented words were cut off as one of Lia's hands swung up and made contact with the hardness of his chiselled cheek, leaving several smears of blood on his flesh from the small cuts in her palm.

'No!' He held up his hand to stop two dark-suited men who would have stepped forward in response to her attack. 'That is the second time you have slapped my face, Amelia. I will not allow it a third time.'

The second time?

Oh, goodness—yes. Her father had introduced them in a restaurant two months ago. They had both been dining with other people, but Lia had been totally aware of Gregorio de la Cruz's gaze on her, following that introduction. Even so, she had been surprised when she'd left the ladies' powder room partway through the evening to find him waiting for her outside in the hallway. She had been even more surprised when he'd told her how much he wanted her before kissing her.

That was the reason she had slapped his face the first time.

She had been engaged at the time—he had been introduced to her fiancé as well as her that evening—so he had stepped way over the line.

'Your father would not have wanted this.' He kept his voice low, no doubt so none of the other mourners gathered about the graveside would be able to hear his response to her attack.

Lia's eyes flashed with anger. 'And how the hell would you know what my father would have wanted when you don't—*didn't*—know the first thing about him? Except, of course, that he's dead!' she added vehemently.

Gregorio knew far more about Jacob Fairbanks than his daughter obviously did. 'I repeat—this is not the time for this conversation. We will talk again once you are in a calmer state of mind.'

'Where you're concerned that's never going to happen,' she assured him, her voice harsh with contempt.

Gregorio bit back his reply, aware that Amelia Fairbanks's aggression came from the intensity of her understandable grief at the recent loss of her father—a man Gregorio had respected and liked, although he doubted Jacob's daughter would believe that.

The newspapers had featured several photographs of Amelia since the start of the worldwide media frenzy after her father had died so suddenly two weeks ago, but having already met her—*desired her*—Gregorio knew none of the images had done her justice.

Her shoulder-length hair wasn't simply red, but shot through with highlights of gold and cinnamon. Her eyes weren't pale and indistinct, but a deep intense grey, with a ring of black about the iris. She was understandably pale, but that pallor didn't detract from the striking effect of her high cheekbones or the smooth magnolia of her skin. Long dark lashes framed those mesmerising grey eyes. Her nose was small and pert, and the fullness of her lips was a perfect bow above a pointed and determined chin.

She was small of stature, her figure slender, and the black dress she was wearing seemed to hang a little too loosely—as if she had recently lost weight. Which he could see she had.

Nevertheless, Amelia Fairbanks was an extremely beautiful woman.

And the sharp stab of desire he felt merely from looking at her and breathing in the heady spice of her perfume was totally inappropriate, considering the occasion.

'We will talk again, Miss Fairbanks.' His tone brooked no argument this time.

'I don't think so,' she said, scorning his certainty.

Oh, they *would* meet again. Gregorio would ensure that they did.

His gaze was guarded as he gave her a formal bow before turning on his heel to walk across the grass and get into the back of the black limousine waiting for him just outside the graveyard.

'Señor de la Cruz?'

Gregorio looked up blankly at Silvio, one of his two bodyguards, to see the other man holding out a handkerchief towards him.

'You have blood on your cheek. Hers, not your own,' Silvio explained economically as Gregorio gave him a questioning glance.

He took the handkerchief and rubbed it across his cheek before looking down at the blood that now stained the pristine white cotton.

Amelia Fairbanks's blood.

Gregorio distractedly put the bloodied handkerchief into the breast pocket of his jacket as he glanced across to where she stood beside a tall blonde woman at her father's graveside. Amelia looked very small and vulnerable, but her expression was nonetheless composed as she stepped forward to place a single red rose on top of the coffin.

Whether she wished it or not, he and Amelia Fairbanks would most definitely be meeting again.

Gregorio had wanted her for the past two months—he could wait a little longer before claiming her.

CHAPTER ONE

Two months later

'I NEVER REALISED I'd accumulated so much *stuff*.'

Lia groaned as she carried yet another huge card-board box into her new apartment and placed it with the other dozen boxes stacked to one side of the tiny sitting room. The other half was full of furniture.

'I'm sure I don't need most of it. I definitely have no idea where I'm going to put it all.' She looked around the London apartment with its pocket-size sitting room/kitchen combined, one bedroom and one bath-room. It was a huge downsize from the three-storey Regency-style townhouse she had shared with her fa-ther.

Beggars couldn't be choosers. Not that Lia was ex-actly a beggar—she had a little money of her own, left to her by the mother—but the comfortable lifestyle she'd known for all of her twenty-five years no lon-ger existed.

Every one of her father's assets had been frozen until the extent of his debts had been decided and paid by his executors—which would take months, if not years. Considering the dire financial situation her father had been in before his death, Lia doubted there would be anything left.

Their family home had been one of those assets, and although Lia could have continued to live there until everything was settled she hadn't wanted to. Not without her father. The business sharks were also circling, ready to snap up the assets of Fairbanks Industries as soon as the executors had decided when and how they were going to be sold off to pay the debts.

Lia had used her own money to pay her father's funeral expenses and the deposit on this apartment, plus the few bits of furniture she had deemed necessary to fill the tiny space. She hadn't been allowed to remove anything from the house except personal items.

She had resigned from all the charitable work that had taken up much of her time—with her father dead and his estate in limbo those charities no longer considered the name Fairbanks as being a boon to their cause!—and she'd looked for, and found, a job that paid actual wages. She needed to be able to earn enough at least to feed herself and continue paying the rent on this apartment.

She had taken charge of her own life, and it felt strangely good to have been able do so.

Cathy shrugged. 'You must have thought you needed it when you did the packing.'

She didn't add what both of them knew: a lot of the contents of these boxes weren't Lia's at all, but personal items of her father's she had packed and been allowed to bring from their home. Items that had no value but which had meant something to him, and which Lia couldn't bear to part with.

Lia had put all these boxes in storage for the past

two months, while she'd stayed with her best friend Cathy and her husband Rick. That had been balm to her battered emotions, but a situation Lia had known couldn't continue indefinitely. Hence her move now to this apartment.

She was over the absolute and numbing shock of finding her father in his study, slumped over his desk, dead from a massive heart attack the paramedics had assured her would have killed him almost instantly. Cold comfort when they'd been talking about the man Lia had loved with her whole heart.

In some ways she wished that previous numbness was still there. The loss of her father's presence in her life never went away, of course, but now a deeper, more crippling agony at the loss would suddenly hit her when she least expected it. Standing in the queue at the local supermarket. Walking in the park. Lying in a scented bubble bath.

The loss would hit her with the force of a truck, totally debilitating her until the worst of the grief had passed.

'Time for a glass of wine, methinks,' Cathy announced cheerfully. 'Any idea which one of these boxes you put the wine glasses in?' The tall blonde grimaced at the stack of unopened boxes.

'I'm space-challenged—not stupid!' Lia grinned as she went straight to the box marked 'Glassware', easily ripping off the sealing tape to take out two newspaper-wrapped glasses. 'Ta-da!' She held them up triumphantly.

Lia had no idea what she would have done without Cathy and Rick after her father died. The two women had been friends since attending the same boarding school from the age of thirteen, and Cathy was as close to her as the sister she had never had. Closer, if what she'd heard about sisterly rivalry was true.

Luckily Cathy worked as an estate agent, and was responsible for helping Lia find this affordable apartment. But, even so, there was only so much advantage she could take of Cathy's friendship.

'You should go home to your husband now,' she encouraged as the two of them sat on a couple of the boxes drinking their wine. 'Rick hasn't seen you all day.'

Rick Morton was one of the nicest men Lia had ever met—as much of a friend to her as Cathy was, especially this past two months. But the poor man must be longing to have his wife and his apartment to himself.

'Are you sure you're going to be okay?' Cathy frowned.

'Very,' Lia confirmed warmly.

Rick had been persuaded to go off and enjoy a football match with his friends that afternoon. A welcome break for him, it had also allowed the two women to move Lia into her new home. But there had to be a limit to how much and for how long Lia could intrude on the couple's marriage.

'I'm just going to unpack enough to be able to make the bed and cook myself something light to eat before I go to sleep.' Lia gave a tired yawn: it had been a long day. 'I don't just have a new apartment to organise, but a new job on Monday morning to prepare for too!'

Cathy slipped her arms into her jacket. 'You're going to do just fine.'

Lia knew that. After the past two months she had no doubt that she was capable of looking after herself. Nevertheless, she still had to fight down the butterflies that attacked her stomach whenever she thought of all the changes in her life since her father had...*died*. She still choked over that word—probably because she still couldn't believe he was gone.

And he wouldn't be if Gregorio de la Cruz hadn't withdrawn De la Cruz Industries' offer to buy out Fairbanks Industries. The lawyers might have presented that death knell to her father, but there was no doubt in Lia's mind that it was Gregorio de la Cruz who was responsible for the withdrawal of that offer.

Her father had watched the decline of his company for months and, knowing he was on the edge of bankruptcy, had decided he had no choice but to sell. Lia firmly believed it was the withdrawal of the De la Cruz offer that had been the final straw that had broken him and caused her father's heart attack.

Which was why all of Lia's anger and resentment was now focused on the man she held responsible.

Futile emotions when there was no way she would ever be able to hurt a man as powerful as Gregorio de la Cruz. Not only was he as rich as Croesus, but he was coldly aloof and totally unreachable.

The man had even been accompanied by two bodyguards at her father's funeral, for goodness' sake. They hadn't been able to prevent Lia from slapping him, though. Was that because Gregorio de la Cruz had *allowed* it? He had certainly indicated that the two men should back off when they would have gone into protection mode.

She was thankful it had been a private funeral, and that there had been no photographs taken of the encounter to appear in the newspapers the following day and stir up the media frenzy once again. There'd been enough speculation after her father's sudden death without adding to it with her personal attack on Gregorio de la Cruz.

Nevertheless she had found a certain satisfaction in slapping the Spaniard's austerely handsome face. Even more so at seeing *her* blood streaked across his tautly clenched cheek.

As the days, weeks and then months had passed, and Gregorio de la Cruz's chilling promise that they would talk again hadn't come to fruition, Lia had mostly been able to put the man out of her mind. Just as well, because she only had enough mental energy to concentrate on the things that needed her immediate attention. Such as packing up the house, with Cathy and Rick's help, and finding herself an apartment and a job.

But she had successfully done all those things now—including securing a job as a receptionist in one of London's leading hotels.

Having no wish to start answering awkward questions from a prospective employer or, even worse, become the recipient of sympathetic glances that just made her want to sit down and cry, Lia had applied for several jobs under the name Faulkner—her mother's maiden name.

Nevertheless, she had no doubt it was her years of being *the* Amelia Fairbanks that had given her the necessary poise to secure her job. The manager of the hotel had obviously liked her appearance and manner enough to give her a one-day trial. He had admitted afterwards to being impressed with her warmth and the unflappable manner with which she'd dealt with some of their more difficult clientele.

The poor man had no idea she was usually on the

other side of the reception desk, booking in to similar exclusive hotels all over the world.

So—new apartment, new job.

Cathy was right: she was going to be just fine.

But not if one of her new neighbours was going to ring her doorbell at nine o'clock at night, when she was soaking in a much-needed bath after having pushed herself to empty half a dozen of the boxes once she'd eaten a slice of toast.

It had to be one of her new neighbours, because Lia hadn't sent out new address cards to any of her friends yet. It was the next job she had to do—once she had unpacked completely and arranged her furniture ready for receiving visitors.

Not that she expected there to be too many of those. Amazing how many people she had thought were friends had turned out not to be so once she was no longer Amelia Fairbanks, daughter of wealthy businessman Jacob Fairbanks. Even David had broken their engagement.

But she refused to think about her ex-fiancé now!

Or ever again after the way David had deserted her when she'd needed him most.

Going to answer the door wrapped only in a bath towel was far from the ideal way to meet any of her new neighbours, but it would look even worse if Lia didn't bother to answer the door at all. It must be obvious she was in from the amount of noise she'd been making unpacking boxes and moving furniture around.

Impatient neighbours, Lia decided as the doorbell rang again before she'd even had chance to wrap the towel around herself.

She might be new to living in an apartment, but she

knew at least to look through the peephole in the door before opening it. Except she couldn't see anyone in the hallway—which meant they had to be standing out of view. Well, there was always the safety chain to prevent anyone from coming in if she didn't want them to. And she *didn't* want them to. She was nowhere near ready—or dressed!—to receive visitors.

The reason her visitor had been standing out of the view of the peephole became obvious the moment Lia opened the door and saw Gregorio de la Cruz standing in the hallway!

'I do not think so.' He placed his handmade Italian black leather shoe in the six-inch gap left by the door chain, effectively preventing Lia from slamming the door in his face.

'What are you doing here?' Lia demanded, her hands gripping the door so tightly her knuckles showed white as she stared at the tall Spaniard.

He was once again dressed in one of those dark bespoke tailored suits, with a pristine white shirt and a perfectly knotted dark grey silk tie. Along with that slightly tousled hair, he looked like a catwalk model.

'You seem to have asked me questions similar to that several times now,' he answered evenly. 'Perhaps in future it might be wise of you to anticipate seeing me where and when you least expect to do so.'

Lia didn't want to *'anticipate'* seeing this man anywhere. Least of all outside the door to her apartment. An apartment he shouldn't even know about when she had only moved in today.

Except he was the powerful Gregorio de la Cruz, and he could do just about anything he wanted to do.

Including, it seemed, finding out the address of Amelia Fairbanks's new apartment.

'Go to hell!' She attempted to close to door. Something that wasn't going to happen with that expensive leather shoe preventing her from doing so.

'What are you wearing? Or rather, not wearing...?'

Gregorio found himself totally distracted by the view he could see of Amelia's bare shoulders, where tiny droplets of water dampened her ivory skin, and what appeared to be a knee-length towel wrapped around the rest of her body. Her hair was loosely secured at her crown, with several loose tendrils curling against the slenderness of her nape.

'None of your damned business!' There was a flush to her cheeks. 'Go away, Mr de la Cruz, before I call the police and ask them to forcibly remove you.'

He arched a dark brow. 'For what reason?'

'Stalking. Harassment. Don't worry, I'll think of something suitable by the time they get here,' she threatened.

'I am not worried,' he assured her calmly. 'I merely wish to speak with you.'

'You have nothing to say that I want to hear.' She glared at him, her eyes a deep metallic grey, the black rings wide about the irises.

'You cannot possibly know that.'

'Oh, but I do.'

Gregorio was not known for his patience, but he had waited for two long and tedious months before seeking out this woman again. Two months during which he had hoped her emotions would not be quite so volatile. Obviously time had not lessened her resentment towards him. Or the blame she felt he deserved for her father's death at the age of only fifty-nine.

To say he had been shocked by Jacob Fairbanks's demise would be an understatement. Although it must have been a strain for the man—and his company—to have been under close scrutiny of the FSA financial regulators. They were still investigating, and all of Jacob Fairbanks's assets would remain frozen until their investigation was complete.

Gregorio had no doubt that it had been the withdrawal of De la Cruz Industries' offer to buy Fairbanks's company that had caused the FSA's investigation. But he would not be held responsible for the bad business decisions that had brought Jacob Fairbanks to the brink of bankruptcy. Or the man's fatal heart attack.

Except, it seemed, by Amelia Fairbanks...

'No bodyguards this evening?' she taunted. 'My, aren't you feeling brave? Facing a five-feet-two-inches-tall woman all on your own!'

Gregorio's mouth tightened at the jibe. 'Silvio and Raphael are waiting outside in the car.'

'Of course they are,' she scorned. 'Do you carry a panic button you can press, if necessary, and they'll come running?'

'You are being childish, Miss Fairbanks.'

'No, what I'm *being* is someone attempting to get rid of an unwanted visitor.' Her eyes flashed. 'Now, take your damned foot out of my doorway!'

His jaw tightened. 'We need to talk, Amelia.'

'No, we really don't. And Amelia was my grandmother,' she dismissed. 'My name is Lia. Not that I'm giving *you* permission to use it. Only my friends are allowed that privilege,' she added with a sneer.

Gregorio knew he was most certainly not one of those. And nor did *'Lia'* intend for him ever to become one.

It was unfortunate for her that Gregorio felt differently on the subject. He didn't only want to be Lia's friend, he had every intention of becoming her lover.

When his parents had died twelve years ago they had left their sons only a rundown vineyard in Spain. As the eldest of the three brothers, Gregorio had made it his priority to rebuild and expand, and now he and his brothers owned a vineyard to be proud of, as well as other businesses worldwide. He had done those things by single-mindedly knowing what he wanted and ensuring that he acquired it.

He had wanted Lia from the moment he'd first set eyes on her. He would not give up until he had her.

He almost smiled—but only almost—at the thought of her reaction if he were to state here and now that that was his intention. No, he knew to keep that to himself. For now.

'Nevertheless, the two of us need to talk. If you would care to open the door and put some clothes on…?'

'There are two things wrong with that demand.'

'It was a request—not a demand.'

She raised auburn brows. 'Coming from you, it was a demand. I don't *care* to open the door, *or* go and put some clothes on. And nor,' she continued when he would have spoken, 'as I've already said, do you have anything to say that I want to hear. Because of you my father is dead.' Tears glistened in those smoky grey eyes. 'Just leave, Mr de la Cruz, and take your guilty conscience with you.'

Gregorio's jaw clenched. 'I do not have a guilty conscience.'

'Silly me—of course you don't.' She eyed him scornfully. 'Men like you ruin people's lives every day, so what does it matter if a man had a heart attack and died because of you?'

'You are being melodramatic.'

'I'm stating the facts.'

'Men like me?' he queried softly.

'Rich and ruthless tyrants who trample over everyone and everything that gets in your way.'

'I was not always rich.'

'But you were always ruthless—still are!'

For the sake of his brothers and his own future, yes, he had become so. Had needed to be in a business world that would have eaten him up and spat him out again if not for that ruthlessness. But ruthless was the last thing he wanted to be where Lia was concerned.

He shook his head. 'You are not only being overly dramatic, but you are also totally incorrect in your accusations. In regard to your father or anyone else. As you would know if you would allow me to come in and talk to you.'

'Not going to happen.' She gave a firm shake of her head.

'I disagree.'

'Then be prepared to take the consequences.'

'Meaning?' Gregorio's lids narrowed.

'Meaning I'm being extremely restrained right now, but if you persist in this harassment I promise you I *will* take the appropriate legal steps to ensure you are made to stay away from me.'

He raised his brows. 'What legal steps?'

'A restraining order.'

Gregorio had never experienced this much frustrated anger with another person's stubbornness before. He was Gregorio de la Cruz, and for the past twelve years no one had dared to oppose him. Lia not only did so, but seemed to take delight in it.

He had never felt so much like strangling a woman and kissing her at the same time, either. 'Would you not have to engage the services of another lawyer in order to be able to do that?' he retaliated.

Colour blazed in her cheeks at his obvious reference to the fact that David Richardson was no longer her family lawyer *or* her fiancé.

'Bastard!'

Gregorio had regretted the taunt as soon as it had left his lips. At the same time as he couldn't take it back when he only spoke the truth. David Richardson had left this woman's life so fast after her father's death and Fairbanks Industries being put under investigation, Gregorio wouldn't be surprised if the other man hadn't suffered whiplash.

He took his wallet from the breast pocket of his jacket before removing a card from inside. 'This has my private cell phone number on it.' He held out the white gold-embossed business card to her. 'Call me when you are ready to hear what I have to say.'

Lia stared at the card as if it were a viper about to strike her. 'That would be *never*.'

'Take the card, Lia.'

'No.'

The Spaniard's jaw clenched as evidence of his frustration with her lack of co-operation. She doubted many people stood up to this arrogant man. He was far too accustomed to *telling* people what to do rather than asking.

Lia had acted as her father's hostess for years, so she had met high-powered, driven men like him before. Well…perhaps not *quite* like Gregorio de la Cruz, because he took arrogance to a whole new level. But she had met other men who believed no one should ever say no to them. Probably because no one ever had.

She had no problem whatsoever in saying no to Gregorio.

Lia didn't remember her mother, because she had died in a car crash when Lia had still been a baby. But for all Lia's life her father had been a constant—always there, always willing to listen and spend time with her. Their bond had been strong because of it. When her father had died Lia hadn't just lost her only parent but her best friend and confidante.

'I'm asking you to leave one last time, Mr de la Cruz.' She spoke flatly, sudden grief rolling over her, as heavy as it was exhausting.

Gregorio frowned at the way Lia's face had suddenly paled. 'Do you have anyone to take care of you?'

She blinked in an effort to ward off her exhaustion. Which in no way stopped her from continuing to fight him verbally. 'If I tell you that I'm alone are you going to offer to come in and make hot chocolate for me? Like my father did whenever I was worried or upset?'

'If that is what you wish.' He gave an abrupt inclination of his head.

'What I wish for I can't have,' she said dully.

Gregorio didn't need her to say that her wish was to have her father returned to her, because he could already see the truth of that in the devastation of her expression: the shadowed grey eyes, those pale cheeks, her lips trembling as she held back the tears.

'Is there anyone I can call to come and sit with you?'

'Such as…?'

Not her ex-fiancé, certainly. David Richardson could not have truly loved Lia, otherwise he would have remained at her side and helped her to weather the storm that had followed her father's death. Instead he had distanced himself from any scandal that might ensue once the investigation into Jacob Fairbanks's finances was complete.

Gregorio had no such qualms. He had no interest in the outcome of that investigation, nor in what other people might or might not choose to say about Lia or himself. His private life was most definitely off limits. He might not be in love with Lia but he certainly wanted her, and he would be pursuing that desire.

Lia appeared to be swaying now, and there was not a tinge of colour left in her face. She looked so fragile that a puff of wind might knock her off her bare feet.

What had she been doing when he'd arrived? She was obviously naked beneath the towel wrapped about her, but she claimed she was alone so she obviously wasn't entertaining a lover. The obvious explanation was that Lia had been taking a shower or a bath in order to wash away the dust of having moved in to her apartment today.

The loosely secured hair and the droplets of water that had now dried on the bareness of her shoulders would certainly seem to indicate as much.

'Take off the safety catch and let me in, Lia,' Gregorio instructed in his most dominating voice. It was a voice that defied anyone to disobey him.

She attempted a shake of her head, but even that looked as if it was too much effort. Her head seemed too heavy to be supported by the slenderness of her neck.

'I'm not sure I can,' she admitted weakly.

'Why not?'

'I… My fingers don't seem to be working.'

Gregorio stepped up close against the partially open door. 'Move your right hand slowly, then slide the catch along until it releases.' He held his breath as he waited to see if she would do as he asked.

'I don't want to.'

'But you will,' he encouraged firmly.

'I… It's… You…'

'Move your hand, Lia. That's it,' he encouraged gruffly as she hesitantly moved her hand towards the safety chain. 'Now, slide the lock along. Yes, just like that,' he approved softly. 'A little more—yes.'

Gregorio breathed softly as the safety chain fell free and he was able to push the door open. Not quickly or forcefully, but just enough to allow him to enter the apartment.

To be alone with Lia at last.

CHAPTER TWO

THE APARTMENT LOOKED to be in absolute chaos to Gregorio's gaze. There were boxes everywhere, and furniture stacked haphazardly in the tiny sitting room. The kitchen looked as if there had been an explosion of cooking utensils in its midst, and not a single surface was visible beneath pots and pans and cutlery.

Gregorio had never seen this side of moving to a new home before. The vineyard in Spain had belonged to his family for years, and the three de la Cruz brothers had grown up there. The rambling ranch-style house was full of family heirlooms as well as memories. And he had hired an interior designer to decorate and furnish the apartments he had acquired in New York and Hong Kong, as well as his houses in Paris and the Bahamas.

No wonder Lia was exhausted.

Lia managed to rouse herself slightly as she heard the finality of the closing of the door to her apartment. She wasn't completely sure how, but Gregorio de la Cruz was now standing inside her apartment, rather than outside in the hallway.

She remembered now… She had opened the door and let him in. Not because she'd wanted to but because she had felt *compelled* to. His voice, deep and mesmerising, had ordered her to unlatch the safety chain, and because she had been consumed by that black exhaustion she had done as he'd instructed.

He seemed taller and larger than ever in the confines of her untidy apartment. Taller, darker, and just plain dangerous. Like a huge jungle cat preparing to pounce on its unsuspecting prey.

The almost-black hair was in that tousled style again, and his face was set in harsh lines. His shoulders looked huge beneath the tailored suit, his chest defined and muscular, waist slender, hips and thighs powerfully muscular.

Lia could smell the aftershave he wore, easily recognising it as one that cost thousands of pounds an ounce. Even so there was a fine stubble on his chin, as if he was in need of his second shave of the day.

Her gaze moved quickly upwards and was instantly ensnared by glitteringly intense almost black eyes. 'I—'

'You need to sit down before you fall down.' Gregorio stepped across the room to remove several items from one of the armchairs before lightly grasping Lia's arm to support her until she was seated. 'Do you have any brandy?'

She somehow looked more fragile than ever seated in the chair.

'Wine,' she answered with a vague wave of her hand in the direction of the kitchen area.

Wine would not revive her as well as brandy, but it was still alcohol and better than nothing. Gregorio found a half full bottle of red wine on the breakfast bar, a used glass beside it. Predictably, it wasn't one of the de la Cruz vintages.

'Here.' Gregorio held the glass of wine in front of

her until she took it from him with slender fingers that shook slightly. 'Have you eaten anything today?'

'Um…' Her forehead creased as she gave the matter some thought. 'A bowl of cereal this morning and some toast this evening. I think…' she added doubtfully.

He scowled his displeasure before turning on his heel to stride through to the kitchen area. There was a loaf of bread on one of the units, a tub of butter and a carton of milk—and nothing else when he pulled open the fridge door and looked inside.

'You do not have any food.' He closed the fridge door in disgust.

'Maybe that's because I only moved in a few hours ago.'

Gregorio held back a smile at the return of her sarcasm. Evidence that Lia was feeling slightly better? He hoped so.

'Which begs the question—how did you know I'd moved in here today?' She eyed him suspiciously.

Gregorio had known about the apartment in the same way he'd known about everything Lia had done in the two months since her father's death. He was given daily reports on her movements by his head of security.

No doubt it was an intrusion into her personal life that Lia would take exception to if she knew about it. But it was Gregorio's belief that the Fairbanks's situation was not yet over, and until it was she would accept his protection whether she wanted it or not.

'Drink your wine,' he ordered dryly as he took his cell phone from his pocket.

'Look, Mr de la Cruz—'

'Gregorio. Or Rio, if you prefer,' he added huskily. 'That is what my family and close friends call me.'

'Of which I'm neither. Nor do I intend to be,' she added dismissively. 'What are you doing…?' She frowned as he made a call.

'I had intended inviting you out to dinner, but now that I see how tired you are I am ordering dinner to be delivered to us here instead.' Gregorio put the cell phone to his ear, his gaze remaining challengingly on Lia as he waited for the call to be picked up.

Lia was starting to wonder if she had fallen asleep in the bath and was having another nightmare. Because Gregorio de la Cruz couldn't *really* be in her apartment, ordering dinner for both of them. Could he?

He certainly seemed real enough. Tall, muscular, and bossy as hell.

It seemed surreal after the months of torment she had just suffered through. Because of *him*.

Being a little unfair there, Lia, a little voice taunted inside her head.

Gregorio wasn't responsible for the decline of her father's company, nor the ailing economy. He had also been perfectly at liberty to withdraw his interest in buying Fairbanks Industries if he had decided the company wasn't viable.

Lia *did* believe it was the withdrawal of that offer which had resulted in her father's company being put under investigation, though, and only weeks later in her father's heart attack and premature death.

She had to blame someone for all that, and Gregorio de la Cruz was the obvious person.

He had ended his call now, and was once again looking at her with those fiercely penetrating black eyes.

Lia's heart skipped a beat. Several beats. The blood rushed hotly through her veins as she saw something stirring in the cold depths of those dark orbs. Gregorio continued to stare at her. Something that looked like a flickering flame was growing stronger, hotter by the second, and was sucking all the air from the room as well as Lia's lungs.

She swallowed. Her heartbeat was now sounding very loud to her ears. So loud that surely Gregorio could hear it too? Lord, she hoped not! This man had kissed her once, and although Lia had slapped his face for it she had never forgotten it.

'I'm really not hungry.' She stood up to place the empty wine glass on the breakfast bar. Only to falter slightly as she realised how close to Gregorio she was now standing.

'I doubt you have felt hungry for some time now,' he acknowledged softly. 'That does not mean your body does not need sustenance.'

Why did that sound so...so *intimate*—as if Gregorio wasn't talking about food at all?

Maybe because he wasn't?

Lia recognised the flame in his eyes for exactly what it was now. Desire. Hot, burning desire. *For her.* A desire he had demonstrated four months ago and which he obviously still felt.

She took a step back—only to have Gregorio take that same step forward, maintaining their close proximity.

She moistened her lips with the tip of her tongue. 'I think you should go now.'

'No.' He was standing so close his breath was a light caress across the soft tendrils of hair at her temples.

'You can't just say no.'

'Oh, but I can. I *have*,' he added with satisfaction.

Lia blinked up at him, her heart thumping wildly now, her palms feeling damp. 'This is insane.' *She* was insane. Because a part of her—certain parts of her—was responding to the flickering flames in those coal-black eyes.

Her skin felt incredibly sensitised. Her nipples were tingling and between her thighs she was becoming slick with arousal.

'Is it?' Gregorio raised a hand and tucked a loose curl behind her ear before running his fingertips lightly down the heat of her cheek.

'Yes…' she breathed, even as she felt herself drawn to leaning into that caress.

Her father's death and David's defection meant it had been a long time since anyone had touched her, held her, apart from Cathy's brief reassuring hugs. Lia's body cried out for another kind of physical connection.

From Gregorio de la Cruz?

This man was a corporate shark who felt no compunction in gobbling up smaller fish. He was also a man who had a different woman on his arm in every news photograph Lia had ever seen of him. He bought and sold women—usually tall and leggy blonde women, who looked good on his arm and no doubt filled his bed at night—as easily as he bought and sold companies.

Lia wasn't tall, leggy or blonde.

Nor was she for sale.

She stepped back abruptly—only to give a shiver as she immediately felt the loss of the heat of Gregorio's body.

'I'm going to my bedroom to dress. I advise that you be gone by the time I come back.'

His sculpted lips curved into a smile. 'I make it a rule always to listen to advice, but I rarely choose to take it.'

Her chin rose challengingly. 'Is that because you're always right?'

His smile widened, revealing even white teeth. 'I have a feeling that however I answer that question you will choose to twist it to suit your own purposes.'

He was right, of course.

As always?

'Or should I say to suit the opinion you have formed of me without actually knowing me,' he added harshly.

Lia eyed him impatiently. 'I know enough to know I don't want you here.'

'And yet undoubtedly here I am,' he challenged.

'That's because you... Because I... You know what? Get the hell out of my apartment!' Her earlier agitation had returned, deeper than ever. 'Whatever sick game you're playing, I want no part of it.'

He sobered. 'I do not play games, Lia, sick or otherwise.'

'That's odd, because I'm pretty sure you're playing one now.'

Gregorio drew in a deep and controlling breath. Lia made no effort to hide her distrust and dislike of him. And right now her body couldn't hide her physical reaction to him.

Her breasts had plumped, her nipples hard as they pressed against the covering towel, and Gregorio's nostrils flared as they were assailed with the scent of her sweetly perfumed arousal.

Lia might distrust him, might think she had every reason to dislike him, but the response of her body told him she also desired him as much as he desired her.

He could wait to satisfy that desire. If he had to. And for the moment it seemed he must.

'I agree—you should go and put some clothes on.' He nodded abruptly. His self-control was legendary, but even *he* had his breaking point. And Lia, wearing only a towel to cover her nakedness, was it.

'Thanks so much, but I really don't need your permission to do anything!'

A nerve pulsed in his tightly clenched jaw. 'Dinner will be here shortly.'

'I've already told you I don't want any.'

Gregorio's eyes narrowed. 'Did your father have a line over which it was not safe to cross?'

'Oh, yes,' she recalled, with a wistful curve of her lips.

'And I am sure you knew to the nth degree how close to that line you might venture?'

'Yes...' She eyed him warily now.

'I have now reached my own line,' Gregorio informed her calmly.

'Is that supposed to scare me?'

Her bravado was admirable. Unfortunately it was nullified by the rapidly beating pulse visible in her throat: Lia was well aware of exactly how close she was to crossing over his line. And to paying the consequences for that trespass.

Gregorio's mouth thinned. 'You are—' He broke off as the doorbell rang. 'That will be Silvio, delivering our dinner.'

Her eyes widened. 'Wow, you must be a regular customer for the restaurant to have delivered so quickly.'

Their dinner had been prepared at and delivered by the staff at Mancini's, one of the most exclusive and prestigious restaurants in London. If Lia thought they were going to dine on pizza or Chinese food she was mistaken.

'Go and dress,' he instructed harshly. 'Unless you wish Silvio to see you wearing only a towel.'

Lia had a feeling the thought of that bothered Gregorio more than it bothered her. She was half inclined to remain exactly as she was—if only so that she could annoy Gregorio even more than he already was.

The fact that she knew she would feel more comfortable fully clothed was the deciding factor in her turning on her heel and walking down the hallway to her bedroom. But she was aware of Gregorio's devouring black gaze following her every step of the way.

Once in her bedroom, Lia slumped back against the closed door and drew in several deep breaths. Exactly what was going on here? Because something most certainly was.

Gregorio had not only kept the promise he'd made two months ago, that the two of them would talk again, but now that he was here in her apartment he was making no secret of the fact he still desired her.

Her body's traitorous response to him was harder for Lia to accept, let alone make sense of.

He was *Gregorio de la Cruz*, for goodness' sake. The man who'd had a hand in driving her father to his death.

When did I stop holding him completely responsible?

She hadn't. Had she…? No, of course she hadn't.

Gregorio was hard, ruthless, and scary as hell. He was also at least ten years older than she was, with the added experience that came with those extra years.

Dear God, she must be more desperate for human

warmth than she'd realised if she'd been physically aroused by a man she should *hate*!

'Good?'

Lia's only response was a throaty 'mmm' as she dipped another piece of asparagus into melted butter before eating it with obvious enjoyment.

Gregorio had removed his suit jacket and tie, and rolled up the sleeves of his shirt to just beneath his elbows by the time Lia had returned fully dressed from her bedroom. Her hair was loose about her shoulders, in the style he preferred—but if Lia had known that he was sure she would have scraped it back into a severe bun! She was wearing tight black jeans with a deep grey sweater that perfectly matched the colour of her eyes.

He had placed their food in the oven to keep warm, cleared the breakfast bar, found cutlery and laid two places so they were ready to eat as soon as Lia returned.

After stating that she wasn't hungry she had devoured succulent prawns and avocado with obvious relish, and steak, asparagus and dauphinoise potatoes were now being enjoyed with the same enthusiasm. The fact that she had drunk two glasses of the red wine Gregorio had ordered to be delivered with the meal—he'd had the foresight not to order one of the vintages from the de la Cruz vineyard—would seem to indicate she approved of that too.

Gregorio had found the food to be as delicious as always, but most of his enjoyment had come from watching Lia as she placed the food delicately in her mouth before eating with relish.

More colour returned to her cheeks the more she ate, and there was now a sparkle to her eyes. Evidence that she really had been starving herself the past two months? Not deliberately, but because food had simply become unimportant to her with her life in such turmoil.

Gregorio intended to ensure that didn't happen again.

Lia was enjoying the food so much, and Gregorio seemed to be enjoying watching *her*, that there had been very little conversation between the two of them as they ate together.

Which was perhaps as well. Lia felt the need to argue with this man every time they engaged in conversation.

She finally placed her knife and fork down on her empty plate. 'I'd forgotten how much I enjoyed the food at Mancini's.'

Past tense, Gregorio recognised with a tightening of his mouth. Because Lia's world had been turned upside down and she could no longer afford to eat in such exclusive restaurants.

Which was his cue to resume their conversation about her father's death. A subject guaranteed to bring back the contention between the two of them, but also one that stood between them as an invisible barrier.

Gregorio would accept no barriers between himself and Lia—invisible or otherwise. He intended knowing everything there was to know about this woman. Inside as well as out. Intimately. And he intended her to know him in the same way.

'That was delicious. Thank you,' she added awkwardly. 'But it's been a long day, and now I think what I really need is to get some sleep.'

She did look tired, Gregorio acknowledged. Well-fed, but tired. And what did a delay of one more day or so matter when he had already waited this long for her?

He glanced at the disorder about them. 'Would you

like me to come back tomorrow and help you with the rest of your unpacking?'

'Why are you being so nice to me?' Lia frowned her puzzlement, more confused than ever now that she had satisfied a need for food she hadn't realised was there until she'd begun eating.

Her stomach and her appetite had perked up at the very first taste of the food from Mancini's—a restaurant she had enjoyed going to several times in the past, alone and with David or her father.

'You are a person it is easy to be nice to,' Gregorio dismissed with a shrug of his broad shoulders.

Shoulders that looked even wider and more muscular now that he was no longer wearing his jacket. In fact the whole casual thing he had going on—losing the jacket, taking off his tie, unfastening the top button of his shirt and rolling back the sleeves—had succeeded in making him more approachable and even more lethally attractive.

Which was perhaps his intention?

Lull the poor befuddled woman into a state of uncertainty and then pounce?

Cathy was never going to believe her when the two of them spoke on the phone tomorrow as they usually did, and Lia told her friend about Gregorio's visit and the fact the two of them had eaten dinner together.

Lia wasn't sure she believed it herself.

It was becoming more and more difficult to continue thinking of this man as the monster who had helped to destroy her father when he was being nothing but attentive and kind to her. No matter how rude she was, he continued to treat her with respect and kindness.

It's just his way of worming his way into my good graces before he goes for what he really wants!

Which Lia had now realised appeared to be *her*.

He was obviously a man who enjoyed a challenge if he thought he was going to win *that* battle.

'No, I'll be fine, thanks.' She stood up as indication that he should leave.

A hint he ignored as he remained seated at the breakfast bar. 'We have not eaten dessert yet.'

'Take it with you,' she dismissed. 'I couldn't eat another thing.'

'I could not deprive you of Mancini's celebrated chocolate cake.'

Lia gave a soft gasp. 'He really sent you some of his famous chocolate cake?' The dessert was Mancini's secret recipe, and it had always been Lia's choice when she had dined at the restaurant. It was rich and decadent, and the taste of the cake was orgasmic.

'He sent *us* some of his chocolate cake,' Gregorio corrected.

'He didn't know I would be dining with you.'

'Oh, but he did. I spoke to Mancini personally and requested he send all your favourite foods.'

She widened her eyes. 'You *told* him we were having dinner together?'

Gregorio studied her from beneath hooded lids. 'Is there a problem with that?'

'Not for me, no.'

'Or for me.'

He certainly didn't *look* concerned at having announced to a third party that he was having dinner with the daughter of Jacob Fairbanks. Considering the speed with which some of her so-called friends and her fiancé had disappeared in a cloud of smoke, she found Gregorio's behaviour odd to say the least.

'You're a very strange man,' she said slowly.

'In a bad way or a good way?' he prompted as he stood up.

'I haven't decided yet.'

The grin he gave softened the harshness of his features. 'When you do, let me know, hmm?'

'You're different than I imagined.'

'In what way?'

'That night at the restaurant when you—when you kissed me, I thought you were just another arrogant jerk who doesn't like to hear the word no.'

'One out of the two, certainly,' he mused.

Lia didn't need him to tell her it was the word no he didn't like to hear. There was no doubting he was arrogant too, but there was something else. Something she couldn't quite equate with the ruthless bastard she'd labelled him. Perhaps it was the fact that, whatever his reasons, he was actually attempting to take care of her.

'You said you weren't always rich?'

'No.' He settled more comfortably on the bar stool. 'When I graduated from university with a business degree and returned to Spain it was to find that my father had allowed the family vineyard to decline. Several years of bad harvest…diseased vines.' He shrugged. 'There were still my two brothers to go to university. I put my own life on hold and set about ensuring that happened.'

'By founding the de la Cruz business empire?'

'Yes.'

'And is your life still on hold?'

He looked at her admiringly. 'Obviously not.'

Lia gave a shake of her head. 'I don't think it would be a good idea for the two of us to meet again.'

He looked displeased. 'Why not?'

Lia avoided meeting his gaze. 'Besides the obvious, I don't belong in that world any more.'

'The obvious…?'

'I hold you partly responsible for my father's death.' There—she'd stated it clearly, so there could be no lingering doubts as to her reason for staying away from this man.

Was she protesting too much?

Because of her earlier reaction to him?

Maybe. But that didn't change the fact that she really didn't want to see or be alone with Gregorio again. He…unsettled her. Disturbed her. In a deep and visceral way Lia could never remember being aware of with any other man. Including the man she had once been engaged to and had intended to marry.

'I am sorry you feel that way,' he answered evenly. 'And you can belong in whatever world you choose to be in,' he announced arrogantly.

'You really can't be that naïve! My father is dead. My engagement is over. Most of my friends have deserted me. I've lost my home. My father's business is under investigation. None of the charities I worked for want the name Fairbanks associated with them. I now live in this tiny apartment, and I start a new job on Monday.'

'None of those things changes who *you* are fundamentally.'

'I no longer *know* who I am!' If there had been enough room to pace then Lia would have done so, as she was suddenly filled with restless energy. 'I try to tell myself none of those other things matter. That this is my life now…'

'But…?'

'But I'm mainly lying to myself.' She inwardly cursed herself as her voice broke emotionally. Gregorio was the last man she wanted to reveal any weakness to. 'And you're lying to *yourself* if you think that being nice to me, buying me dinner, will ever make me forget your part in what happened,' she added accusingly.

'No barrier is insurmountable if the two people involved do not wish it to be there.'

'But I *do* wish it to be there.'

'Are you sure about that?'

When had Gregorio moved to stand so close to her? She felt overwhelmed by both his size and the force of his personality—a lethal combination that caused her heart to start pounding loudly again.

'You have to go,' she told him.

'Do I?'

'Yes!'

Despite the food she'd eaten, Lia had no reserves of energy left to resist the pull of those dark and compelling eyes. No defences to fight the lure of that hard and muscular body. Even the reminder that he was Gregorio de la Cruz wasn't working. She was caught like a deer in the headlights of a car as his head slowly began to lower towards hers.

Gregorio was going to kiss her…

No matter how exhausted and defenceless Lia felt, she couldn't allow that to happen.

'No!' She raised enough energy to put a restraining hand against his chest, and that brief contact was enough to make her aware of the tensed heat of Gregorio's body and the rapid beat of his heart. 'You really do have to leave. *Please.*'

His lips remained only centimetres away from her own, his breath a warm caress against her cheek.

His nostrils flared as he breathed long and deeply before slowly straightening and then finally stepping away. 'Because you asked so nicely…'

Lia gave a choked laugh, able to breathe again now that he was no longer standing quite so close to her. 'As opposed to threatening to call the police and having them kick you out?'

'Exactly.' He rolled down the sleeves of his shirt and fastened them before shrugging back into his jacket. 'Think of me tomorrow when you eat all that chocolate cake,' he added huskily, and then the door closed softly behind him as he let himself out of the apartment.

Lia breathed easily at last once he had gone. What the hell had happened just now? She had almost let Gregorio kiss her, for goodness' sake. She—

Lia froze as she saw the business card sitting on top of the breakfast bar.

The same business card she had refused to take from him earlier, with his personal mobile number embossed on it in gold.

CHAPTER THREE

'GOOD MORNING, LIA.'

Lia felt all the colour drain from her cheeks as she stared up at the man standing on the other side of the reception desk at the London Exemplar Hotel.

She had always thought that a person feeling the colour leeching from their face was a ridiculous concept: people couldn't actually *feel* the colour leaving their cheeks.

Except Lia just had. In fact the blood seemed to have drained from her head completely, settling somewhere in the region of her toes and leaving her feeling slightly light-headed as she continued to gape across the reception desk at Gregorio de la Cruz.

He tilted his head, a mocking smile playing about those sculpted lips as he saw her reaction to his being here. 'I did warn you that in future you should anticipate seeing me where and when you least expected to do so.'

Yes, he had—but it hadn't occurred to Lia that Gregorio might turn up at her new place of employment.

Deliberately so?

Or was it purely coincidence that Gregorio had come to the Exemplar Hotel on the morning she began working there?

Lia very much doubted that. With a man as powerful and well-connected as Gregorio there was no such thing as *coincidence*.

Which meant he had known she would be here. How he knew was probably by the same means he had acquired the address of her new apartment.

She narrowed her eyes. 'Are you having me followed, Mr de la Cruz?'

'Followed? No,' he dismissed. 'Am I ensuring your safety? Yes,' he admitted without apology.

Lia's brows rose. 'Why on earth does my safety need ensuring?'

'You are now alone in the world.'

'We both know why *that* is!'

'Lia—'

'Is there a problem here—? Mr de la Cruz!' Michael, the hotel manager, quickly hid his surprise as he greeted the other man warmly.

'Good morning, Michael,' Gregorio returned smoothly as the two men shook hands. 'And, no, there is no problem. I just came down to say hello to Miss… Faulkner,' he finished, with a knowing glance at the badge Lia had pinned on the left lapel of her jacket.

It was a surname Gregorio knew didn't belong to her.

And he also apparently knew the manager of this hotel by his first name'

An uneasy feeling began to churn in Lia's stomach, growing stronger by the second and making her feel slightly nauseous.

There was no such thing as coincidence where Gregorio de la Cruz was concerned.

Which meant he had known exactly where she would be starting her new job this morning.

He really was having her followed—might he even have had some influence in her attaining this job too?

For what reason?

The churning in Lia's stomach became a full-blown tsunami as she searched for the reason Gregorio was doing these things.

That guilty conscience she had accused him of having?

No, he had denied feeling any guilt in regard to her father's death.

The only other reason Lia could think of was to make her feel beholden to him. Not just beholden but trapped, when she badly needed to keep this job in order to pay her rent and bills as well as to buy food.

Trapped enough to give him what he wanted?

Namely herself.

'Of course.' Michael accepted Gregorio's explanation. 'If you would care to take your lunchbreak early, Lia, I'm sure we can accommodate—'

'*No!* No,' she repeated in a calmer voice as she realised how rude her previous vehemence must have sounded. 'I'm sure a busy man like Mr de la Cruz has somewhere else he needs to be right now.' Her eyes glittered in challenge.

Whatever was going on here, and whether or not Gregorio had had a hand in her acquiring this job, she did not want her co-workers seeing her on the receiving end of deferential treatment from the manager on her very first morning. There were already several curious glances being sent their way—goodness only knew what conclusions the people she had only just started working with were drawing about this conversation alone!

'Thank you for the offer, Michael.' Gregorio answered the other man smoothly. 'But, as Lia says, I have another appointment in a few minutes.'

'Oh. Okay. Fine.' The other man looked slightly flustered. 'I'll leave the two of you to talk, then.' He hurried off in the direction of his office behind the reception area.

'I do not like your hair pulled back in that style.'

Lia raised an irritated gaze. 'I really don't give a—'

'Language, Lia,' Gregorio drawled.

'Down?' she repeated abruptly. 'You told Michael you had come *down* to say hello to me…' she said as Gregorio raised a questioning brow.

'I occupy the whole of the penthouse floor of the hotel,' he admitted without apology.

Lia's heart sank down to wallow in all the blood that had already drained and congealed in her feet. 'Is it possible that you own the Exemplar Hotel?'

'It *is* part of the De la Cruz Hotel Group, yes.' He gave a smile of satisfaction.

Trapped!

Lia had absolutely no doubt now that for reasons of his own Gregorio was involved up to his arrogant neck in her being given this receptionist job.

Gregorio's satisfaction faded, his eyes narrowing as he recognised the flush gathering in Lia's cheeks for exactly what it was. Anger. White-hot burning fury.

'Do not do anything you will regret,' he warned softly as she stood up.

'The only thing I regret is actually thinking you were being nice to me on Saturday.' She bent to retrieve her bag from under the desk, her eyes glittering accusingly as she glared across at him. 'I'm going to take that early lunchbreak, after all. Perhaps you would like to clear *that* with your buddy Michael?'

'He is not—'

'Stay away from me, Gregorio!' she hissed, leaning across the desk so that only he could hear. 'Find some other mouse to ensnare in your trap, but leave *me* alone!'

Her cheeks were ablaze with colour as she marched the length of the reception desk, appearing on the other side of it before striding the length of the hotel lobby and out through the front door.

Gregorio very much doubted it was the right time to tell Lia that the staff of the Exemplar Hotel were not allowed to use the front entrance.

Well, that hadn't gone as well as he might have hoped.

Hope.

That seemed to be all he had where Lia Fairbanks was concerned, when she continued to resist and deny him at every turn.

Maybe ensuring she was employed at one of the de la Cruz hotels hadn't been his best idea, but at the time, knowing of her lack of funds and the problems she was having finding suitable employment, it had seemed the right thing to do. Besides which, he knew Lia could do the job standing on her head.

She was warm, gracious, well-spoken, beautiful... And, having been her father's long-time hostess and companion, she knew exactly what was required of a receptionist in a prestigious hotel.

He should have waited until a more suitable time, of course, to inform her that he owned the hotel where she now worked. But, having spent a frustrating day yesterday, wondering what Lia was doing and who she was with, and knowing she was downstairs working in the lobby of the hotel, Gregorio hadn't been able to resist coming down at least to look her again.

Once he had seen her—as cool, calm and collected as he had known she would be—he hadn't been able to stop himself from actually speaking to her.

Considering Lia's fury when she left, he wasn't sure she would be coming back.

'So, how was your first morning at work?' Cathy prompted excitedly the moment she sat down at the table where the two women had arranged to meet for lunch. 'Met any gorgeous unmarried billionaires yet?' she teased as she made herself more comfortable by shrugging off her jacket.

Oh, yes, Lia *had* met an unmarried billionaire. But Gregorio de la Cruz's looks were compelling rather than pretty-boy gorgeous.

But he was a manipulator. He was having her followed. He had arranged for her to be employed at his hotel. He had literally taken away all her options. Until he owned her body and soul.

Body and soul?

Lia would be lying to herself if she didn't acknowledge her physical reaction to Gregorio. She only had to glance at him to be totally aware of him. Only had to look into those dark and compelling eyes to feel her body heating from the inside out.

Much as she might wish it wasn't true, she was physically attracted to Gregorio de la Cruz.

'Never mind,' Cathy sympathised, obviously misunderstanding the reason for Lia's silence. 'It was only your first morning, after all.'

For some reason, when the two women had spoken on the phone yesterday Lia hadn't told Cathy about Gregorio's visit to her apartment the evening before. Usually she told Cathy everything—had done since the two of them were at school together—but when it came to the subject of Gregorio, Lia didn't know quite what to say.

Maybe because yesterday she had still been a little uncertain in her conjecture as to the reason for Gregorio's visit the evening before—had still been wondering if perhaps she wasn't imagining things...desires... that simply hadn't been there.

On Saturday he had said he wanted to talk to her— which he hadn't. He had told her he would feed her dinner—which he had. And he had almost kissed her. He *would* have kissed her if Lia had allowed it.

His appearance at the hotel this morning—*the hotel he owned*—left her in no doubt that for reasons of his own Gregorio was weaving a spider's web about her. One made out of expensive dinners and the job she desperately needed, but still a spider's web.

Was he only doing these things because he *wanted* her?

Because he knew he couldn't have her any other way?

Lia found it hard to believe it was because Gregorio desired her. She had been complimented on the way she looked since men had first begun to take notice of her in her mid-teens. But she didn't fool herself into believing Gregorio was so bedazzled by her he would go to any lengths to have her. He only had to snap his fingers to have any woman he wanted, when he wanted her, so why bother even trying with a woman he knew had every reason to continue resisting him?

Maybe, despite his denials, he *did* feel some guilt in regard to her father's death?

'You okay, Lia?'

'Fine.' She determinedly shook herself out of her mood of despondency as she picked up the menu. 'Let's order, shall we?'

Until she knew what Gregorio was up to she had no intention of telling Cathy she had even seen him again, let alone that he was now pursuing her.

Relentlessly.

'Can I offer you a lift home?'

'No, thank you.'

Lia didn't need to look at the driver of the dark sports car driving slowly beside the pavement she was walking along to know it was Gregorio. Illegally kerb-crawling, of course—but then he seemed to be as cavalier towards the law as he was to everything else.

'You would prefer to take public transport rather than be driven home in the comfort of my car?'

'I would prefer to crawl home on my hands and knees than accept a lift from *you*!'

'You are being childish.'

'I am being the independent woman I now am— despite your efforts to make me otherwise!' Lia's hands clenched as she turned to glare through the open passenger window at Gregorio.

She had half expected to see him at the hotel again when she'd returned from lunch, and had breathed a sigh of relief when the afternoon had passed by without any more unwelcome interruptions from him.

She should have known he wouldn't give up that easily.

The car came to a stop and she stepped forward to bend down and talk to him directly through the open window. 'I realise you're a man accustomed to taking what he wants, and to hell with anyone else's feelings, but let me assure you I can't be bought or seduced into your bed with a few expensive dinners and a job— What are you doing?' she gasped as Gregorio turned off the car's engine before opening his door and climbing out of the low-slung vehicle.

His expression was dark and thunderous as he strode round the back of the car towards her. Lia instinctively took a step back.

He was dressed less formally than Lia had ever seen him before, in a black polo shirt open at the throat and worn beneath a soft black leather jacket, with jeans resting low down on his hips. The former emphasised the broadness of his shoulders and toned chest and abs, and the latter added to that rugged attraction. Gregorio looked breathtaking in a formal suit, but in casual clothes he was even more dark and dangerous.

Gregorio took a tight grasp of her arm as he opened the passenger door of the car. 'Get in,' he bit out between gritted teeth.

'I—'

'Get in the damned car, Lia, before I pick you up and put you there.' His voice was low and controlled. As if he might start shouting if he allowed himself to speak any louder.

It made Lia even more reluctant to put herself in the vulnerable position of being alone in his car with him. At least out here in the street she had somewhere to run.

She raised her chin challengingly. 'I believe you are stepping way over *my* line now.' She reminded him of their conversation on Saturday.

Those black eyes glittered dangerously. 'You just made an outrageous accusation. One I do not intend to dignify with an answer when we are standing out here in the street, where anyone might overhear our conversation.'

Her cheeks warmed. 'You made the purpose of your interest in me obvious on Saturday evening. Or am I wrong in thinking you want me in your bed?'

A nerve pulsed in his clenched jaw. 'No, you are not wrong.'

She nodded. 'Which is why, after discovering you're now my employer, I have come to the conclusion I have.'

Gregorio never lost control. *Never.* He considered it a weakness to do so. And weakness could be exploited... manipulated.

Nevertheless, he knew he was seriously in danger of losing control at this moment. No one had ever accused him of the things Lia just had. No one would ever *dare*. No matter what she believed, he had no reason to manipulate her into an intimate relationship with him.

Not when he knew she felt the same desire for him that he felt for her...

Even if it *was* a desire she obviously didn't want to feel.

Gregorio's only motive in protecting and helping her was the fact that she no longer had anyone else in her life who would do so. The wealth she had grown up with and no doubt taken for granted was no longer there as a buffer either.

So, yes, Gregorio might have put in a word with Michael Harrington regarding employing Lia at the hotel, but his only reason for doing so had been an effort to give her back some of what she had lost.

For Lia to have reached the conclusion she had, that he was blackmailing her into a relationship with him as a result of his actions, was unacceptable. An insult of a kind Gregorio had never faced before.

The nerve in his jaw throbbed. 'We are having dinner together.'

'Did you not hear what I just said?'

'Of course I heard you,' Gregorio snapped. 'How could I do otherwise? But, as *I* said, I will not answer any of your accusations on a public street.'

His bodyguards had parked their SUV behind his sports car and the two men were now standing on the pavement a short distance away, watchful and alert to any and all danger.

'I have no intention of being alone with you. Anywhere,' Lia added with finality.

Gregorio stilled to regard her through narrowed lids. That last remark had been made so vehemently…

Lia's eyes were glittering brightly, her cheeks flushed and her lips full and pink. The evening was warm, and she had removed the jacket of her business suit as soon as she'd left the hotel. The cream blouse beneath was so sheer Gregorio could see the outline of her light-coloured bra. Her breasts were quickly rising and falling as she breathed deeply, the plumpness of her engorged nipples showed as a darker pink through the lace of her bra.

Gregorio slowly moved his gaze back up to her face. 'You want me too,' he stated.

'That's a lie!' Lia recoiled as if Gregorio had struck

her, pulling her arm from his grasp as she did so. 'How could I possibly want you?' Her breathing became even more erratic. 'When you're the callous man who helped hound my father to his death?'

Lia heard herself say the words, saw Gregorio's reaction to them—his expression hardened and his eyes were once again those fathomless black pits—and all the time knew Gregorio was right. That she'd spoken so vehemently because she *did* want him. And she shouldn't. For all the reasons she had just stated.

Except her traitorous body was refusing to listen to her. Her breasts felt fuller and more sensitive and she felt the ache of arousal between her thighs.

'You are lying to yourself, Lia,' Gregorio dismissed scornfully. 'We both know that.'

'Your arrogance is only exceeded by your conceit!'

He gave a hard smile. 'When you are ready to hear the truth about your father I suggest you give me a call. Until then…' He turned to nod at the two bodyguards, indicating his intention of leaving.

'The truth about my father?' This time Lia was the one to place a restraining hand on Gregorio's arm, able to feel his tension through the soft material of his jacket. 'What are you talking about?'

He looked at her between narrowed lids. 'As I said, call me when you are ready to listen.'

'And my job…?'

He drew himself up to his full height, a couple of inches over six feet. 'Your continued employment is not conditional upon you agreeing to see me or listen to me. Or anything else.' His mouth was a thin line.

Lia's hand slowly dropped back to her side. 'I don't understand you…'

'Perhaps that is because—as you admitted the other evening—having now spoken with me, you find I do not fit with the preconceived prejudice you felt towards me?' he taunted.

There was some truth in that. No, there was a *lot* of truth in that, Lia conceded heavily. Gregorio was arrogant, and used to having—taking—whatever he wanted. But equally there had been no doubting his anger when Lia had made her accusations about his manipulating and trying to force her into a relationship with him.

He had also been considerate and unthreatening at her apartment on Saturday evening. If he really was as ruthless as Lia had thought him to be, then surely he would have forced the issue of wanting her then? He wouldn't have taken no for an answer when there had been a convenient bedroom just down the hallway.

After all, *she* might not have been aware of it at the time, but Gregorio had already known he held all the power.

And now he had implied that he knew something about her father that she didn't.

Lia gave a slight nod as she came to a decision. 'I'll have dinner with you in exchange for you telling me what it is you think you know about my father that I don't.'

She held her breath as she waited for Gregorio's response.

CHAPTER FOUR

'I THOUGHT WE would be having dinner in a restaurant.' Lia looked dazedly around the interior of the luxurious de la Cruz jet she and Gregorio were now seated on, being flown off to goodness knew where after boarding the jet at a private airfield fifteen minutes ago. 'I don't have my passport with me.'

'We are not going to land anywhere,' Gregorio assured her. 'And we do not need to go to a restaurant when I have persuaded Mancini to join us on board for the evening.'

If Lia had needed any convincing that Gregorio was super-rich—up there in the stratosphere wealthy—then the private jet and exclusive services of the chef were proof enough.

Except she hadn't needed any further proof of this man's wealth and power.

'We're just going to fly around while we eat our meal?'

'Why not?' He shrugged. 'It ensures our privacy.'

Privacy was the last thing Lia wanted with this particular man. A man she knew was starting to get to her, in spite of herself.

Gregorio knew the information he had about Lia's

father was her only reason for allowing him to take her to dinner. Unfortunately his self-control was currently balanced on a very fine edge where Lia was concerned.

She hurled her insults at him as barbs meant to wound. They had succeeded in doing that, but her open defiance of him had also deepened the desire Gregorio felt to make love with her. To be consumed by the fire that burned between them whenever they were alone together. He wanted to strip every item of clothing from her body and gorge himself on her succulent flesh before burning in those flames.

'*Now* will you tell me what you think you know about my father that I don't?'

His gaze became guarded. 'Our agreement was that we would have dinner first.'

She gave a frustrated sigh. 'In that case we might as well eat.'

'So gracious,' Gregorio drawled as he stood up to remove his jacket.

A delicate blush coloured her cheeks. 'Why don't you just open and pour the wine?' she instructed him abruptly.

'Do you like to take charge in bed too?'

'Gregorio!' She gasped.

He raised speculative brows as he opened the white wine cooling in the galley, revealing none of the pleasure he felt at hearing her use his given name for the first time. 'I wasn't complaining. I merely wish to be pre-warned if that is the case.'

She looked more flustered than ever. 'I didn't accept your invitation—I'm only here because you promised to give me information about my father,' she reminded him flatly.

'All the while knowing how much I want you.'

'I was only— I didn't— Why do you always have to turn everything back to—?'

'My wanting you?' Gregorio finished softly. 'Perhaps because possessing you has obsessed my mind for some time now.'

She snorted. 'I find that very hard to believe!'

He poured the wine into two glasses before pushing one towards her, an indication that she should drink some of it. 'That I want you? Or that I have thought of you constantly since I first saw you?'

'I was engaged to another man!'

Gregorio gave a brief glance at her bare left hand. 'An engagement is not a marriage.'

'Obviously not,' she acknowledged heavily. 'But I find it difficult to believe you felt an instant attraction to a woman you had only just met.'

'Possibly because you prefer to continue believing me a man capable of *hounding* people to their deaths.'

She winced at this reminder of her earlier accusations. 'Talking of *possessing* someone—me—isn't exactly normal behaviour,' she defended.

'You would prefer that I flatter and seduce you with words before I attempt to make love to you?'

'That's the way it's usually done, yes.'

He gave a dismissive shake of his head. 'I have no time for such games.'

'And, personally, I would prefer it if you never referred to the subject again.'

'Then you are lying to yourself.'

'You—'

'Would you like me to show you how much you are lying?'

'No!' Lia could see the raw passion burning in his dark gaze.

He drew in a deep breath as he continued to study her for several long seconds. 'Drink some of your wine,' he finally encouraged huskily.

'And you call *me* bossy!' She eyed him impatiently.

He studied her over the rim of his glass as he took a sip of what proved to be a very good glass of white wine. He waited until Mancini had served their first course before speaking again. 'You believe me to be a male chauvinist?'

She grimaced. 'Maybe it's just a cultural difference?'

'You do not believe that any more than I do,' he observed dryly. 'And you should have met my father—compared to him I am a fully enlightened man who believes in equal opportunity for all three sexes.'

'He's...no longer with you?'

'Neither of my parents is still alive.' Gregorio inwardly berated himself for unthinkingly introducing the painful subject of the death of a parent. 'My father believed it was my mother's role to be a wife to him and to bring up their three sons.'

'And you don't?'

Lia took her glass of wine. Their conversation was far too personal for her liking. Combining that with how casually dressed Gregorio was this evening, this situation—the private jet, the personal chef—was all too disturbing for her peace of mind.

'My mother ensured my two brothers and I have a more modern attitude.' Gregorio shrugged. 'For instance, she insisted all of us learn how to cook.'

'How did your father react to that?'

'As a man who had never had to learn how to so

much as boil an egg, he was horrified,' Gregorio recalled with one of those smiles that changed his face from austerely attractive to devastatingly handsome. 'My mother loved my father enough to allow him to believe he was the patriarch of the family, when in actual fact she was the one who decided what, when, where and how.'

'She sounds amazing.'

Gregorio heard the wistful note in her voice—a reminder that Lia had grown up without a mother. It seemed as if every subject they touched upon had the potential to blow up in his face.

'She was,' he dismissed briskly.

'But you've never married?'

'There has been no time for a woman in my life.'

'That isn't what the newspapers say!'

'I was referring to a woman I might wish to marry.'

'Rather than go to bed with?'

His jaw tightened. 'Yes.'

'What happened to the woman you were having dinner with that night at the restaurant?'

'*Happened* to her…?'

Lia nodded. 'She looked nice.'

Gregorio's company had been in negotiations to buy Fairbanks Industries for some weeks before he had recognised Jacob Fairbanks in the restaurant that evening. Both of them had been dining with other people. David Richardson was known to him as Fairbanks's lawyer. But he'd never before met the woman seated between the two men.

She had been exquisite.

Gregorio had seen his dining companion seated before immediately going over to Fairbanks's table to seek an introduction to the beautiful redhead. Amelia Fairbanks—Jacob's daughter. And the lawyer was her fiancé.

When Amelia had stood up to go to the powder room half an hour later, Gregorio hadn't been able to resist following her. Or kissing her. Only to receive an angry slap to his cheek as soon as the kiss had ended.

The evening hadn't gone at all as Gregorio had originally intended it should. Not only had he mainly ignored his dining companion for the rest of the evening, in favour of staring at Amelia Fairbanks, but he had also put the other woman in a taxi as soon as they'd left the restaurant, rather than accepting her invitation to go back to her apartment for the night.

He straightened. 'I never saw her again after that evening.' Nor had he dated any other women in the past few months.

'Why not?'

He gave her a pointed glance. 'Because I saw you that night and I wanted you.'

Lia turned away from the intensity of that dark gaze. 'I can't imagine you allowing anyone—least of all me—to disrupt a single part of your life.'

'Can't you?'

She was so aware of everything about this man she was finding it hard to maintain the distance necessary if she was going to continue resisting him. Even more so after those revelations about his parents and his childhood. She didn't *want* to know things about Gregorio's life, to think of him as having been a child with loving parents and two younger brothers he had no doubt argued and fought with but would likely defend to the death if one of them was in danger. Knowing those things made him more a flesh-and-blood man and less the ruthless monster, Gregorio de la Cruz. Which had no doubt been his intention all along.

She must never forget who or what he was. Nor that he had revealed himself as someone who was not averse to using manipulation and machination to get what he wanted. And there could be no doubt now that he wanted *her*.

She glared at him. 'I'm not interested.'

'No?'

'No,' she snapped, seeing his knowing expression. But she knew he was right; she could never remember being this aware of a man before. Ever.

She had known David for over a year before he'd asked her out and she'd accepted. They had dated for another year before he proposed and she had accepted. They had been engaged for just over a month before David had invited her back to spend the night at his apartment, and again she had accepted.

Up until the night David had ended their engagement he had been every inch the gentleman throughout the whole of their courtship.

Gregorio wasn't a gentlemen, and nor did he ever *ask* for anything he wanted. He just assumed it was his right and took it.

But wasn't it better that way?

To be simply swept off one's feet and not have to think about whether or not it was sensible, or consider the possible repercussions—?

No, of course it wasn't! Now that Lia was completely on her own it was even more important for her to be on her guard. Most especially so with Gregorio de la Cruz.

* * *

'You cheated,' Lia complained two hours later as she let the two of them into her apartment.

'I merely suggested we bring dessert back here.' Gregorio followed her inside.

'And so delayed answering my questions for even longer. Well, don't make yourself too comfortable,' she warned as Gregorio sat down at the breakfast bar. 'Because you aren't staying.'

'You *are* bossy in bed,' he said knowingly.

'You'll never know,' she assured him tersely.

Gregorio made no reply. Why bother contradicting her when it would only lead to another disagreement? When he was fully aware that Lia, in spite of herself, wanted him as much as he wanted her.

Besides, he could afford to concede a single battle when he had no intention of losing the war.

'Do you *want* any dessert?'

'I couldn't eat another thing after that delicious meal.'

'That's what I thought.' She put the dessert in the fridge before straightening. 'I've had dinner with you, fulfilled my part of the agreement, now it's time for you to start talking.'

She leaned back against one of the kitchen cupboards, arms crossed defensively in front of her chest.

'Of course.'

Gregorio stood up in what was now a very tidy apartment. All the boxes had been emptied and removed, the furniture was neatly arranged, and several photographs of Lia and her father had been placed in prominent places.

'I liked your father very much—but obviously you

choose not to believe that,' he said impatiently, acknowledging her sceptical snort.

'I have no reason to believe anything you say.'

'And *I* have no reason to lie to you.' He scowled. 'Lia, De la Cruz Industries did *not* withdraw from the negotiations to purchase your father's company.'

'Of course you did—'

'No,' he stated evenly. 'Your father was the one who withdrew from our offer.'

'That's ridiculous.' Lia pushed away from the kitchen unit, her movements restless as she walked into the larger area of the sitting room. 'Why on earth would he do that when he was on the verge of bankruptcy and so badly needed to sell Fairbanks Industries?'

'In light of the current FSA investigation into the company, I think we may assume it was because he had discovered some…discrepancy.'

'What sort of discrepancy?'

'I believe several million pounds were transferred from the company accounts to offshore bank accounts.'

'You *believe* or you *know*?'

'I know,' he confirmed quietly.

'My father did *not* steal from his own company, if that's what you're implying!' Her hands were clenched at her sides.

'Of course not.'

'Then who did?'

Gregorio shrugged his shoulders. 'Only a limited number of people had the means, and access to the bank accounts affected.'

She frowned as she thought over what Gregorio had told her.

He'd said her father had withdrawn from the negotiations to sell Fairbanks Industries. That he had done so because he had discovered someone had been stealing from his company.

But who?

As Gregorio had said, only a few people had access to the company bank accounts.

Her father, obviously.

And Lia, as a precaution—in case anything should ever happen to him and she needed access, he'd explained. How ironic that was, in the circumstances.

The two vice presidents of the company...

The accounts department only had limited access—not enough to be able to transfer funds from company accounts to another one.

There was no one else except—

Lia gave Gregorio a startled glance. 'Do you happen to know who he suspected?'

'I think you have already guessed the answer to that question.'

There was only one answer, if she eliminated everyone else. But it simply wasn't an answer Lia could give any credence to.

David had not only been her father's lawyer but her fiancé when the embezzlement had supposedly taken place. Besides which, his family was incredibly wealthy. There was no incentive for David to steal money from her father's company.

Lord knew she had no reason to think kindly of David, after he had let her down so badly, but she simply couldn't believe the man she had intended to marry was capable of the things Gregorio had just revealed to her.

CHAPTER FIVE

'YOU'RE WRONG.' SHE gave a firm shake of her head.

Gregorio had watched the play of emotions on Lia's face. Puzzlement. Dawning realisation. Shock. Doubt. Followed seconds later by this outright denial.

'Are you saying that because you *know* I'm wrong or because you hope that I am…?'

She looked at him blankly for several seconds. 'I'll admit David ultimately proved not to be the man I thought he was when I agreed to marry him, but he isn't the thief you're implying he is either.'

'Again, I ask—is that because you know for certain I'm wrong or because you don't want to believe I'm right?'

She straightened her shoulders defensively. 'David comes from a wealthy family. He's a partner in one of the most prestigious law firms in London. His father *owns* that law firm, for goodness' sake.'

'And you consider that proof of his innocence?'

'Well. No. Of course it isn't proof.' She shot Gregorio an impatient glance. 'But there is absolutely no reason why he would have stolen from my father.' Her chin rose in stubborn denial. 'David is a wealthy man in his own right.'

'My sources tell me that Richardson has a serious gambling habit.'

'Then *your sources* are wrong.' She gave a disgusted shake of her head. 'I went out with David for a year, was engaged to him for three months. David doesn't gamble.'

'I'm afraid he does. Excessively so. I am reliably informed that he lost over sixty thousand pounds in one casino alone last month.'

She gave a pained frown. 'But I never saw... There was never any hint... Can I really have been so wrong about him?'

Gregorio had known this was going to be a difficult conversation, and that was the reason he had delayed having it for as long as he could. He had known Lia would have a problem believing her ex-fiancé was guilty of theft on a grand scale, despite the other man having deserted her when she'd needed him. It was for this reason that Gregorio had been skirting around the edges of the subject for the past three days. He had known that once his suspicion was out in the open he would have no way of retracting it. That Lia would hate him all the more because of it.

Gregorio had no doubt the FSA would eventually find the missing funds, and the offshore bank account, but that would be the end of their investigation. They would have absolutely no jurisdiction in another country.

Gregorio wasn't hampered by such legalities. His own security people were even now following the money trail to the offshore bank account in the name of Madras Enterprises. He had no doubt they would eventually unravel the maze surrounding this mysterious company, and when they did Gregorio was sure they would be able to identify the owner of that company as being David Richardson.

If Richardson *was* involved, then he had probably considered it prudent to distance himself from the Fairbanks family after Jacob's death—starting with breaking his engagement to Lia. There was also the fact Lia was no longer wealthy, and Richardson was going to need a *very* wealthy wife with his obsessive gambling habit to satisfy.

'If— Whoever is responsible... My father *died* because of the strain he was put under!' Tears glistened in her eyes.

Gregorio's mouth thinned. 'I will get to the bottom of who is responsible, Lia, this I promise you,' he assured her grimly. 'And when I do they will be made to pay for what they did.'

'It won't bring my father back.'

'No.' What else could he say to a statement like that?

She dropped down into one of the armchairs. 'Then it really doesn't matter who's to blame, does it?'

She leaned her head back, closed her eyes.

It mattered to Gregorio. If David Richardson was responsible for the embezzlement then he couldn't be allowed to get away with what he'd done to the Fairbanks family. Nor could he be left in a position of power where he could do the same thing to other clients who put their trust him as their lawyer.

'Did you tell me these things so that I won't hate you any more?'

Gregorio's eyes narrowed as he looked across to see Lia now watching him guardedly. He could read nothing from her expression.

'I told you so that you would know the truth,' he said cautiously.

'But also so that I don't hate you any more?'

'Is this a trick question?' He eyed her warily. 'Do I damn myself whichever way I answer it?'

'Probably.' She gave a humourless smile as she stood. 'I think you should leave now. My head is buzzing with all that you've just told me, and I need to get my things ready for work in the morning.'

His gaze became searching. 'Are you going to be okay?'

'Yes.'

Lia wished she felt as positive as she sounded. The things Gregorio had told her tonight were disturbing, to say the least. She still didn't believe David was involved, but if her father really *had* discovered that someone was embezzling funds from Fairbanks Industries, and had withdrawn from the de la Cruz offer because of it, then she very much doubted that both men could be wrong in their suspicions.

She had only just started to put her life back together, and now she felt exposed and vulnerable again.

Moving in to her apartment and starting a new job had been positive things. A fresh start. Moving forward after weeks of feeling as if she were stuck in a quagmire of emotions with no way out.

Gregorio had given her a lot of information to think about tonight. Information about David that, if true, meant he was responsible to driving her father to his death. It also seriously brought into question the reason he had pursued her and asked her to marry him.

And her own ability to know if a person was trustworthy or not.

She had trusted David, and even if it turned out that he was innocent of Gregorio's accusations, David had still let her down by leaving her to deal with her father's death alone.

She had distrusted Gregorio the first timeshe met him, and yet he had done nothing but try to help her. Albeit for reasons of his own, he had apparently been protecting her this whole time—had been instrumental, she was sure, in helping her to acquire her job. By doing that he had given her back some of the pride and confidence in herself she had lost.

Was it possible that the good guy was really the bad guy and the bad guy was really the good guy?

Lia was giving herself a headache, trying to make sense of it.

'I'll walk you to the door,' she offered distractedly.

Gregorio knew he had no choice but to accept that it was time for him to leave and he slowly followed Lia down the hallway to the apartment door.

Lia had a lot of new information to think about. But he didn't doubt for a moment that David Richardson was involved in this up to his pretty-boy handsome neck.

'Thank you.'

Gregorio blinked as he focused on Lia standing hesitantly beside the still closed door to her apartment. 'Sorry?'

She lifted her chin. 'I appreciate it must have been difficult for you to tell me those things.'

Gregorio drew in a slow and steadying breath, aware that Lia was placing a tentative trust in him.

'That doesn't mean I forgive you.' Her eyes narrowed. 'Only that for the moment I'm cautiously giving you the benefit of the doubt.'

He couldn't help but smile at her begrudging trust. 'I can live with that.'

'And call off whoever you have following me,' she added with a frown. 'It makes me uncomfortable to think of someone watching my every move.'

Gregorio would rather Lia felt a little discomfort than any harm came to her. If Richardson thought for one moment she knew of his duplicity there was no knowing what he would do. For the moment the other man felt secure, with his funds in an offshore company, but if Richardson ever began to doubt that security that might quickly change.

'Gregorio?'

He grimaced. 'Your father would have wanted someone to take care of you.'

She raised auburn brows. 'I doubt he ever imagined it would be you.'

'No,' he conceded wryly. 'Am I allowed a goodnight kiss?'

Lia burst out laughing. Which was pretty incredible after the conversation she'd just had with this man. But she couldn't help her response. It was so ludicrous for a man like Gregorio to *ask* if he could do something he had decided he wanted to do.

'When did you last ask a lady's permission to kiss her?'

'Never,' he acknowledged dryly.

She continued to chuckle. 'That's honest, anyway.'

'Your answer...?'

Despite the lightness of Gregorio's tone, Lia could sense his inner tension. It was there in his expression, in the stiff set of his shoulders and the hands clenched at his sides.

Long and elegant hands she had found herself studying as they ate dinner together. Everything about Gregorio was elegant and controlled. The way he moved. The way he ate. The way he talked. All calmly and elegantly done, and all firmly under his control.

A part of Lia wanted to shake that control—if only for a few minutes.

Besides, it was very narrow in this hallway, and made even more so by Gregorio's physically overwhelming presence. She could feel the heat of his body so close to her own, and breathe in that seductive aftershave...

'Yes.' She looked directly into his fathomless black eyes.

His brows rose. 'Yes?'

Lia felt a smile parting her lips. It felt good to smile again. In a genuine show of happiness rather than the polite curving of her lips she had been showing everyone for months now. Besides, she had just succeeded in surprising the hell out of Gregorio.

'Yes,' she repeated, more firmly.

She didn't need the warmth of another human being tonight, she *wanted* it—and not just anyone's warmth either. Gregorio's. She very badly wanted to know how it felt to be held and kissed by Gregorio de la Cruz.

Gregorio hesitated no longer and moved in closer to Lia, his hands moving up to cup her cheeks as he lifted her face, his gaze holding hers as he slowly lowered and tilted his head to claim her lips with his own.

Soft lips parted slightly beneath his as he continued to kiss her. Tasting. Sipping. Lia's hands moved up to grasp hold of his wrists and she moved up on tiptoe to increase the pressure of her lips against his.

Gregorio felt as if he had been in a constant state of

arousal for days…weeks—which he had—and now he was actually kissing Lia again he never wanted to stop.

His arms moved about her waist and he pulled her body in tight against the hardness of his as he deepened the kiss. His tongue swept lightly across and then between her lips to enter the welcoming heat beyond.

It felt as if he was *inside* Lia as she sucked his tongue in deeper still, her cheeks hollowing around his invading tongue in a parody of how it would feel to have him thrusting between her thighs. Hot and wet, and oh-so-good.

Gregorio gave a groan and began to stroke his tongue in and out of her mouth, his arousal throbbing hot and heavy in response as he placed his hands on Lia's bottom and pulled her body in even tighter against his own.

Lia gave a low moan, her breathing ragged as she felt the length of Gregorio's arousal pressing against the softness of her abdomen. Heat built between her thighs in response. Her nipples felt hard as unripe berries, and achingly sensitive against the restricting lace of her bra.

She pressed in closer still as she released Gregorio's wrists to slide her hands up his chest, until her fingers became entangled in the dark and silky hair at his nape. She couldn't seem to get close enough—she wanted more, *ached* for so much more.

Gregorio broke the kiss to trail his lips hotly down the arched column of her throat. 'Can I stay?' he asked throatily. 'Please, Lia, let me—'

'Yes.'

She didn't even allow him to finish. She didn't want to talk—she wanted…*wanted*…him. She wanted Gregorio, and the mindless pleasure she already knew they would have together.

David had been her only lover to date, and Lia had always assumed that her lack of orgasm was a fault on her part, not his. Had thought that they needed time to adjust and become accustomed to each other in that way. That pleasure would come with the physical familiarity of being married to each other.

But just a few minutes of being in Gregorio's arms, of having his lips and hands on her, and Lia felt as if she was about to spontaneously combust. As if something inside her was about to burst free, taking her to a place she had never been before.

'I said yes.' She frowned as Gregorio continued to look at her searchingly.

'Are you going to hate me again in the morning?'

'I might hate you again later on tonight, but right now *hate* is the last thing I'm feeling. Can we not dissect this, Gregorio?' She frowned as those black eyes continued to question her. 'Conversation is very overrated, you know.'

His tension broke as he smiled. 'You *are* going to be bossy in bed,' he decided with satisfaction.

'I'm going to be bossy *out* of bed if we don't go to my bedroom very soon!'

Gregorio chuckled softly as he placed his hands beneath her bottom and lifted her up off the floor. 'Wrap your legs around my waist,' he encouraged.

'Now who's being bossy…?'

Lia trailed off, her breathing becoming erratic as Gregorio turned to walk down the hallway towards her bedroom.

'Oh, God…'

Her arms clung tightly about his neck and she buried her face against his throat as each step he took ground her body sensually against his, sending wave after wave of pleasure coursing through her body.

'That is so... Gregorio!'

She gasped as the tension between her thighs intensified before suddenly being released, engulfing her in heat and an overwhelming pleasure that caused the whole of her body to tremble and shake as she rode out that release to its last shuddering throb.

So *that* was what the ultimate in physical pleasure felt like!

That connection men and women throughout the ages had killed for.

Lia now understood every one of those emotions.

Her orgasm had been a pleasure such as she had never dreamed of. Pure ecstasy. It had connected her to Gregorio in a way she had never experienced before with anyone else.

There was none of the awkwardness or embarrassment she had always felt with David as Gregorio carried her across her darkened bedroom and lay her down on the bed before lying on his side next to her.

'Are you okay?' He lifted a hand to caress the hair back from her temple.

'Better than okay.' She nodded, still trying to catch her breath.

'Light on or off?' he queried softly.

'On,' Lia decided, and she turned to switch on the lamp on her bedside table.

She moved up onto her knees, wanting to see all of Gregorio as she slowly undressed him. That hard and muscled chest. The taut abdomen. The long length of his arousal. Those long and muscular legs.

She already knew he was going to look like a mythological god. All golden flesh and hard muscles.

'Arms up,' she instructed as she lifted and then removed his T-shirt completely, revealing his chest covered in a light dusting of dark hair, his nipples like bronzed pennies. She touched them lightly, glancing up at him as she heard his sharp intake of breath and felt his nipples pebble against her fingertips. 'You like that?'

'Yes.'

Gregorio had no idea what Lia's sexual experience had been before tonight, and he didn't want to know either. Here and now, the two of them together, it was so highly charged, so intensely pleasurable, that everything and every other woman he had ever known before Lia faded into insignificance. Forgotten. All he could see and feel was narrowed down to this woman. To seeing and feeling only Lia.

Her orgasm a few minutes ago had come as a complete surprise to him. He had barely touched her before she'd found her release.

He could only hope that quicksilver response was uniquely for him.

He sucked in a breath as Lia scraped her nails lightly over the hardness of his nipples, a slight smile curving her lips as she watched and obviously enjoyed seeing his response to her touch.

She could pleasure and torment him for hours if it meant he could see that smile on her lips while she did it.

Her eyes glowed dark grey, her cheeks were flushed, and her lips were curved into that seductive smile, slightly swollen from their earlier kisses.

'*Dios!*' Gregorio's back arched off the bed as Lia's

tongue rasped moistly across one sensitised nipple, his fingers becoming entangled in the auburn hair draped across his chest as her lips completely engulfed his nipple with the heat of her mouth and she suckled deeply.

Gregorio was used to being the lover, the aggressor, and while women always responded with kisses and caresses he had never had one take charge of him in quite this way before. It felt strange, and yet somehow liberating at the same time—a measure of the trust that was slowly building between the two of them. Fragile as yet, but growing stronger the more time they spent together.

The things Lia was doing to him with her mouth and tongue made Gregorio's body throb and ache.

Lia lifted her head to smile at him, her eyes sultry as her hands moved down to unfasten the top button of his jeans, quickly followed by the other three. Gregorio sighed his relief as his desire was no longer constricted by material, only to suck his breath in again as Lia's hand caressed the length of him outlined against his black boxers.

'I want to feel your lips and your hands on my bared flesh,' he encouraged huskily. 'Please...' He lifted himself up and pushed his jeans and boxers down to his thighs.

Lia's breath caught in her throat as her gaze feasted on his fully naked body. She moistened her lips with the tip of her tongue.

'You're— *No...!*' she cried as the ringing of the doorbell sounded, shrill and intrusive. 'God, no...' she groaned as she buried her face against Gregorio's chest.

'Ignore it—' A second loud ring, longer this time, cut across Gregorio's protest.

'It's probably one of the neighbours, come to say hello to the new tenant.' She sighed as she sat up.

'That has never been my experience.' He frowned.

'That's probably because you live in a hotel. I have to answer that,' Lia snapped with impatience as the bell rang for a third time. Whoever was on the other side of that door was *not* going to receive a warm welcome from her—that was for certain. 'Stay exactly where and how you are,' she instructed Gregorio as she got up from the bed.

'*Sí, señorita.*' Dark eyes glittered with humour.

Lia cast one last, longing look at the lean and muscular length of Gregorio's body before turning to hurry from the bedroom, straightening her clothes as she went.

The doorbell rang for a fourth time just as she wrenched the door open.

'Oh, thank goodness!' A relieved Cathy stood outside in the hallway, Rick at her side. 'I was *so* worried about you.' She gave Lia a hug.

'I'm fine,' Lia assured her, her mind racing as she wondered what she was going to do about Cathy and Rick standing on her doorstep when Gregorio was half naked in her bedroom.

No immediate answer came to mind.

'You seemed so down at lunch,' Cathy said. 'I was worried about you, and Rick and I just had to come over and see if you were okay.'

'I'm really fine,' Lia repeated distractedly, her mind racing as she tried to find a solution to this dilemma.

There was no way she could get out of inviting Cathy and Rick inside her apartment. Not when they were giving up their evening to visit her. But, conversely, she couldn't expect Gregorio to spend all evening hiding out in her bedroom.

As if that was really an option! Gregorio went where he wanted and did what he wanted. It went without saying that hiding in a woman's bedroom would *not* be what he wanted.

'You look a little flushed.' Cathy looked at her in concern. 'Maybe you have the start of a cold?'

'Er… Cat…' Rick said hesitantly beside her.

'Or maybe it's the flu?' His wife continued to fuss. 'There's a lot of it about at the moment, and—'

'Cat!'

'What is it, Rick?' Cathy turned to her husband impatiently.

Lia winced as Rick ignored his wife and continued to look past Lia into the hallway beyond. She knew without looking that Gregorio had left her bedroom, after all, and was now standing behind her.

She just hoped he had put his clothes back on first!

CHAPTER SIX

'Perhaps I should introduce myself?'

A fully dressed Gregorio—thank goodness—looked at Lia as the four of them stood awkwardly in the sitting room of her apartment. Lia really hadn't had any choice but to invite the other couple inside.

'Fine.' It was the only word she'd seemed able to say since she had opened her apartment door and found Cathy and Rick standing outside in the hallway.

'Oh, I know *exactly* who you are, Mr de la Cruz,' Cathy assured him with a sideways glance at Lia. 'We're Cathy and Rick Morton. Friends of Lia's.'

Lia winced as she sensed Cathy's censorious gaze on her after that last announcement. It was questioning why, when they were such close friends, Lia hadn't confided in Cathy regarding her friendship with Gregorio. She was going to have some serious explaining to do once Gregorio had left. Whenever that was going to be. Because of the four of them he seemed to be the most relaxed and the least intimidated by this situation. He also showed no inclination to leave.

Lia felt bad for not telling Cathy about Gregorio's previous visit, or that she was working for him. At the time she had thought it was the right thing to do—that she would be avoiding Gregorio as much as possible in future, so telling Cathy about him was a waste of time. Look how well *that* had turned out!

But at least he had all his clothes back on and had tidied himself before he'd come out of her bedroom. Although the slightly creased T-shirt and tousled dark hair indicated that hadn't been the case minutes ago.

Lia knew Cathy was going to want to kill her once the two of them could speak privately.

'I remember seeing you with Lia at the funeral,' he answered Cathy as the three of them shook hands. 'And, please, you must both call me Gregorio.'

The pleasantries over, an awkward silence once again fell over the room.

'Wine.' Lia had finally found another word to say. 'Let's all have a glass of wine. I have red or white. Which would you prefer? The white is dry, the red fruity.'

Now she'd regained her voice Lia didn't seem able to stop babbling, but at the same time her gaze couldn't quite meet Cathy's or Rick's, and she was avoiding Gregorio's completely.

She felt so stupid. Like a child who had been caught out not being honest. Not that Cathy or Rick were in the least judgemental—it was Lia who felt as if she had somehow disappointed them.

'You sit and chat with your friends and I'll pour the wine.' Gregorio spoke dryly, obviously knowing the topic of their conversation would be him.

'I'll help you.' Rick hurriedly followed the other man into the kitchen area.

'Cathy—'

'He seems to know his way around your kitchen,'

Cathy observed softly as the two women sat down, Her brows rose as she watched Gregorio remove a bottle of red wine from the rack before taking glasses from the cupboard above.

Lia tried again. 'Cathy—'

'I have to say he's an improvement on the last guy,' her friend murmured appreciatively.

Lia's eyes widened. It was the last thing she had expected the other woman to say. 'You didn't like David?'

'He was your choice, so of course I liked him.' Her friend shrugged. 'Except I didn't, if you know what I mean.'

No, Lia *didn't* know what she meant. She had always thought Cathy and Rick *liked* David: the four of them had often gone out to dinner together, and they had always seemed to get on.

'He could be rather condescending,' Cathy added with a grimace.

Thinking back to those evenings, she realised David *had* talked down to Cathy and Rick. As if they weren't quite of his social standing. Which was ridiculous. Cathy's father was a politician, currently in government, and Rick's family owned and ran a huge farm in Worcestershire. Rick himself was senior manager at a software firm here in London.

It made her wonder what else she hadn't noticed about David during the months they had dated and been engaged. Whether Gregorio's suspicions about him were well-founded. David had certainly proved himself to be a less than supportive fiancé after her father's death.

Unlike Gregorio…

She might not particularly *like* the idea of Gregorio having his security men keeping an eye on her, but there was also a certain…reassurance—a warmth in know-ing that someone cared enough about her to do that.

Lia chewed on her bottom lip. 'About Gregorio—'

'Don't worry about it, sweetie.' Cathy smiled as she leaned forward to give Lia's arm a reassuring squeeze. 'It's a surprise, but not an unpleasant one. The man is *gorgeous*, isn't he?' She lowered her voice even more.

Lia glanced across to where Gregorio and Rick were chatting together like old friends—as it turned out, as she listened briefly to their conversation, they were two men who both liked football but supported oppos-ing teams. Gregorio was laughing at something Rick had said, his dark eyes warm with humour, a relaxed expression lightening his austere features.

'Yes, he is,' Lia acknowledged softly.

'He doesn't seem at all cold and remote this evening,' Cathy added approvingly.

Gregorio had been anything *but* cold and remote in her bedroom a few minutes ago. Burning hot and very close better described the two of them together. Just thinking about all Gregorio's naked and respon-sive flesh was enough to cause Lia's cheeks to warm in a blush.

Cathy gave her a knowing grin. 'Do you want us to leave as soon as we've drunk our wine?'

'*No!* I mean… No,' she repeated softly as the two men turned curiously at her vehemence. 'I think I may need saving from myself,' she told Cathy with a groan. 'I don't know what I was even thinking. He's just so—'

'Overwhelming and sexy as hell?' her friend sup-plied lightly.

Lia's gaze could no longer meet Cathy's. 'Yes.'

'Here we go,' Rick announced in an over-hearty

voice as he handed Cathy a glass of red wine. No doubt as a warning to the two women that they were no longer alone.

'Lia.'

She glanced up at Gregorio as he stood beside her chair, holding out a glass a red wine for her to take. The humour gleaming in those dark eyes told her he had overheard Cathy's last comment—and Lia's response to it.

She turned her gaze away, her hand shaking slightly as she took the wine glass from him.

'So, what do the two of you have planned for the rest of the evening?' Rick prompted politely—and immediately had to thump Cathy on the back as she began to choke on a mouthful of wine. 'What did I say?' Rick looked bewildered by his wife's reaction.

'Never mind, love,' Cathy answered once she'd caught her breath. 'Let's just drink our wine and pick up a Chinese takeaway on the way home.'

'Lia and I have already eaten, but we could always order in food for you to eat here?' Gregorio suggested lightly. 'Alternatively, we could all go out for a drink together somewhere the two of you could have some food?'

Lia slowly turned her head to look at him. Who *was* this man and what had he done with the cold and arrogant Gregorio de la Cruz? Because *this* man certainly wasn't the ruthless businessman who swallowed up companies with the voracity of a shark. Or the playboy billionaire she'd read about in the newspapers who had a different blonde on his arm every week.

'Okay, this is getting a little weird now.'

Lia stood up decisively. She might have been in

shock since Cathy and Rick had arrived, but she was recovering fast. And the four of them spending the rest of the evening together wasn't going to happen.

'Cathy and Rick are far too polite to say so, but they don't want to spend the evening with the two of us—'

'Hey, don't put words in my mouth,' Cathy protested.

'Because they are both totally freaked out right now,' Lia continued determinedly. '*I'm* freaked out right now, so I know they have to be too.' She frowned at Gregorio. 'The two of us aren't a couple and we aren't going out for the evening with anyone—least of all my two best friends. What happened earlier...' She gave Cathy and Rick a self-conscious glance. 'Shouldn't have happened.'

'I believe *you* are the one embarrassing your friends.' Now Gregorio looked every inch the coldly arrogant man Lia had met at her father's funeral: his eyes were narrowed and no longer warm, but hard as the onyx they resembled, and his sculptured lips were thin and unsmiling.

'Not at all.' Cathy stood up. 'It's time the two of us were going anyway. Rick?' she prompted sharply as her husband made no move to get up out of his chair.

'What? Oh. Yes. Sorry.' He rose abruptly to his feet, then seemed to realise he still had a glass in his hand and looked around for somewhere to put it.

'Here.' Cathy took the glass and placed it on the coffee table next to her own. 'I'll call you in the morning, okay?' She gave Lia a hug. 'Nice to meet you, Gregorio.' She nodded. 'Say goodnight, Rick,' she instructed dryly. Her husband still looked slightly dazed by the speed of their departure.

'Goodnight, Rick,' he repeated as he was pulled down the hallway by his wife.

The apartment door closed quietly behind them seconds later.

Leaving an awkward silence.

A very cold and very uncomfortable silence that caused Lia to give a shiver as the chill seemed to seep into her bones.

'Your rudeness was completely uncalled for,' Gregorio snapped finally.

'No.' Lia's chin rose as she faced him. 'No, it really wasn't. I don't know what happened between the two of us earlier, but it isn't going to happen again. I won't *let* it happen again,' she added firmly. She was totally unsettled by their earlier passion. 'And we certainly aren't ever going out for the evening with any of my friends, as if the two of us are together.'

Gregorio was having to exert great willpower so as not to lose his temper. He made a point of never losing his temper—no matter what the provocation. But he had not encountered anyone as stubborn as Lia before.

He had been disappointed when he'd realised Lia's visitors had to be Cathy and Rick Morton, the couple he had seen her with at her father's graveside two months ago. He knew, from the daily security reports he received, that Lia had lived with the other couple before moving into her apartment at the weekend.

Rather than remaining in Lia's bedroom like a dirty little secret she was keeping hidden away, Gregorio had decided to dress and join them.

He had no experience of being in the company of a woman's friends or family, but he had thought he was doing quite well. Being charming to Cathy. Talking football with her husband. Pouring them all wine. It had seemed perfectly logical to him, as the other couple were obviously close to Lia, to suggest they all spend the rest of the evening together.

Lia's vehemently negative response to that suggestion had been immediate. And, to his surprise, her words had hurt.

He was close to his two brothers. Well…as close as he could be when he was based in London, Sebastien was in New York, and Alejandro was taking care of the estate and vineyards in Spain. He also had a large extended family, of which *he* was the recognised patriarch.

He had sex with the women who flitted in and out of his life, but he did *not* become involved with their family or their friends. He rarely even *met* any of their friends, let alone their family. He had been willing to make an exception with Lia, and he'd received a verbal and public slap in the face for his trouble.

He would not make the same mistake again.

'What happened earlier is that you used me for sex,' he bit out coldly, his accent more clipped in his anger. 'No doubt any man would have sufficed. I am pleased I was able to give you *one* orgasm, at least, before we were interrupted.'

The colour had drained from her cheeks. 'You *bastard*!'

Gregorio shrugged his shoulders. 'You were the one at such pains to explain exactly what we have between us, I am merely agreeing with you. When you feel in the need for sex again perhaps you should give me a call? If I have the time I— No, I do not *think* so.' Gregorio grasped hold of Lia's wrist as her hand arced up towards his cheek. He used that grip to pull her up close against him. 'I warned you the last time you did that I would not allow you to do it again without retaliating.'

Her top lip turned back in a sneer. 'I should have known you were the type of man who would hit a woman!'

Gregorio's jaw tightened. 'Any man who strikes a woman, for whatever reason, no longer has the right to call himself a man. My retribution will be of quite a different kind, I assure you.'

Lia swallowed. Gregorio's threat was all the more disturbing because he'd delivered it in such a calm and conversational tone. As if they were discussing the weather rather than his retribution.

'Let go of me,' she said evenly.

He quirked one dark brow. 'Are you going to slap me again?'

'No.' That impulse had passed. Besides, she had never felt tempted to hit anyone before Gregorio.

'Pity.' He bared his teeth in a humourless smile as he released her wrist and stepped back. 'I believe I would have enjoyed punishing you. Perhaps I still will...' he mused.

Lia breathed shallowly. 'Punishing me?'

Black eyes glittered through narrowed lids. 'You are not someone who likes to feel out of control, are you?'

That sounded more like a statement than a question, and Lia treated it as such. 'Neither are you,' she defended.

'I do not remember objecting when you made love to me earlier.'

The warmth in her cheeks deepened as she recalled her aggression. And her pleasure...

Which was another reason she wasn't going to allow

herself to be alone with Gregorio again. He affected her, drove her wild with passion in a way no other man ever had. Including the man she had intended to marry.

She and David had spent the night together regularly after their engagement. Nights she had enjoyed even as she had known there had to be *more*. Although she had enjoyed David's lovemaking she had never reached the pinnacle of physical pleasure when they were together.

A few minutes of just being kissed by and kissing Gregorio and she'd had her first orgasm. He hadn't even touched her. The stimulation had come from those kisses alone.

Just being with him physically excited her.

As much as it disturbed her.

Because she wasn't sure she even *liked* Gregorio.

Lia moistened her lips with the tip of her tongue. 'I really think you should leave now.'

Gregorio had given her far too much to think about. Not just what had happened between the two of them, but the truth about David's involvement in the demise of her father's company.

Because, no matter how confused she was about her feelings for Gregorio, she knew he wasn't a liar. In fact, he was the opposite: Gregorio tended to be brutally honest.

Lia knew she had to see and talk to David again. To find out for herself if what Gregorio had said about him having a gambling habit was true, at least. To try and get David to tell her the part he had played—or not played—in the downfall of Fairbanks Industries.

CHAPTER SEVEN

'THIS ISN'T PART of my job description.'

Gregorio quirked one dark eyebrow as he looked at Lia, standing in the doorway to the office in his penthouse suite. 'My PA has called in sick this morning. I'm not sure it's altogether wise for you to refuse to assist your employer on only your second day of employment.'

Lia wasn't sure it was either. But neither did she think it was coincidence that Gregorio had requested *she* be the one to assist him. Although he certainly *looked* businesslike, in one of those perfectly tailored suits—dark grey today—with a pale grey shirt and striped blue tie.

After a very disturbed night's sleep Lia had tried to put yesterday evening from her mind and treat today as a new start. It had proved not altogether possible when—as promised—Cathy had telephoned her first thing this morning, wanting to know all the juicy details of Lia's relationship with Gregorio.

Lia had told her friend what she felt comfortable with Cathy knowing. Mainly that she really had no idea what last night had been about. Only that she wasn't going to allow Gregorio that close to her again.

After making another phone call Lia had forced herself to shower and dress before coming in to work today. Knowing that Gregorio might appear at any moment and shake what little self-confidence she had managed to dredge up and wrap around herself like a protective cloak.

Having Michael Harrington send her up to the penthouse floor to assist Mr de la Cruz within minutes of her arrival at the Exemplar Hotel had succeeded in tearing a great hole in that protective cloak!

'Is this what you meant when you spoke about punishing me?'

Gregorio narrowed his eyes as he sat back in his chair to look across the width of his desk at Lia. She was once again wearing a black business suit and a cream blouse—the uniform of all the hotel receptionists—and her hair was swept up in that confining style he didn't like. Mainly because it hid all the gold and cinnamon highlights amongst the red. Her face was slightly pale, but there was a defiant glitter in those dark grey eyes.

'You consider assisting your employer to be a punishment?' he challenged.

'That would depend on what he wants my assistance with.'

'The history and accounts of some of the companies I am interested in buying.'

Her eyes widened. 'And why would you think I have any knowledge on either of those subjects?'

Gregorio gave a confident smile. 'Because your father told me you very often assisted him when he worked at home in the evenings.'

Her hand reached out blindly to allow her fingers

to grasp hold of the doorframe for support. 'My father told you…?'

'Jacob and I met several times.' He nodded. 'Once we had finished our business discussions you invariably came into the conversation.' He stood up to move around to the front of his desk. 'He was very proud of you.'

Lia could find no answer to that statement. Instead she blinked back the tears stinging her eyes and prompted briskly, 'Just tell me what I can do to help you.'

Gregorio had to bite back his immediate response. Which was, *you can get down on your knees and relieve me of the throbbing ache of arousal that kept me awake all night*. He was pretty sure that wasn't the sort of help Lia was offering.

He had been coldly angry when he'd left Lia's apartment the evening before. Something that seemed to have become a common occurrence around Lia. A couple of glasses of brandy had eased some of that anger, but nothing had succeeded in taking away the sexual tension that had kept his body hard and throbbing for release.

Not even a freezing cold shower.

The moment he thought of Lia again—and that was becoming an occupational hazard too—his desire sprang back to life as if it had never gone away.

Receiving a phone call earlier this morning from Tim, his PA, explaining that he was sick with the flu, had seemed to set the tone for today too.

Until Gregorio had realised exactly *which* member of the hotel staff he could ask to assist him in Tim's place…

Was it a punishment for Lia for the fact that he couldn't seem to stop wanting her?

Maybe. Whatever his motive, Gregorio already knew that the next few hours were going to be as painful for him as they would for Lia. If for different reasons.

He had been aware of Lia's perfume the moment she entered the penthouse: that light floral scent with an underlying note of womanly musk. And he couldn't stop his gaze from returning again and again to the swell of her breasts, visible where the top two buttons of her blouse had been left unfastened.

They had been interrupted yesterday evening before he'd had a chance to remove any of Lia's clothing. He had not been allowed to see those breasts bared. His jaw clenched and his teeth ached with how much he wanted to remove her blouse and bra before gorging himself on her naked breasts. Starting with her plump and soon-to-be-aroused nipples…

'The files are on Tim's desk,' he said stiffly instead.

If he had set out to punish Lia, as she'd suggested, then during the course of the morning, working so closely with her, Gregorio knew that his intention had come back to bite him on the butt. Or on another part of his anatomy that was even more sensitive.

Despite the fact that she was sitting across the room from him, at Tim's desk, her perfume continued to fill the air and invade his senses. And Gregorio was aware of every move she made—especially when she stretched her back and arched her neck to ease the tension of sitting at a desk for several hours.

Physical awareness danced along his skin every time she spoke to him, even on such a mundane subject as company accounts.

Flu or not, Tim had better be back tomorrow, or he could start looking for another job!

'I'm scheduled to have an early lunch today.'

'What?' Gregorio scowled across the room at her.

'Michael has given me an early lunch today,' Lia repeated as she glanced at her wristwatch. 'I'm meeting someone just after twelve.'

'Who?' The demand was out before Gregorio's brain had connected with his mouth. 'We still have work to do,' he added with a scowl.

'I'm entitled to a lunchbreak,' she reasoned. 'I'll make sure I finish here when I get back.' She stood up to push her chair neatly beneath the desktop, making no attempt to answer his query as to who she was meeting for lunch.

Gregorio scowled his frustration. He wanted to tell Lia that she couldn't go. That it was more important that they finish this work and he would order lunch for them both to be brought up by room service.

Most of all I want to know who she's having lunch with!

'Say hello to Cathy for me,' he tested lightly.

Lia's smile was enigmatic. 'I'm not meeting Cathy for lunch, but I'll be sure to pass your message along the next time I speak to her.'

Gregorio stood, feeling too restless to remain seated at his desk. 'Are you going anywhere nice?'

She shrugged. 'Just a little Italian bistro quite close to here.'

Gregorio thought he knew the place she meant. It was tucked away in a side street a couple of blocks from here, and run by a middle-aged Italian couple. The food was both good and inexpensive. Something Lia no doubt now took into consideration with her changed circumstances.

'I could order some chocolate cake from Mancini's to be delivered here,' he tempted.

Her smile was rueful as she shook her head. 'I'm happy with the selection of cheesecakes at the bistro.'

Gregorio's eyes narrowed. 'Do you go there often?'

'I used to in the past, yes,' she answered cautiously.

'With David Richardson?' The offices of Richardson, Richardson and Pope weren't too far from here, so it seemed logical to assume that Lia might have met her fiancé for lunch at the bistro for the sake of convenience.

Lia frowned. 'You may be my employer, but I don't believe that where I have lunch and who with, in my own time, is any of your business.'

Of course it wasn't. And Gregorio was well aware that his questions were intrusive. It wouldn't even have occurred to him to ask another employee about their lunch plans. Tim had worked for him for two years now, and the two men worked well together, but he had zero interest in Tim's private life.

But Lia wasn't only his employee.

She was also the woman Gregorio wanted, and he wanted her more the more time he spent in her company.

Which meant it was time—*past* time—to call one of the women he'd occasionally had lunch with in the past. An afternoon in bed with another woman would certainly ease his physical frustration.

Having made that decision, Gregorio found himself still in his office fifteen minutes later, waiting for the call from one of his security team to tell him exactly who Lia was meeting for lunch.

* * *

Lia hadn't known how she would feel when she saw David again—the first time they had met since the evening he'd broken their engagement. David had been in Scotland—conveniently?—when she'd buried her father, and his own father had represented Richardson, Richardson and Pope. It had been an awkward situation for both of them, and they hadn't spoken apart from Alec Richardson's murmured condolences as he moved along with the procession of other people offering their sympathies for her loss.

Her first thought, when David entered the bistro where they had agreed to meet for lunch, was that he looked different from how she remembered him.

Or maybe she was just looking at him from another perspective? Through lenses that were less rose-coloured? After all, she had once thought herself in love with this man.

What a difference three months could make. What a difference *one evening* had made: David had shattered every one of her illusions about him when he'd walked out of her life and left her to the mercy of the media wolves.

He was still male-model-handsome. His hair was the colour of ripened corn, his eyes as blue as the sky on a summer's day. His body looked lithe and fit in his tailored dark suit, and he wore a blue shirt that was perfectly matched in colour for his eyes, and a meticulously knotted navy blue tie.

Yes, on the surface David still gave the appearance of being a confidently handsome lawyer. But Lia was able to look past that veneer today. To see the lines of dissipation beside his eyes and mouth. The slight lax-

ness to the skin about his jaw. To note that his strides
through the bistro seemed less purposeful and more
full of nervous energy.

Was that an indication that David was far from comfortable with this meeting that Lia had requested when
she'd rung him earlier that morning?

It was a meeting he had tried to avoid, and only ac-
quiesced to once Lia had explained that she had found
some papers amongst her father's things she thought
David might be interested in seeing. It wasn't true, of
course, but the fact that he had changed his mind about
the meeting based on that comment had filled Lia with
misgivings. Perhaps the things Gregorio had told her
about David were the truth, after all.

David was a thief and a liar...

'You're looking well,' David commented, but he
made no move to touch her or to kiss her in greeting
before sliding into the seat opposite hers in this relatively private booth at the back of the bistro.

Lia didn't return the compliment. Mainly because it
wasn't true. 'I'm very well, thank you,' she answered
with cool formality.

He waited until they had placed their drinks order
with the waitress and she had left them menus before
asking, 'Are you still living with the Mortons?'

'I have an apartment of my own in town now. And
a job,' Lia added.

'One that pays actual wages or another job at one of
your do-good charities?'

Cathy was right, Lia realised. David *did* condescend.
He was doing it right now.

Her fingers itched to wipe the mocking smile off
his lips.

When had she developed these violent tendencies?

She had never struck anyone in her life until she'd lashed out at Gregorio in that restaurant. Now she wanted nothing more than to slap David too.

Was it because she knew, deep down, that Cathy's comments about him had been correct? That Gregorio's suspicions about David's involvement in her father's downfall might also prove to be correct...?

'I'm a hotel receptionist.'

The words instantly made her think of the morning she had just spent, working in Gregorio's penthouse suite.

The suite was furnished differently from the others Lia had been shown around on her first morning—it was part of her job as a receptionist to know exactly what each of the rooms had to offer people wanting to stay at the hotel. And the office was definitely personal to Gregorio, indicating that he really did live there all the time.

It made a certain sense. Gregorio had all the conveniences of the hotel—like room and laundry service, restaurants, a spa, et cetera—and none of the inconvenience that came along with owning his own house or apartment.

Even if it *had* seemed a little strange to know that his bedroom was just down the hallway from where the two of them were working...

'How the mighty have fallen,' David sneered.

The gloves really *had* come off today, hadn't they?

It made Lia feel slightly foolish for not having seen David's true nature before now. No doubt he had hidden the worst parts of himself from her while they were dating and then engaged, but even so Lia had always believed herself a good judge of character. Obviously she had been wrong.

Had she been wrong about Gregorio being the bad guy?

She'd already acknowledged that might be the case. Now she was convinced of it.

Quite what she was going to do about it, she had no idea. Gregorio was…overwhelming. Forceful. And he made no secret of his desire for her.

At least he *hadn't*…

But the way they had parted last night, and the stiltedness between them this morning, seemed to indicate he might have put that feeling behind him and moved on.

Could she blame him?

He had been very polite and friendly with Cathy and Rick last night—*she* was the one who had been rude and dismissive towards *him*. In front of the other couple. No wonder Gregorio had been so angry.

She owed him an apology, Lia realised.

'Lia…?'

She narrowed her gaze on the man sitting opposite her. 'Did you ever love me or were you just using me from the start?'

David looked taken aback by her direct attack. 'The niceties are over, I take it?'

'Very much so.' She nodded abruptly. 'So answer the question. Were you using me, and my father's name and wealth, right from the start of our relationship?'

His scowled. 'I only agreed to meet with you today because you said you had some papers you needed to discuss with me.' His eyes narrowed. 'There *are* no papers, are there?'

'No.'

'Damn it.' He swore softly under his breath. 'I have no intention of hashing over ancient history—'

'It's only been a few months, David,' she snorted. 'I would hardly call that ancient *anything*!'

Their conversation stopped briefly while the waitress put their drinks down on the table. Lia shook her head when the young girl asked if they were ready to eat yet. Lia very much doubted they would get as far as eating anything. Just the thought of food made her feel nauseous.

David leaned forward across the table once the two of them were alone again. 'I don't appreciate being spoken to by you in this insulting manner.'

Her eyes narrowed. 'And *I* don't *appreciate* learning that I was going to marry a dissolute gambler!'

David reared back, a look of total shock on his face. 'I have no idea what you're talking about.'

But he did, Lia realised. The truth was there in his guarded expression and in the way his face had paled.

'Let's not play any more games, David,' she scorned. 'Your parents can't possibly know about your gambling, or they would have done something to help you.'

She had always liked the couple she had believed would one day be her in-laws, and knew that Daphne and Alec Richardson would be devastated to learn the truth about their only child.

'Are you threatening me?'

Lia felt a shiver down the length of her spine at the underlying malice in David's tone. It reminded her of something her father had once told her: a cornered animal almost always attacked. The look of rage on David's face said he was getting ready to do just that.

'Not at all,' she assured him smoothly. 'I was merely thinking how disappointed they would be if they knew the sort of man you really are.'

'Stay away from my parents!' David grated.

'I intend to. Oh, I almost forgot.' Lia turned to search through her handbag. 'You might want to give this to the next unsuspecting idiot.' She placed a ring box down on the table in front of him. The engagement ring inside had belonged to his grandmother. 'Or perhaps you could just sell it to pay off more of your gambling debts? But then, you don't need to, do you?' she continued in a hard voice. 'Not when you have the money you stole from my father's company stashed away in an offshore account.'

'You don't… I didn't… You can't possibly know…' David's face was now an ashen grey rather than just white.

'I *do* know. And, yes, you *did* do exactly what I've just accused you of doing. I don't have all the proof as yet, but I will. Believe me, I *will*,' she assured him vehemently.

She would never wish to harm Daphne and Alec deliberately by revealing the truth about their son, but neither could she allow David to get away with having destroyed her father.

'I don't think so,' David sneered as he recovered quickly. 'You're no longer the privileged daughter of the wealthy and powerful Jacob Fairbanks. Now you're just Lia Fairbanks, who has to work for a living. You have all the power and influence of a toothless dog.'

'You—'

'Sorry I'm a little late, Lia.'

Lia had recognised Gregorio's voice the instant he spoke, but that didn't stop her from staring at him as he slid into the seat beside her. Or drawing in a shocked breath as he kissed her lightly on the lips before turning his narrowed gaze on the man seated on the opposite side of the table.

'Richardson.' He nodded tersely.

If Lia was surprised at Gregorio's being there then David had obviously gone into complete shock. So much so he couldn't even answer the other man.

Gregorio turned to Lia, one dark brow raised in innocent query. 'Have you said something to upset your ex-fiancé? What's this?' He picked up the dark blue velvet ring box and flicked the lid open to reveal the two-carat solitaire diamond ring David had given her on their engagement. 'No wonder you gave it back—it isn't right for you at all.' Gregorio snapped the lid closed and put the box back where he had found it. 'I much prefer the natural yellow diamond ring *I* have picked for you.'

The ring Gregorio had picked for *her*?

A natural *yellow* diamond?

Lia had only read about natural yellow diamonds, and seen photographs of them. They were so unique, so rare, that most reputable jewellers claimed they never expected to see one in their lifetime, let alone have the privilege of selling one.

Gregorio reached over and linked his fingers with those of her left hand before lifting it up and kissing her ring finger. 'It's going to look perfect on you.'

'What...? I... You... Are the two of you...?' David at least made an attempt at speech, even if not very successfully.

Talking was still beyond Lia. It was surprise enough that Gregorio had come to the bistro at all, but that he should now be giving David the impression that the two of them were… That they were…

'Yes, we are,' Gregorio stated challengingly. 'Have the two of you ordered yet?' he continued, as if he *hadn't* just rendered the two people seated at the table with him dumb. 'I worked up quite an appetite this morning.'

The look he gave Lia could only be called intimate. Except…

When Lia looked into his eyes she could see the dangerous glitter so at odds with his pleasant tone and demeanour. Gregorio was angry. Coldly, furiously angry.

With her? Because she had met up with David?

Lia was pretty sure that was the reason.

Earlier she had refused to tell Gregorio who she was meeting for lunch, but she'd never had any intention of keeping the identity of that person a secret: how could she when she knew one of Gregorio's men would have followed her when she'd left the hotel earlier? Lia had known that the other man would report back to Gregorio as to *who* she was meeting. She just hadn't expected it to be so soon—or that, knowing she was meeting David, Gregorio would decide to join them.

Or that he would intentionally give David the impression that the two of them were *together*.

What on earth was all that about?

Did Gregorio think David would physically hurt her?

Why else would he have assigned one of his own bodyguards to protect me?

Before today Lia would have dismissed the idea of David ever hurting her as ridiculous. But the dangerous glitter in his eyes a few minutes ago, when he had taken her comment about his parents as a threat, said she would have been wrong.

David was more than capable of hurting her.

And Gregorio was obviously taking no chances.

His protectiveness really was quite... Well, not sweet, because Gregorio was the least *sweet* man Lia knew. But his concern for her definitely gave her a warm and fuzzy feeling inside.

'No, we haven't ordered yet.' She gave him a warm smile. 'I'm not sure David is staying.'

Her ex-fiancé was still staring at Gregorio, and at their linked hands, as if he had seen a ghost. Or his own demise? David must surely realise that with Gregorio beside her—literally—she wasn't the defenceless little nobody he had implied she was earlier.

He gave himself a visible shake before answering her. 'You're right. I have to get back to the office.' He slid to the end of the bench seat.

'Don't forget to take this with you.' Gregorio picked up the ring box, but retained his hold on it as David would have taken it from him. 'Stay away from Lia in future, Richardson.' Gregorio spoke softly, but he was no less threatening because of it. 'If I see you near her again I might not be quite so understanding.'

David's face flushed with annoyance. '*She* was the one who asked for this meeting.'

'Lia always tries to see the good in everyone.' Gregorio nodded. '*I* don't suffer with the same affliction.'

The other man's chin rose defensively at the challenge in Gregorio's tone. 'You don't frighten me.'

'I have no intention of frightening you,' Gregorio said pleasantly as he finally released the ring box. 'But *they* can—and will if I think it necessary.' He gave a nod in the direction of the two men standing outside the restaurant.

Lia had to choke back a laugh as she saw the look of horror on David's face as he looked at the two burly bodyguards. One of them had obviously accompanied her, and Gregorio had brought the second man with him. Both men were at least five inches over six feet in height, with shoulders that looked to be almost as broad.

David didn't say another word, pushing the ring box into his jacket pocket as he turned on his heel and strode out of the bistro. Lia saw him give the two bodyguards a wary glance before he hurried off in the direction of his office building.

Leaving a tense silence behind him.

Lia shot Gregorio a nervous glance from beneath her lashes. She could feel his tension, and see it in the stiff set of his shoulders. His eyes were narrowed, his lips thinned.

She breathed in deeply before speaking. 'I thought—'

'You didn't *think* at all,' Gregorio rasped. 'If you had then you would have known not to arrange to see or speak to Richardson alone.'

'I—'

'You will *not* defy me in this way again, Lia,' he bit out evenly. 'Do you understand me?'

'But—' She broke off as the unfortunate waitress chose that moment to come back and take their order.

'We are not staying,' Gregorio informed her abruptly as he took out his wallet to remove some money, handing it to the waitress as he slid out of the booth and pulled Lia with him.

'Where are we going?' She just had time to grab

her shoulder bag as he marched them both towards the exit.

'Somewhere we can talk privately,' came the grimly determined reply.

Lia didn't like the sound of that.

At all.

CHAPTER EIGHT

'WILL YOU JUST ease up—before I either fall over or you pull my arm out of its socket?' Lia complained as Gregorio continued his march down the street, his fingers firmly around the top of her arm as he pulled her along beside him. Everyone instinctively stepped out of his way, and consequently hers too. They obviously knew from looking at Gregorio's face not to get in his way.

His expression was... Dark and dangerous. That was the only way Lia could think of to describe it. Thunderous brows were lowered over even darker and stormier eyes, his jaw was tight, lips still thinned, his jaw clenched. His whole body language said, *Get out of my way or risk being trampled underfoot.*

An impression no doubt added to by the two men who were six and half feet of pure muscle following just a couple of steps behind them.

'Gregorio—'

'It would be better if you did not speak to me right now,' he bit out, without so much as glancing at her.

'But—'

'*Dios*, do you *ever* do as you are told?' He maintained his hold on her arm as he turned to face her, his eyes glittering darkly as he glowered at her from his superior height. 'Do you have *any* idea what you risked by meeting Richardson alone?'

She did now. 'I wasn't exactly *alone* when one of your men follows me everywhere I go. Besides, David would never—' She broke off with a wince, knowing that the David she had met today was not the man who had wooed and won her. Today he had been that cornered animal. Feral. Likely to strike out and maim or kill without warning.

Gregorio eyed her scornfully. 'Do not try to convince me of something you no longer believe yourself!'

Her cheeks warmed. 'That isn't true—'

'Do you still have feelings for him? Is that it?' Gregorio snapped disgustedly. 'You want to believe he is not involved because you are still in love with him?'

'No!'

Gregorio couldn't miss the vehemence in her denial. 'Then why meet with him at all? Why would you even *do* something like that when I have told you of my suspicions regarding him?'

'Because I needed to know—to see for myself— whether or not David is capable of doing what you suspect he has!' She glared at him.

'And?'

She gave a shiver. 'He's more than capable. In fact I was about to excuse myself from having lunch with him when you arrived and started acting like a caveman.'

Given the circumstances, Gregorio considered his behaviour earlier to have been quite circumspect. What he had really wanted to do was rip David Richardson's head from his shoulders for daring to so much as breathe the same air as Lia.

If Lia thought he had behaved like a caveman when

he'd joined her and Richardson, then she should have seen him when he'd first received Silvio's phone call telling him exactly who she was meeting for lunch.

Gregorio had left the hotel immediately and walked the short distance to the bistro. Seeing Lia sitting cosily in a booth with Richardson had only made him angrier. Overhearing Richardson's scornful comments to her, mocking her social fall and her need to work for a living, had made Gregorio want to slam his fist into the other man's face.

'I consider myself to have been very restrained,' he assured her tightly.

'Is your restraint an excuse for all that nonsense about an engagement ring too?' She eyed him disgustedly.

Gregorio felt warmth staining his cheeks. 'It was my way of letting Richardson know that you aren't alone in the world, no matter what he may think to the contrary.'

'By giving him the impression that I'm now engaged to *you*?'

A nerve pulsed in his jaw. 'It worked, didn't it?'

'And what if he decides to tell someone else about our bogus engagement? Maybe the media?' Lia challenged. 'Did you even think of that?'

Of course Gregorio hadn't thought of that. His only objective had been to protect Lia.

Really?

Was he being honest with himself?

Knowing Lia was with David Richardson had filled him with a blinding rage. Seeing her in the company of the other man, her hair a loose tumble about her shoulders in the way that he liked it, had sent every thought from his head except getting rid of Richardson.

And one word.

Mine.

Lia *was* his—whether she knew it yet or not.

Perhaps it was time that she did.

'Gregorio!' Lia squeaked in protest when he didn't answer her but instead resumed pulling her along the street beside him, his face set in grim lines.

Lia wasn't sure she altogether trusted that expression. And she felt even less reassured when they entered the hotel through the underground car park, where one of the lifts for the penthouse floor was situated. Gregorio scanned his key card to open the doors and pressed the button for the penthouse floor once they were both inside.

Lia could only assume the two bodyguards would either remain downstairs or come up later. Because Gregorio obviously wasn't willing to let them travel in the same lift as them.

Lia could feel the heat and tension radiating from Gregorio now they were together in this small confined space. He didn't so much as look at her—because he was so disgusted with her?—but his harsh expression said he was every inch the arrogant and ruthless Gregorio de la Cruz at this moment.

She ran the tip of her tongue over the dryness of her lips before speaking. 'I believe I owe you an apology for the way I behaved and spoke to you yesterday evening—'

Her words were cut off abruptly as Gregorio pressed her back against one of the mirrored walls, grasping both her wrists in one of his hands before lifting her hands above her head and holding them there as he fiercely claimed her lips with his own.

The length of his body was pressed intimately against Lia's, allowing her to feel how aroused he was. And she was aware of the response of her own body.

She kissed him back with all the pent-up emotions from last night and from this morning, parting her lips to allow Gregorio's tongue to claim the heat of her mouth. Possessively. The victor with his captive. Exactly like that conquistador Lia had once likened him to.

She loved it.

Was she *falling in love* with Gregorio?

It was far too soon for her to know that for sure. Besides, right here and right now she just wanted to kiss and devour him in the same way he was claiming her. To lose herself in the desire that was never far away when the two of them were together.

She pressed even closer against him as she returned heated kiss for heated kiss. Neither of them was even aware of it when the lift doors opened and then closed again—until the lift started to go back down again.

'Dios mio!' Gregorio reluctantly dragged his mouth from Lia's, his forehead resting on hers as he kept her pressed up against the wall. 'You are driving me so crazy we risk being stuck in this lift for the rest of the day.'

Lia laughed softly under her breath. 'I'd much rather we spent our time in a bed!'

Gregorio drew his breath in sharply. 'Me too.'

She smiled teasingly. 'That's it? Just "me too"?'

He grimaced. 'As you said, conversation seems to be our downfall. I do not want to ruin the moment as I obviously did yesterday evening.'

She sobered. 'That was completely my fault. I felt defensive after Cathy and Rick arrived. But I should never have talked to you in that way.' She moistened lips slightly swollen from the force of their kisses. 'You drive me crazy too, Gregorio.'

'I—'

Gregorio turned away as the lift reached the ground floor and the doors opened automatically to reveal a surprised Silvio and Raphael, waiting outside.

Gregorio made no move to separate himself from Lia. 'Could you inform Mr Harrington that Miss Fairbanks will be spending the rest of the day with me in my suite?' he told them, before once again pressing the button for the penthouse floor.

Lia giggled, and buried her face against Gregorio's chest as the lift doors closed and they began their second ascent in as many minutes.

Gregorio had never heard Lia giggle before. It was pleasant. Warming.

An indication that she was happy?

Dios, he hoped so. Because there was no way he was going to be able to let her walk away from him again today.

Lia's confidence faltered slightly as they stepped out of the lift into Gregorio's suite. He was ten years older, and so much more experienced than she was. He'd had dozens of lovers, whereas she'd only had one—and not a very satisfactory one at that.

She had believed sexual compatibility to be of minor importance when she'd been with David. They'd loved each other, mixed in the same social circles, and their families had approved of the match. Her lack of sexual pleasure with David hadn't seemed that important.

What an idiot I was.

A stupid, naïve idiot who, after reaching a climax in

Gregorio's arms while still fully clothed, couldn't wait to experience that sexual release again.

David had always ensured he took his own pleasure, but what if she couldn't satisfy Gregorio? What if—?

'You think too much.' Gregorio reached up and smoothed the frown from her brow. 'First we will take a shower together.'

He clasped her hand in his as they walked down the hallway.

Was Gregorio expecting her to take all her clothes off and get in the shower with him?

Lia had a sick feeling in the pit of her stomach. She had seen photographs of the women Gregorio usually went to bed with, and although she took care of her body she knew she didn't match up to those model-thin, toned-bodied blondes. Despite her weight loss, her breasts were firm and up-tilting, but a little too big for the slenderness of her waist. Her hips were too curvy—

'You are still thinking too much,' Gregorio murmured indulgently, turning to face her as the two of them stood in the middle of the terracotta-tiled bathroom. 'You are very beautiful, Lia.'

He gently claimed her lips with his. Sipping. Tasting. *Claiming.*

Lia was so lost in her rising desire she wasn't even aware of Gregorio removing her jacket, and then unfastening her blouse before dropping it to the floor with her jacket. Or of his unfastening of the zip of her skirt before that too slid down to join her jacket and blouse.

Heat blazed in her cheeks as Gregorio ended their kiss, stepping back, making her painfully aware that she was now wearing only a cream bra and matching panties, along with suspenders and stockings. And for some inexplicable reason she was still wearing her high-heeled shoes!

Lia wondered what Gregorio saw as his hands tightened about hers. His eyes were dark as he looked his fill of her from the top of her head to her ridiculous high-heeled shoes.

'You are every one of my fantasies come to life,' he approved darkly.

Lia somehow doubted that. 'Aren't you a bit over-dressed for taking a shower?' she said lightly, changing the subject.

He released her hands and stepped back and out of his shoes before stretching his arms out at his sides. 'Undress me. No—keep your shoes on,' he added gruffly as she would have stepped out of them.

'Now who's bossy?' she teased.

'Those high heels are *very* sexy.'

The burning in her cheeks seemed to have become a permanent fixture as Lia slipped the jacket from Gregorio's shoulders and down his arms before placing it neatly on the vanity: the suit had probably cost more than Lia was going to earn in a month.

His eyes glittered down at her as she stepped forward to unfasten and remove his tie before undoing the buttons on his shirt.

Lia's breath caught in her throat as she bared his chest, her fingers caressing lightly over that olive-toned flesh as she took off his shirt. His body really was beautiful—as perfect as any sculpture of a Greek god and yet, unlike a statue, warm and firm to the touch.

Her fingers were slightly clumsy as she unfastened the button of his trousers and tugged the zip down. The material slid down his hips and thighs before he stepped out of the trousers altogether, revealing that he wore a pair of black boxers beneath, the bulge of his arousal once again visible against the fitted material.

Forget all the gods: Gregorio was pure perfection.

Wide shoulders, toned pecs and abs, long muscular legs…

Just looking at him made Lia's heart beat faster and louder.

'Take them off.'

Lia's breathing became ragged as she raised her hands to the waistband of Gregorio's boxers, hooking a finger at each hip before slowly pulling the material downwards. Which, considering Gregorio's large and obvious erection, wasn't as easy as it sounded.

She had to ease and stretch the material over that pulsing flesh, before falling down on her knees in front of him as she slowly moved the material downwards and then off completely, along with his socks.

Her gaze returned hungrily to Gregorio's fully engorged and fiercely jutting arousal.

'Lia…!'

She knew what Gregorio wanted, what his husky voice was begging for. Not demanding. *Begging*.

Had Lia fallen to her knees deliberately? For just this purpose?

Absolutely.

She wanted to hear Gregorio's groans of pleasure as she took him into her mouth. To taste and lick him. To suck him.

Just thinking of that, and of how the two of them must look right now—Gregorio completely naked and fully aroused, her wearing only bra, panties and stockings— caused her own level of desire to increase achingly.

Gregorio drew his breath in sharply, his knees almost buckling as he watched Lia's fingers encircle him. She slowly licked her parted lips before bending forward to take him into the heat of her mouth.

His hands moved, his fingers grasping her bared shoulders as her other hand cupped him beneath his arousal. At the same time she took him deeper into the heat of her mouth. She pulled back again—slowly, firmly—her tongue a hot rasp over the sensitive tip, her cheeks hollowed as she sucked.

Gregorio thought the top of his head was going to explode as Lia set a tortuous rhythm. Taking all of him, deeply. Followed by the slow and tormenting drag of withdrawal. The continuous hot stroke of her tongue on his sensitised flesh. The rhythmic squeeze of her hands.

And all the while she looked so damned sexy in her bra, panties and stockings, her hair a wild tumble of auburn, gold and cinnamon about her shoulders, Gregorio couldn't take his eyes off her.

He could feel the heat of his release building, every muscle in his body straining as he fought for control of that release. The pleasure was too much...too much—

'No...!' He pushed her away from him, fingers digging into the soft flesh of her shoulders when she looked up at him with sensual dark eyes. 'Lia...' He pulled her up to her feet, his arms going about her waist as he drew her in tightly against him. 'That was incredible.'

Oral sex had been a definite no-no with David, so this was the first time Lia had ever...

Having no interest in exploring the boundaries of their sexual relationship was surely another sign that David had just been using her.

What an idiot she had been!

'I liked it too,' Lia acknowledged huskily.

'I do not want it to be over too soon.'

Gregorio gave one of those sensual smiles that transformed his face from austere to breathtaking.

'My turn,' he murmured with satisfaction, and he reached behind her and unfastened her bra before removing it completely. *'Dios!'* He spoke almost reverently as his gaze feasted on her pertly bared breasts. 'I love these...' His hands cupped beneath her breasts as he lowered his head to suckle each engorged nipple in turn.

Lia groaned, clinging to Gregorio's shoulders as she was engulfed in pleasure, heat instantly spreading to her core.

'I want to taste you...'

Gregorio straightened before lifting her up in his arms and carrying her out of the bathroom and down the hallway to his bedroom. He lay her down carefully on the bed, kneeling beside her to hook his thumbs in her panties, pulling them slowly down over her hips and thighs and then off completely, leaving Lia dressed only in the suspenders and stockings.

His eyes darkened as he looked at her. 'You are the sexiest woman—'

'You've seen today?' she teased, sure that Gregorio had been with women a lot sexier than her.

He tilted his head as he studied her. 'Why do you do that? Is it your way of pushing me away?'

She gave a splutter of laughter at the ridiculousness of that statement when they were both naked. 'Do I *look* as if I'm pushing you away?'

Gregorio didn't return her smile. 'We both have

pasts, Lia. I can no more take mine away than you can. But there is just the two of us here. Now. Together.' He lay down on the bed beside her, his hand cupping her cheek as he turned her face towards him. 'Beauty is in the eye of the beholder, Lia, and you are the most beautiful woman it has been my privilege to make love to.'

Her cheeks heated, although at the same time she still felt sceptical. 'I think we're both agreed that it's best if we don't talk.'

'Because you do not believe me?'

'Gregorio—'

'It is okay.' His thumb caressed her full bottom lip. 'I have every intention of showing you how beautiful you are to me.'

And if that was Gregorio's intention then that was exactly what he did as he made love to her tenderly, appreciatively, *savagely*. Squeezing and caressing her breasts as he drove her wild with his lips and tongue, driving Lia over the edge of release time and time again. Until she was so sensitised that his lightest touch inflamed her senses and she crashed into another orgasm.

And still she hungered for more. More of Gregorio's lovemaking. More of *him*.

'I need to be inside you *now*,' he finally rasped, his hair tousled from where Lia had grabbed hold of its darkness at the height of her pleasure.

'Please…' She arched up, needing to be filled, needing to have Gregorio inside her as much as he wanted to be there.

Lia's unease returned during the time it took him to open the foil packet he had taken from the bedside drawer and roll the condom on with an expertise that indicated he had done it many times before.

Gregorio frowned slightly, obviously seeing the uncertainty flickering across Lia's face. 'I realise this is not in the least romantic, but it is my responsibility to protect you.'

There was no arguing with that comment. None that made any sense in the circumstances, anyway.

And Lia totally forgot about that moment of unease as Gregorio knelt between her thighs and slowly, erotically, eased himself into her. Stretching her, filling her, as if they were two parts of a whole, finally joined together.

'That feels so good,' Gregorio groaned as he lay down on top of her, taking his weight on his elbows and claiming her mouth with his as he slowly began to thrust inside her. '*You* feel so good, Lia.'

Lia groaned as Gregorio's movement sent off tiny explosions inside her, wrapping her legs about his waist and pulling him in deeper still. Their breathing became loud and ragged and those thrusts became less co-ordinated as the pleasure built, higher and higher.

Gregorio broke the kiss to groan, his body tense. 'Come with me, *bella*. Now!' he rasped, and he began to pulse inside her, taking Lia with him in an orgasm so strong and intense she screamed out her pleasure.

CHAPTER NINE

'LUNCH HAS ARRIVED.'

Lunch? A glance at her wristwatch told her it was almost five o'clock in the afternoon, and Lia didn't want to move out of the warm comfort of the bed where she and Gregorio had spent the whole afternoon making love. They had left the bed only once, to take the shower they had forgone earlier. Gregorio had made love to her again against the shower wall once they had soaped, washed and caressed each other all over. The third time had been just a few minutes ago.

Every part of Lia ached, but it was a pleasurable ache. An ache that came from knowing Gregorio's possession so intimately, so many times in such a short time.

Which was surprising, because Lia hadn't thought a man could recover sexually so quickly. David certainly hadn't…

'Whatever you are thinking about has put a frown on your brow,' Gregorio reproved as he crossed the room to stand beside the bed, wearing a towel knotted loosely around his hips.

Probably so that he could open the door when Room Service delivered their late lunch, Lia realised.

'It was nothing of any importance.' And it wasn't. None of it. David. Their less than satisfying relationship. Their broken engagement. *My lucky escape*—that seemed more appropriate. 'I'm too comfortable to get out of bed.' She gave Gregorio a satiated smile.

His smile was indulgent. 'Would you like me to bring the food to you in here?'

'That sounds like an excellent idea.' Lia tucked the sheet about her breasts as she sat up against the pillows.

Gregorio sat on the bed beside her. 'You are very beautiful to me, Lia.' His fingertips ran lightly down one of her flushed cheeks.

Lia believed him this time. How could she not after the exquisite way Gregorio had made love to her for hours? After he had *shown her* time and time again how *beautiful she was to him*.

So why was he now the one frowning?

'I want you to promise me you will not see Richardson alone again.'

Ah.

Gregorio's eyes narrowed. 'Why are you looking at me like that?'

'Probably because I'm wondering if this is the reason you've made love to me all afternoon.' She eyed him suspiciously. 'To distract me, and also so I'd be more amenable to whatever you ask of me.'

He stood up abruptly. 'You have never for a single moment been *amenable*, Lia,' he bit out impatiently. *'Dios mio.'* He ran a hand through his already tousled dark hair. 'Is that what you think of me?' He glared down at her. 'That I would use sex to manipulate you?'

Exactly. *Sex.*

She had been making love…*falling in love*…while

Gregorio had been *having sex*. Very good sex, but none-theless it was just sex.

Lia wondered why some women—herself included, apparently—had to pretty it up by calling it 'making love'. Maybe because that was exactly what it did—it prettied up what was basically a primal sexual urge. There was a much more crude word Lia could have used to describe it, but she was too much of a lady to use it.

Gregorio scowled his impatience at Lia's lack of a reply. 'I do not remember having to force you into doing anything this afternoon.'

On the contrary, after her initial shyness Lia had proved to be a very adventurous lover. Satisfyingly so.

So why were the two of them arguing again?

Because their conversations *always*—usually sooner rather than later—became an argument. One of them would take umbrage at something the other had said, and a disagreement would ensue.

'I think I should leave.' Lia avoided his gaze, keeping the sheet wrapped about her breasts as she moved to swing her legs out onto the carpeted floor on the other side of the bed.

'Is this how you usually behave?' Gregorio snapped in frustration. 'You run away whenever you are con-fronted with a situation you cannot control?'

Her eyes flashed as she turned to glare at him. 'I don't have control over a single part of my life right now. Including this part, it seems,' she added vehemently, standing up and taking the sheet with her. 'I no longer *think* I should leave—I *am* leaving.'

She kept the sheet wrapped around her as she marched over to the door.

'Lia!'

She turned in the doorway. 'Let me go, Gregorio.' Tears glistened in her eyes.

Gregorio's shoulders dropped in defeat. He knew he had no desire to force Lia into doing anything. 'As long as you agree not to see Richardson again on your own. My investigation into his lifestyle, and the money missing from your father's company, is still ongoing.'

And Lia's interference would not only put that investigation in jeopardy but also Lia herself.

'You really believe he did it?'

'I do, yes.'

'And that caused my father's heart attack?'

'Yes.'

'Very well.' She nodded. 'But you'll keep me informed?'

'I will,' he conceded tautly. 'Now I insist you allow Silvio to accompany you home and remain outside your apartment building.' After what she had revealed during her conversation with Richardson earlier today, he believed it was now even more necessary that Lia be protected.

She breathed deeply as she obviously fought a battle within herself. 'Do you really think David would hurt me?'

Gregorio's mouth tightened. 'I believe that today you challenged and cornered a man who does not like to be thwarted in any way. By meeting him, saying the things you did, you have now made Richardson aware of some of your suspicions regarding him—if not all of them. It is never a good idea to allow the enemy to know what you are thinking or feeling.'

Lia eyed him quizzically. 'Is that how you've become so successful? By treating everyone else as the enemy?'

He breathed in deeply. 'You are angry with me and deliberately twisting my words.'

Lia was angry with herself—not Gregorio. After all that had happened these past few months she had still allowed herself to be a naïve romantic where Gregorio was concerned. She was twenty-five years old, and had already been used and manipulated by one man for his own selfish purposes. It was time she stopped romanticising and accepted that she and Gregorio had simply spent a pleasurable afternoon in bed together.

And now the afternoon was over.

She forced the tension from her shoulders and half smiled. 'Let's not part as bad friends, hmm, Gregorio?'

Gregorio's eyes narrowed. Friends? Lia believed the two of them to be merely *friends*? After the afternoon they had just spent together?

'Will we be friends with benefits?' he mocked harshly.

'No.' She kept her gaze downcast. 'What happened this afternoon will not happen again.'

'You truly believe that?' he scorned. The sexual tension between them crackled and burned even now. When they were arguing or when they weren't.

She raised her chin as she looked at him, her gaze clear and unwavering. 'It's time I took charge of my own life, Gregorio,' she stated flatly. 'And that includes who I go to bed with.'

'And it will not be me?'

'No.'

Gregorio nodded abruptly. 'Silvio will be waiting downstairs to accompany you when you are ready to leave.'

'Thank you.' Lia disappeared into the hallway, and

there followed the sound of the bathroom door closing seconds later.

Gregorio made his call to Silvio and then turned to stare out of the window at the London skyline, his reflection showing him his expression was grim. This afternoon with Lia had been a revelation. She was correct in her belief that in the past twenty years he had bedded many woman. So many he had forgotten some of their names.

He would never forget Lia's name.

Would never forget Lia.

She was unforgettable.

Not because she was the most beautiful woman he had ever seen. Which she was.

Nor because she was the best lover. Which she was.

No, he would never forget her because she was Lia.

Fiery of temperament. Passionate of nature.

Lia.

'What happened to you yesterday—? Careful,' Cathy warned as Lia's hand jerked so suddenly she almost tipped her glass of water all over the table. The two women had met up at the gym after work, and were now enjoying a relaxing cold drink together in the bar there. 'I expected you to telephone last night, but now I really want to know what happened yesterday.'

The other woman eyed Lia knowingly.

'Which part?' Lia couldn't quite meet her friend's gaze.

She had gone to bed early last night—had pulled the covers over her head and slept for almost twelve hours. Today she was back working behind the reception desk at the Exemplar Hotel, so obviously Gregorio's PA had recovered enough to come in today. Or maybe not? Maybe Gregorio was doing the same as Lia? Trying to ignore her existence as she was trying to ignore his. She certainly hadn't seen anything of him in the hotel today.

'The part that's making you blush,' Cathy said with relish.

Lia winced. 'I'd rather not.'

'At least tell me if it involves Gregorio de la Cruz?'

She sighed. 'It does.'

'Wow!' Cathy had a dreamy expression on her face. 'I love Rick to bits, but being married doesn't make me blind and Gregorio is something else.'

Yes, he was. But quite what that something else was Lia had no idea.

She knew she hadn't been able to stop thinking about him since she'd left his apartment late yesterday afternoon. Since she had made… Well, it hadn't quite been the walk of shame, because it hadn't mattered that the clothes she was wearing were the same ones she had worn to work that morning. But it had certainly been an embarrassing exit from the hotel after Lia had collected her coat from the staffroom. Made more so by the fact that the other receptionists had cheerfully wished her goodnight before she left—just as if it had been a normal working day at the Exemplar Hotel.

There had been nothing *normal* about yesterday as far as Lia was concerned.

The pleasurable aches and pains in her body when she'd woken up that morning had seemed to agree with that sentiment. Which was why she had suggested meeting up with Cathy at the gym after work. The two women had been using different apparatus since they'd arrived, so sitting in the adjoining bar, sipping iced water, was the first opportunity they had found actually to chat.

'I can see by the smile on your face that he's every bit as satisfying as I thought he might be.'

'Cathy!' Lia's cheeks were ablaze with revealing colour.

'Lia!' she came back teasingly. 'You never had that cat-that-got-the-cream expression on your face after spending the night with David.'

Lia sobered at the mention of her ex-fiancé. 'I saw David yesterday too.'

'What?' Cathy sat forward. 'When? Why?'

She sighed heavily. 'Gregorio told me some things about him and I wanted to know if they were true.'

'And were they?'

'Yes.' Lia had no doubt now that Gregorio's suspicions about David would prove to be correct. Or that he was right to be cautious about to what David might do once Gregorio had evidence against him.

'More secrets?' Cathy eyed her sympathetically.

Lia blinked back the tears that never seemed to be far away nowadays. 'Gregorio thinks David is responsible for my father's financial problems and subsequent heart attack. I'm inclined to agree with him.'

'Oh, Lia.' Cathy placed her hand over Lia's and gave it a squeeze. 'I'm so sorry.'

'But not surprised?' Lia quirked a rueful brow.

'Not really, no,' her friend acknowledged with a pained wince.

Lia laughed softly. 'You really will have to be more honest with me in future regarding the men I date!'

'Gregorio has my full approval,' Cathy supplied instantly.

He had Lia's full approval too. But that didn't change the fact that she was just another sexual conquest to him. Unfortunately she had to accept that her emotions didn't function in the same compartmentalised way as his. She already cared more for Gregorio than she should, and she didn't need to have her heart broken for a second time in a matter of months.

Had David's desertion broken her heart?

If Lia was honest, the answer was no. It had hurt that he had ended their engagement so abruptly after her father's death, but she hadn't been heartbroken in the way she would be if she allowed her emotions to become fully engaged where Gregorio was concerned.

If they weren't already...

'I was wondering when you were going to arrive home.'

Lia stiffened as she stepped out of the lift and saw David standing in the hallway, directly outside her apartment. 'How did you get in here?'

There was no reception at this small apartment complex, but it did have a key-coded panel outside the front door, and a security number that had to be logged in before the door could be opened.

She had also left Raphael, her protector for the day, sitting outside in his SUV on the other side of that locked door.

David gave an unconcerned shrug. 'I told one of the other tenants I was a new neighbour and I'd forgotten the door code. She was only too happy to let me inside.'

Lia was pretty sure there had been a lot of David's false charm involved in that conversation. Although she really would have to introduce herself properly to the other tenants, so that they knew exactly who their new neighbour was in future. They also needed to be more cautious about letting unknown people into the building.

In the meantime, she had to deal with David's unwanted presence. 'How did you find out where I'm living now?' she demanded as she walked down the hallway.

He shrugged. 'It wasn't that difficult. A friend of a friend who works for the telephone company.'

Lia eyed him warily. 'Why are you here?' He was dressed casually, in an open-necked pale blue polo shirt and designer label jeans, so he had obviously been home and changed after work before coming here.

He gave her one of his most charming smiles. 'I felt we parted badly yesterday, and I wanted to put things right between us.'

'Really?' She quirked a sceptical brow.

'Yes, really.'

The smile stayed firmly in place, but Lia knew David well enough to realise it hadn't reached his eyes.

'You said some unsettling things to me yesterday, and I wanted to set the record straight.'

Lia thought saying *really* again might be a little too much. 'That's no longer necessary,' she said.

He tensed. 'Oh?'

'I think we both know the truth, David. Which means we have nothing more to say to each other.'

'You aren't being very friendly.'

She snorted. 'Do I have reason to be?'

'We were engaged…'

'*Were engaged* being the appropriate phrase.'

'Look, I know I let you down when you needed me to be strong for you. I made a mistake, okay?' His smile became ingratiating. 'I obviously don't handle sudden death well—'

'I will *not* discuss my father with you,' Lia snapped. *'Ever,'* she added vehemently. 'Now, I would like you to leave.'

'I just want to talk to you, Lia,' he cajoled. 'I've missed you.'

'Oh, please!' She glared her disgust. 'I realise now how completely naïve I was until a few months ago. Maybe I was just too busy being "the privileged daughter of the wealthy and powerful Jacob Fairbanks",' she said, repeating his insult of yesterday. 'If I hadn't been then perhaps I would have seen through you much sooner.'

'This isn't like you, Lia…'

David had returned to the condescending voice that was really starting to grate on Lia.

'You don't talk like this. I can only conclude that it's the influence of de la Cruz.' He gave a shake of his head. 'What on earth are you doing with a man like that anyway? He's a womaniser—and a corporate shark of the worst kind.'

'He's a more honourable man than you'll *ever* be!'

Lia knew that was the truth. In all his dealings with her Gregorio had been nothing but honest. Even when the two of them had spent the afternoon in bed together Gregorio hadn't made any false declarations or promises—before or after.

'Now, I really want you to leave, David.' She searched agitatedly through her shoulder bag for her door key.

'What if I don't want to?'

Lia looked up sharply, butterflies fluttering in her stomach as she realised that David had moved and was now standing much too close to her in the hallway. Uncomfortably so. There was no charm nor an ingratiating smile on his face now.

'One of Gregorio's men is sitting in his car outside this building,' she challenged tensely.

David raised is brows. 'He has men watching you?'

'Protecting me, yes.'

'Protecting you from whom? *Me?*' David questioned when Lia gave him a pointed glance. 'You never used to be paranoid, Lia,' he scorned.

'I never *used to be* a lot of things that I am now.'

'So I've noticed. And not all of those changes are for the better,' David assured her. 'But de la Cruz and his men aren't here. There's just the two of us.'

Lia was aware of that. Very much so. And she didn't like it one little bit. Didn't trust or like *David* one little bit.

'I said I want you to leave,' she repeated through gritted teeth.

'Wouldn't you like to know what *really* happened the night your father died?'

'What?' Lia gasped as she stared at him with wide eyes.

David returned her gaze challengingly. 'I said—'

'I heard you,' she dismissed agitatedly. 'What I want is an explanation of what you meant.'

He shrugged. 'I was with your father when he died.'

'I… But… There was never any mention…' She gave a shake of her head. 'I was the one to find him—slumped over his desk in the morning.'

'Our meeting was lawyer/client confidential.' David shrugged. 'When he suddenly collapsed… Well, as I said, I don't handle sudden death well.'

'He had a heart attack in front of you and you just left him there to die?' Lia reached out to place her palm on the wall for support as she felt herself sway.

'He died almost instantly.' David's mouth was tight. 'There was nothing anyone could have done.'

'You don't know that!' Lia stared at him incredulously. 'You all but *killed* him!'

'Your father died of a heart attack,' he maintained evenly.

'But heart attacks are usually brought on by stress or shock. Did you do or say something to cause his heart attack?' Lia was having difficulty keeping down the waves of nausea churning in her stomach.

'Invite me in and I'll tell you exactly what happened.'

Lia didn't like the smug expression on David's face. Smugness caused by the fact that he knew she would want to know exactly what had happened the night her father died. That she *needed* to know.

But to do that David had said she must invite him in to her apartment.

Did she dare to be alone with him in there?

CHAPTER TEN

GREGORIO TRULY BELIEVED what he had told Lia: a man could no longer call himself a man if he ever raised his hand in anger to a woman. But right now he was very angry. With a red-hot, blinding anger.

Which meant he would have to punch a wall or something to alleviate his tension before seeing Lia. Or he could just punch David Richardson in his too-handsome face and kill two birds with one stone—or one punch.

But for now Gregorio had to concentrate on driving to Lia's apartment so that he arrived in one piece.

He had deliberately avoided the reception area of the hotel today. Had avoided Lia. She had made it clear yesterday that she didn't want to continue seeing him.

That was about to change—whether Lia liked it or not.

Raphael had telephoned him just fifteen minutes ago to report that as a routine precaution he had checked all the numberplates and owners of the cars parked in the street where Lia's apartment was located. He had found Richardson's sports car parked at the other end of the street, neatly—deliberately?—hidden between two SUVs.

Gregorio had left his hotel suite in such a hurry he

had still been talking to Raphael on his cell phone when he'd stepped into the lift and impatiently punched the button for the basement car park.

If Lia had invited Richardson to her apartment, against all Gregorio's advice for her to stay away from the man…

The thought had Gregorio pressing his foot down hard on the accelerator, his expression grim.

'I'm still waiting,' Lia challenged as David stood unmoving and silent in the sitting room of her apartment.

A mocking smile tilted his lips. 'This place is a bit of a come-down for you, isn't it?'

Her gaze remained fixed on him. 'I like it.'

And she did. The apartment was compact and easy to keep clean. It was also her first very own space. She had enjoyed living with her father, but there had been a formality to it, with meals served at set times and an army of staff to cook for them and clean the house. And consequently very little privacy. Here she could do exactly as she pleased, when she pleased—including eating what and when she wanted. In the nude if she so chose.

'If you say so,' David derided sceptically.

'Well?' Lia's impatience deepened.

'Aren't you going to offer me a coffee or something?' He made himself comfortable on the sofa.

'No.'

He chuckled. 'I think I like this new, outspoken Lia after all. *Very* sexy.' His gaze ran slowly over her, from her head to her toes and back again.

Her hands clenched at her sides. 'Will you just tell me what happened the night my father died?'

David's expression became guarded. 'He invited me over. We talked. He had a heart attack. I left.'

Anger welled up, strong and unstoppable. 'You already told me that much in the hallway.'

Had her father *known* David was responsible for the missing money? Had he confronted the other man and then David had simply let her father die when he collapsed?

Why hadn't her father confided in *her*?

The answer came to Lia so suddenly and with such force she almost bent over from the pain.

David had been her fiancé. The man her father had believed she loved and intended to marry. At the time she had believed that too. She had no doubt her father had loved her enough to want to protect her from knowing the truth about her future husband.

'My father confronted you about the embezzlement of Fairbanks Industries funds.' It wasn't a question but a statement.

David's mouth twisted derisively. 'He said that if I returned the money then no one else needed to know what I'd done.'

'But you no longer have the money, do you?'

'Not all of it, no.'

'Because you're addicted to gambling.' Lia looked at him with disgust.

'I'm not addicted!' There was an ugly expression on David's face. 'I just enjoy the thrill…the excitement.'

Addiction.

'Can't you see how it's ruining your life?' Lia frowned. 'How it's turned you into a man who steals from his clients to feed his addiction?'

'You sound just like your father,' David scorned.

'He said if I returned the money no one else need ever know about it and the two of us could live happily ever after. He withdrew from the de la Cruz negotiations to give me time to make the adjustments.'

Which proved Gregorio had been telling the truth when he'd told Lia her father had been the one to withdraw from the negotiations with De la Cruz Industries, even though the sale of the company would have saved her father and the people who worked for him.

Because he had hoped to resolve the situation of David's embezzlement from the company without anyone being any the wiser. Certainly without Lia knowing what David had done.

My father confronted David alone that evening for the same reason—because he wanted to avoid hurting me.

And David—thief, liar and manipulator that he undoubtedly was—had no doubt used her in the same way to try and blackmail her father into silence. The strain had finally proved too much for her father and he'd had a heart attack.

Lia hadn't been in her father's study that evening, nor had she heard any of the conversation between the two men, but she knew with certainty that that was exactly what had happened.

'Get out,' she told David coldly.

His brows rose. 'We haven't finished talking yet.'

'Oh, we've finished,' Lia assured him evenly. 'We're *way* beyond finished,' she added vehemently. 'My father acted the way he did out of love for me, and now I'm going to do exactly the same out of my love for him. I am going to ruin you, David, as you ruined and eventually killed my father. I'll expose you for the cheat and a liar you really are— Take your hand off me!' she protested as David stood and moved across the room so quickly she was unable to avoid his painful grasp about her wrist.

Instead of releasing her David twisted her arm and held it at a painful level against her back, stepping behind her and bringing himself nauseatingly close to her.

'I don't think so,' he murmured viciously as he bent his head close to her ear. 'Why don't you just agree to be a good girl, hmm? Otherwise...'

'Otherwise?' she echoed sharply.

He shrugged. 'Well, you're grieving for your father... Not adapting well to your change of circumstances. People would understand if you were to take a bottle of pills and just fall asleep...'

'You're insane!' Lia truly believed it at that moment: no man in his right mind would threaten to kill her so cold-bloodedly.

'Desperate,' David corrected grimly. 'And you should know better than to threaten a desperate man, Lia.'

Gregorio had tried to warn her. *Had* warned her. Lia just hadn't listened.

Gregorio...

'You would never get away with killing me,' she warned him as she struggled and failed to release herself from David's painful grip. 'Gregorio would know I hadn't killed myself, and he would hound you until he caught you.'

'Wouldn't change the fact you were dead,' David reasoned.

There was no arguing with that logic.

Lia let out a scream as David suddenly twisted her

arm so viciously she thought she was going to pass out from the pain.

'Stop fighting me and I'll stop hurting you,' he ground out harshly.

Lia ceased her struggles. She slumped weakly forward the moment David reduced that painful pressure.

Gregorio tensed in the hallway when he heard Lia scream inside the apartment, not hesitating for so much as a second before he raised his booted foot and kicked the apartment door open.

He stepped through the flying wood splinters from where the lock had been detached from the doorframe and carried on down the hallway, his eyes narrowing as he took in the scene in front of him.

David Richardson stood behind Lia, one of his arms about her waist as he held her against him, his face buried in her hair, his lips against her throat.

Had Gregorio imagined that scream?

Or perhaps the reason for it…?

He knew from personal experience that Lia was a passionate lover. She was also a noisy one. She had screamed several times when they were in bed together yesterday afternoon. Usually when she had an orgasm…

Richardson and Lia were both still fully dressed. But, again, that was no guarantee that Lia's scream hadn't been a pleasurable one: she'd still been wearing all her clothes the first time she'd had an orgasm in his arms. Had he interrupted Richardson while he was pleasuring Lia?

Gregorio returned his narrowed gaze to Lia's face. The wide and startled eyes. The pale cheeks. The trembling lips.

The pale cheeks...

Lia's face was always flushed with pleasure when she orgasmed with him. Her eyes would glow. Her lips would be a deep rose colour.

He took in her body language, noting her tension and the fact that one of her arms was behind her back. Held there by Richardson.

Gregorio's jaw tensed. 'Let her go, Richardson.'

The other man's gaze was insolent as he looked at Gregorio over Lia's shoulder. 'She likes it here. Don't you?' he prompted Lia confidently as his arm tightened about her waist.

'I—' Lia broke off with an indrawn hiss as David gave her arm another painful twist.

She had been completely shocked when the door to her apartment had been kicked or shouldered open— so savagely the lock had come out of the doorframe, wood splintering everywhere, the door itself crashing into the wall behind.

And she had never been more pleased to see Gregorio as he stepped through that ruined doorway, looking for all the world like a dark avenging angel in a black T-shirt, black jeans and heavy black boots, the darkness of hair tousled into disarray.

She had no idea what he was doing here after the way they had parted yesterday—she was just grateful that he *was* there.

At least she would be if David hadn't given her arm that warning and very painful twist.

It was a threat that he intended to hurt her more than he already was if she attempted to alert Gregorio to the fact she was being held against her will.

To hell with that!

'He has my arm twisted behind my back—'

Lia broke off with an agonised yelp of pain as David jerked her arm up even further, the movement accompanied by a snapping sound.

Pain such as Lia had never known before radiated from her arm to the rest of her body. Black spots danced on the edge of her vision as she was thrust forward towards Gregorio, and then the blackness became all-consuming…

'Gently,' Gregorio warned softly as Raphael lifted a still unconscious Lia into his waiting arms where he sat in the back of the SUV.

The other man closed the door and got in behind the wheel to drive them to the hospital.

It was probably as well Lia was still unconscious, because Gregorio had no doubt that her arm was broken. He had heard the distinctive sound of bone cracking as Richardson had pushed her towards him.

Gregorio's arms had moved up and caught her instinctively. All of his attention had been centred on Lia as she'd fainted in his arms—probably from the added pain he had caused by catching her as she fell.

By the time Gregorio had lifted and cradled Lia carefully in his arms, and then looked around, Richardson had gone.

Gregorio had wasted precious more seconds placing Lia gently down on the sofa, before taking out his cell phone and calling down to Raphael. The bodyguard had reported that Richardson had left the building and already driven away. Not Raphael's fault: he couldn't possibly have known that Richardson was fleeing the building rather than just leaving because Gregorio had arrived.

It didn't matter. Gregorio would find Richardson—wherever he ran to. There wasn't a place on this earth where the other man would be safe from Gregorio's wrath for his having dared to physically harm Lia.

In the meantime they had to get Lia to hospital as quickly as possible. Her broken arm needed to be reset and immobilised.

And Gregorio knew her well enough to know she was going to be one seriously angry Lia when she regained consciousness.

The voices were fading in and out of Lia's consciousness, and the pain in her arm was making it impossible for her to make any sense of what was being said.

But she did recognise the three voices speaking. Cathy. Rick. And Gregorio.

Memory came rushing back to her.

David waiting for her outside her apartment... His threats...

Gregorio's unexpected and physically violent arrival...

The snapping sound in her arm as David had pushed her away from him.

The pain.

Blackness.

And then the pain again, when she'd woken up in what she presumed was the A&E department at the local hospital, having her arm X-rayed. Despite the painkillers she had been given, she had passed out again when they'd reset the broken bone.

And throughout all that Gregorio had been at her

side. Not speaking. Just *there*. His face had been set in grimly austere lines. The only words he'd spoken had been to the doctor as the other man had reset her arm. Before she'd blacked out again.

She had no idea when Cathy and Rick had arrived, but she realised Gregorio must have called them. There was no other way they could have known she was at the hospital.

Talking of which…

She opened her eyes to look at the three people sitting beside the gurney she was lying on, obviously all waiting for her to wake up. She seemed to be in some sort of curtained-off area—probably still in A&E. The cast felt like a heavy weight on her left arm.

'At last the lady awakens.' Cathy beamed her pleasure.

'Thank goodness.' Rick heaved a sigh of relief. 'You had us worried for a while there, Lia.'

Only Gregorio remained silent, and a quick glance in his direction showed her that his expression was as grim as it had been earlier, his eyes a glittering black.

Lia turned away to moisten her lips before speaking. 'Can I go home now?'

'Of course.'

'Yes.'

'No!'

She winced as all three of them answered her at once. 'Conflicting answers there, guys.'

'You *can* go home…' Cathy shot Gregorio a puzzled glance—his had been the negative answer.

'But you aren't going to.' He spoke up firmly. 'Not to your own apartment, anyway.' He stood up restlessly and began to pace the confined area behind the curtains.

'I have arranged for the lock to be repaired, but Richardson is still out there somewhere,' he added grimly.

A nerve pulsed in Lia cheek before she spoke quietly. 'He was threatening to kill me and make it look like suicide before you arrived,' she told Gregorio.

'God, no...' Cathy gasped.

'Bastard!' Rick muttered furiously.

Lia moistened the dryness of her lips. 'I don't think he would have done it— Okay, maybe he would,' she conceded heavily when Cathy gave a sceptical snort.

The murderous rage Gregorio had been holding in check for the past two hours threatened to overflow like molten lava from the top of a volcano.

If he could have got hold of Richardson during the past two hours...!

He had debated long and hard as to whether or not to call the police immediately in regard to Richardson's attack on Lia. He had finally decided not to do so—not this evening, at least. He would call the police once he had Lia safe. They would add assault to the rest of the charges he was going to ask the police to bring against David Richardson once they caught him.

Raphael and Silvio were out looking for the other man now, but they had already reported back that Richardson wasn't at his apartment or his parents' house. Considering the amount of money the other man had embezzled from Fairbanks Industries, there was every possibility he had decided to leave the country. Richardson had to know that, having hurt Lia in front of Gregorio, he would now be being hunted.

Gregorio had no intention of stopping that search until he had found the other man and eliminated any further danger to Lia.

'You will stay at the hotel with me,' he stated. He couldn't concentrate his attention on the search for Richardson without knowing that Lia was completely safe.

'Oh, I'm sure there's no need—'

'We'd be more than happy—'

'There will be no discussion on the subject. Lia is coming back to the hotel with me.' Gregorio spoke over the protests of both Lia and Cathy. 'She will be safer there,' he said more gently to Cathy.

Lia inwardly questioned whether she *would* be safer at the hotel.

With Gregorio.

Alone with him day and night in that sumptuous hotel suite.

Not that she was in any condition for a seduction, and nor had Gregorio shown any signs of wanting to seduce her, but even so…

She wasn't comfortable with the idea of staying with him.

'You and Rick both have jobs to go to.' Gregorio continued to talk to Cathy in that soothing tone. 'I can work from my hotel suite, and very often do. Lia will not be left alone at any time until Richardson has been apprehended.'

Oh, great—now she was going to have a babysitter—no doubt Silvio or Raphael—whenever Gregorio had to go out.

'I'd really rather not—'

'The matter is settled,' Gregorio rasped, and those glittering black eyes were challenging as he looked at her.

When Gregorio announced that a matter was settled

it was well and truly settled, Lia acknowledged a few minutes later as she sat beside him in the back of the SUV while Silvio drove them back to the hotel.

She couldn't deny there was a certain logic to her staying with Gregorio. David was obviously more dangerous than she had realised, and she didn't doubt his threat to kill her had been very real. The penthouse floor of the Exemplar Hotel was completely private to Gregorio, and he already had his own security team in place.

Besides, she accepted that going back to her apartment was a bad idea. Even though Gregorio had already had the lock and the door repaired, she didn't trust David any more.

She certainly didn't want to put Cathy and Rick in any danger by accepting their offer to stay with them.

Lia had never thought she would say it—even think it—but Gregorio's hotel suite *was* the safest place for her to stay right now.

CHAPTER ELEVEN

'YOU ARE GOING to need help undressing, and I will put something waterproof over the cast on your arm before you have a shower,' Gregorio informed her evenly as he unpacked the bag of Lia's clothes and toiletries that Cathy and Rick had just collected and brought over from Lia's apartment.

Lia gave a grimace as she sat on the side of the bed in what had turned out to be one of six spare bedrooms in Gregorio's suite. Not that she had expected to be invited to share Gregorio's bedroom, but this impersonal guest room told her exactly the place she occupied in his life.

She really hadn't thought things through enough when she had accepted that Gregorio's suite was the safest and best place for her to be right now. She hadn't thought about where she would actually sleep. Nor taken into account the mechanics of not being able to move her right arm properly, or the fact that she was going to be encumbered with a heavy plaster cast for the next six weeks, and a sling for two of them.

Which meant she couldn't undress herself without assistance, and showering was going to be a big problem. She would probably need to have her food cut up into tiny pieces too, so she could eat with one hand.

But right now her thoughts sounded like those of a whiny, ungrateful brat. 'I'll take a bath instead of a shower,' she announced brightly. 'And I'm sure I'll be able to take my own clothes off.'

She knew the strong painkillers she had been given at the hospital were preventing her from feeling the worst of the pain. Luckily she had been prescribed a whole plastic container full of them!

Gregorio arched a dark brow. 'I have already seen you naked, Lia…'

She shot him an irritated scowl. 'Not under these circumstances, you haven't!' She sighed as she realised she sounded ungrateful. 'I'm sorry, Gregorio. I haven't even thanked you yet for coming to my rescue earlier.'

'Luckily Raphael recognised Richardson's car and called me immediately.' Gregorio leaned back against the tall chest of drawers he had placed her clothes in, arms folded across his chest, his expression unreadable. 'What exactly did Richardson threaten to do to you?'

Lia wasn't fooled for a moment by his relaxed posture, or the mildness of his tone. 'I'm sure he wouldn't really have— No, I'm not.' She admitted with a grimace. 'He was… I had no idea he could be like that. I owe you an apology, Gregorio. Another one. Everything you said about David is true.'

'He is responsible for embezzling the money from your father's company?'

'Oh, yes.'

'He admitted this to you?'

'Amongst other things.'

She related everything David had said to her earlier that evening.

'He was *with* your father the night he died…?' Gregorio frowned.

Lia closed her eyes briefly before opening them again. 'He said there was nothing to be done. That my father died almost instantly. But—' She broke off, unable to say anything more on the subject without breaking down.

'But,' Gregorio acknowledged harshly, 'you think he is responsible for killing your father?'

'Only indirectly—in as much as he caused my father so much distress it brought on the heart attack.'

His mouth thinned. 'I will find him, Lia. No matter what rock Richardson hides under, I *will* find him.'

'I know you will.' She nodded. 'Would you mind very much if I don't take a bath or a shower tonight? I'm tired and aching and I just want to go to sleep.'

'Of course. Whatever you are comfortable with,' Gregorio reassured her as he straightened away from the chest of drawers and crossed the bedroom to her side. 'But I *am* going to help you undress.'

Lia knew that tone only too well: it was one that told her Gregorio wasn't going to be talked out of doing exactly what he said he would. And there was no arguing with the fact that he *had* already seen her naked.

'Did Cathy pack something for me to sleep in?' She stood up—only to have Gregorio reach out and grasp her uninjured arm to steady her as she tilted to one side. It was ridiculous how a little thing like a plaster cast and a sling could affect her balance.

'Something that looks like an oversized T-shirt…?'

'That's it, yes.'

Lia almost laughed at the look of disgust on Gregorio's face. No doubt he was used to the women in his life wearing silk and satin to bed—if they bothered to wear anything at all. Even when she'd been able to afford those things Lia had always preferred practicality and warmth in bed over appearing sexy.

'Thank you for calling Cathy and Rick for me earlier. I— They're the closest thing to family I have.'

'I am aware of that.' Gregorio spoke softly. 'And I have already left instructions that they are to be admitted at any time.'

'Thank you.'

He gave a rueful smile. 'You are very polite this evening.'

'About time, hmm?'

Gregorio shrugged. 'You felt you had good reason to be…less than polite to me before.'

'And I was wrong.' She sighed. 'About everything.'

'Do not upset yourself. You know the truth now, and that is the important thing.'

It was. And yet…

She didn't like it that Gregorio was treating her with the polite distance of a concerned acquaintance, rather than a lover. Not that she didn't fully deserve it, but Lia missed the intensity of passion radiating from him. That had never been far from the surface when the two of them had been together in the past.

She drew in a shaky breath. 'Let's get this over with, shall we?'

'Of course.'

Gregorio forced himself to remain detached and impersonal as he aided Lia in removing her clothes. He had never acted as nursemaid to anyone before—let alone a woman he had been in bed with all yesterday afternoon. But how difficult could it be?

More difficult that he had imagined once he had removed Lia's jacket, blouse and bra. Which had proved easy enough once he had removed the sling.

The physical removing of Lia's clothes wasn't the problem. It was being this close to her when she was completely naked from the waist up, the fullness of her nipples just a tempting breath away. That was enough to tax the restraint of any man—least of all one who had already enjoyed having those succulent nipples in his mouth.

Gregorio attempted to remove temptation by taking the long red T-shirt from the chest of drawers and quickly putting it on Lia before refastening the sling. The nightshirt covered her to mid-thigh.

He drew in a deep, controlling breath as he unzipped and removed her skirt, but his resolve to remain detached was shaken again as he looked at her wearing sexy panties, suspenders and stockings.

He could *do* this, damn it. He wasn't an animal or a callow youth. He was a man of sophistication and experience. He shouldn't be aroused just by looking at an injured woman dressed in an unbecoming red nightshirt—even if she *was* also wearing sexy suspenders.

Except he was.

Thank goodness the restrictive material of his jeans prevented that arousal from being too obvious.

'Gregorio…?'

His distraction obviously wasn't quite so easy to hide!

He dealt with the rest of Lia's clothing with the minimum of contact with the heat of her silky skin, breathing a sigh of relief once he had her safely tucked beneath the bedcovers and could straighten and move away from the bed.

Lia looked...fragile. Her hair was a silky auburn cloud on the white pillow behind her, and her face was almost as pale. The outline of her body was slender beneath the duvet.

But it wasn't just a physical fragility. Lia's eyes were a smoky and unfocused grey, with dark shadows beneath them. No doubt some of that had been caused by the agony of having her arm broken, along with the medication she had been given to relieve the pain. But Gregorio had a feeling it was also an outward show of the turmoil of emotions she had to be feeling inside.

It must have been a shock when Richardson had attacked and threatened her in that way: the animal had broken her arm, damn it. She had intended marrying Richardson once—would no doubt have done so if her father hadn't died and Richardson hadn't revealed his true colours by breaking their engagement.

As far as Gregorio was concerned Lia had escaped being married to a man who one day would have become an abusive husband.

Lia, on the other hand, must feel not only foolish for ever having been taken in by Richardson, but also disillusioned with the whole concept of falling in love.

'Try to get some sleep.' Gregorio's voice sounded harsher than he'd intended, and he made a concerted effort to control his anger. It was Richardson he was angry with, not Lia. 'I will leave the door open, and I'll be in my office or my bedroom if you need anything.'

'Thank you.' The heaviness of her lids was already making them close.

Gregorio hesitated at the door. 'Would you like the light left on or turned off?'

'On!' She half sat up again in the bed. 'Off.' She

grimaced as she sank back against the pillows. 'I don't know…' She groaned.

'We will compromise.' He nodded. 'I'll leave the door open and the light on in the hallway, okay?'

'Okay…' She sighed wearily.

Gregorio adjusted the lighting before quietly leaving the bedroom. As promised, he left the door open.

Only once he had reached the sanctuary of his office did he release the anger that had been building and building inside him by slamming his fist against the door. It hurt him more than it hurt the wooden door, but he needed the release, the physical pain, after remaining calm for Lia's sake for so long.

He wanted to hurt someone. And that someone was David Richardson. Because Lia was suffering the emotional and physical repercussions of the other man's abuse.

He had known she was suffering physically, but her emotional trauma had shown itself in her immediate reaction to the thought of being left alone in the darkness of the bedroom. Lia was frightened, but too determined to appear strong to want Gregorio to see that fear. He had seen it anyway.

His expression was grim as he flexed his bruised knuckles before pouring himself a glass of brandy, carrying the glass across the room to sit in the chair behind his desk.

He swung his booted feet up to rest on the edge of the desk and turned his head to stare out of the window at the night-time skyline. Was Richardson still out there in the city somewhere, hiding? Or had he already left the country? Not that it mattered, because Gregorio wouldn't give up the search—no matter how far Richardson had run.

Gregorio had no idea how long he sat there, sipping brandy and staring sightlessly out of the window, totally aware of Lia just feet away, almost naked in bed. He felt a certain relief when his cell phone vibrated in his jeans pocket and interrupted his reverie. His thoughts had been going round and round in ever decreasing circles, none of them pleasant.

He took out his cell phone and checked the caller ID before taking the call. 'Sebastien,' he greeted his brother tersely.

'Who's annoyed you *now*?' Sebastien didn't waste any time on pleasantries.

'It is too long and too complicated a story to tell.'

'Try…' his brother drawled.

Gregorio gave him a condensed—and censored—version of the events of the past week.

The three brothers had always been close, having shared a common enemy: their father's sometimes overbearing machismo. As adults the siblings had also become friends, and Sebastien was the closest thing Gregorio had to a confidant.

'So Jacob Fairbanks's daughter—Lia—is there with you now, in your hotel suite?' Sebastien prompted speculatively.

'She is asleep in one of the guest rooms, yes,' Gregorio stated. 'She has a cast on her broken arm and no particular liking for *me*,' he added firmly. 'Sebastien…?' he prompted at his brother's continued silence.

'Just give me a second while I choose my words carefully, Rio…' Sebastien spoke slowly. 'Our proposed deal with Jacob Fairbanks was called off months ago, and you told me she slapped you on the face at his funeral—so what is Lia Fairbanks doing in your life *now*?'

Trust Sebastien to go straight to the heart of the matter.

The heart…?

Gregorio had physically wanted Lia from the moment he saw her in that restaurant four months ago. This past week he had come to know the Lia behind that physical beauty. To like her. For her strength. Her principles. Her loyalty—even if it occasionally proved to be misplaced!—and her love for her father and her friends. Her work ethic was also exemplary: Michael Harrington had already told Gregorio he believed Lia would become one of their most competent receptionists.

Had Gregorio come to *like* her or to *love* her?

Until this mess was sorted out and Lia was safe he had no intention of delving too deeply into what his feelings for her might be.

'Taking a long time to answer, there, Rio,' Sebastien mocked.

'You are my brother—not my conscience!'

Sebastien chuckled. 'And…?'

'I feel a sense of obligation to ensure Lia's safety,' Gregorio answered him carefully.

'Why?'

'Because she is— Sebastien, her father—the only parent she had—is dead. David Richardson, her ex-fiancé, deserted her when she most needed him. He has now admitted to embezzling from her father's company, and that is the reason Jacob called off his deal with us. Richardson left Lia alone until he knew the two of us were…acquainted…' He substituted the word he had intended using. One afternoon in bed together did not make him and Lia lovers, and she had made it clear she didn't intend to repeat the experience. 'And then he attacked her, threatened her. He broke her *arm*, dammit!'

'And you feel responsible for her?'

'Yes, I feel responsible for her,' he repeated evenly.

Lia, standing outside in the hallway, overhearing Gregorio's side of the conversation with his brother, hadn't realised how much hearing those words spoken out loud would hurt until Gregorio said them. It was one thing to *think* that was what had motivated Gregorio's continued interest in her—another entirely to hear him state as much to his brother.

She had slept for a couple of hours, only to wake up suddenly, totally disorientated until she remembered where she was and why. Once awake she had realised how thirsty she was, and had got out of bed, quietly leaving the bedroom so as not to disturb Gregorio on her way to the kitchen for a glass of water.

She hadn't meant to eavesdrop on his telephone conversation with his brother, but once she'd heard her name mentioned she hadn't been able to walk away either.

Gregorio had saved her again this evening. He was always saving her from one disaster or another.

Because he feels responsible for me.

Well, that had to change. Maybe not right now, because it was far too late for her even to think of moving out of the hotel and finding somewhere else to stay tonight, and she was determined not to involve Cathy and Rick in any further acts of violence from David. But tomorrow, when she was feeling stronger and able to make other arrangements, she was going to stop being a burden on Gregorio and take control of her own life—as she had said she was going to.

Tomorrow.

'Wake up, Lia! It is not real, *bella*, only a nightmare. *Lia?*' Gregorio prompted more firmly as she continued to scream, the tears streaming from her closed eyes and down her cheeks as she fought off his attempts to take her in his arms.

Gregorio had drunk several more glasses of brandy before going to bed, knowing he was going to need the relaxant if he stood any chance of sleeping at all.

It had taken some time, but he had finally dozed off into a fitful slumber. Only to be woken—minutes... hours later?—by the sound of Lia screaming.

At first he had thought someone—Richardson—had managed to get past his security and Lia was being attacked. It was only once he had entered her bedroom and found her there alone, screaming as she tossed from side to side in the bed, that he realised she was obviously in the middle of some horrendous nightmare.

His efforts to calm her had so far been unsuccessful.

'Lia!' He was careful not to knock the cast on her arm as he grasped her shoulders. 'Open your eyes and look at me, Lia,' he instructed firmly.

She'd stopped screaming, at least, and her eyes were open, but her body was still being racked by intense sobs.

'It was just a nightmare...it isn't real,' he continued to soothe as he took her in his arms.

It seemed very real to Lia!

She was running, knowing that something...someone...was pursuing her. She couldn't see him when she dared to take a quick glance behind her, but she could feel him, hear him breathing—could almost *feel* that hot breath on the back of her neck. And then he was there—in front of her—not behind her at all. An indistinct dark shadow and yet she knew it was a man. Knew it was David. And he wanted to kill her.

'You are safe now, Lia.' Gregorio held her tightly. 'No one will harm you while I am here. I promise you.'

But he wouldn't always be there, would he? She was just a woman Gregorio felt a fleeting obligation to protect. Because she was alone in the world and she needed his help. He didn't *really* care about her. They'd had sex yesterday afternoon, and that was the reason he probably felt even this much obligation. Right now he was probably regretting that he had ever shown an interest in her at all. She brought too much baggage with her, and Gregorio de la Cruz wasn't interested in a woman with baggage.

'I'm okay now.' She was very aware of the fact that Gregorio wore only a pair of loose jogging trousers, and his chest was completely bare. The warm and muscular chest he was holding her against... 'I'm sorry if I disturbed you.' His half-nakedness was certainly disturbing *her*! 'I'll be fine now.'

She kept her gaze lowered as she attempted to pull away. Gregorio's arms only tightened in reaction.

'Lia, look at me.'

She didn't want to look at him. At any part of him. Bad enough that her hand that wasn't restricted by the sling was now pressed against Gregorio's chest, that his flesh was warm and sensual to the touch.

'Lia?'

She glanced up at Gregorio's face and then quickly

down again. His hair was tousled from sleep, his eyes black, and dark stubble lined his jaw. He looked incredibly sexy. And he smelt edible. A cross between the lingering aroma of that expensive cologne he wore and something else—a male musk that was uniquely Gregorio.

She felt her body's response to all that overwhelming male lushness.

Gregorio simply felt an obligation to look out for her, Lia firmly reminded herself. That was the only reason he had been around this past couple of months.

And in return she had slapped him at her father's funeral, been incredibly rude to him before asking him to leave her apartment, and then yesterday—yesterday she had told him she didn't want him. That she never wanted to go to bed with him again.

Liar, liar, pants on fire.

She could lie to Gregorio, but there was no longer any chance of lying to herself.

She was in love with Gregorio.

Not infatuated, not sexually enthralled by him—although she was that too!—but one hundred per cent in love with him.

He was everything a man should be. Honourable. Truthful. Protective of those he deemed weaker than himself. A man Lia knew instinctively her father had liked as well as respected. And the reason she knew that was because her father had recognised those traits in Gregorio.

In the same way her father had known that David was none of those things. If he had lived, would her father have told her the truth about David? Or would he have continued to lie and cover up for the younger man because he wouldn't have wanted to hurt Lia by exposing the true nature of the man she loved?

Lia hoped it would have been the former, and that her father would have realised she was strong enough to accept the truth.

None of which changed the fact that she had now fallen deeply in love with a man who was never going to want her as more than a friend with benefits.

'I'll be fine now,' Lia assured Gregorio lightly as she pulled out of his arms. 'Please go back to bed. *Please.*'

'Sure?' He studied her closely.

'Sure.' She nodded, keeping that bright look on her face until Gregorio had left the bedroom.

Which was when Lia closed her eyes and allowed hot tears to fall down her cheeks.

CHAPTER TWELVE

'MIGHT I ASK what you are doing here, Sebastien?'

Gregorio's brother had arrived at the hotel just minutes ago. Considering it was only eight o'clock in the morning, Sebastien had to have flown here in the second company jet overnight from New York. Almost immediately after the two men had concluded their telephone conversation the night before, in fact.

His brother stepped back from their brotherly hug. 'You didn't sound at all yourself when we spoke on the phone last night, Rio.'

He arched dark and sceptical brows. 'And that was reason enough for you to immediately fly to London?'

Sebastien gave him a boyish grin. 'That, and I wanted to see Lia Fairbanks for myself.'

Gregorio tensed. 'Why?'

Sebastien's grin grew even wider. 'I wanted to meet the woman who has my big brother so tied up in knots.'

'Stop talking nonsense,' Gregorio snapped. 'No doubt you would like a cup of coffee?'

He turned away to pour some of the strong brew he always made to accompany his breakfast. He had already drunk two full cups this morning, having been unable to fall asleep again after Lia's nightmare. He had wanted to stay alert in case Lia needed him again.

'No changing the subject, Rio.' Sebastien made himself comfortable at one of the high stools at the breakfast bar as he accepted the mug of coffee. 'What's so special about Lia Fairbanks?' He kept his eyes on Gregorio as he took a swallow.

Everything.

The thought had leapt unbidden into Gregorio's head, and once there he couldn't seem to dislodge it.

Lia was special. *Very* special. A woman who remained strong through adversity. Most women would have been hysterical after Richardson's attack last night, but Lia had remained calm. And this was after she had lost her father only two and a half months ago and her engagement had ended—although after the events of yesterday she was probably relieved that it had.

As for the way the two of them were in bed together...

Lia was like none of the women Gregorio had known in the past. She gave not only with her body but with all that she was. Gregorio had never known a lover like her before.

Would he ever know another lover like her again?

'Perhaps I'll know the answer to that once I've met her?' Sebastien was still eyeing him speculatively.

Gregorio felt an unaccustomed surge of possessiveness at the thought of Lia meeting Sebastien. Would she find Sebastien attractive, as so many other women did? The two brothers were very alike in looks, with their dark hair and dark eyes, and a similar build and height.

Would Lia find his brother easier to get along with than Gregorio?

That was a given. Gregorio was well aware that he lacked the charm and ease of manner Sebastien could so easily adopt if the need arose. And meeting a beautiful woman was definitely one of those occasions.

The thought of Lia gravitating towards Sebastien was enough to cause Gregorio's hand to clench at his side and his fingers to tighten about his coffee mug until the knuckles turned white.

'I'm guessing you don't like that idea.' Sebastien grinned.

Gregorio gave his brother an irritated glance. 'Do not see emotions where they do not exist.'

Sebastien openly chuckled now. 'If you don't stop gripping the handle of that mug so tightly you're going to snap it right off.'

He relaxed that grip. 'You would be better spending your time thinking of ways to help me locate David Richardson than commenting on things you know nothing about.'

'I know nothing about Richardson, either.'

Gregorio's lids narrowed on his brother. 'This situation needs to be resolved, Sebastien. Quickly.'

'But then Miss Fairbanks would move back to her own apartment.'

'Exactly.'

'Rio—'

'Why are you *really* here, Sebastien?' Gregorio looked at his brother searchingly, noting the lines beside his brother's mouth and eyes that didn't gel with his light-hearted banter. 'What's wrong?'

Sebastien sighed heavily. 'Nothing a hot and meaningless fling wouldn't cure.'

Gregorio winced. 'Do you have someone specific in mind?'

His brother grimaced. 'Maybe.'

Definitely, in Gregorio's opinion. 'Who is she?'

'Could we just concentrate on *your* problems rather than my own?' Sebastien prompted impatiently.

'This woman is a *problem*, then?'

'Monumentally so,' his brother conceded. 'But don't worry. I'll handle it when I get back to New York.'

'Handle it or handle her?'

Sebastien gave a hard grin. 'Both.'

'I hope I'm not interrupting?'

Gregorio turned sharply at the sound of Lia's voice, a scowl darkening his brow as he saw she was only dressed in that over-large thigh-length red T-shirt, with her arm in its sling over the top of it and her hair dishevelled from sleep.

'I'm Sebastien de la Cruz.' His brother stood politely. 'I hope we didn't wake you?'

'Lia Fairbanks,' she returned stiltedly. 'And, no, you didn't wake me. I just woke up and felt in need of coffee.'

'My big brother is in charge of the coffee pot. Rio...?' he prompted as Gregorio made no move to pour a third cup.

It was the first time Lia had heard anyone address him by the affectionate diminutive; it made him seem less the powerful and arrogant Gregorio de la Cruz and more the older brother. The casual navy blue polo shirt and faded jeans he wore added to that illusion.

She hadn't been able to help overhearing at least part of Gregorio's conversation with Sebastien—again. The little she had heard made it clear Gregorio wanted her out of his hotel suite as soon as possible.

Not that it came as a surprise. She already knew Gregorio had only insisted she come here at all because of that sense of responsibility he felt towards her. Nevertheless, hearing him reiterate those feelings to his brother made it all too real.

'You are not dressed appropriately to receive visitors,' Gregorio bit out tautly. 'I suggest you return to your bedroom and put on a robe, at least.'

Lia frowned at the censure she could hear in his tone. And at the continued lack of coffee. 'I can't manage on my own.' She gave a pointed glance at the sling immobilising her arm.

'Then I will come and assist you.' Gregorio straightened. 'If you will excuse us, Sebastien?'

'Don't bother on my account.' Sebastien resumed his seat on the bar stool. 'I think you look charming just as you are. Rio has explained that your arm is broken,' he said sympathetically.

Lia was sure, from the conversation she had overheard, that Sebastien de la Cruz was well aware of exactly how she had broken her arm. Or rather, how it had been broken for her.

Now that she was no longer in excruciating pain, and the effects of the painkillers had worn off a little, she was aware of the shock of exactly what David had done to her. Of what else he had threatened to do to her if she didn't back off.

She really hadn't known the true David at all until last night.

She gave a grimace in answer to Sebastien's comment. 'It could have been worse.'

'So I understand.' He nodded. 'I'm sorry you've had to go through this.'

'The princess had to be woken by the frog some time. It's what my father called me,' she explained emotionally as both men looked at her. 'His princess.'

A princess he had protected from seeing or hearing any of the harsh realities of life. Until he'd died from the strain of trying to protect her from the harshest reality. Well, Lia was well and truly awake to all those realities now—she had the plaster cast on her broken arm to prove it.

'I will accompany you to your bedroom and help you into your robe,' Gregorio announced into the silence.

Lia turned her frowning attention on him. 'I haven't had any coffee yet.'

'Because I have not poured you any. Nor will I do so until you are wearing your robe.'

'I'm perfectly decent as I am.' The nightshirt covered her from her neck to a couple of inches above her knees.

'I will be the judge of that.' His mouth was thin, his dark eyes glittering.

Lia gave a squeak of protest as Gregorio grasped her shoulders and turned her in the direction of the hallway and her bedroom, walking her forward in front of him. 'I can walk unassisted!'

'Then do so.' He released her, but his presence behind her continued her impetus out of the kitchen.

'What is *wrong* with you?' Lia demanded impatiently once they were outside in the hallway.

His eyes narrowed. 'You are virtually naked in front of a complete stranger.'

'He's your *brother*, for goodness' sake.'

'And you met him for the first time five minutes ago—which makes him a stranger to you.'

'"Virtually naked" would be wearing only my underwear,' Lia defended. 'And I don't remember you complaining the last time I was in your suite dressed like that,' she challenged.

Gregorio could feel that nerve pulsing in his cheek again—a common occurrence, it seemed, when he was with this stubbornly determined woman. 'And I would not complain if you were to be dressed like that again—as long as the two of us were alone together when you were.'

'Sebastien didn't seem to mind the way I'm dressed,' she taunted.

His lids narrowed to slits. 'If you are trying to annoy me you are succeeding!'

Lia snorted. 'I obviously don't have to try very hard.'

Gregorio frowned. 'What do you mean?'

'Never mind.' She shook her head before turning to continue walking down the hallway.

Gregorio caught up with her as she reached her bedroom. 'What did you mean by that remark?' he repeated as he followed her inside.

She turned to face him. 'I'm obviously nothing more than a nuisance to you. Even more so now that your brother has arrived.'

Lia was *so* much more to Gregorio than a nuisance. More than he was prepared to admit. Even to himself.

'Well?'

He scowled his irritation. 'Do not take that aggressive tone with me!'

'Or what?'

'What is wrong with you this morning?' he snapped.

'You've refused to give me my first cup of coffee of the day.'

Gregorio drew in a deep breath in order to hold on to his temper. 'Only until after you have put your robe on.'

'And I'm still waiting for the assistance you so gallantly offered.'

Gregorio ignored her sarcasm as he helped her to put her robe on. Lia was obviously spoiling for a fight this morning, and he wasn't about to give her one.

'Did you know that your accent gets stronger when you're angry?'

He finished tying the robe of the belt about her waist before stepping back. 'Then I must presume it is always stronger when I am with you.'

Lia arched a mocking auburn brow. 'Did you just make a joke?'

'Doubtful,' he drawled dryly.

'Irony *is* joking.'

'Then I must make jokes all the time.'

'When you're with me.' She nodded.

'When I am with anyone.'

Lia eyed him quizzically. 'You and your brother aren't much alike, are you?'

He tensed. 'In looks—'

'Oh, I wasn't talking about the way you look—that's a given,' she dismissed without further explanation. 'What is your youngest brother like?'

'Alejandro is...complicated,' he replied cautiously.

Alejandro's problems were not discussed outside the family.

'Like you, then.' Lia nodded. 'He was married, wasn't he?'

That was part of Alejandro's problem. And what did Lia mean by saying that *he* was complicated?

His life was an open book. He was a successful businessman. Wealthy. Single. He had a healthy sexual appetite, as the newspapers were so fond of reporting, and he didn't hide the fact that he had zero patience with incompetence or triviality. Or that he was bored very easily.

Something he had certainly never been when he was with Lia…

'You're taking too long to answer, which probably means you aren't going to.' Lia sighed. 'Can we go back to the kitchen now? The coffee is calling to me.'

Gregorio gave an exasperated laugh as he followed her out of the bedroom. 'You are obsessed with your morning coffee!'

'He left with a scowl on his face and returns smiling,' Sebastien observed mockingly as Lia and Gregorio entered the kitchen together. 'You're a miracle-worker, Lia.'

She grimaced. 'I think you'll find Gregorio was laughing *at* me rather than with me.'

Sebastien shrugged. 'A smile is still a smile, for whatever reason.'

'Is that such a rare occurrence?' Lia seemed to recall that Gregorio had laughed quite often when the two of them were together. When they weren't arguing or making love…

'I would say unique rather than—'

'When the two of you have quite finished discussing me as if I am not here…' Gregorio raised pointed brows as he handed Lia the mug of coffee he had just poured for her.

Oh, Lia was only too aware that Gregorio was there. As she'd said, Sebastien was as dark and handsome as his brother. But he possessed an easy charm that was lacking in Gregorio—although, on closer inspection, the sharp intelligence in Sebastien's eyes gave the impression that that might be a veneer over a deeper, darker nature. But it was Gregorio she was constantly aware of. Every minute. Every second.

Lia chose to concentrate on drinking her coffee rather than make any reply to Gregorio's comment. Until the silence in the kitchen became uncomfortable. 'What were the two of you discussing when I came in?' Apart from the fact that Gregorio couldn't wait to move her out of his hotel suite.

'Your ex-fiancé.' Sebastien was the one to answer her.

She winced. 'I would rather not be reminded of that fact.'

'As would we all,' Gregorio put in harshly.

Lia gave him a sharp glance, knowing she deserved the admonition in his tone. Thank goodness she was no longer that naïve nincompoop who had fallen for David's charm. 'Any news on his whereabouts?'

'None,' Gregorio answered grimly. 'Lia, the police will be coming here to interview you in just under an hour—'

'The police?' she echoed sharply.

He nodded. 'We can and will find Richardson, Lia, but it's better if the police bring him to justice for the things he has done. As such, I telephoned the police and reported his attack on you last night first thing this morning. The story will be backed up by the broken door and the hospital report on your broken arm.'

She carefully placed her empty coffee mug down on the breakfast bar. 'You should have consulted me before doing that.'

'Why?'

'*Why?*'

'Uh-oh—I think I'll go and take a shower and grab a couple of hours' sleep, if no one minds.' Sebastien glanced between the two of them. Lia was glaring at Gregorio and he looked genuinely perplexed by her anger. 'Obviously no one is even going to notice I've gone!'

Lia waited only as long as it took for Sebastien to leave the room before answering Gregorio. 'You had no right to contact the police without talking to me first.'

'I had *every* right.' A nerve pulsed in his tightly clenched jaw. 'I should have called them last night, once we reached the hospital, but I decided to wait until today—'

'It wasn't your decision to make—'

'God knows what would have happened to you last night if I hadn't kicked open the door to your apartment!'

She was well aware of how much she owed Gregorio. 'But the *police*, Gregorio...' She groaned as she sank down onto one of the bar stools.

Gregorio frowned as he saw how pale her cheeks had become. 'Do you not see that this is the best way to put Richardson in the spotlight of the authorities? The police will want to know the motivation for his attack on you, and I will hand over to the police all the information I have gathered so far in regard to Richardson's illegal dealings with your father.'

Lia saw *Gregorio's* motivation. It had been very cleverly done.

He had taken care of two problems at the same time. He would pass on the information he had concerning Fairbanks Industries to the police and at the same time ensure that this situation ended as quickly as possible. The two of them would then be able to get on with their own respective lives.

Which was what she wanted too.

Wasn't it?

CHAPTER THIRTEEN

LIA LAY HER head back against the sofa in exhaustion after the police had asked all their questions and finally left the hotel. But she wasn't too tired to remember that she was supposed to be working today. 'I need to contact Mike Harrington to tell him I won't be in today.'

Gregorio's brow rose at hearing Lia call the hotel manager *Mike* Harrington; he had only ever known the other man by the more formal Michael. 'I have already spoken to him.'

'Why am I not surprised?' Lia muttered.

'At the time I was unsure of what time you were going to wake this morning,' he defended.

'Fair enough.' She sighed. 'I'm just wondering whose life you ran before taking over mine?'

'Lia—'

'It's okay.' She held up a defeated hand. 'I understand.'

'Understand what, exactly?'

'That the quicker this is resolved the sooner I'll be out of this suite and your life.' She stood. 'I think I'll take some more painkillers and then follow Sebastien's example of taking a nap for a couple of hours.'

She left the sitting room.

Gregorio was so stunned by her first comment that he was barely aware of the second one.

Lia believed he wanted to hasten her departure—not just from this suite but from his life. What had he ever said or done to make her think that?

His only motivation in ending this situation with Richardson was to ensure that nothing like last night ever happened again. He also wanted to clear her father's name. Again for Lia's sake, more than anyone else's.

Lia had been very defensive this morning. Spoiling for a fight. Earlier Gregorio had put it down to late reaction to the shock of Richardson's attack last night. But what if it was for another reason entirely? Her barbs and sarcasm had been directed solely at him, Gregorio now realised. Much to Gregorio's annoyance she had joked with Sebastien a couple of times this morning. Usually at Gregorio's expense. And she had been calm and polite when she answered the questions put to her by the police.

He didn't understand why. What had he and Sebastien been discussing shortly before Lia joined them in the kitchen earlier?

Damn it!

Sebastien had been teasing Gregorio about his responses to Lia, and he had reacted defensively to that teasing. Had denied that Lia had any importance in his life amongst other things. One of those things being stating his need to resolve the situation quickly and to agree that it was so that Lia could move back to her apartment.

He hadn't meant that the way it had sounded— had only been fending off Sebastien's too-personal comments.

Perhaps he shouldn't have said it? Especially in a place where there had been a chance that Lia might overhear the comment.

Damn, damn, *damn* it.

Lia's first thought on waking up was that there was something heavy lying across her. Then she realised it had to be the unwieldy plaster cast she had on her arm.

Except… This weight felt lower down than the plaster cast. Warmer too. More flexible.

She carefully lifted the duvet so she could see what it was.

An arm.

A bare and muscular *male* arm, lightly dusted with dark hair.

An arm she easily recognised as belonging to Gregorio.

Gregorio is in bed with me!

Lia was sure he hadn't been there when she'd fallen asleep earlier, almost the instant her head had touched the pillow. She had been exhausted from talking with the police for over an hour, and then the painkillers had finally kicked in.

Gregorio must have come to her bedroom and got into the bed with her some time after that.

A part of her knew she should be annoyed, at the very least, at his having taken advantage of her sleeping. Another part of her just wanted to curl up in his arms and go back to sleep.

She also couldn't help wondering if the rest of him was as naked as his arm…

She took care not to wake Gregorio as she scooted backwards until her bottom came into contact with his

groin. She was more than a little disappointed to feel
the brush of denim against her skin where her nightshirt had rucked up as she'd moved about in her sleep.

'If you move back a little further you will discover
that I am fully aroused.'

Lia instantly tensed at the unexpectedness of discovering that Gregorio was awake. Was it because she
had woken him? Or had he already been awake when
she'd been fidgeting about trying to discover what was
curved about her waist? And in her careful—and obvious—efforts to discover if Gregorio was naked…?

She moistened her lips before speaking. 'What are
you doing in here?'

'Until a few minutes ago I was sleeping.'

'I meant—'

'I know what you meant, Lia.' Gregorio moved up
to roll her gently onto her back so that he could look
at her, careful not to jar her arm. Her face had more
colour than earlier, thank goodness. Her eyes no longer had that haunted look, either. 'I wanted to be here
when you woke up.'

'Why?'

'Two reasons.'

'Which are?'

'Silvio contacted me shortly after you had gone
to sleep. He and Raphael discovered Richardson was
booked on a flight to Dubai.'

Her eyes widened. 'He was fleeing the country?'

'I believe in the beginning, with your father dead,
he thought he could weather the storm and his life here
in England would go on as before, with no one any the
wiser as to what he had done. But—'

'But yesterday I alerted him to the fact that wasn't

going to happen.' She winced. 'I'm *so* sorry, Gregorio. I just wanted him to know I wasn't as stupid as he thought I was, but all I did was give him the opportunity to leave England as soon as possible.'

'Do not feel bad about that. Richardson's response to your warning was damning in the extreme. Besides,' he added with satisfaction, 'he is now in police custody, after an anonymous phone call informing them he was booked onto the Dubai flight.'

She gave a shudder. 'He's a lawyer, Gregorio—do you think the charges against him will stick or will he manage to wriggle out of them?'

'His attack on you will certainly stick. The FSA will also be very interested in Richardson's behaviour. Especially as I have now given them all the information I have so far on his having embezzled money from Fairbanks Industries. It may take some time but, yes, I believe eventually Richardson will be made to answer for all his crimes.'

Lia gave a shaky sigh. 'I can't believe it's over.'

'In *time* it will be,' Gregorio cautioned again.

Lia had no doubt that with the powerful Gregorio de la Cruz's involvement that time would come sooner rather than later, and that David would one day end up in jail—as he fully deserved to.

'You said there was a second reason you wanted to be here when I woke up?' she reminded him softly.

Gregorio felt the frown lift from his brow. 'I believe you are suffering under a misapprehension in regard to something you overheard me say earlier.'

Lia's tension was immediate in the wariness of her expression. 'Oh…?'

He nodded. 'I am not…comfortable with emotions.'

She smiled ruefully. 'I noticed.'

'Let me finish, Lia,' he reproved gently. 'Sebastien was being his usual irritating younger brother self this morning.'

'Obviously I can't speak from personal experience, but I believe that's part of a sibling's job description.'

'Perhaps,' Gregorio allowed dryly. 'Sebastien seems to think it is, at least.' He sobered. 'What I said to him, about resolving the situation with Richardson so that you could return to your apartment, was not meant as literally as I believe you have taken it.'

She frowned her puzzlement. 'I don't understand...'

'Nor did I until I tried to find a reason why you were being so dismissive of me,' he admitted. 'Lia, *you* were the one who brought an end to our...relationship.'

'Our going to bed together, you mean? Well... Yes.' Her gaze didn't quite meet his. 'It was clouding the issue. Obviously, having known and liked my father, you feel some sort of responsibility towards me. But I assure you—'

'I feel *concern* for you, not responsibility.'

'Oh.'

He nodded. 'I realise some of my actions and comments may have come across that way to you, but I assure you that *responsibility* is the last thing I feel when I look at you or touch you.'

'Oh.'

'Now you are worrying me,' he drawled. 'The Lia Fairbanks I know always has plenty to say on any subject,' he explained as she frowned. 'Lia, has it occurred to you that I could just as easily mistake *your* responses to *me* as gratitude?'

Her eyes widened. 'You think I went to bed with you out of *gratitude*?'

He smiled slightly. 'What I think is that we should start being honest with each other, so that in future we avoid these misunderstandings.'

The only words Lia heard were *in future*. That implied the two of them were going to *have* a future. Maybe not as anything more than friends, but even friendship was better than *responsibility* or *gratitude*.

'I'm waiting for you to start being honest,' she prompted after several long seconds of silence.

Gregorio chuckled at her guardedness. 'I have been honest with you from the beginning. I told you when we met again last week that I'd wanted you from the first night I saw you in Mancini's with your father and Richardson.'

'And now you've had me.'

'Yes.'

'I… This is in the spirit of honesty, you understand?'

'I understand.'

'Well. I… You're only the second man I've… Well, that I've…'

His brows rose. 'I am only your second lover?'

'Yes.' Lia breathed a sigh of relief that she didn't actually have to say the words. 'And in comparison the first one was awful,' she said with feeling. 'Not that I'm comparing you to David in any way,' she added quickly. 'I just want you to know that our lovemaking was spectacular. Wonderful. Special.'

'In the spirit of honesty?'

She frowned up at him. 'Are you mocking me?'

'Not at all.' Gregorio chuckled. 'In the spirit of the same honesty, can I say that our lovemaking was—

Lia…?' He prompted against the fingertips she had placed over his lips.

'I really don't want to hear how I measured up to the legion of women you've had in your bed.' She grimaced.

'I seem to recall that a Roman legion comprised about five thousand soldiers, and while I *have* been sexually active for some years, I very much doubt the total of my bed partners comes anywhere near that number.'

'You *are* mocking me!'

'Only a little,' Gregorio acknowledged huskily. 'And only because I am honoured to have been your second lover—especially as the first was such a failure.' His voice lowered. 'What I would *really* like above all things is to be your last lover too.'

'Sorry?' Lia's mouth had gone dry. Did Gregorio mean…? Was he asking…?

No, of course he wasn't. Gregorio didn't *do* for ever. She must have misunderstood him.

'Lia…' His hands moved up to cradle each side of her face as he looked down at her intently. 'Beautiful Lia. Our lovemaking was spectacular to me too. Wonderful. Most of all, special.'

'It was?' Lia wasn't sure she was still breathing. She couldn't possibly be awake.

'It was,' Gregorio confirmed gently. 'I wanted you from the moment I saw you, but in just a few days I have also fallen in love with you.'

Her eyes widened. 'You *love* me?'

'So very much.' Gregorio had only realised how much earlier, when he had contemplated the huge gap Lia would leave not only in his hotel suite but in his life, his heart, when the time came for her to leave and return to her own apartment.

Lia swallowed. 'Really?'

'Really,' he confirmed. 'Perhaps I always did. I have never believed in love at first sight, but...' He leant over to pull open a drawer in the bedside cabinet and remove something from inside. 'This is the handkerchief I used to wipe the blood from my cheek the day you slapped my face at the funeral.'

'You keep it in your bedside drawer?'

'Silvio gave it to me that day.' He smiled ruefully. 'I placed it in this drawer when I returned home, and it has been here beside me every night since.' He dropped the handkerchief back in the drawer. 'I couldn't bear to part with it.'

'You *love* me?'

'I do.' He nodded. 'More than life itself. Rather than wanting you to leave, as you believe, if I could I would keep you here with me for ever. But all of this is too soon for you.' He sighed. 'You lost your father such a short time ago. Your engagement ended badly. You need time to heal. To make a life for yourself. To prove to yourself that you *can* make a life for yourself.'

'You can understand that?'

His smile became warmer. 'You would not be the Lia I love if you did not feel that way.'

She looked up at him searchingly, noting the love and pride shining in his eyes as he steadily returned her gaze, leaving himself and his emotions wide open for her to see.

'Gregorio.' She reached up and touched his cheek. 'I've fallen in love with you, too.' She spoke clearly, firmly, wanting there to be no more misunderstandings between them. 'I love you,' she said. 'So very much.'

Gregorio felt as if someone had punched him in the

chest, stealing all the breath from his lungs and rendering him incapable of speech. Lia *loved* him?

'How can you possibly…?' He was finally able to force words past his shock. 'You cannot possibly… You believed… You accused me of…'

'Yes. Yes. Yes. And yes,' Lia acknowledged emotionally. 'I did, and I believed all of those things. And *still* I fell in love with you. Because you're none of those things, Gregorio. You're honourable. Truthful. Protective. You have been nothing but kind to me even in the face of my less than gracious behaviour towards you. How could I *not* fall in love with you?'

'Dios mio…' Gregorio continued speaking in Spanish as he buried his face against her throat.

'I have no idea what you're saying, but I don't care because I'm sure it's something beautiful.' Lia laughed happily, her arm about his shoulders as she clung to him.

He lifted his head, his mouth now only inches away from Lia's. 'I said you are beautiful. My heart. My world.'

'I love you, Gregorio. I love you so very much.'

She lifted her head and claimed his lips with her own.

'I said you would be bossy in bed,' Gregorio murmured indulgently a long time later, when the two of them were lying naked in bed together, Gregorio on his back, Lia nestled against his side with her head on his shoulder.

Their lovemaking had necessarily been gentle, because of the cast on Lia's arm, but no less beautiful because of it. Perhaps more so, because they had taken the time to explore and appreciate every inch of each other. Not just in passion and pleasure, but in love.

'Lia, when this is over there is a question I wish to ask you.'

Lia felt as if her heart had leapt into her throat. 'Why can't you ask me now?'

'For all the reasons I stated earlier.' He sighed. 'I want you to be sure—*very* sure—when you give me your answer.'

She frowned. 'And what happens in the meantime? Between us, I mean? Do we go our separate ways and meet up again in three months' time, say, to see if we both still feel the same way?'

'No!' Gregorio's arms tightened about her possessively. 'Absolutely not. We will see each other every day. And we will share the same bed every night,' he stated firmly.

Lia could barely hold back her smile of happiness.

Gregorio loved her. She loved him.

And whether Gregorio ever asked her that question or not was unimportant, because she had absolutely no doubt they would be spending the rest of their lives together.

EPILOGUE

Three months later

'YOU LOOK BEAUTIFUL,' Cathy said emotionally as she adjusted Lia's veil outside the church in her role as matron of honour.

Today was the happiest day of Lia's life. The day she and Gregorio were to be married.

She glanced down at the engagement ring she had transferred to her right hand for the duration of the ceremony. A solitaire yellow diamond, as Gregorio had said it would be. To Lia it was a symbol of their love and happiness together, and a promise for their future.

'Do stop fidgeting, Rick,' Cathy teased her husband as he stood beside Lia, ready to escort her inside the church and give her into Gregorio's safekeeping for the rest of their lives together. 'You look gorgeous,' she reassured him with a light kiss to his lips.

Lia found it hard to believe that this was happening. Six months ago she had thought her world was coming to an end—now she knew it was just beginning.

This was the first day of the rest of her life with Gregorio, as his wife.

'Ready?' Cathy prompted brightly.

'Oh, yes,' Lia confirmed without hesitation.

The last three months had been a rollercoaster of emotions. Gregorio's telling her he loved her. David's arrest and charges of embezzlement and fraud having been added to the charge of grievous bodily harm for his attack on Lia. Her days being occupied with making a success of her job at the Exemplar Hotel—which she had. And all her nights being spent in Gregorio's arms.

Throughout it all Gregorio had been the constant. Always there. And always, *always* assuring her of his deep love for her.

Today was their wedding day. A day when they would reaffirm their love for each other before family and friends.

She placed her hand on Rick's forearm before stepping forward, which was the signal for the two ushers to open the church doors and for 'The Wedding March' to be played.

And there, waiting for her at the altar, stood Gregorio, love and pride shining unreservedly in his eyes as he looked at her.

An unshakable love Lia knew she would return for the rest of her life.

* * * * *

DOCTOR ON
HER DOORSTEP

ANNIE CLAYDON

CHAPTER ONE

Jenna had been longing for this moment. She slid her car into the parking space outside the rambling Victorian house that had once been her family home and killed the ignition. A shower and a pizza were waiting for her inside and nothing now stood between her and the solitary, relaxing evening she had promised herself.

There was something, though. Some*one* to be more precise, and he was sitting on the steps, in the shade of the wide arch of the porch, his elbows propped on his knees, legs stretched out in front of him. His demeanour said he was waiting for someone, and since that someone was unlikely to be her, he must be another of Janice's endless stream of boyfriends.

It was a shame, but she couldn't do anything about it. Janice had moved out of the ground-floor flat three weeks ago, and if she hadn't seen fit to share her forwarding address with him, then Jenna certainly wouldn't. The best she could do for him was to take a contact number and promise to pass it on.

Okay. This won't take long. Pity really. She didn't like giving people the brush-off and there was something about his relaxed pose that said he was someone you'd like to spend time with. Jenna hauled the two heavy shopping bags out of the boot of her car and manoeuvred her way through the front gate, kicking it closed behind her, rather harder than she had meant to. The low sun dazzled her, and she was halfway down the front path before she could get a proper look at the stranger.

He looked like a rock star. Distressed leather jacket, jeans and boots. Light brown hair streaked with gold, which was just long enough to slick behind his ears, and the kind of tan you didn't get from a two-week Easter break. His eyes were hidden behind dark glasses but the tilt of his head indicated that he was watching Jenna as she walked towards him and dumped her shopping bags at his feet.

'Hello. Can I help you?'

'I'm looking for Dr Weston.'

'Oh! That's me.' Something crawled up Jenna's spine, and she wondered whether a bug had got into her shirt. A bug that was somehow making her fingertips tingle as well.

'I'm Adam Sinclair. Dr Greene told me he'd mentioned my name to you.' His accent was English, but he'd obviously been in America for a while. Mid-Atlantic. Rolling between the familiar, cut-glass consonants of home and a heart-stopping drawl.

'He said…' Jenna gulped back the words. It wasn't tactful to repeat what Rob Greene had said in his email. 'I thought you weren't going to arrive until next weekend.' Jenna's reflection stared back at her from the dark lenses of his glasses.

He seemed to realise that the sunglasses were unnerving her and he pulled them off, hooking them into the open neck of his shirt. 'I flew in from America this morning, and I'm driving down to Exeter tonight for the week. I thought I'd swing by and try to see you on the way.'

His tawny gaze looked as if it had been kissed by the

same sun as his hair and was a hundred times more unsettling. Jenna fixed her eyes on a point somewhere between the bridge of his nose and his hairline and issued a mental instruction to pull herself together. 'That's something of a detour. North London's not exactly on the way from Heathrow to the M3.'

'Well, I did say swing. Implies an arc.' He shrugged off the twenty miles of crowded roads as if they were a minor obstacle. 'Is there a problem?'

'No.' Jenna didn't move. It wasn't really a problem. He just wasn't quite what she'd been expecting. To be absolutely honest, she wouldn't have known *how* to expect someone like this, appearing out of nowhere, on her doorstep.

'I should show you some ID.' He'd mistaken her bewilderment for mistrust, and pulling his wallet out of his jacket pocket he opened it and handed it to her. Credit cards. A Florida driving licence. A photograph of a woman. Jenna closed the wallet and handed it back.

'Thanks.' She reached for her bags of shopping, but he got there first, picking them up as he got to his feet. 'You'd better come inside.'

Adam followed her up the stairs to her flat in silence, keeping his distance as she opened her front door and waiting for her to motion him in. He followed her through to the kitchen and put her bags onto the counter.

'I'll just put my shopping away, and then show you the flat.' Jenna threw her keys down on the countertop and slipped out of her jacket, rolling up the cuffs of the plain white shirt she wore underneath. 'Would you like a cup of tea?'

'Tea would be nice, thanks.' He had retreated back to stand in the doorway, obviously intent on not crowding her. 'I'm getting the feeling that I'm not quite what you expected.'

He could say that again. 'Well, actually, I somehow got the idea that you were a woman from Rob's email. But it makes no difference.'

There was a whole world of difference in the wry grin that melted his chiselled good looks. No medical doctor had any business even being in possession of a smile like that, let alone using it.

'Ah. Sorry about that. If you'd prefer not…'

'It's not a problem. Rob does tend to write as if he's being charged by the word.' Rob's characteristically staccato email had, as usual, provided more questions than answers. *Travelling alone, concerns about hotel. Security and quiet needed. Speak on return from hols.* Rob wasn't back for another week and in the meantime Jenna had jumped to the conclusion that Dr Sinclair was a woman.

'Yeah. When Ellie was born he emailed me a photo of her and Cassie, and wrote *"7 lbs. Beautiful"* underneath. I sent him a text demanding details and he replied *"Girl".*'

Jenna snorted with laughter. 'He sent you a photo? You were honoured, most of us just got *"Born"* with a couple of exclamation marks. You've known Rob a while, then, as Ellie's nearly five.'

'Ever since med school. Ellie was born just after I went abroad.' He gave her a confiding grin and Jenna hung on to the countertop for support. 'If it wasn't for Cassie I'd never know what he was up to, though. She sends photos, letters. Even had a copy made of that drawing they have in their sitting room of Ellie and Daisy.'

He was clearly aware that she was alone in the house, and was trying to drop as many reassuring details into the conversation as he could. By chance, the reference turned out to be particularly appropriate. 'That sketch is one of mine. Cassie asked me to do a second copy for a friend who was overseas.' Someone who was going through a tough time, Cassie had said.

Laughter escaped his studied reserve. 'Really? That drawing is remarkable, I have it hung in my study at home. It always makes me smile.'

It was only a pencil sketch. Jenna had been pleased with how it had turned out, but it was nothing all that special. He seemed to want to say more, but she cut him short before he got the chance. 'I hear Florida's a beautiful part of the world. What do you do there?' Jenna opened the refrigerator and started to stack her shopping away.

'I'm a plastic surgeon.'

So this was the image that sold nose jobs and liposuction to the rich, was it? Adam probably did pretty well out of it. Jenna reckoned that a good percentage of the female population would go through hell, high water and even general anaesthesia to see approval in Adam Sinclair's face.

Taking advantage of the fact that the open fridge door hid her from him, Jenna rolled her eyes. 'And that's what you're going to be lecturing on?'

'Yes. I was looking to spend some time back in the UK and when I got the offer of a month here as a visiting lecturer, I jumped at it. I'm spending a week visiting family, and I'll be back here on Sunday week for my first lecture.'

'On a Sunday? It's a public lecture, then.' Not that she was even vaguely interested.

'Yeah. Three o'clock in the Fleming Lecture Theatre.'

He didn't invite her to come, and Jenna didn't express any interest in doing so. Instead, she straightened up, flashing him a brisk smile. 'I'll make the tea and take you downstairs to see the flat.' Perhaps she'd been too harsh in judging him. Okay, so Adam wasn't a woman. That was hardly his fault, neither was it a crime, although that smile of his ought to be kept under house arrest. If he chose to use his talents and an expensive education to carry out largely unnecessary surgery, that was a matter for his own conscience. He was what he was.

As a sign of penitence she picked up a packet of chocolate biscuits, along with her mug and the keys to the ground-floor flat, before leading him down the stairs. 'I've just had the walls done, and it stinks of paint at the moment, but it'll air out by next week.'

'That's fine. I just want somewhere to stay. Rob offered to put me up, but with two children and another one on the way he doesn't have the room. And I don't like hotels much.'

'No. Rob mentioned that.' Jenna led the way into the lounge and plumped herself down on the dust sheet that covered the sofa.

'He did?' The look he shot her was half-wary. Three-quarters guilty.

'In passing. I don't much like hotels either.' It wasn't her business. Jenna reached for the biscuits as a change of subject, opening the packet and offering him one. 'Why don't you take a look around? There isn't much furniture, I'm afraid, just the basics.'

'That's what I like about it.' He ignored the biscuits and walked over to the window, drawing the shutters back to let the evening sun spill into the room, slanting across the walls and floor. 'And there's plenty of light.' He turned to Jenna. 'This will be fine, if that's okay with you.'

'Don't you want to look at the rest?'

'Should I?' He gave her a quizzical look, and Jenna felt the back of her neck begin to burn.

'It's the usual practice. I'll stay here if you don't mind.' She felt awkward under his gaze, the way the corners of his mouth twitched slightly when he looked at her spare frame and her dark red hair, scraped back off her face and secured tightly at the back of her head. His profession, and those smouldering tawny eyes, seemed to make a constant, unspoken judgement of her.

'So you're not going to come with me and point out the finer features of the property?'

'No, I take a relaxed approach. Drink tea and let you show yourself around.'

He chuckled. 'Fine. I can take a hint.' He disappeared out into the hallway, the sound of his footsteps indicating his progress around the flat. He was back again almost before she could extract a second biscuit from the packet. 'One of the doors is locked.'

'Ah, yes. That's the second bedroom. My last tenant went to Spain to work and she's left some of her stuff here for me to send on when she gets settled. I can clear the boxes out if you want that room, but the main bedroom's through here.' Jenna led him the full length of the hallway and opened the door.

He strode inside and looked around. 'Big room.' He sat down on the bed. 'Decent mattress. That's a real bonus.'

'I think you'll find that's my line. As I'm here, I'll also point out that there's plenty of cupboard space.'

'Which would be my cue to look inside.'

'Absolutely. Let me know if you find any skeletons. I don't think Janice left any behind, but you never can be sure.'

Adam opened the doors wide, inspecting the interior of the wardrobe. The smile that was playing around his lips broadened when Jenna jumped as he flinched back suddenly. 'Nope. She must have taken them all with her.'

'Well, that's a relief.' Jenna brushed a few crumbs from the front of her shirt. 'What do you think, then?'

His eyes travelled around the bedroom. 'May I see the other room, please? The one that's locked.'

'Of course.' Jenna led the way down the hallway. 'This room's a little smaller and there isn't so much cupboard space. I like it better, though, there are doors out on to the patio and you get the early morning sun.' Most tenants preferred the extra cupboard space.

The soft leather of his jacket brushed against her arm as he walked past her into the room. 'I like it too. Would it be okay if I swapped the boxes over to the main bedroom and brought the bed through here?'

Jenna shrugged. 'I'll do that some time next week for you.'

He shook his head. 'No. I'll do it.' He didn't wait for her answer and turned to walk over to the French doors, staring out into the garden. 'Big garden. What's the area at the end there that's attracting the butterflies?'

Her beloved butterfly garden. Jenna was both pleased and slightly embarrassed that he'd noticed it. 'That's part of the garden too. My grandfather and I planted it when I was little. There are herbs and shrubs to attract the butterflies, but it's getting a bit out of control now.'

'So this was your family home?'

'Yes. It was my grandparents' house. I split it into two flats after they died. I was a student then and the income came in handy.' He nodded as if he understood, but there was no way that he could have done. Jenna herself didn't fully understand what had happened with her parents.

'You lived with your grandparents?'

'Yes, I've lived here since I was ten.'

He said nothing. Jenna began to wish that either she'd not said so much or that he would question her more. Anything but this half-story, which he seemed to accept so unquestioningly. Or maybe it wasn't acceptance. Maybe he simply didn't care.

Adam turned away from the window and followed her through to the sitting room. 'So, do we get to haggle over the rent now?'

She'd rather he didn't. That way he had of quirking his eyebrow gave him an unfair advantage. 'It's seven hundred for the month. I'll stock the fridge up for you.'

'You will not. Seven hundred pounds is daylight robbery, this place is worth twice that. I may have been away for a while, but I haven't lost touch with London property prices.'

'I keep the rent low so I can pick and choose who I have here. Anyway, you can't haggle upwards.'

'Why not?' He lifted one eyebrow.

'You just can't. I won't have it.'

He held up his hands in a gesture of surrender. 'Okay. Done.' Adam reached into his jacket and brought out his wallet. 'Would you like a deposit?'

'Not particularly. The place is empty anyway.'

'Fair enough.' He picked his mug of tea up from the coffee table and took a final swig. 'I'd better get back on the road, then, and leave you to get on with your supper.'

Jenna flushed. He'd noticed that she was already on her third chocolate biscuit and was regarding the packet pointedly. So what? She was on her feet all day in a busy A and E department, not sitting in a leather chair behind a swanky desk, and she worked up an appetite. And she might not have curves, but at least her figure owed nothing to silicone. 'Thanks. I'll see you in a week's time, then.'

CHAPTER TWO

SUNDAY morning. Ten-thirty. Jenna should have been drinking tea and reading the paper, but instead she was studying the street outside. A car drew up and she twitched the muslin curtains back into place, stepping away from the big bay windows.

The bell sounded when she was halfway down the stairs. As soon as she opened the door, a four-year-old bundle of energy launched itself at her.

'Hello, Ellie. Did you have a nice holiday?' She nodded at Rob and crooked her finger at him. 'Come in. You've got some explaining to do.'

Nothing was going to dent Rob's good humour this morning or dim the violent hue of his Cornwall Surfers T-shirt. He followed Jenna up the stairs, replying indulgently to Ellie's chatter, and flung himself into an armchair while Jenna fetched some juice, a pad of paper and a box of assorted pencils and crayons for Ellie.

'Don't give her that pad, Jen. She'll only make a mess of it.' Rob was looking at the thick, white cartridge paper that Jenna had put in front of Ellie.

Jenna nodded at Ellie, who was smoothing her hand across the pad. 'You're never too young to be able to appreciate the texture of nice paper.' She bent and tore one of the thick sheets from the pad, clipping it on to a board for Ellie, and selected a soft pencil from the box. 'Here you are, sweetie, try using this.'

Rob rolled his eyes. 'Well, if she turns out to be the next Picasso, then I suppose we'll have you to thank. Look, sorry about the mix-up last week.'

'We managed.' Jenna walked through to the kitchen to make some tea and Rob followed her. 'You might have told me, though.'

'Well, it's a bit tricksy, you know how these things are.'

'No, not really, not until you tell me.'

'Okay, well, Adam's a decent bloke. One of the best people I've ever known, in fact, but he's not had it easy these last eighteen months. I've been trying to find him somewhere to stay where he can have some peace and quiet, get back on his feet.' Rob shrugged. 'Tactfully, you know?'

Rob was no good at tact, he usually left that kind of thing to Cassie. 'Which explains all that cloak-and-dagger stuff in your email.'

'Yeah.' Rob brightened. 'Yeah, that's it.' It wasn't it at all. There was a whole list of other questions that sprang to mind.

'So he's not staying with you and Cass?'

'No. We offered, of course, but he says that we've no room. And what with Cass being pregnant and everything...' They both jumped as the doorbell went. If that was Adam, he was early.

'Can you get the intercom?' Jenna reached up into the kitchen cabinet for another cup. 'And don't worry. He'll be fine here, and I'll keep an eye on him.'

'Thanks, Jen.'

Rob disappeared out of the kitchen and Jenna gave the teapot a swirl, even though she'd already done so once, and dumped it down on the tray. It would have helped if she knew what on earth she was meant to be keeping an eye out for, but Cassie would be a much better bet than Rob when it came to straight answers.

The commotion in the hallway indicated that the object of her speculation had arrived and that he was being greeted by both Ellie and her father at the same time, the child squealing with laughter and demanding a hug.

Jenna popped her head around the kitchen doorway. He was a picture of health and good humour, tanned, taller and broader than Rob and grinning as he lifted Ellie up so she could fling her arms around his neck. No trace of whatever it was that Rob was so concerned about.

'Hello, there.' His head jerked upwards as Jenna spoke.

'Hi.' He came forward, still carrying Ellie, who looked as if she was going to have to be prised away from him with a crowbar. 'I hope we're not crashing in on your morning.'

'Not at all. Welcome back.' She held her hand out to him, and he took it, his touch cool, measured. He seemed to be less careful about keeping his distance now that he was not alone with her, and held on to her hand for one moment too long before Jenna pulled hers back again.

'Where *is* my present?' Ellie was demanding now, beating her hands against his shoulders.

'In a minute, honey. We'll just collect the keys from Jenna and get out of her hair first.' He was smooth, she'd give him that. Perfect poise. Nothing but easy charm.

'I've just made tea.' Jenna waved him into the sitting room. 'And Ellie's been doing some drawing, I expect you'll be wanting to see that. Let her open her present here if she'd like to.'

When she brought the tea in, Ellie was already working on the package that Adam had given her. Pink paper on the outside, a pretty bow and layer upon layer of paper underneath, firmly bound with sticky tape.

'Hope it lives up to all this anticipation.' Rob was making no move to help his daughter as she whooped with delighted frustration, trying to rip the parcel open.

'Me, too.' Adam too was letting Ellie get on with the task of unwrapping her present unaided. 'So how was the holiday? Catch any waves?'

'Fabulous. We were on the north coast, and the hotel was close to this great little surf beach, so I could go out first thing in the morning and make it back in time for breakfast.'

'Nice one. You'll have to come back to Florida soon.' Adam accepted a mug of tea from Jenna, taking a grateful sip.

'We will. You can sit on the beach with Cassie and the kids and I'll show you how it's done.'

'Yeah, right, in your dreams.' He shot a bright grin at Jenna. 'Takes more than a hideous T-shirt to make a surfer. What was Cassie thinking, letting you go out in that?'

Rob laughed. 'She reckons that if I go out in it then she won't have to put up with it around the house.' He ran his hand over the garishly coloured fabric. 'What, don't you like it?'

Ellie's delighted squeal meant that Adam never did get to deliver his verdict. She'd reached the inside of the package and was holding up a string of beads.

'Aren't they pretty?' Ellie brought the beads to Jenna to show her and when she examined them carefully she could see they were hand painted, each one different.

'I got them in Mexico.' Adam watched as Jenna carefully wound the beads around Ellie's neck for her, nodding with approval. 'You look beautiful, honey.'

Ellie was climbing up on the sofa, between Adam and

Rob, to catch a glimpse of herself in the mirror over the fireplace, and Rob tugged at her sleeve. 'What else have you got, then, El?' He gestured to the folded fabric that still lay amongst the ruins of the wrapping paper.

Ellie pulled the fabric out, turned it around a couple of times then held it up against herself, and Jenna caught a glimpse of colourful embroidery on a white cotton background.

'It's a bit big, isn't it, mate?' Rob was surveying his daughter. 'She'll be sixteen before she grows into that.'

'No, idiot. It's a dress.' Jenna smoothed the fabric and held it against Ellie. It was roomy, but the drawstring at the waist meant that it could be adjusted to fit her perfectly.

'Can I wear it?' Ellie was jumping up and down with excitement.

'Not until you've said the magic word.' Rob smiled at her.

Ellie launched herself at Adam, nearly knocking his tea over and flung her arms around his neck, kissing his cheek. 'Oh, that's nice... Can I have another one? Right here?' His finger was on his other cheek and Ellie obliged eagerly. 'Thank you.'

'I drew you a picture.' Ellie's hands were on Adam's shoulder, pulling as hard as she could, and Jenna saw alarm flare in Rob's face.

'Gently, El. Adam's shoulder isn't properly mended yet.'

Adam waved him away. 'I'd love to see your picture, Ellie, will you show me?'

Ellie fetched her drawing and climbed up onto Adam's knee. 'That's Mum...and Dad...me and Daisy...and that's you.' Her finger was moving across the paper.

'That's very good. And who's this, up there?'

Ellie shook her head, as if the stupidity of adults never

ceased to amaze her. 'That's your friend. Mum says she's in heaven.'

Rob's face tightened, but Adam's smile never faltered. 'That's lovely, honey. I'm so pleased you drew her too, along with the rest of us.'

'Will you tell her?'

'Ellie…' There was a note of anxiety in Rob's voice but Adam's glance quieted him.

'Of course I'll tell her. She'll be so happy, I expect she'll tell all her friends up there.'

Ellie glared up at the ceiling and nodded, as if satisfied. 'Can I wear my dress?'

This time Adam allowed Rob to step in. 'Not yet, El. We've got some things to move around downstairs and I don't want you getting it all dirty. Later on, when we've finished.'

The circular face that Ellie had drawn, giving no hint of who Adam's friend might really be, released its grip on Jenna's attention and she bumped back down to earth. 'Oh, no, that's okay, I already did that.'

Adam's gaze was on her now, so palpable that it almost tickled her skin. 'You did what?'

'I moved the boxes and the bed. And put a few things in the fridge, just essentials, to keep you going until tomorrow.'

His eyes slid down her thin bare arms, and her fingers jerked in her lap. 'On your own? I thought I said I'd do that.'

Rob came to her rescue. Kind of. 'What I love about this woman is that you can say anything you like to her, and she'll hear you, but she won't listen. Eh, Jen?'

Adam pursed his lips thoughtfully. 'In that case, perhaps I can just put my bag downstairs and take you all to lunch before my lecture.' He glanced at Ellie, his face breaking into a smile. 'Go and ask your dad if you can wear your new dress.'

The dress fitted perfectly. Adam and Rob had disappeared downstairs with the keys, while Jenna stripped off Ellie's jeans and T-shirt and drew the dress over her head, running her fingers over the hand embroidery and arranging it just so.

'Can I have some perfume?' Ellie was obviously keen on playing the lady.

'No, you know what your mum says about perfume.' Ellie's idea of a dab behind her ears was to tip half a bottle of Cassie's anniversary gift over her head. 'Tell you what, this is much better.'

She trimmed a couple of stalks of lavender from the bunch in the fireplace and tied them firmly with a ribbon from the drawer. 'Here, I'll fix it onto your dress… like this…and you'll smell nice and look nice as well.' She leaned back and admired her handiwork. Ellie looked beautiful.

'Are you going to dress up, too?' Ellie had unpinned Jenna's hair and was arranging it around her shoulders.

'No, I'm fine as I am.' Jenna looked down at her jeans and cotton, sleeveless top. This was about as good as it got, and however much she wanted to make an effort to look nice today she wasn't going to do anything that might betray that to either Rob or Adam.

'Perfect.' Adam's voice boomed behind her and she jumped. He obviously meant Ellie.

'Doesn't she look pretty?' She flashed a smile at him.

'Yes, she looks perfect, too.' His mouth twisted in a smile as Jenna flushed. 'Thank you for the flowers.'

She'd arranged lavender and sweet-smelling greenery in a vase, putting it downstairs in the hearth to break up the stark, white walls and bring a little of the garden into the flat. And he'd noticed them. 'They're not really flowers.'

He shrugged. 'Thanks anyway. You have a good eye, they look stunning.' He ignored the redness, which was now spreading across her cheeks, and turned his attention to Ellie. 'And you look like a proper young lady.'

Ellie seemed to take as much delight as Jenna did in Adam's approval, but she was more straightforward about showing it. 'I did Jenna's hair, too. Look.' She tugged at one of Jenna's curls.

'Maybe I'll just fix it back up again.' Jenna gathered her hair behind her head, looking for the elastic tie that Ellie had discarded somewhere on the floor. She'd never quite got around to liking her hair much. Too many memories of her mother tugging mercilessly at the tangles and bemoaning the fact that it wasn't smooth like her sister's. And that, horror of horrors, it was red.

'Don't.' Something about Adam's tone made her freeze, stock still. 'It really suits you like that.' There was no indication in his face that this was anything other than a polite compliment.

Rob came to her rescue again. Friendly, open and perfectly unmoved by the intensity of Adam's voice. 'Yeah. Fiery, eh, Jen? Doesn't take any nonsense from anyone.' He gave Adam a pointed look and held his hand out to Ellie. 'Come on, then. If we're going, let's go.'

'Flame-haired.' Rob missed Adam's quiet comment in the kerfuffle of getting Ellie out of the door and down the stairs, but Jenna caught it, as she guessed she had been meant to. She shot him a glare and he grinned innocently, as if he'd meant nothing by it. Maybe he hadn't.

'So what's the story with Julie, then?' Adam had waited until Rob had taken Ellie home and he and Jenna were sit-

ting alone in the open-air enclosure on the pavement outside the restaurant.

'Julie? You mean Julie Taylor?'

'Yes. Her consultant, Iain Simms, emailed me on Friday
evening, copying you in.'

'Oh. I haven't had time to look at my email for the last
couple of days.' He was making her feel self-conscious
again. His eyes had wandered towards her far too many
times already, cool, assessing, as if he was sizing her up,
and Jenna couldn't help wondering what he saw. Wishing
that it wasn't what she saw in the mirror. Pale limbs, un-
touched by the sun. A slim waist, but precious few curves.
Red hair.

If he noticed her agitation, he paid no heed to it, leaning forward across the table towards her. 'Too busy drag-
ging furniture and boxes around, eh?'

Actually, yes. Those golden eyes were far too perceptive for Jenna's liking. And she didn't want him to see the
effect they had on her when she met his gaze. 'Shall we
walk?' Walking seemed a better option than sitting here,
staring straight at him.

'If you like.' He stretched his arms, flexing his shoulder as if it was stiff, and signalled for the bill. 'Along the
river? Somehow the river always makes me feel as if I'm
home again.'

Jenna nodded. The pavement to one side of them dipped
and meandered its way down to the south bank of the
Thames. Tower Bridge was in the distance to the right.
The footbridge to their left, with a stream of Sunday afternoon day-trippers dawdling their way across the river.
'I've never been away long enough to have that feeling of
coming home. I'd like to travel. Learn a little about life.'

'You don't need a plane ticket to learn about life.' His
eyes focussed somewhere else for a moment, as if he was

straining to catch a last glimpse of the place he had left behind. 'Let's walk. I'll tell you what Iain's email said.'

They strolled together down the broad steps that led to the river path. He was all sun-drenched charm, relaxed grace, and Jenna allowed herself to wonder what it would be like to walk arm in arm with him. She gave herself twenty seconds to feel the warmth of his body next to hers and then consigned the fantasy to the breeze that blew in from the river.

'So I guess we'll be working together on this one.'

'Uh?' If she'd been listening then she would know what they were working together on. 'You mean you're going to be working at the hospital? As well as lecturing?'

The slight twitch of his eyebrow told her that he'd already said that. 'Yeah. Iain's asked me to work with him on a few specific cases. I'm also working down in A and E for one or two days a week, while Dr Bryant's on paternity leave. I'm hoping to get the chance to observe some of the techniques and practices you employ.'

'And teach us a thing or two as well?' The idea of being observed for any length of time by those amber eyes was… well, it would be interesting, if nothing else.

'Yes. That too. I do have something to offer in return.'

'I'm sure you do.' Jenna wasn't even going to think about what Adam had to offer. 'So why your particular interest in Julie? We're hoping that she won't need much reconstructive surgery.'

'It's not all about surgery.' He grinned down at Jenna. 'Iain suggested that since you've been visiting her every day, I should speak to you about her.'

'Well, I only really know about her case in a general sense. I saw Julie when she came into A and E after she was the victim of an acid attack. She saw it coming and shielded her face, but she has burns on her arm and shoulder. Iain and his team are dealing with that, though I'm really more concerned about her emotional state.'

'Which is where I come in.'

Jenna turned to him in surprise. There was nothing in his face, no clue of what he was thinking. As she stared, a small muscle at the side of his jaw broke free of his control and began to flicker. 'You know something about trauma?'

He knew something all right. That muscle was going crazy. 'I do. Many of my patients are in the same position as Julie, and I try to deal with that as well as their physical needs.'

Jenna narrowed her eyes. 'And there's no counselling help? In Florida?'

He seemed to relax a little. 'I work for a charity. We work all over South America, bringing medical aid and surgery to poor communities. Florida's our home base. We have a facility there where patients who need specialised care are brought.'

'So…' Embarrassment trickled down the back of her neck and made her shiver. She'd misjudged Adam.

'So what?' It appeared he wasn't going to let her off the hook.

'I thought…' She heaved a sigh. She might as well spit it out. 'When you said plastic surgery and Florida, I thought you meant nip and tuck.'

'Ah.' Amusement sounded in his voice. 'No, I mostly deal with cleft lips, cleft palates, facial tumours, injuries. Mostly children and teenagers, some adults. I imagine the rich and famous expect their surgeons to turn up to work in something other than ripped jeans and a T-shirt.'

Jenna swallowed hard. He would be eye-catching enough in pretty much anything, and she didn't want to even think about ripped jeans. His neat chinos and plain, casual shirt were quite enough for the time being. 'Then I owe you an apology. Your work sounds amazing.'

'It has its rewards.' The warmth in his face told Jenna that those rewards weren't measured in pounds and pence. 'Many of my patients are traumatised, either from their injuries or from having been mocked or shunned because of their appearance. I told Iain that I was especially interested in seeing how that was dealt with here.'

Jenna shrugged. 'That's just the trouble. Julie won't see a counsellor.'

'So I hear. I also hear that she trusts you and that you've been doing your best to fulfil that role for her.' He fixed her with an enquiring look. 'Not a particularly easy path to tread. Difficult not to become over-involved, I imagine.'

Jenna pressed her lips together and he shrugged as if he had already proved his point. 'My lecture starts in an hour. Would you like to come?'

'I might just do that. Were you thinking of covering trauma?'

'I was considering touching on the fact that a small team with limited resources needs to take a more holistic approach.'

'In other words you need to treat the person, not just the injury.' It was a private dream of Jenna's. Not just to be a doctor but to be a healer. 'Difficult not to become over-involved, then.'

A smile spread slowly across his face. 'I'm going to have to take the Fifth on that.'

'If you do that, the jury's going to assume that the answer's yes.'

'Nothing I can do about that. They can assume whatever they like.' For a moment Jenna thought that she had broken through his reserve. Then the fire died in his eyes. 'I'll drop in and see Julie tomorrow.'

Jenna nodded. He wasn't making a request and she supposed that she was going to be stuck with his input, whatever that might be. She may as well accept it gracefully. 'I'd be interested to hear what you think. You know where to find me.'

'I do.' He looked at his watch. 'It's time I headed over to the lecture theatre. Will you fill me in on some more of Julie's details on the way?'

It was the dream that had haunted him for the last eighteen months, sometimes once every week or two, sometimes every night. He woke up with a stifled cry, icy sweat against his cheek. For a moment, he couldn't work out where he was, and then the dim glow of the nightlight brought him to his senses. The muslin drapes, drawn across the half-open French doors, fluttered in the night breeze and he slowly got out of bed, shaking his head, trying to reclaim his place in the waking world.

Slipping outside onto the moss-lined stones of the patio, he took a deep draught of air, inhaling the smell of the city, mingling with the softer scents of the garden. He started, instinctively drawing back into the shadows, as a sharp click sounded above his head.

Jenna had opened the door, which led on to an iron railed balcony above his head, and was standing beside the steps that snaked down to the patio, just a few feet away from where he stood. In the darkness Adam could see only that she wore something loose, swirling around her bare feet, and that her hair was a wild shadow around her head.

He held his breath. She was leaning over the balcony, craning round towards him, and he guessed that she could see the open French doors and the light inside. Adam flattened himself against the wall and watched as she seemed to sniff the air, like some shy, nocturnal creature of the forest.

A fox trotted across the lawn. Her head jerked upwards and she followed its progress, waiting until it had disappeared into the shrubbery before she turned and slowly walked back into the house. Adam heard the catch on the door being fastened and then there was silence.

He swiped his hand across his face. Tomorrow was going to be a busy day, and he should try to sleep again. The thought that she was there, perhaps even watching over him, calmed him. Tomorrow would be time enough to probe the intriguing contradictions of his flame-haired, disturbingly gorgeous landlady.

CHAPTER THREE

'Look, she's here now.' Julie's face lit up into a grin and Adam turned to see Jenna entering the ward. Red hair, bound tightly at the back of her head, white shirt and dark slacks. Even in such severe attire she looked like an angel. Not one of those sweet, dimpled ones, looking down dispassionately from the safety of a cloud. She was a warrior angel, the kind you'd really like to have on your side when things got tough, who rushed in where everyone else feared to tread and plucked you out of danger.

'She comes every lunchtime, does she?' Adam knew that she did. Iain had already told him that.

'Yes. Just for half an hour. Sometimes less.' There was a hint of resentment in Julie's voice and Adam reflected just how precious that time was for Jenna. A snatched half-hour when most of the A and E staff were happy just to grab a sandwich and get their breath for a few minutes.

Before he had time to answer, Jenna was at the foot of the bed, her fingers grasping the rail where Julie's notes hung. 'Hi, there.' She was all smiles. 'How are you, then? You're looking better.'

Julie flashed her a grin. 'Yeah, I feel better. That other doctor says I'm doing okay. They've got the pain control sorted now.'

'Good.' Jenna's gaze caught Adam's and he basked in

its warmth for a moment before her attention was back on Julie. 'I see you've met Dr Sinclair.'

'Yes.' Julie turned her wide blue eyes on to Adam. 'He's going to monitor my progress.'

Jenna's face lit up. She looked a great deal more enthusiastic about it than she had the other day but, then, she'd obviously enjoyed his lecture, questioning him about it all the way home. 'Really? That's good. You've made plenty already.'

'Suppose so.' A porter wheeled a squeaking trolley into the ward and Julie flinched. Adam remembered that reaction all too clearly. All your senses on red alert, every moment of the day. Alarm at any sudden noise.

Jenna had leaned forward, her hand tapping Julie's foot gently. 'Hey. Earth to Julie. It's okay, honey, just a porter.'

'Yeah. Just a porter.' Julie's eyes filled with tears and Jenna's helpless gaze flipped to Adam.

'Listen, Julie, these feelings are natural.' Adam repeated what he'd been told so many times. 'It will pass. You just have to hang in there until it does.'

'When?' Julie almost spat the word at him. 'When will it pass?' Adam recognised that sudden, volatile fury too. As if his heart was already full to the brim with anger, and only a drop more would make it spill over.

'I can't tell you. There are ways we can help you...' Adam tailed off as Julie turned her head away from him. He was losing her.

'What do you want, Julie?' Jenna's voice cut across the space between them. 'Dr Sinclair can lie to you if you like. Give you a time and a date when everything will be back as it was. Or he can respect you enough to tell you the truth.'

The warrior was back. The woman who took life by the shoulders and shook hard until she got what she wanted.

Adam grinned and took Jenna's cue. 'I *could* lie. Do you want me to?'

'Of course not.' Julie shot an imploring look at Jenna. 'But it's all so much talk, isn't it?'

Adam saw Jenna's knuckles whiten as she gripped the rail at the end of the bed. She'd done a good job with Julie. She'd gained her trust, and she'd used it to help Iain and the other doctors do their work. But she'd hit a brick wall here.

Unless… Adam hadn't planned on this, but the agonised look in Jenna's eyes spurred him on. 'That's what I thought when the doctors said that to me. So they sent me to a counsellor and I didn't believe her either. In the end you have to find out for yourself.'

He had Julie's attention. Jenna's too, only she was trying not to look at him with such overt interest as Julie. 'What do you know about it?'

'I've been there. Not in the same way as you, but I think I understand part of what you're feeling. I was shot, and ended up in hospital in Florida.'

Julie's eyes were as round as saucers. 'Like on TV?'

Jenna huffed quietly. 'No, it's not the same as on TV, Julie…' Adam waved her to silence. Now wasn't the time for her to spring to his defence, however much it pleased him to hear her do it.

'The thing is that being shot changed my view of the world. Before, I'd thought that I was pretty much unbreakable, but I realised that I wasn't. I had to relearn how to do the smallest things without panicking. But I did, which is how I know that you can. And that you will.'

Julie stared at him, and then gave him a curt nod. Slowly, her eyes left his face and focussed on Jenna. 'Did you bring me some chocolate?'

Jenna reached into her pocket and held up a pound coin.

'It's in the machine if you want it. Dr Sinclair will come with us, it's right outside the doors of the ward.'

Julie fingered the blanket that lay over her legs. 'I don't want to disturb my skin grafts.'

'You won't.' Adam tapped the thick file that he had brought with him. 'I've read all of your notes and the skin grafts have taken nicely. You can get up and move around gently now. In fact, it'll be good for you, stimulate the circulation.'

Julie wrinkled her nose. 'They look horrible. I've seen them when they do the dressings.'

'I know.' He fingered the envelope he had tucked inside the file, wondering whether now was the time to bring it out. 'They'll look better. You know that, don't you?'

'Yeah. S'pose so.' Julie huffed a sigh. 'Every day, in every way it just gets better and better, is that it?'

Adam suppressed a grin. He could see why Jenna had taken to Julie. Underneath all that teenage petulance the kid had spirit. 'Well, yeah. Some days are always going to be better than others, but if you look at it in the long term, things do get better.' He was getting there. He got a grin in return. 'You look better when you smile, you know.'

'Yeah, I've heard that one before too.'

Adam came to a decision and pulled the envelope he had brought out of the file. 'I brought you a picture. One of my patients, I treated her for burns.'

Julie focussed on the envelope. 'So I'm supposed to look at this and see how much progress she's made, am I?' Petulant *and* bright. Adam could see why Julie was such a handful.

'I had a lot of fears when I was hurt. A lot of feelings that I couldn't come to terms with.' The look on Julie's face told Adam that she did, too. 'So did the girl in the picture.

It's a tough road, but sometimes knowing that you're not walking it alone makes it a bit easier.'

He was delving much deeper into his own pain than he'd expected to. But somehow, with Jenna sitting quietly beside him, and Julie, whose need was so much greater than his own, it felt okay. Almost a relief.

'Okay. I'll look.' Julie reached for the photograph, struggling to get it out of the envelope with just one hand. Jenna didn't move to help her. Tough love. But it was love, all the same, the kind that was going to haul Julie through this, kicking and screaming if necessary.

Jenna craned over to see the photograph. 'Who's the boy that she's with?'

'That's Rick. They're married now.'

Jenna exchanged looks with Julie. 'He's nice. I think he's more of a Ricky than a Rick, don't you?'

Julie giggled. 'Yeah. Pretty neat guy.'

It wasn't exactly textbook stuff, but it was working. The last thing that Julie was seeing were the faint scars on Claudia's leg. She was seeing a young woman, happy and in love, her handsome boyfriend at her side. Jenna worked round to the scars, but only after she'd made her point about Rick not caring about them. Adam's hand strayed absently to his shoulder. She was almost making him feel better.

'Can you make me a copy of this?' Julie regarded Adam, obviously assessing his age and likely technical competence. 'Do you know how to do that?'

'I've got a copy. Take this.'

'So you like the younger man, do you?' All the way down to the canteen, Adam had been smiling at something, and that was obviously it.

'Oh, go boil your head.' Jenna stuffed her take-away

sandwich into his hand while she rummaged in her bag for her purse, then grabbed the sandwich back again. She wasn't best pleased with him, but tact prevented Jenna from challenging him here and now on the matter.

He shot her a puzzled look and her exasperation began to cool. Not before he'd noticed it, though. 'Want to talk about it?' Before she could stop him, he'd taken her sandwich back, showing it to the cashier and then walking away with it to a quiet spot in the far corner of the canteen.

As soon as she reached the table where he was sitting, she made a lunge for the sandwich, but he was too quick for her, holding it out of her reach. 'So you're going to starve me into submission now, are you?'

'If necessary.'

'I do have money, you know. I can go and get another one.' Jenna plumped herself down on the chair opposite.

'You're not going to, though.'

She probably shouldn't have shown her hand by sitting down. 'No. I'm not.' He pushed her sandwich across the table towards her with one finger, and Jenna took possession of it. 'You might have told me about being shot. That you know about trauma first hand.' She lowered her voice, hissing the words across the table at him.

'I might have done.' He rubbed thoughtfully at his shoulder. 'I would have done, if I'd known that I was going to tell Julie.'

'That's not the point. Do you really think that you're best placed to help her if you've still got issues of your own to deal with?'

'Who says that I do?'

The look in his eyes, for a start. And Jenna was sure that she'd not been mistaken when she'd thought she'd heard his stifled cry last night. Even though she hadn't seen him, she'd sensed his presence out on the patio. 'Well, do you?'

'Not where Julie's concerned. I have it under control.' Maybe he saw the disbelief in her eyes. 'If you want to know, you should just ask. Rob drives me crazy, tiptoeing around what happened as if it's some guilty secret.'

'Well, tact never was Rob's strong point.' She got a grin in response. 'I would like to know, but the canteen's probably not the best place in the world to have this conversation.' Jenna looked around awkwardly.

'It's okay. My fiancée and I were both shot eighteen months ago in Guatemala, in a roadside ambush that went bad. Elena died, and I pulled through. I struggled with it, for a long time.'

The mixed emotions jostling in her chest drained away, leaving only horror and shock. 'Adam, I'm so sorry.'

He slid his hand across the table towards hers, as if he should be the one to comfort her. 'It happened and I won't say that it hasn't changed me. But I'd never let it compromise the welfare of any patient.'

'No.' Her fingers were trembling, and she pressed them down onto the tabletop to steady them. 'I'm sorry, I shouldn't have insinuated that.'

'But I still should have told you?'

'Yes, I think you should.'

He nodded. 'So do I. And I want you to promise me something.'

Anything. She'd do anything she could to help him. 'Okay.'

'If you ever think that a personal issue is getting in the way of my treatment of a patient, you'll tell me. I don't mean dropped hints or concerned noises, but words of one syllable.'

'I can do that. I'm better at words of one syllable than I am at hints.'

He grinned. 'Thought you might be.' He looked at his watch. 'As we're here, do you have time for some coffee?'

'Yes, of course.' Those honest eyes of his. Never once countenancing pity, but demanding respect. Jenna could almost feel them drawing her in, inch by inch. 'I've another twenty minutes of my lunch break left, and they'll page me if they need me.' He went to stand and she beat him to it. 'Stay there, I'll get them.'

Things were beginning to make sense. He'd papered over the cracks of his own trauma so effectively that it only surfaced at night when he couldn't suppress it with an effort of will. And by the time Jenna returned with the coffee, setting his cup down in front of him, he had already moved on and was thinking about something else.

'Acid's a very personal way to attack someone.'

'It was personal. Kind of.' Jenna tipped some milk into his cup. 'Julie has a sister, a year older than her. They're very alike, could be twins. She'd borrowed her sister's blouse and jacket to go out in.'

'And the acid was meant for her sister?'

'Yes. An ex-boyfriend who held a grudge. The parents knew there was a problem there, and had been keeping an eye on Julie's sister.'

'And no one thought to stop Julie from going out dressed in her sister's clothes?' Anger suffused every line of his face.

'Easy to be wise after the event. I've talked to the parents and put in an urgent request for counselling for Julie's sister, but she's not at the top of the priority list.'

He sighed, his finger and thumb massaging the bridge of his nose. 'Do you think it would help if you and I had an informal chat with the whole family?'

Jenna turned the idea over in her head, and decided to trust him. 'Yeah. Yes, I think that would help a lot.'

* * *

He'd seemed glad of her company over coffee, and almost relieved when Jenna had steered the conversation round to lighter topics. Relaxed now, he strolled with her all the way back down to A and E, staying to chat to Jenna's colleague Brenda while Jenna went to the locker room. And he was still there when she returned.

'I saw penguins last year when I went to New Zealand. I wasn't too keen on the little blighters but my friend was mad to see them.' Brenda's blond hair, piled up on the top of her head in a messy confection of highlights and lowlights, was shining, along with her smile.

'Yeah?' Brenda had caught Adam's interest and he hardly noticed Jenna's return. 'I'd love to go to New Zealand.'

'Great place. We stopped off in Hong Kong on the way.' Brenda was a seasoned traveller, saving her money and her annual leave for somewhere far-flung every summer. 'I'm planning to go to India this year.'

His arms were folded on the counter in front of him and he leaned forward towards Brenda. 'Are you? Whereabouts?'

Brenda had his full attention now and they were swapping stories about places they'd been, things they'd seen. Jenna didn't have much to contribute to that conversation. Sure, she got itchy feet from time to time, who didn't? But her yearning to see the world had been smothered by the need for security, her home, her career. One day, maybe, she'd have that sufficiently sorted to venture out a little.

'Tell him to come along, Jen.' Brenda was nudging her elbow.

'Uh? Where?' She'd lost track, reckoning that Brenda and Adam were doing fine on their own.

'To the softball match next Friday evening.' Brenda turned her attention back to Adam. 'All the hospitals have teams, and we have a kind of league. We're playing the Marylebone Medics, and they take it all very seriously, you know, practising and not drinking beer until afterwards.' Brenda's eye assessed the full breadth of Adam's shoulders with something more than professional interest. 'I bet you're pretty handy with a bat. We might just stand a chance if I can persuade Rob to play as well.'

'Where do you play?' Adam seemed to be weighing up the offer.

'Hyde Park. Over in the southern section, there's always plenty of room on the sports field to stake a pitch. Our team's the Bankside Cheetahs—because we cheat, not because we resemble a graceful, fast-moving animal.' Brenda giggled. 'Although Jenna has her moments.'

'Right. Like last month when I tripped over your foot.'

'That was just unlucky. Anyway, we're never too proud to welcome a ringer on to the team.'

'I work here. Part time for the next month, anyway.'

'Oh, well, that's even better.' Brenda was scenting victory. 'I thought you were lecturing at the university. They've got their own team but you don't want to be with that lot. Far too young and enthusiastic.'

Adam chuckled. 'I'm filling in with a couple of shifts a week here, as well as working with the reconstructive surgery team.' He grinned. 'We're all sharing knowledge. So, assuming that I'm old and cynical enough for the Bankside Cheetahs, I'm totally legit.'

'Well, that's sorted, then.' Brenda turned her green eyes on to him, full force. 'I was wondering what that orange circle on the roster was. Stands for knowledge-sharing, does it?'

'Guess so.' Adam glanced at his watch. 'But since I'm supposed to be sharing elsewhere today, I'd better make myself scarce.' He gifted Brenda with a devastating smile and nodded at Jenna. 'Later.'

Brenda watched Adam through the automatic doors, chewing speculatively on the end of her pencil. 'How did it go with Julie?'

'Good. He really got through to her. And he was honest with her, didn't treat her as if she was stupid, just because she's young. From what I saw of his case notes at the lecture yesterday, he's an exceptional surgeon.'

'Praise indeed.' Brenda shot a querying glance towards Reception and received a signal that all was quiet. 'So you're practically living with him. What's the story, any lady visitors?'

'Give him a chance, he's only been here two days.' Jenna could see exactly where this conversation was headed. 'You interested, then?'

Brenda shrugged. 'Don't want to step on anyone's toes.'

Jenna shrugged. There was no reason why he shouldn't be dating again. She doubted that Adam was short on offers.

'I wouldn't know. You'll have to ask him. Or Rob, he'd probably know.'

'I didn't mean that.' Brenda was looking at her pointedly.

'Me?' Jenna flushed, shaking her head. 'What are you, mad?'

'What's wrong with that? He's good-looking, seems like a nice guy. Unless you've still got an arrangement with Joe…?'

'Joe? He's been gone nearly a year now.'

Brenda pursed her lips. 'I thought that maybe you were waiting for him or something. You two did seem very cosy right before he left. Didn't strike me as if it was the end of the road somehow.'

Cosy was not the word for it. It had been more like agonised prayer on Jenna's part that a miracle would happen and he wouldn't leave. Or that he'd want her to go with him to Australia. Something, anything other than the harsh reality that he'd just felt like a change of scene and she wasn't included in his future plans.

'No. We split up for good.'

'I'm sorry. I didn't realise, Jen, you seemed so okay with it all that I thought that you two had worked something out.' Realisation dawned on Brenda's face. 'But you were just playing nice, weren't you?'

Jenna shrugged away the hurt. It had been the same when her parents had left, easier to pretend that she didn't care and just get on with her life. 'Joe's ancient history. And Adam's not my type.'

'I would have thought he was pretty much anyone's type.' Brenda shot her a suspicious look. 'But, then, he's not around for long, is he.'

'Exactly. Having one boyfriend leave the country is bad luck. Two looks like carelessness.' Add her parents to the list and it was criminal negligence. Jenna swallowed the thought and grinned at Brenda. 'I could ask you round some time if you're interested, though.'

The idea seemed to appeal to Brenda, but she shook her head. 'No. You know me, I don't run after men. Always better to let them come to you.'

Fair enough. On the evidence of his reactions, Adam might just do that. Brenda was good-hearted, pretty and she knew how to have a good time. No tangled strings. No stupid hang-ups. Just as long as he remembered to close the French doors at night, if he did decide to take Brenda up on the offer that Jenna reckoned she was pretty much certain to make.

CHAPTER FOUR

IT was his fourth night in the flat, and the fourth night in a row that the dream had come. He guessed that it was the change of scene that had brought the dreams back so often. So vividly. Adam gritted his teeth and got on with it. Get out of bed. Shake the dream off. Walk a little and then go back to bed and hope that this time his sleep was untroubled.

The dream clung to him as if he had fallen into a pit of stinking mud. Maybe his talk with Julie and her family that afternoon hadn't helped. It had gone well, but he hadn't been able to get the haunted look in Julie's sister's eyes out of his head.

He padded through to the kitchen and got himself a glass of water, drinking it down in one go. Throwing on jeans and an old T-shirt, he slipped noiselessly through the open French doors and onto the patio to get some air.

'Okay?' Her voice sounded above him, making him jump. Adam wondered whether any of the cries that had sounded through his dream had been real and had woken her.

'Yeah. Warm night again.'

'Yes. I can't sleep.' They both skirted carefully around the real reason for Adam's wakefulness. And perhaps for hers. He'd heard the click of the balcony doors above him more than once these past couple of nights.

Adam sat down on the wide steps of the fire escape. 'Join me?' It was probably a bad idea, but he couldn't help himself. He'd seen her often enough over the last couple of days, but she had seemed remote, less willing to connect with him, and it had chilled him to the marrow.

Her footsteps were silent behind him, but he felt the silky material of her dressing gown brush against his arm as she walked down the steps and sat down next to him. She smelled just lovely. Like an English country garden after a downpour of rain, sweet and clean, with a touch of the deep scent of the earth.

'Is this why you wouldn't stay with Rob and Cassie?' Her voice was quiet, measured. Soothing, like the dark stillness of the night. 'They wouldn't have minded, you know.'

'I do.' The hairs on the back of his wrist were standing on end where the silky material had touched him. The brief sensation had almost made him cry out.

'For Ellie and Daisy?'

'Yeah. The drawing that Ellie did...'

Her soft laugh echoed through his empty heart. 'That was beautiful. Bright colours, smiley faces. It didn't seem like a sad picture to me.'

'To me either. A year ago, six months even, I couldn't have looked at it without breaking down. But now it makes me smile. Elena would have loved it.' He shifted a little, working at the tension across his shoulders. 'This... The dreams aren't for Ellie to know about, though. They're something different.'

'How?'

All he'd wanted these past few days had been for her to challenge him, help him break free of the shackles that were stopping him from doing what all his instincts clamoured for. He'd asked her to be honest with him, speak plainly, and she had. But it wasn't enough.

'I don't want to go there, Jenna.'

He felt her shrink away from him. 'I'm sorry. Fools rush in...'

He was suddenly so sick of this. Sick of the complex dance they'd been doing, never getting too close but unable to keep their distance. 'Angels don't fear anything.'

'I wish I could take a leaf out of their book.'

Maybe he should too. Act as if he was on the side of the angels. Pretend that what he'd told her already was all there was to it, and that there wasn't another part of him that had been irrevocably broken that day on the road.

'Perhaps they should take one from yours.'

She laughed quietly into the moonlight, shaking her head. 'I don't think so somehow.'

Something whispered against his arm, feather soft. The wings of a moth, maybe, or one of the butterflies from her garden, out on a late-night spree. Or maybe it had been a lock of her hair.

'You underestimate yourself. You can teach them a thing or two.' He dipped in a little closer and found that her lips were already there. Euphoria swamped the voice of reason. It would just be one kiss. A man didn't have to fall in love, risk everything again, just for one kiss.

If she'd have stayed still, quiet, maybe he could have resisted her. But he felt her fingers on his jaw, skimming across the night's stubble. Then she whispered his name, and ripped every last thread of his resolve to tatters.

His hands found her waist and she slid onto his lap. He kissed her, heat banking and flaring in his chest until his head began to swim.

'Mmm. That was foolish.' Her lips brushed warmly against his, full of the promise of what he hadn't yet tasted.

'Very.' If the first kiss could be explained away as a heat-of-the-moment thing, the second trashed that particular excuse. They both knew exactly what they were doing. Her gaze locked with his and he was lost, drowning in the deep blue waters of her eyes. Adam poured everything he had, everything he was into the kiss, letting the long, slow beat of their passion take him.

Finally, he let his lips slip from hers and he held her gently to his chest, not caring that she could surely hear the urgent pumping of his heart. She was silent for a long time and when she did speak her voice was almost a whisper. 'Adam, I...'

He rested his cheek against her hair. 'I know. The most foolish things can be the sweetest.'

She laughed quietly and he was glad that he had pleased her. 'Got a little carried away, I guess.'

She knew it wasn't only that just as well as he did. But Adam already cared about her too much to short-change her by taking this any further. 'Yes. Something about a hot summer night. Jenna, I'm sorry if...'

'It's okay. I know.' She hung her head, moving to get up off his lap, but he pulled her down. He may not be able to take this any further, but he wouldn't have her believe what she so obviously seemed to think.

'When I kissed you, Jenna, it was you that I wanted. Just you.'

She gnawed at her lip uncertainly, seeming to be unable to take that fact in. Reality was closing back in on both of them, wrenching them apart, but he couldn't let her go without knowing that these last moments had been special. He dropped a kiss onto the end of his finger, pressing it against her lips, and felt them curve in a smile.

'I suppose I'd better go. Before either of us starts anything we can't finish.' She didn't move from his lap.

'That would be best.' He'd committed himself once to a woman. But that was when he had believed in love without loss. And he had a ready-made excuse not to take this any further. 'I'm only here for a month and then I have to leave.'

'I know.' She seemed almost relieved, as if that had settled some conflict that was going on in her head. A flash of mischief crossed her face. 'Great kiss, though.'

'Yeah. One of the best.' *The* best, as far as he could remember, but saying that would only get him into more trouble than he was already in.

Wordlessly she jumped to her feet, almost running past him and up the steps of the fire escape. Seconds later the click of the door catch above him told him that she had gone straight inside.

He sat for a moment his head in his hands. It was one thing to join forces with Jenna to help Julie, but anything else was out of the question. He was going to have to be very clear on that from now on. Slowly he stood, making his way back through the open French doors, shedding his T-shirt and jeans and throwing himself back onto the rumpled sheets of his bed.

Jenna watched as Brenda shaded her eyes, scanning the park anxiously. 'He said he'd be here. He was tied up with something but he'd definitely be here.' She gave an exaggerated grimace.

'He'll be here, then. Or he won't. One of the two.' Jenna had tried to forget that kiss of a couple of nights ago. Or at least disregard it. It seemed that was what Adam was doing too.

'Well, if he doesn't make it in the next fifteen minutes,

I'll have to put Sue in to bat. And you know how she hates it, she only really comes to watch Andrew.'

Jenna lay back on the rug that was spread under the trees at the edge of the softball pitch. 'I'll go in again. We can do that if we don't have a full team.'

'Yes, but we do have a full team. You can't go twice if we have a full team, those are the rules.' Brenda was stripping the seeds from an ear of wild grass, in much the same way that a vexed child pulled the legs off an insect. 'I suppose we could say Sue's hurt her ankle. Then we wouldn't have a full team.'

'They're all medics too. They can spot a fake injury just as well as we can. You can't fool them with a bandage and some red felt-tip.'

Brenda stared at the opposing team, all dressed in matching sports shirts, huddled together, obviously discussing tactics. 'Yeah, you've got a point. This lot take it all far too seriously, they'd probably want a doctor's note and a second opinion.'

'We'll just have to hope he makes it, then.' Jenna scanned the path leading down from the car park. 'Look, isn't that him there? With Rob?'

'Yes-s-s!' Brenda was already scenting victory and jumped to her feet, waving and cupping her hands around her mouth. 'Come on, you two. Get a move on.'

Adam arrived, was thoroughly chastised for being late, and then sent straight in to bat. Rob sat down on the rug, cracking open a can of beer from the cool box, making exaggerated noises of disgust when the bowler threw a foul ball at Adam.

The next ball was good, and the crack of the bat was accompanied by Rob's roar of approval. The ball whizzed over their heads and Jenna ducked as three fielders from the opposite team thundered past her into the trees.

'Run!' Brenda's screamed instruction was unnecessary as Adam had already dropped the bat and was running. 'No, Erica, don't hang around like that. You'll block him. You run as well.'

Erica obeyed, cantering home just slowly enough to leave Adam stranded behind her on third base. Brenda waved her in to bat, moaning with frustration as a curved ball slipped past her and she was caught out.

'You next, Rob.' Brenda confiscated his beer and pushed Rob to his feet. 'And no daisy cutters.'

'Aren't you supposed to encourage them? You are team coach after all.' Jenna was watching Rob's back as he trudged onto the pitch, picking up the bat.

'I brought the beer, what more do they want?' Brenda watched with approval as Rob took a swing at the ball, sending it off to the corner of the pitch. 'With any luck, they'll clock up a few runs between them.'

By the time Adam and Rob had finished, Jenna and the rest of the Bankside Cheetahs were cheering along with Brenda. Twenty runs, six of them home runs, which more than doubled their score and put them in with a chance.

At half-time Brenda delivered a short inspirational message, which amounted to threats of physical harm if anyone dropped a catch, and then deployed her team, Adam and Rob close in for the weaker batters and in the outfield for the stronger. Jenna was in her usual position at third base, with Brenda herself floating, shouting instructions that no one took a great deal of notice of.

It was a draw. Thanks to a few lucky catches on her own part, some impressive teamwork between Adam and Rob and an almost superhuman catch by Adam, which prompted universal applause. The Marylebone Medics swallowed their incredulity and took it in good part, breaking out their own supplies of beer.

Adam was deep in conversation with one of the opposing team, obviously someone he knew from the way they'd greeted each other. Jenna tried not to watch him, but Brenda had no such scruples.

'Great catch, that. Perhaps we could all practise together next week.'

'Practise?' Jenna's mouth dropped open. 'Since when have we practised? Anyway, getting everyone together for games is difficult enough, what with half the team being on shift at any one time.'

'Suppose so.' Brenda finished gathering the bats and balls together into the large holdall that housed their kit. 'Are you going to take this?'

'Yes, I've got my car with me. Want a lift?'

Brenda grinned. 'No, thanks. That guy from the Marylebone team that Adam's been yacking with all evening lives in my neck of the woods. Adam's going to drop him, and then my place is on the way back to yours from there, so I'll tag along.'

A sour taste suddenly caught in Jenna's throat. So what? It was only a lift. And she'd told Brenda already that she wasn't interested in Adam. One measly kiss wasn't going to change that. Even if it hadn't been one, and if describing the way that Adam kissed as measly was actionable in any court of law.

'Okay. Will you give me a hand over to the car park with the kit, then?'

Brenda helped Jenna to carry the holdall to the car park and dump it into the boot of her car. She could see Adam and Rob strolling forty yards behind them and left Brenda leaning on the bonnet of Adam's car as she accelerated away. Whatever was, or wasn't, going to happen next, she didn't want to be around to see it.

* * *

The next day had dawned bright, clear and, best of all, Saturday. If Jenna had been in the mood to let off steam, and she wasn't saying that she was, then attacking some of the weeds in her butterfly garden would be an ideal way to do it.

She spent some time hacking at the mint, which had run riot across the whole area. Cutting it down and then digging out the network of long, stubborn roots that ran under the soil was hard work, and as the sun climbed in the sky she seemed to get more hot and bothered, rather than less.

'Morning.' She had been tugging at a particularly recalcitrant root, and didn't hear Adam's approach across the grass. Jenna turned, slipping her gardening gloves off and wiping her forehead as if the redness of her face was due to heat and exertion.

'Morning.' He looked tired and a little bleary-eyed, as if he'd had no sleep last night. Probably hadn't.

'You're working on the garden, then?'

That was self-evident. But, then, if he had any sense of decency, he was just as much at a loss for words as she was. 'Yes. I thought it was time I did some tidying up.'

'Looks like hard work.' His eyes rested on the garden fork, stuck into the earth next to her, as if he was considering offering her a hand.

'It's this mint, it sends out runners all over the place. It's a job to dig it all out.' Jenna grabbed the fork. 'I reckon that's enough for today.'

He nodded, stifling a yawn. If he had the temerity to do that again, she'd probably be justified in stabbing him with the fork. If he stretched then she'd do it slowly.

Jenna looked at her watch. 'Well, I'd better get on. I said I'd meet some friends for lunch.' Let him get back to bed, he obviously hadn't had any sleep last night. Or if he had, it hadn't been here. He'd been quiet enough when he'd slipped in at seven o'clock this morning, but she'd been awake, just as she had been off and on for most of the night.

'Yeah, sure. I just wanted to have a quick chat with you. About last night.'

Oh, no he didn't. It was one thing to kiss. Telling was quite another. And Brenda was Jenna's friend, she didn't want to hear about what had happened last night. Certainly not from him. 'I've got to go.' She looked at her watch again to emphasise that there was no time to stand around talking.

He gave her a questioning look and Jenna gathered up her gloves and fork. 'I'll catch you later.' Much later.

'Sure. Later, then.' He watched her march across the lawn and up the fire-escape steps into her flat. When Jenna tiptoed up to the kitchen window a few minutes later and peered out, he was still standing on the lawn, alone, seemingly deep in thought.

'You look tired. What have you been up to?'

Jenna could well ask the same of Brenda. But instead she pulled her shoulders back and smiled. 'Oh, nothing.'

'And of course today had to be the busiest day since written records began.' Brenda glanced around her quickly. 'I think it's settling a bit now, though.'

'Hope so. Where's Adam? Have you seen him?' Jenna didn't actually want to know where Adam was. She just wanted to know whether the coast was clear to grab a coffee from the machine.

'Booth six, I think. He's been flat out all morning, too.' Brenda peered at her with an air of professional concern. 'You really do look shattered. You need an early night tonight.'

'I'm okay.' Jenna had worked it all out in her head now. About a thousand times. She'd told Brenda herself that she wasn't interested in Adam, and he'd obviously told her nothing to contradict that. She should just keep her head down and not make waves.

Brenda puffed out a breath. 'Catch you for coffee later, then. You look as if you need some. Are you taking the accident victim that's coming in?'

'Yes.' Jenna nodded as the automatic doors to Casualty swished open. 'Looks like he's here already.'

She motioned the porter to take the trolley over to an empty cubicle then turned to the ambulance paramedic. 'What've you got for me, Joel?'

'Young lad, dislocated shoulder that seems to have snapped back into place, bruising around the rib cage. He was thrown off his bike in a three-car pile-up. He was all over the place when we got there, took a swing at Andy before we could get him calmed down and onto a back-board.' Joel shook his head. 'I wish people wouldn't do that.'

Jenna nodded. 'Hopefully it's just the shoulder, then. Has he been breathalysed?'

'Yep. Nothing significant. He's just an aggressive little so-and-so. Watch him, Jenna, his left arm's useless but he's got a handy right.'

'Thanks. I'll keep an eye out.' It happened. People in pain, their systems flooded with adrenaline after an accident. The fight-or-flight instinct kicked in, and the very people who were trying to help got on the end of a fist for their pains. 'You and Andy okay?'

'What, scrawny kid like that? We've seen worse.'

So had she. All the same, Jenna left the door of the cubicle open behind her and stood on the youth's left side, out of reach. 'My name's Jenna and I'm a doctor. I see you're hurt. May I take a look?' She injected what was hopefully the right mix of warmth and firmness into her tone.

'Yeah, okay. Just my arm.'

'All right.' That would do for starters. After that, Jenna would work her way around to giving him a full examination. 'Your name's Peter?'

'How did you know that?' His face was very pale, but two red spots had appeared on his cheeks.

'It's on your notes.' Jenna twisted the clipboard around so he could see the writing and flipped it back again before he could read it. 'Do you have any pain in your neck? Your back?'

'No. I told those idiots in the ambulance. It's my shoulder that hurts. It went out when I came off my bike.'

'Okay.' She reached for the scissors in her pocket. 'I'm going to cut the sleeve of your shirt so I can have a look without hurting you too much. And I really need you to lie still for the moment.'

'Do I get compensation, then? This is a new shirt.'

Jenna refrained from rolling her eyes. If she had a pound for the number of times she'd heard people complain when emergency staff cut their clothing, she'd be a rich woman. 'No, you don't. And, look, it's torn already.'

Peter grimaced at her and allowed her to carefully cut the sleeve of his shirt. The shoulder was red and swollen, but seemed to be back in place. 'It looks as if you've saved me a job. I'll take an X-ray to make sure, but from what the ambulance crew say your shoulder's popped back in again.'

'I don't need any X-ray. I felt it.'

'Well, we need to make sure. And it's important we make sure that you've no injury to your back, as well.' Jenna walked round to the other side of the bed. He wasn't exactly docile, but she couldn't examine him if she didn't get in close. 'Is it okay with you if I take your blood pressure?'

Clearly it wasn't okay. Peter was skinny but strong, and the straps that were intended to immobilise him had left his arms free. When he grabbed the front of her scrubs, pulling her towards him, she couldn't resist him. 'I told you I don't want any of that shit.'

She knew exactly how to hurt him so badly that the last thing he'd be thinking about was grabbing her. Instead, Jenna gripped the edges of the mattress, her nose two inches from Peter's contorted face. 'Okay. Okay, whatever you say.'

'And get me out of this lot.' He'd managed to work free of some of the restraints, and he howled in pain as he tried to use his other arm to get rid of the brace on his neck.

'Peter, stop it. You need to stay still.'

He yanked on her scrubs and her hips slammed painfully against the bed frame. The urge to fight swelled in her chest and she ignored it.

'Let her go. Now.' She couldn't see who was standing behind her, but she knew anyway. Adam's voice was quiet, measured, but as cold as ice.

Peter didn't move.

'Let her go.' Repeat the instruction. Let that be the only thing in Peter's head. His only thought. Jenna took a deep breath.

'Let me go, Peter.' Peter's fingers loosened and she pulled herself free, stumbling backwards with the momentum, feeling Adam's hand on her arm, steadying her.

'Okay?' Those tawny eyes flashed with concern. She didn't want it. She didn't need a knight in shining armour, and even if she did, Adam was the last person she wanted to fulfil that role.

'Yes, fine. Thank you.' She steadied herself, pulling her arm away from him.

Adam ignored her silent plea to leave. He moved in close, between her and Peter, giving Peter a glare that would have cowed a grizzly bear. Maybe, on this occasion, Adam did have something to add to the mix.

'Right.' Adam was firm and clear, brooking no argument. 'You've been hurt and we're here to do what we can about that. What you need to do right now is cooperate and lose the attitude.'

'Or what? The rozzers don't scare me.' Peter's tone of exaggerated defiance gave the lie to his assertion.

Adam let it go and picked up the clipboard containing Peter's notes, scanning them quickly. 'I see you've been breathalysed and you've got some alcohol in your system but not much. Probably from last night. Anything else?'

'Nothing. I'm clean.' Peter cursed Adam comprehensively.

'Yeah, I've heard that one before, but my parents deny it.' The hint of a smile flickered around Adam's lips. 'I can do a drug test if you like, but it's a great deal easier if you just tell me. You can't get arrested for what's in your system.'

True enough. On the other hand, Peter had been driving. Adam had conveniently neglected to mention that. Jenna wondered what he would do if what he obviously suspected turned out to be true.

'Couple of smokes. Last night.'

'Okay. Anything else?'

'Nah. What do you think I am?'

Adam refrained from giving an answer and shot Jenna an amused look. 'Are you happy to examine him now?'

'Of course.' She didn't want Adam waltzing in and taking over. 'If you're busy, I'll call someone else in.'

'That's okay, I'm free for the moment.' He twisted back to face Peter. 'You've got one more chance. Don't blow it.' His glare said it all. Lay one finger on her and you'll have to answer to me.

Jenna didn't much like it, but she knew the rules. You didn't go near a violent patient without someone else in attendance. Peter hardly looked at her as she went about her examination but Adam's looming presence was enough to keep him compliant.

'Any other pain, Peter?' Peter's eyes momentarily flicked to his leg, before he turned on her and snarled in the negative.

'Did your bike roll onto your leg?' That kind of injury was common. Motorbike riders whose legs were crushed when the bike rolled. Peter wasn't old enough to be driving a big machine, but even a smaller one could do a fair bit of damage.

'I said…' Peter stopped short at Adam's warning growl. 'It's okay. Thanks.'

Nothing like a bit of thanks. And this was nothing like it. 'All the same, I'd like to take a look at it, please.' Jenna flipped a look at Adam. Peter was wearing heavy boots, laced up tight around his ankles. She might need some help from him if she was going to avoid being kicked in the face.

'Don't even think about it, mate.' Adam issued the warning and moved to Peter's leg, unlacing one of his boots, taking it off and dropping it onto the bed. When he touched the other foot, Peter's hiss of pain was quiet but unmistakeable.

Adam carefully cut the laces this time, opening the sides of the boot as wide as he could. As he did so, blood plumed over his hands. He reacted quickly, removing the boot, and a deep cut on Peter's ankle gouted blood.

'I need something to put this into.' He was holding the boot away from him, blood dripping from it onto the floor. Peter's thick socks and the tight lacing of the boot had obviously acted like a compress, stopping the wound from bleeding until now.

Jenna moved quickly, grabbing the plastic wastepaper bin, pulling the top off and dumping the liner and its contents onto the floor. 'Here, this'll do.' She held out the bin and Adam dropped Peter's boot carefully inside.

'Don't touch it!' His tone was urgent and when Jenna looked inside the bin she saw the reason for Peter's injury. A small, razor-sharp blade nestled inside the blood-soaked boot and sock. Adam's head swivelled round to Peter, who had suddenly become very pale. 'Okay, mate, you've got a cut on your ankle. All under control.'

Jenna wasn't so sure. He was doing all the right things, but there was something about the look in his eyes, the dead, dull horror when the blood had suddenly covered his hands that set alarm bells ringing in her head. 'Want a hand?'

'I've got it.' His voice was level now. Perhaps she'd been mistaken. 'Can you hand me that gauze, please?' He was still gripping the wound tightly, and taking the gauze pad that she proffered, he quickly slipped it over the jagged cut and reapplied pressure.

The set of his jaw was a little too tight and his eyes had lost their fire. But Adam was a professional, and he never faltered, working quickly to bind the wound and elevate the leg, even taking time to reassure Peter. For the time being Jenna had to allow him a measure of respect. As soon as they were out of this cubicle, she could go back to contempt.

CHAPTER FIVE

'Hey!' Jenna had thought that now Peter's leg had been dealt with, X-rays ordered and a member of the hospital security team was keeping a discreet eye on him, Adam would lay off being stern and commanding. It appeared not.

She turned slowly. Too slowly, as it looked like a comment. So what? It *was* a comment. 'Yes?'

'I want a word.'

'Can it wait?' Jenna looked around her. A and E was currently experiencing one of those lulls between storms, and she could see nothing that required her immediate attention.

'No, it can't. One minute. It's important.'

'The other ambulance from the crash will be here any minute.'

'No, it won't. Brenda says they're still cutting the driver out of the car.'

Jenna pressed her lips together. She didn't want to talk to him, not after he'd found his way into someone else's bed just days after kissing her like that. But it didn't look as if she had much choice. He knew how to act like a professional and she should show that she could, too.

'What can I do for you?' They were in the open area,

right next to the nurses' station. What could he say to embarrass her here?

'It's about Julie.'

'What about Julie?' Alarm supplanted resentment in a second.

Adam seemed to relax now that he had her attention. 'She had a bad time on Friday night. She heard that the lad who threw the acid was getting out on bail and she started to panic.'

'Is she all right?' The temptation to run upstairs to Julie's ward was almost irresistible. But Jenna couldn't. It would have to wait. The doctors and nurses there were doing their jobs, and she had to do hers here.

'Yeah. I sat with her, talked it through. When I dropped in on her on Saturday she was much better.'

Jenna swallowed hard. If she'd taken the time to listen to Adam on Saturday, she would have known. She'd had the time to go and see Julie over the weekend, she could have done that.

'I got a page from the hospital just after I left Brenda's on Friday night.' His gaze caught hers and then flipped away again. 'About ten-thirty.'

The significance of the time was not lost on Jenna. She'd driven out of the car park, leaving Adam to take Brenda home at just before ten. It was half an hour's drive to Brenda's. If he'd been back on the road by ten-thirty then he must have just dropped her straight off.

'Ten-thirty.'

'Yep.'

She'd made a mistake. She'd shown that the time he'd got the call was important to her. Jenna tried to gloss over that. 'So you stayed with Julie all night?'

'Yes. How did you know?'

'I heard you come in on Saturday morning.' Joy battled with guilt. Guilt won out. 'I...I should have been there.'

He shook his head. 'Her mother was there. Between us we pretty much had everything covered. I would have called you if we'd needed you. Julie's okay.'

'Are you sure?' Joy made a late comeback, seeping through her system like an insidious drug.

'She's okay. She's going to be discharged as planned in a couple of days' time. She's doing well.'

'I...I guess I owe you...'

'Yeah, you do.' He broke in before she could offer the apology. 'You owe me a coffee, and I'm collecting after this shift's done.' He looked at his watch. 'Two hours, in the courtyard.'

When he disappeared at the end of their shift without a word to anyone, Jenna knew where he'd be. She found him sitting on one of the benches in the courtyard, his body relaxed and at rest, his eyes scanning the comings and goings around him. Watching the world go by always seemed an active and worthwhile pursuit with Adam.

Jenna sat down next to him, not too close, and handed him the coffee from the cardboard carry-container. 'Oh. Thanks.' He regarded the logo on the cup. 'This isn't hospital coffee.'

'No, I popped out. This is nicer.'

'Yeah, much. Thanks.' He took a sip and leaned back, throwing his arm across the wooden backrest. 'I can do with this.'

'Me, too. Adam, I'm sorry...' This time she got the word out before he stopped her.

'Nothing to be sorry about. You didn't know where I was.' That could be taken two ways. She didn't know that he'd been with Julie. Or that he hadn't been with Brenda.

'I could have given you the chance to tell me.'

He shrugged. 'I could have made you listen.'

He could have. But the tone of his voice told Jenna that perhaps he hadn't fully understood the reason for her attitude until now. 'Anyway.' He obviously didn't want to talk about it anymore. 'I called Patient Services about Peter.'

'Yes, Brenda said.' Jenna had seen Adam talking to Peter again as he'd stitched his ankle. 'They're sending someone?'

'Jake Something-or-the-other. Apparently he's a volunteer but he doesn't stand any nonsense.'

'No, he doesn't. Jake's an ex-fireman, and he's taken on a few kids who are headed in the wrong direction. He's worth his weight in gold.'

'That much? I saw him, he's no flyweight.' Adam chuckled.

'Did you notify the police?'

'Jake said he'd deal with it.' Adam stared out through the high iron railings at the busy street, where two cars had met, bumper to bumper, and neither seemed disposed to back down to let the other through. 'What would you have done if he'd been carrying acid?'

Jenna knew what he was asking. There had been no way of knowing whether Peter had a victim or an aggressor. Probably a bit of both, that was the way vicious circles started. 'I don't know. I would have let someone else take the decision. Backed out on the grounds of personal feelings.'

Adam nodded. 'That's what I reckoned. Jake's better equipped to deal with it objectively.' The bloody knife had obviously affected him more than he'd said.

'Teenagers are almost always a product of their experience.' If she knew nothing else, she knew that, beyond a shadow of a doubt.

'You think so?'

'Don't you?'

He took another sip of coffee. 'Yeah, I do. Just wondered why you did.'

Her heart was beating a warning tattoo in her chest and Jenna ignored it. This craving for him to know everything about her was probably unhealthy, or at the very least inadvisable, but right now it was impossible to resist.

'I was on that knife edge. When I was adopted by my grandparents, I thought I was alone in the world, and was ready to wage war on everything and everyone.' She shrugged. 'I was only ten, so I didn't get very far. Without them, though, who knows where I would have ended up?'

'You were adopted? My brother and sister are adopted.' He grinned. 'My sister says that Mum and Dad saved her from what she might have become if they hadn't been around.'

'That's it exactly. How old was your sister when she came to you?'

'Five. She'd been through a lot. Lost her mother to drugs. Her father wasn't on the scene.' He shrugged. 'She didn't say one word for the first three months she was with us. She used to tag along after me with this solemn look on her face, clutching this awful old teddy bear.'

'And now?'

'Now you can't shut her up. She graduated from medical school the year before last.'

'What's her name?'

'Mattie.' The look on his face said it all.

'You're very proud of her.'

He chuckled. 'Don't tell her that. But I couldn't love her more if I tried.'

His face was open, full of warmth. So handsome that Jenna could have wept. And he was so close that all she needed to do was to reach out, touch him.

Why did she want him so much? Was it *because* he was leaving? Was she just trying to re-create the pattern she'd been through with her parents and with Joe, somehow make it right this time? Maybe she could make it right this time. Adam was different from Joe in so many ways.

It was too complex a question to consider right now. 'I want to pop in and see Julie before I go home. If you're in tonight, can I give you a knock later?' She made it sound casual, like a friend popping in for coffee. It was, wasn't it?

'Sure.' That smile. The one that left her slightly breathless, as if she'd just run up a flight of stairs. Joe had never made her feel like that, not even in the first bright months of their romance. 'That'd be nice, I'll look forward to it.'

His mistake began to dawn on Adam as he made his way home on the Underground. Just as the crowded train drew out of King's Cross station, he realised that he was smiling. A woman who was crushed against him and trying not to jab him in the ribs with her handbag smiled back and he made an amiable comment on the discomfort of being jammed up in such close proximity to his fellow travellers and looked away.

He hadn't understood Jenna's reaction to him on Saturday, but now he did. And he'd caught himself revelling in the idea that Jenna had been jealous and upset over where she thought he'd been on Friday night. Wondering whether the kiss they'd shared had been so foolish after all.

The train was beginning to empty out at each stop. Adam stood aside and waved the woman next to him into an empty seat. What kind of person took pleasure in another's discomfiture? He did, obviously. And what kind of person acted on it? Well, he could stop himself from doing that, at least.

Fresher, cooler air hit him as he made his way up the steps from the station to pavement level. The walk home seemed to clear his head a little and he dropped his bag in the hall, making straight for the sofa and throwing himself down on it. He was tired. Hadn't slept at all on Friday night, and not much for the two nights since. Slowly, his eyelids began to droop.

Adam tore himself from the grip of a dream of visceral intensity only moments before he heard her knock on the door. Shaking his head, trying to throw it off as best he could, he called to her. 'Just coming. Won't be a minute.'

He took the time to splash some cold water on his face and found her waiting at the front door. She nodded, almost shyly, as he motioned her inside.

'You okay?'

He felt as if the dream was branded across his face. 'Yeah. Sorry, have you been knocking? I fell asleep.' Adam wiped one hand across his face, struggling to dispel the feeling of hollow, aching emptiness.

'Want me to make you a cup of tea?' She was looking at him steadily, frank concern in her eyes.

'No. Thanks.'

She followed him through to the sitting room and sat on the edge of the sofa. 'Adam, please, don't. You're not okay. These dreams…'

He hardly heard what she said for the anger bursting through his veins. Self-loathing at his own deceit. He wasn't some tragic hero struggling through a difficult patch. He was broken, finally and irrevocably, a man who'd failed to do the one thing that he'd promised he would always do, and who had the scars to prove it.

'It's nothing.' His voice sounded harsh, but she didn't

flinch. Stared him down with those beautiful blue eyes of hers.

'Pull the other one. It's got bells on it.' Her chin jutted slightly.

'You don't want to go there, Jenna.' He tried to turn away from her but he couldn't.

'Don't tell me where I want to go. That's my decision to make.'

Fine. If that was the way she wanted it. Let her see what kind of man he really was, and then she'd go. Adam caught her hand, pulling her to her feet, and pressed it against his shoulder, knowing that the thin material of his shirt wouldn't disguise the mutilated flesh beneath it.

As soon as her fingertips touched his shoulder, he knew that this was wrong. He let go of her hand, praying that he hadn't hurt her, shaking with guilt and shame.

'Earth to Adam.' She was standing close, her soft voice penetrating the static in his brain, her fingers gently tapping out some kind of call sign on his.

'Are you reading me?' Her voice again. Seemingly miles away but still clear, still something for him to hang on to.

'I read you. I…I'm sorry.' He heard his own voice, broken and weak but trying now to reach out to her.

'Forget the sorry. Just keep this wavelength open.'

He forced himself to take a deep breath. Took a step back, but then the coffee table behind him blocked his retreat, and she moved with him, keeping up the connection. 'I'm sorry, Jenna. I shouldn't have done that. Taken hold of you like that.'

She tossed her head. She may be small, certainly no match for his strength, but she was completely unafraid. Like an angel. 'Let me see them, Adam.'

'You don't want…' He fell silent as her eyes flashed dangerously. She'd already told him about that.

He was unable to stop her as she unbuttoned his shirt, pulling it away from his shoulder. Adam closed his eyes. He'd prefer not to see her reaction. He didn't want to watch and see the same revulsion in her eyes that he saw in his own when he looked into the mirror.

He felt her fingers on his shoulder, cool, gentle like a cleansing balm. Heard her voice, clear and sweet, with no trace of anything but concern. 'Through and through.'

'Yes.' He was speaking almost automatically, powerless to resist her. 'I was lucky. Couple of inches to the right and it would have shattered my shoulder. An inch to the left and it would have hit an artery.'

'Any more?'

He could have said no. Perhaps in some other life, where her candid eyes and soft touch didn't compel the truth from him. Adam unbuttoned his shirt, pulling it free of his jeans and away from the scar beneath his ribs on his right side.

She made no comment but slid her fingers downwards. He sucked in a breath, willing his muscles not to convulse at her touch, his body not to react to her. 'That one they had to dig out.'

'Yes, I can see.' She ran her finger along the small surgical scar that traversed the jagged one made by the bullet's entry. 'Is that it?'

'No.' He sank down onto the coffee table behind him and indicated the line of the red weal that started just above and behind his ear and felt her carefully part his hair so she could see it.

'That one…' She let the sentence drop for an excruciating moment. 'Do you remember anything about what happened?'

'No. Nothing. Elena and I were alone together on the road, and no one really knows.' Hot tears sprang to his eyes and he scraped his hand across his face. 'I don't know if I did anything to help her.'

He heard her breath catch. This final admission, the one he most hated himself for, had been too much. One step too far. He tried to pull away from her, but she was standing in between his legs and he would have had to physically compel her to move to do so. He'd done that once too often already this evening.

'You don't know that you didn't do anything.'

'I know that I didn't do enough. These road bandits aren't out to kill, they just want to rob. We were travelling in a clearly marked vehicle and they must have known we were aid workers and probably foreign nationals. Something must have gone badly wrong.'

'And you assume that it's your fault.'

'I know that I promised to look after her. And that makes me responsible. Whatever I did or didn't do led directly to Elena's death.'

'I don't believe it.'

Four words. Friends, family had talked with him for hours, telling him all the reasons why he shouldn't blame himself. But those four words, spoken with such certainty, meant more to him than any of it. 'You can't just ignore…'

She could. He felt her arms around his neck, drawing him in, and he pressed his cheek against her body, winding his arms around her waist. For a moment he let himself take the comfort that she offered, and then he gently moved her backwards so he could stand again.

'I want you to go, Jenna.' He needed her to go. Before he did anything that he would hate himself for afterwards. Before he did the unthinkable, and began to fall in love with her.

She looked up at him, tears in her eyes. 'Are you sure?'

'Yes, I'm sure. This can't work for either of us. I'm leaving in three weeks' time.'

He had wondered whether she feared anything and here was his answer. She seemed to retreat back from him, without moving an inch. 'Yes. So you are.' She turned and almost ran out of the room, and Adam heard the door slam behind her.

CHAPTER SIX

ADAM lay in bed, staring at the ceiling, listening to Jenna's footsteps down the stairs and the muffled thud of the front door closing. For the whole of this week he'd been up and out of the house before her and home late, but he'd swapped his Friday shift and had the day off today.

Kicking the tangled sheet away from his legs, he padded through into the bathroom, glaring at himself in the mirror. He didn't much like what he saw. A man who had maintained a cool distance from a woman who deserved more than his polite detachment. She wanted more, he knew that for a fact. And he did, too. Didn't they both deserve the chance to be friends and to let that friendship run its course, wherever it might lead?

He reached into the shower, turning the stream of water on full. If he was going to take that step into the unknown, he may as well do it right. And since doing it right was going to take some effort, he needed to stop messing around and get moving.

It was like déjà-vu, only Adam knew exactly when he had done this last. He was sitting on Jenna's doorstep on a Friday evening, waiting for her to come home. Just as before, he knew exactly when she caught sight of him. That little nervous twitch of her free hand, reaching for her face and then falling to her side. The way she tried not to stare at him but looked anyway.

'Locked yourself out?'

He shook his head, looking up at her. She just didn't know how beautiful she was. 'No. Waiting for you. We've been doing a fair job of missing each other for the last few days.'

She pressed her lips together, her eyes searching his face. Then she smiled. 'Yes. Complicated, isn't it?' She sat down on the step next to him. 'Perhaps we should work out a timetable for the coffee machine. You can take odd hours and I'll take evens.'

'Not going to work. Not unless we include the chocolate machine as well.'

'You don't eat chocolate.'

'You do. And they're right next to each other.' Adam felt the smile working through his bones and breaking through on to his lips. He'd missed her so much. 'Tell you what, you can have both machines any time. I'll go to the one next to Haematology.'

She nodded. 'That's very civil of you.' She was fiddling with the strap of her handbag. 'Or I suppose it wouldn't do any harm if we acted like adults.'

'You mean share the same drinks machine?'

She shrugged. 'As long as we're not too obvious about it.' She was starting to relax and her tiredness seemed to lift as she did so.

'I don't want to leave things this way, Jenna. I wish we could be friends.' He'd said it and there was no going back now.

She smiled up at him, that tense, slightly worried smile that she gave when she was thinking. 'We are friends. It just seems that there are an awful lot of rules to it at the moment.'

'Is that what you want?'

'It strikes me that putting limits on a friendship rather defeats the object.'

'Me, too. Can I admit to having broken the rules today, then?'

'What, you went to my coffee machine?'

'Worse than that. Want to come and see?'

She hesitated. He gave her an encouraging smile, and the investment yielded a massive return when she grinned back at him. 'Okay.'

She followed him around the house and through the side gate. Her little cry of astonishment made all of the sweat and the blister on his hand worth it. 'Oh! Adam!' She stopped short, one hand flying to her mouth.

'Like it?' He turned, grinning. He'd done the best job he could, weeding and tidying up her butterfly garden, finding the patterns of the original planting and restoring them.

'No, I love it. Thank you.'

'I got you some things to plant as well, to fill in a few of the gaps.' He gestured over to the tubs on the patio. Pink and white lavender to complement the blue she already had. Hebe. Lilac.

For a moment he thought she was going to hug him, but instead she dropped her bags and ran over to the tubs, bending down to take in the scent of the flowering plants. She had lost all of the weariness in her step and was laughing with delight. 'You must have spent all day on this.'

Pretty much, but her reaction rewarded him ten times over. His heart beat a little faster as he moved on to his next piece of rule-breaking. 'Are you too tired to come out for a spot to eat?'

She hesitated again, just long enough to make it seem like a victory when she nodded. 'I am quite hungry. Where did you have in mind? Most of the places around here are packed on a Friday evening.'

'I know somewhere that won't be. It's quiet, just the two of us, and we can…' What? Adam deliberately hadn't thought that far yet. It needed the two of them to decide what happened next. 'We can talk.'

'I'll, um… Can you give me fifteen minutes, just to take a shower and get changed?'

His heart practically jumped into his throat. He hadn't realised how very much he wanted this until she'd said yes.

'Do I need to bring anything special? Wellington boots? Sun hat? Sou'wester and a pair of walking shoes?'

He laughed. 'No. Just bring yourself.'

He still wouldn't tell her where they were going. He drove north, and in thirty minutes they were on an open road, houses and shops behind them and countryside ahead. 'It's nice to be out of town once in a while.' Jenna was watching the sun slanting across the fields and wondering whether she could do that warm light justice if she tried to paint it.

'I thought you might like to get out of town for a change.' He glanced across at her. 'You look nice tonight. Very retro, it suits you.'

'It's not really retro.' Jenna smoothed the skirt of her dress across her legs. 'This is one of my grandmother's dresses. She had loads of clothes that she didn't wear any more, all in storage. She got a lot of them cut down for me, because I liked them so much.'

She was pleased he liked the dress. She liked it too, and she'd worn it for a reason. Live for today, Grandma had always told her. And tonight she had an opportunity to listen to that advice.

He chuckled. 'So that's a genuine Horrocks summer dress.'

'Yes. How did you know?'

'One of my sisters went to the London College of Fashion. She loves vintage clothes and I've learned how to tell one label from another over the years.'

'Really? You'll have to ask her over sometime, I've still got a load up in the attic. Gran was always very well dressed.'

He laughed. 'It's a nice offer, but you don't know what you're letting yourself in for. Ask one and you're likely to get flattened in the rush when they all turn up.' His eyes twinkled with amusement. 'And I won't be able to save you.'

'How many sisters do you have?'

'Oh, there's a whole gang of them. Five at the last count, and a brother.' He laughed at her stifled gasp. 'Christmas is always interesting.'

'It must be…' His tone told her just how it must have been, growing up in such a large family. Warm. Loving.

'Noisy. It's pretty noisy when we all get together. And now that three of my sisters are working on grandchildren, it's even noisier.' He chuckled. 'My mum loves it. My dad keeps threatening to move out for a bit of peace, but it's just bluster.'

'So where do you come in the pecking order?'

He grinned. 'I have two older sisters, Nell and Sophie, then there's me, then Rachel and Caroline who are twins and then my brother Jamie, and Mattie, who's the youngest.'

Jenna was struggling to get her head around him being one of seven. 'So your parents had five children, and then adopted two more?'

'Yeah. Gluttons for punishment, my mum and dad. But we all looked after each other quite a bit.'

'You must think my house very strange and silent.' The

admission just popped out before Jenna had time to think about it.

'It's…different. I like it, though. You've filled it with life—your art, your garden.' He grinned. 'Anyone with six siblings gets to know the value of silence.'

'Stop it. You wouldn't be without them.'

'No, you're right, I wouldn't.' He flipped his eyes towards Jenna for a moment and then back on to the road. 'Mattie's a lot like you.'

'I guess I should take that as a compliment.'

'It is. To both of you. If it's okay to compliment you, that is.'

Tonight she'd let it pass. 'I'd like to meet her.'

'Yeah, she'd *love* to meet you. She's been nagging me for a while now about dating.'

'Oh, so this is a date, is it? You might have told me.'

He flashed her a wicked grin. 'Well, I've got a clean shirt on. We're on our own in the car and I'm taking you somewhere nice. You look gorgeous. Go figure.'

'Where *are* you taking me?' The bit about looking gorgeous wasn't lost on Jenna but she decided to let that pass, too.

'It's a surprise date.' Adam slipped out of the fast lane, slowing as he approached the junction to exit the motorway.

'I'm surprised already.'

'Ah. Well, hold on to your hat, then. What do you say we…? Huh. What do you say we just go round this roundabout again? I've missed my exit!'

Jenna kept silent, letting him concentrate on driving until they were on the right road. By the time they were, he'd obviously thought better of whatever it was that he'd been about to say. *What do you say we leave the ghosts behind, just for tonight?* Maybe. *What do you say we stop try-*

ing to ignore the past and think about the future? Maybe. *Wouldn't that be nice?* Wouldn't it just.

They drove through a couple of small villages, and then Adam turned off the road, pulling up outside a gate and jumping out of the car. Ignoring a sign that said that the land beyond was private, he swung the gate open, and they bumped along a mud track that seemed to lead to the middle of nowhere.

'Is this it?' Jenna was starting to wonder whether a dress had been the right choice of attire for the evening.

'Nearly.' He shot a grin at her. 'You won't get it out of me, you know. I want to have the pleasure of surprising you.'

It was a pleasure, was it? Warmth flowed through her veins, like molten gold. Jenna drew her arms across her body, hugging herself as they drove up a steep incline, to the top of a hill that was crowned by a knot of trees.

He drew to a stop and jumped out of the car, opening her door. Jenna got out, stretching her limbs. The view was magnificent. She could see for miles across fields and woodland, dotted with houses and small villages. It was breezy enough that she was glad of the thin cardigan she had slung around her shoulders, but the wind was still warm from the heat of the day. 'This is lovely.' She took a deep breath. 'Just the thing to blow away the cobwebs.'

He grinned. 'And we're not even there yet.'

He took her hand and led her through the canopy of trees. Up ahead there was a wall, old bricks, weather-beaten and worn, which seemed almost as much a part of nature as the trees around her. She strained to see what was beyond it, but it was too high.

'Close your eyes.' He'd come to a halt by a carved wooden door, cut into the wall, and pulled a set of large, old-fashioned keys from his pocket.

Jenna obeyed, placing one hand over her eyes and hanging on to Adam's shoulder with the other. He'd brought her to some mysterious, magic place and she shivered with expectancy. She heard the sound of a key turning in a lock, and then Adam's hand on her waist guided her carefully ahead.

There was the sound of a door creaking closed behind her. She could smell lavender, and when something brushed on her cheek she reached out to touch it. 'Lilac.'

'That's right.' His voice was quiet, almost a whisper, and she could feel his breath on her ear. He took her another couple of steps, positioning her just so, as if he wanted her to get exactly the right view. 'You can look now.'

Jenna opened her eyes, clinging on to him still. In front of her was a round structure with a domed roof and old stone steps leading up to an arched doorway. Flower beds radiated out from it, in concentric circles, criss-crossed by paths made from weathered brick paviours. The whole was contained by a high wall, one side of which she'd seen from the outside.

'Adam! This is beautiful. What is this place?' It was like a magical secret garden, deep in the countryside. If a unicorn had appeared from somewhere and ambled up to nuzzle her hand, she would hardly have been surprised.

'It belongs to my uncle. He owns this land and when he bought it the observatory was up here, pretty much in ruins. It's taken him twenty years to restore it, and the garden.'

'But what was it doing here?'

'This land used to be part of an estate connected to a big country house. This was the lord of the manor's own private observatory.' He grinned. 'A rather extravagant version of a garden shed, where he could leave the house behind and do his own thing, I guess.'

'And your uncle did all this himself?'

'Pretty much. Dad used to bring us here a lot in the summer when we were kids, and he worked on it with my uncle. See that brick path over there?' He indicated the line of one of the paths that traversed the garden. 'All my own work. A little rough in places, but I was only fourteen.'

'So this place must be special to all your family.'

'Yeah. It's very special. Come and see the observatory.' He led her through the garden and up the stone steps, unlocking the door and opening it for her. 'It was pretty much a shell when he came here, but Uncle Jim's restored it back to its original use. With a few modern twists.'

In the gloom Jenna could see an upholstered bench running the full circle of the smooth, painted walls. A set of comfortable chairs indicated that here stargazing was not a solitary pursuit. And above her head, suspended by a system of pulleys and supports, was a telescope.

'Shade your eyes.' Jenna obeyed without comment. He seemed to have this worked out, to the last step, one delight after another. Adam operated a large wheel by the door, turning it with ease.

'Adam!' Jenna stared, open-mouthed. The panels of the dome had rolled to one side, leaving only glazing on three of the four sides, and the whole space was flooded with light. She saw cream-painted walls, rich, russet-coloured upholstery and, nestling in the curve of the ceiling, the gleaming telescope. 'How did the roof roll back like that?'

'It's all done with smoke and mirrors.' He grinned. 'My uncle's an engineer by trade, and he spent years designing it all and getting it working.' He pointed upwards. 'You can let the telescope down to a comfortable viewing height when night falls.'

He gave her a chance to wander around, his eyes following her as she ran her hands over the large wheels that rotated the dome, sat to admire the comfort of the chairs, and stood at the centre of the compass pattern in the mosaic floor to stare at the sky above her head.

'So.' He finally rubbed his hands together in a sign that there was more to come. 'Do you want to eat first or see the garden?'

Food. He'd thought of everything. 'Oh. Well, I'm hungry, but I want to see the garden while it's still light.' Smell the scents of the evening before dusk fell.

'Both, then.' He chuckled. 'That's fine. Go outside and have a look around and I'll join you in a minute.'

Adam shooed her away and busied himself on a small paved area at the back of the observatory, carrying out a couple of chairs and fighting with a fold-up table. Left with nothing to do, Jenna wandered the garden, smelling the herbs and flowers.

The whole place was full of little individual touches. One corner planted with medicinal herbs. An old stone bird bath with butterflies, birds and a tiny mouse carved amongst leaves and flowers. Jenna was inspecting it, running her fingers along the pitted surface, when a loud pop made her jump.

'Watch out!' he called. Something thudded against the wall twenty yards away, and Jenna ran to retrieve it. 'Sorry about that. Must have shaken it up a bit.' Adam was grinning at her, holding a foaming champagne bottle in one hand. 'Care for some very fizzy champagne?'

While she'd been immersed in the garden, he'd laid the table. Crisp white linen. Glasses, plates and heavy, old-fashioned cutlery. By the side of the table was an ice bucket.

'Where on earth did you get all that from?' Jenna had been expecting a sandwich and vacuum flask.

He laughed. 'The bench in the observatory is actually cupboards. Jim's latest addition is a solar-powered fridge. Sit down.' He poured two glasses of champagne and handed her one. 'What shall we drink to?'

There was no tomorrow to drink to. Or, at least, not too many of them. 'Tonight. Let's drink to tonight. It's perfect, Adam, thank you.'

He smiled, meeting her gaze, and she was locked into the pleasures of the moment. Forget yesterday. Forget tomorrow. Now was too good to spoil with their corrupting decay.

'Tonight, then.' He tipped his glass against hers and she was lost.

He'd brought food—salads, cold meats, crusty bread, which he produced in succession while they talked and ate, enjoying the cool colours and scents of the garden. As dusk fell, and colours faded to grey, he lit a lantern, which shone a pool of light onto the table.

'So where is your uncle, then?'

Adam laughed. 'Friday night is dance night.' He leaned across the table confidingly. 'He's got a lady friend down in the village. He won't be back home until late, if at all.'

'That's a shame. I'd have liked to thank him.'

His lips twisted in a wry grin. 'You can put a note through his letterbox—we passed the house at the bottom of the hill there.' He took the keys from his pocket and dropped them into her hand. 'We've got this place to ourselves tonight. So as soon as it's dark enough we can do a little stargazing, if you'd like.'

'I'd love it. Strawberries first, though.'

'Of course.' He picked up one of the large strawberries from the dish between them and held it under her nose.

'Mmm. Love the smell of strawberries.' She took a bite. 'And the taste.'

He leaned towards her, dropping the strawberry onto

the white tablecloth. 'Love your smell.' He moved closer, and Jenna leaned to meet him. 'And your taste.'

The kiss was a feather-soft sensation on her lips. There was no way he could get any closer to her as the table was between them. For a moment Jenna thought he would sweep it away with one bold stroke and take her in his arms, but he didn't. Even so, he lingered, stretching towards her, his fingers light on her jaw.

'I'm breaking the rules again.'

Jenna smiled at him. 'You don't seem very contrite about it.'

'Maybe they don't apply up here.'

'So we're lost in uncharted territory.' The earth had turned and the sun had slipped beneath the horizon. 'We'll just have to do whatever feels right.'

'Don't tempt me, Jenna.' His eyes were dark, soft pools of shadow that held unthinkable pleasures.

'Would you give in?' He'd give in. She knew he would. If only for tonight.

'When an irresistible force meets an immoveable object...'

'And you're immoveable, are you?'

'Which makes you irresistible.' He brushed her lips again and Jenna's insides turned to jelly.

She put one finger across his lips and they formed into the shape of a kiss. 'So what about the laws of the universe? Do they apply up here?'

'Maybe.' He smiled at her. 'Shall we check them out? See whether the stars are still where they're supposed to be?'

He carried the lantern into the observatory, holding her hand all the way. It was like being a teenager again. Holding someone's hand in the dark, feeling the thrill of what might or might not happen next. The cautious slide into the unknown. It was as if Joe didn't exist and Adam was the first man who had ever kissed her.

Jenna watched as he heaved on the controls, bringing the telescope down to a comfortable height for viewing and opening a panel in the ceiling to the night air. He consulted a chart and pulled again on a different wheel, this time expending more effort on it, the muscles in his shoulders swelling to take the strain as the dome above her head swung round.

He showed her the moon, bright, filling the lens completely, large craters now plainly visible. Saturn and its rings, low in the evening sky. Then he showed her the stars, naming each one for her. Albireo, at the head of Cygnus, the swan, which the telescope showed to be a bright double star. Vega in Lyra, Corona Borealis. Magical names, which seemed to fit right in with the enchantment of the night.

When she began to shiver, he wrapped a woollen throw around her shoulders. When she exclaimed with the wonder of it all, he seemed to draw closer, caught up with her in the marvels of the universe.

'Let's go home.'

'Yeah? We can get a glimpse of Mars and Venus on the horizon just before dawn, if we're lucky.'

Jenna twisted in his arms, brushing a stray lock of hair away from his forehead. 'Not good enough. I want more than a glimpse.'

He gazed at her, and suddenly she felt as if she were the centre of the universe. Drawing everything around her inwards by some fluke of gravity. 'Are you sure, Jen? This is… Some stars align only once. In our lifetimes, anyway.'

'I know. Is that a reason for us not to take our chance when they do?'

His arms tightened around her. 'Not for me. I want to

write your name and mine across the sky tonight. But when I go, I won't be back.'

That was unlikely. Adam had family, friends here, but that wasn't what he meant. He wouldn't be coming back for her. But at least he was honest about it, and wouldn't leave her agonising over hollow promises to return. 'I know. But tonight we can do as we please. The stars don't care, they'll keep turning without us for a while.'

He kissed her. Long and slow. Earth-moving. She'd found her way back from his last kiss, but this one took her way beyond any possibility of retracing her steps.

'Whatever the lady wants...' He'd already taken the left-overs from their meal to the car, and all he needed to do was stow the telescope back in place, close the overhead window to the heavens and lock the door. Then he caught her hand, leading her through the darkness of the garden.

They hardly touched, hardly spoke. Only his fingers, twined with hers, told Jenna what she needed to know. That he was there still. And that for the moment he wasn't going anywhere.

It was one in the morning, and the drive back to town took less time than the drive out, the dark streets almost empty of cars. It was as if they were in their own small world, not needing anything else. Just being here, with him, was the only thing that Jenna wanted, and she ignored the minutes ticking away on the dashboard clock. It would end. But not right now. Not yet.

CHAPTER SEVEN

SHE had her back against the door of his flat. Nothing mattered, not how she'd got here or what she was going to do next. She felt nothing other than his kiss.

When he had finished kissing her mouth, he moved to her jaw, and her neck. 'Your place or mine?' He hardly stopped to voice the question.

'Mine's too far.' Her legs had gone to jelly and she doubted if she'd make the stairs without help.

The door gave behind her. Somehow he'd had the presence of mind to get the key out of his pocket and slide it into the lock while still kissing her. Without its support Jenna almost stumbled backwards, but his arm around her waist steadied her, pulling her into the safety of his body.

He backed her through the door, kicking it closed behind him, and pinned her against the wall of the hallway. His keys jangled unnoticed onto the floor, along with the bag from the all-night chemist, and now that both his hands were free, he made the best use of them.

One hand was behind her head, and the other… The other explored her body, waiting for each breath that she caught, each quiver of her muscles to tell him which way to go next.

He kissed her throat, bending just enough to cup his free hand behind her leg, pulling it gently upwards until the fabric of her dress tangled around his thigh. A little pressure, the smallest friction, through folds of cloth and Jenna felt her body arch into him and she threw her head backwards, crushing his fingers against the wall.

'Oh! Sorry...your fingers...'

'That's okay, I've got another hand.' That other hand had finally found its way through her skirts and his fingers were sliding along the skin of her thigh.

She was trembling in his arms. Waiting. Waiting, with every nerve screaming for what came next.

'Tell me what you want.'

That was the one thing she hadn't expected. 'I...I... You.'

His low chuckle reverberated against her neck. 'Mmm. I want you too, honey. But that's not all I want.' His lips found the sensitive spot behind her ear, making her shiver. 'I want to know how I can please you.'

His voice was low, insistent. No one had ever asked that of her before, and his point-blank demand melted a shard of ice that had been embedded in her heart for so long that she hardly even knew it had been there. There was nothing she needed to do or say to make him want her. She just needed to be, to feel.

Jenna clung to his shoulders as if he were the most precious thing in the world to her. At this moment he was the only thing in the world. His mouth was on hers again, his hand sliding from the back of her head to her breast, his fingers caressing gently.

He tore a sigh from her throat and then a cry. Not satisfied with that, he slowly stepped up the pace until she choked out his name.

'Do that again. Please.' Was it really her saying these things?

'You mean…this?' His eyes blazed bright, and she no longer cared. She just wanted Adam's hands on her.

'Oh! Yes.' Her fingers found his belt and she tugged at it. 'Bedroom.' There was only one thing on her mind right now, and that involved a bed. And Adam. Not necessarily in that order.

'I like the way you think. But I won't let you out again. Not until…' He let the sentence drift, floating through a myriad of possibilities, each one of them more delicious than the last.

'You asked me what I wanted.'

'So I did.' He lifted her up and carried her into the bedroom, sitting her gently down on the bed and kneeling before her. He stripped off his shirt as if he couldn't wait to be rid of it. No hesitation, no trying to hide his scars. Just for tonight they didn't seem to exist, either.

He was more beautiful than she could have imagined. Sun-burnished skin and lean, finely muscled lines. She looked, and then touched. Then kissed. His skin was smooth, warm and she could almost taste his desire.

'Now you.' He was easing her out of her dress, his mouth and tongue exploring as his fingers exposed more flesh.

'So beautiful.' She was naked now, and his fingers trembled against the sensitive skin of her neck. 'I can hardly bear to touch you, you're so beautiful.'

'Tell me you're kidding.'

He laughed, rolling her back onto the bed, his body covering hers. 'Yeah. I'm kidding.'

The man that Jenna woke up with was a stranger. One who had slept peacefully in her arms. One who had made love as if he had been hungry for life, drinking in every last blissful drop of her pleasure and his own. And there had been a lot of pleasure. He'd made quite sure of that. Adam's eyes flickered open and focussed lazily.

'Hey, honey.' There was no trace of regret. No second thoughts in his golden eyes as he wrapped his arms around her more tightly, pulling her into him. 'What are you doing?'

'Watching you.' The night had been warm and at some time while they'd slept the sheet that covered them had been thrown aside. In the chill hours before dawn his body had kept her warm.

'What do you see?'

She nudged at his shoulder. 'Stop fishing for compliments. You know what I see.' In the end, she'd told him everything. What she wanted. How good it felt when he gave her everything that she dared to ask for, and then more.

'Oh. Can't I have just one? I'll make you a cup of tea.'

'In that case, you can have as many as you like.' She disentangled herself from his limbs, pushing him towards the edge of the bed. 'When you come back.'

He chuckled, pulling her towards him for one last kiss and, too late, Jenna realised her mistake in letting him get out of the bed they'd shared. It was too tender, too full of emotion to be just a kiss. It tasted like the beginnings of a goodbye.

Inch by inch he was leaving her. He had gone into the shower naked and entirely hers. Come back out again with a towel tied around his waist, another draped around his neck, hiding the scars on his shoulder. If his dreams were like an evening mist, dissolved under the heat of a new day, then so was the man who could forget about the past and the future.

But his smile remained. All the way through breakfast,

and as they walked together to the local shops to catch the last few hours of the farmers' market that set up in the station car park every Saturday.

'Which way now?' Adam had two heavy string bags slung over his shoulder and was working on lightening the one that Jenna carried by dipping into the bag of apples he'd bought.

'Do you mind if we drop into the library?' Jenna pointed to the large old building, just along the street.

He shook his head and began to amble along the road. 'Can I carry your books home?'

She laughed. He made everything so easy. No rush, but at the same time he seemed to get an enormous amount done just by moving steadily from one task to the next. 'If you like. Perhaps I should get some talking books, they're not so heavy.'

'Spoilsport. How am I going to earn a big thank-you for lugging four CDs back home?'

'You'll have to use your ingenuity.' She liked Adam's ingenuity. Very much.

His low chuckle drifted in her direction. 'Racking my brains as we speak.'

They climbed the stone steps to the impressive Victorian building, and walked through a pair of glass doors to an old-fashioned reading room. He waited while Jenna took her talking-book CDs from her handbag and handed them to the woman behind the desk for scanning. 'Is there a community noticeboard here?'

'Yes, over there. Why, thinking of joining a club?'

'No.' He had taken the last bite of the flesh of his apple and was working his way through the core, leaving only the stalk. 'Remember the kid with the knife in his boot? Peter?'

'Of course I do.'

'I made a bet with him. If I don't come up with the goods then I owe him a tenner. And since I'm pretty sure I know what he'll spend it on, that's not going to happen.'

'You think we'll ever see him again?' Jenna had heard from Jake that Peter hadn't turned up for his appointment with him, and that he wasn't answering his calls and texts either. 'What's the betting he's back doing all the things he's always done? Carrying a knife. Drinking, taking drugs.'

Adam shrugged. 'No reason to give up on him.'

'You'll have to. You can't keep chasing him from Florida.' The word no longer evoked images of sun and the ocean. It was the word that reminded Jenna that Adam didn't live here, and that soon he'd be going home.

'True.' He seemed to be considering the implications, too. 'But that's something I can't do anything about. I won't give up on him until I have to.'

Right. He couldn't see that moving around as he did was a choice. That making connections and then leaving them behind was part of that choice. Jenna let the thought slide. 'So what's this bet about?'

'He bet me I couldn't come up with a list of fifty things you can do on a Saturday night for a fiver. I'm up to thirty-nine and I'm running out of ideas.' Last night's mischief flashed in his eyes and Adam crowded her backwards in between the shelves of books until they were out of sight, then captured her against him, pulling another apple out of the bag she was carrying.

'Is scrumping one of the thirty-nine?' Florida was suddenly a million miles away and his body next to hers was all that mattered.

'No. Good thinking. That can be number forty.'

They strolled home, discussing the leaflets for clubs and courses that Adam had picked up at the library, then made something to eat. Adam had some work to do for his lecture the next day and he brought his laptop out into the garden, sitting with Jenna under the sprawling oak tree that shaded the far end of the lawn.

Afternoon turned to evening, and Adam snapped his laptop shut, dozing in the shade, while Jenna sketched. When she laid her pencil down, he sat up and stretched. 'Would you like to plant those shrubs?' He indicated the plants he had brought her, still on the patio in their tubs.

'Yes.' She contemplated the butterfly garden. 'Where do you think they should go?'

'Oh, I'm leaving that to you. You're the one with the artist's eye. I'll just do the digging.'

He hauled the tubs down to the edge of the lawn, and Jenna indicated the positions she thought they'd look best in. Smiled when she changed her mind. Chuckled quietly when she changed it back again and apologised awkwardly.

'That's okay. I could do with the exercise. This easy life in London's making me fat and lazy.'

'Fat where?' She ran her fingertips across his hard, flat stomach.

He laughed out loud, pulling her into his chest. 'That's for you to find out.'

She took the bait and ran her fingers across his arms, his back. 'Still looking.'

'Keep going.' He kissed her full on the lips. Could she hope for tonight? Jenna had thought not, but as the sun had fallen, he'd seemed to lose the inhibitions of the day. It would be dark in a couple of hours, and the part of Adam that was wholly hers seemed to have woken, stretching and yawning after a day's slumber.

'I thought you were meant to be digging.'

'Determined to make me sweat, eh?'

'Absolutely.' She nestled into his neck, standing on tip-toe on the broken earth. 'Love the smell of your sweat.'

'Pheromones. You like my smell, I like yours. Mother Nature does the nicest things sometimes.'

Was that all it was? The chemistry of attraction? There seemed to be so much more between them than that. Chemistry blew those thoughts from her head as Adam ran his hand down the full sweep of her back, and she clung to him, pressing her body against his.

'There's always payback, though.'

The word struck cold into her heart. 'What payback, Adam?'

'You make me sweat and I'll make you...' he brushed his lips across her forehead '...glow.'

That kind of payback she could handle. 'Seems fair enough. What else?'

'Wait and see.' He drew back a little, his golden eyes dancing playfully. 'Go and get the spade, and we'll get these planted first.'

Adam dug four deep holes, and Jenna fetched some compost from the bag he'd left on the patio. Together they lifted the plants from their tubs into the ground and Adam shovelled earth around them. When they'd watered them well, Jenna went into the house to fetch a drink and when she returned found Adam back under the oak tree, reclining on the cushions.

'Thanks.' He took the glass from her and drank deeply. 'You'll have to change your sketch now.'

He hadn't touched her sketch pad but it lay open on the rug beside him, her drawing of the butterfly garden plainly visible. 'No, I'll do another. That was how it was at that moment in time. I felt differently about it then.'

'Oh? How?'

She shrugged, sitting down beside him. 'I'm not sure.

Everything changes, moves on from moment to moment. What you see depends on how you feel.' When she'd made that sketch she'd wanted to preserve her memories of yesterday. She hadn't included any of the promise that she now felt for tonight in it.

He nodded slowly. Picked up the leaf of the pad and looked at the next page and broke into laughter. 'So this is how you see me, eh?'

She'd drawn him in cartoon, covered in mud, chasing after a small boy who dribbled a football out of his reach. Jenna bit her lip. Perhaps he wouldn't like it. He might not like the other one either where he was pressing a stethoscope to the furry chest of a small bear, sitting on a bench in a queue of children and adults. 'Just playing around. I got the ideas from some of the pictures you showed at your lecture.'

He was grinning broadly. 'I think they're great. Can I have a copy?'

'Take that one.'

'Thanks. Will you sign them for me?'

'They're only cartoons.'

He rolled over towards her, catching her hand and pressing her knuckles against his lips. 'They're wonderful. Stop underestimating yourself.' He picked up her pencil and pressed it into her hand. 'I want them signed.'

Jenna pretended reluctance as she quickly initialled both portraits, tearing the sheet from the pad and giving it to him. Too late she remembered the drawing that was beneath it.

'Is that how you see me, too?' Alarm flashed in his eyes as he saw the drawing.

There was nothing wrong with the portrait. Adam, asleep under the oak tree, his face relaxed and contented. It was just how he had looked. But seeing it again, Jenna realised that she'd given too much away. There was love in every line of it. Raw longing in each smudged shadow.

She shrugged and put the pad to one side, flipping it closed. 'Kind of.' Her stomach was turning now. If he hadn't seen it in the drawing, he must see it in the blush that was spreading across her cheeks.

He nodded slowly, as if he was turning something over in his mind. 'Jen, last night…'

He was going to say it. Last night had been a mistake. She'd thought he might say it all day, but this evening had chased those fears away. The world had turned again, though, throwing them back to where they'd started out. 'Last night was incredible. It'll always stay with me, wherever I go.'

She suddenly felt sick. If anything, that was worse. 'Yeah… Me, too.'

'I have to leave, Jen. You know that.'

She didn't know anything of the sort. He had a choice, and leaving was what he'd opted for. 'There are people there who need you.' The words almost choked her.

'I've been wondering if…maybe you'd like to come out to Florida. For a holiday. I'd love to show you around.'

She almost punched him. Instead she pretended to think about the offer. 'Perhaps. I'd rather go to South America. See the work you do there. Perhaps even help out a little.' If he went for that, she might just consider it.

'No.' The one sharp interjection pierced that particular bubble before it had even started to float. 'I…I don't think that's a good idea, Jen. It's no place for…' He broke off. 'Don't ask me to take you there.'

'Then don't ask me to come to Florida.' She had thought she could do this. Thought that honesty and certainty would make things all right. But that had been before he had shown her that lovemaking was so much more than just the joining of two bodies.

'But, Jen…' He broke off in exasperation. 'I don't see the difference.'

'Let me tell you the difference, then.' It was either rail at him or burst into tears at this point. Or both. 'My biological parents are Alexis and Daniel Thorn. They're alive and living very nicely, thank you, in the South of France.'

She'd shocked him into silence. Tears were coursing down her cheeks and Jenna rubbed angrily at them with her hand.

'They left me with Gramps and Grandma when my sister, Laura, became ill.' Now that the floodgates were wide open, nothing was going to stop her from finishing.

'What was the matter with her?' His voice was soft now, but Jenna didn't care.

'Anorexia. She was eight years older than me, and it took her three years to die. All that time I spent with Gramps and Grandma, I hoped that Laura would get better and that I could go back home. But when she died of a heart attack, my parents didn't want me back home, they went to France. Said they couldn't bear the memories.'

'They left you behind?' He reached out to her and Jenna jerked away.

'They said they'd come back. Then they said I could go out there for a holiday. But they lied. I didn't see them again until I was eighteen, and by that time I'd made Gramps and Grandma my legal next of kin and taken their name.'

'Jen, I'm so sorry…'

'So am I, Adam. But we made a bargain that we wouldn't carry this on after you left, so don't start bending the rules on me now for your own convenience.'

She'd wounded him, even though he tried not to show it.

Her eyes filled with tears again at the thought of it. Jenna knew she was being unfair. She couldn't demand commitment from him after just one night. But she couldn't give him what he asked either.

If he'd been willing to take her with him to South America, demonstrate that there was some chance he could share his life with her, then maybe. Just maybe. But two weeks on the beach and then another parting. No. Not even if he asked her to stay. He would always be leaving, always be going away to work.

She tried to summon a smile, but couldn't. 'I should go. I'm sorry, Adam, but I think that's best.'

'Yeah. You're right, Jen. However much I wish you weren't.'

Sadness hit her, hard, right in the middle of the chest. But it was too late to repair the damage. About fifteen years too late. Jenna got to her feet and walked away from him, without looking back.

She'd shut herself in her flat and tried to concentrate on something else. Washing up. Checking her emails. Crying over Adam wasn't on her list of things to do, even if it did seem to be about the only thing that was getting done at the moment. It was only when thunder rumbled in the sky that she remembered her sketch pad, still lying under the tree in the garden where she'd left it, and ran down the fire-escape steps to fetch it.

The pad lay on the steps, about halfway up. Just about at the limit of Adam's reach from the patio, she reckoned. It was covered in plastic to protect it from the rain, and on top of it was a yellow rose. Unwilling to leave the rose where it lay, she picked it up and ran back to her flat.

Yellow. Friendship. He'd obviously been out to get it. There were no yellow roses in the garden and this one had a long stem and was perfectly shaped. She brushed the petals against her face, catching the scent of it.

They'd meant to spend the night together, but had ended up making love. And in the aftermath of that earth-turning explosion of emotion Jenna had found that, after all, there was one thing that Adam feared. One by one she picked the petals from the rose, letting them fall onto the kitchen countertop, tears running down her cheeks as she did so. When the stem was bare she dropped it into the bin, scooping the petals after it, to clean up the mess she'd made.

CHAPTER EIGHT

THE last six days had seemed like six months. Jenna had been unable to avoid bumping into Adam and they had both been polite, restrained. And she'd gone over every word that had passed between them, analysed each look, in an agony of self-reproach. Her anger had drained away, and with it some of the shadows from the past. But it was too late. Living for today was a hollow aspiration when Adam was now a part of yesterday.

She had hesitated before paging Adam, but only for a moment. This was work, and her reluctance to see him was of secondary importance. When he strode through the doors to the A and E department, he brought reinforcements in the shape of four white-coated youngsters, who were obviously students. He gave Brenda a cheery wave and made straight for Jenna, his face suddenly solemn.

'What can I do for you?'

'I've a patient who came in with a minor cut, incurred in a fall. I've cleaned and glued it.' The students were hanging on her every word and one seemed to be taking notes.

'With you so far.' Adam spoke for the whole group. His tone was professional, verging on the friendly, but that was about all. His eyes were just as blank as they'd been all week.

'Then I got the "Oh, and by the way...".' Jenna was beginning to feel uncomfortable under the four earnest stares. 'Sometimes people present with very minor things. When you've dealt with that they tell you what they've really come for.'

One of the students nodded condescendingly. 'Doorknob syndrome.'

Jenna focussed on the student's name badge. 'Gaining a patient's trust is half the battle, Mark. It's not easy to talk about some issues.'

Adam nodded, addressing the students. 'People walk out of those doors every day, having decided that they can't talk about what's really worrying them. If we let them do that, then the next time we see them it's often a real emergency.' He turned back to Jenna. 'So what's the problem?'

She proffered her notes to Adam. 'He showed me an area on his arm where his skin has lost its pigmentation. I think he may have Hansen's disease. He told me he comes from Brazil and he's over here studying. He's only been here a couple of months and he has no family in this country.'

'That's leprosy, isn't it?' There was a little rustle of unease and Mark spoke up again.

Adam ignored him. 'Can anyone tell me about Hansen's? Yes, Geeta.'

One of the other students began to reel off a list of the indications of Hansen's disease and Adam nodded her through them. 'It's one of the least communicable infectious diseases there is. Transmission is via respiratory droplets, and casual contact doesn't lead to infection. You have to be resident in an endemic area for several years before the risk of infection becomes appreciable.' Geeta stopped, gulping in a breath, and then continued. 'In Brazil it's referred to as Hansen's disease, because of the stigma surrounding the name leprosy...'

'Very nicely put. Thanks, Geeta.' Adam cut Geeta short, grinning apologetically as he did so, and flipped through the notes in his hand. 'Where is the patient?'

'Examination room two.'

'Shouldn't he be in isolation? The law says…' Mark piped up, and received a nudge in the ribs for his pains from one of his companions.

'The law says we *may* put a Hansen's patient into isolation. It's important that he has treatment now, not just for his own sake but to stop the spread of the disease, but that's an issue that hasn't arisen yet and may well not.' He flipped a glance towards Jenna, fixing his gaze back on to the students quickly. 'Dr Weston's approach, which I advise you all to note very carefully, is holistic. Treat the person, not just the disease.'

'Within the bounds of practicality.' His praise tasted bitter when there was no accompanying warmth in his eyes. 'In A and E that's something you can rarely achieve.'

'But something a good doctor, such as yourself, achieves naturally.'

Jenna cut in before Adam could say any more. 'I think that all six of us in the room might upset the patient.' Perhaps Adam and just one of the students would be appropriate, while she waited outside with the others.

Adam nodded, addressing the group. 'I agree, and it's about time I let you all go, anyway. Dr Weston and I will see the patient, and I'll update you on his progress and treatment tomorrow.' His lips twitched into what might have been a grin if he hadn't stifled it almost immediately, and Jenna tried to ignore the sweet, tingling sensation at the back of her neck. 'Emotionally and physically.'

Did he really need to put it quite like that? Perhaps he did. On anyone else's lips, the words would have been just words. Jenna nodded politely in the students' direction and turned, walking slowly towards the examination room.

'Do you have to?'

'Do I have to what?' His guard dropped for a moment and he was all innocence. Kissable innocence, damn him. She'd hoped she might have got over that by now.

'You know. Embarrass me in front of everyone?'

'I was making a point. Mark might be bright but his bedside manner leaves a great deal to be desired.' He twisted his lips into a brief, wry smile. 'But if you don't like being complimented, I won't do it again.'

She narrowed her eyes at him. Much as she wanted to kick him, it had better wait until after he'd examined the patient she'd called him down to see.

'I guess we'll be talking about this later, then.' Adam bent to whisper the words in her ear and before she had a chance to respond he'd opened the door to examination room two, motioning her inside.

'Hector, I'm sorry to keep you waiting.' Jenna summoned a smile for the young man propped up on the bed, and got a brief one in return. 'This is Adam Sinclair, the doctor I told you about.'

Hector nodded at Adam, suspicion flashing in his dark eyes. Adam approached the bed and held out his hand. 'I imagine your English is better than my Portuguese.'

The ghost of a smile crossed Hector's face as he took Adam's hand and shook it. 'I went to an English-speaking school.'

'English it is, then. How long have you been in London?'

'One month. I start studying here in September.'

'Great. What are you studying?'

'Mathematics. I will study for three years.'

Adam grinned at him with that easy warmth that Jenna

no longer had any right to. 'Rather you than me. I've no head for figures. Where are you from?'

'Manaus.'

'Ah, I know it well. I worked there for a while.' Adam leaned forward and picked up Hector's arm, examining it carefully. 'How long have you had this?'

'A little while.'

'And what about this bump under your eye? Did you do that when you fell today?'

'No.' Hector was still tense, defensive even, and Jenna couldn't fathom why. He'd got over the hard part of actually asking for help. Most people loosened up a bit after that.

'All right.' Adam's voice was soothing. 'I can take a tissue sample to find out what this is, and then I can give you the proper treatment.'

'You cannot give me the medicine now?'

Adam regarded him steadily. 'Not until I have a confirmed diagnosis.'

'If you have worked in Manaus you know what this is.'

'I can't rule Hansen's disease out. But we have to be sure. You know, don't you, that if that's what it turns out to be, then it's in its early stages and we can treat it.'

Hector nodded. 'You get the drugs and you are cured.'

'Yeah, well, just getting the drugs doesn't work. You need to actually take them. And you'll take them here, under supervision, in the hospital.'

'I can take them by myself. I do not need anyone to watch me.'

Adam regarded him thoughtfully. 'I have friends in Manaus. Good people who run a clinic there. If you are worried about someone at home, then I can put you in touch with them. They will help.'

Hector stared at him, insolence creeping into his expression.

'The drugs are free, you know that.' Adam was clearly not about to give up.

Silence.

'Okay, Hector. Who is it? A member of your family?' Adam waited and received a blank look. 'A friend? A girlfriend, maybe?'

Hector's olive skin reddened slightly. 'My family must not know.'

'That's okay, I'm not going to tell them. Neither will my colleague.' Adam gestured towards Jenna and she shook her head emphatically.

'Your friends. They will report her, though.'

Adam nodded. 'That's the law. But no harm will come to her and they can help her.'

'You do not understand.' Hector's chin jutted resolutely. He'd obviously said about as much as he was prepared to say at the moment.

'No, I don't. That's because you're not giving me all of the facts, Hector. Do you want to help your girlfriend or not? Because I'm guessing that if you don't then no one else will.'

He was putting a lot of pressure on the youth, but Jenna didn't stop him. Unless someone got to the bottom of this, a young woman might go without the treatment she desperately needed.

'You don't want to help her?' Adam made a gesture of frustration with his hand that was two inches too expansive to be British in origin. 'Who can she turn to, then?'

Hector broke. He'd put up a good fight, but Adam was too much for him, too determined. 'Her father has it. He will not tell anyone. If I send her the drugs, then she will not get sick.'

'That's not how it works, Hector. Now, listen to me. It's by no means certain or even likely that your girlfriend is infected, however much she's exposed to it. She should get checked over, though, just in case. And her father needs treatment, too.'

'He will never agree. He made her swear that she wouldn't tell anyone. She made me swear.'

'If your girlfriend's being put at risk, don't you think it's your duty to do something about it?' There was a merest hint of a flicker at the side of Adam's eye. Nothing more. 'What's her name?'

'Maria. My parents don't know about her, her family does not have money.'

'So you saw her on the quiet, eh?' Adam was grinning conspiratorially.

'Yes. My parents thought I was studying.' It seemed that now the floodgates had opened, they were well and truly open.

Adam chuckled quietly. 'Pretty name. Is she pretty?'

'Of course.'

'Does she have any symptoms?'

Hector shook his head. 'I do not think so.'

'Well, that's a good start.' Adam folded his arms across his chest. 'Okay, here's the deal, Hector. You stay here and we'll find out what's the matter with you and treat it. Meanwhile, I'll have a word with my friends. See if we can't work something out for Maria.'

'Her father will beat her if he finds out.'

'He's not going to. My friends know how to be discreet, they've done this before. And they can and will make sure that Maria's okay. They'll deal with both her medical needs and the situation with her father. That's what you want, isn't it?'

Hector nodded.

'Good.' Adam's tone was affable but brooked no argument. 'I'm bound by law to notify a case of Hansen's disease to the authorities. That means you not only have my protection, you also have that of the law, too. We'll get the skin samples done, and get you a bed here in the hospital. Once you're settled, I'll come and see you and we can talk about Maria. Is that okay?'

'Yes.' Hector's dark, liquid eyes were fixed on Adam. 'Thank you.'

'All part of the service.' Adam got to his feet. 'I can hear the trolley outside and I for one would kill for a cup of tea. What do you say I go and get some for us both?'

'He's got guts.' Adam had chatted to Hector while Jenna collected the tissue samples, and when she left the cubicle he followed her.

'You think it is Hansen's?'

'I'd be surprised if it wasn't. And he comes from Northern Brazil, where Hansen's is endemic.' He sighed. 'Even though it's greatly feared, he was willing to send the drugs that he needed to his girlfriend.'

'You can help her, can't you? Please tell me you can.' Jenna was almost pleading with him. Hector had been too proud, but she didn't care. Thirty minutes ago she might have, but that had been before Adam had crushed all her defences by going out on a limb to help the young couple.

'I've got a few influential friends who owe me a favour and if the situation's too much for the clinic to handle, they'll pull some strings.' He shrugged. 'It's not the first time I've seen this kind of situation.'

'Thank you.' Words didn't seem to cover it. The slight movement of his hand, gravitating towards her arm, told Jenna that he too felt something.

'Not going to be a problem.' He looked up and his gaze

fell on two figures sitting in the corner of the waiting room. 'What are they doing here?'

Mark and Geeta were in deep conversation together, and when Mark saw Adam he sprang to his feet.

'You'd better go and see. It looks as if it's you they're after.'

Adam let out a sigh and walked over to the pair. A quick conversation, the transfer of a blue plastic bag from Mark to Adam and then, wonder of wonders, a smile and a handshake between the two. Adam strode back towards Jenna, a look of bemused disbelief on his face.

'What's that?' Jenna pointed at the bag.

Adam opened it and peered in. 'They've been on a scavenger hunt. Bits and pieces, some soap, something to read.' He moved the newspaper to one side. 'Pen and paper, chocolate and a couple of oranges.' He looked up at Jenna, his face shining as if he had just witnessed a miracle. 'They listened when you said that Hector didn't have anyone, and went and found some things for him for his first night in the hospital.'

'That's nice of them.' Jenna looked up, and caught Mark's eye, giving him a thumbs-up and a broad smile.

Adam was shaking his head slowly. 'I was wrong about him.' Clearly nothing gave him greater pleasure than to admit it.

'Everyone has the ability to change. I believe that in my heart. If I didn't I couldn't do this job.'

'And we all have the choice.'

'Yes. I see a lot of bad things down here. Knives, acid, drink and drugs, all kinds of violence. I see some good things, too.' She indicated the carrier bag. 'Random acts of kindness.'

He leaned in, just close enough for their conversation to be private, not too close that anyone would remark on it. 'You have the capacity to see what people might be, not what they are. It's a great gift.'

Much good it did her. She saw what Adam could be and how much he'd changed already. An exceptional doctor, skilled, professional and caring, who had somehow reclaimed his passion in the last few weeks, lifting his already considerable gifts to a whole new level. But that did nothing to close the deep crevasse that lay between the two of them. Jenna bit her lip and studied the floor.

'I have to go and give these things to Hector.' He indicated the carrier bag that he was holding. 'Mark and Geeta are hanging around. I said I'd ask if he wanted them to go up to the ward with him. It'd be good for him to have someone of his own age. He needs a friend.'

'Yes. That's a nice idea.' She reached out and touched his arm. It was okay. She knew the score and that was okay.

'Thanks.' His face softened and she saw the man who had haunted her dreams for the last six nights. 'Thanks, Jen.'

CHAPTER NINE

THE dream was different this time. Normally Adam was not aware of having dreamt, only of the terror of waking and the dull horror that followed. But this time the dream seemed to go on for an eternity.

Someone was screaming. His own roar sounded from somewhere in the distance and when he looked at his hands there was blood. The butt of a gun and an arm. Light and shadow. No, not light and shadow, it was patchy, half-pigmented skin. The sun in his eyes then on his back as he tried to crawl to Elena.

He tried to push himself into wakefulness, but the dream held him tight, replaying the disjointed images again and again, like a loop of badly damaged film. Finally, with a cry that seemed to resound through his dreams and into the waking world, he managed to wrench his eyes open.

'Adam.' He was lying on his back, sweat soaking into the sheet beneath him, fighting for breath, and all he could think about was Jenna's voice. This had to stop.

'Adam. It's okay, you've been dreaming. But you're back.'

He jerked himself upright. She was perched on a large linen chest that stood in the corner of the room, deep in shadow. 'Jenna. What the hell…? How long have you been here?'

'Ten minutes. A little longer maybe.'

'How did you get in?' He looked over to the French doors, which he had fastened securely before he had gone to bed but which were now wide open.

'I have a key, remember? I heard you moaning, and when you started yelling I came down and banged on the door to wake you up. When you didn't, I went and fetched the key.'

Why would she do that? The thought of her watching him while he battled his most shameful secret filled Adam with self-loathing. A little bit of it spilled out in her direction and he felt his lip curl. 'You wanted to see, did you?'

'No, not particularly. But I did want to hear.' Her voice was carefully measured, as if she was making an effort not to rise to his bait. 'Take this.' She rose and walked over to the bed, holding out a piece of paper. She was wearing a white cotton nightdress under the silky robe that he liked so much, and Adam noticed that her hand was trembling. 'You were speaking in Spanish. I've written it down, but I don't know what it means.'

He didn't take the paper and she put it down on the nightstand. 'You should look at it now, while the dream's still fresh. Perhaps it'll help.'

She was leaving him alone to read what she had written, not even asking for thanks, although her quiet courage deserved far more than that. 'Wait.'

She froze. The word hung in the air between them and Adam wished he could grab it back. He should have just let her go. She didn't need to see this. He didn't want to show her.

'What is it?' Jenna moved slowly back to the bed, sitting down on the edge of it.

'I…' He couldn't say it. He wanted her to stay, but

couldn't get past the clamour in his head, pulling him back down into the dream and its terrors.

'Would you like me to stay?'

She'd said it for him, and suddenly that was all he wanted. Damn the dreams. Damn the terrors. She could cut through them, with one touch of her fingers. 'Yes. If that's not too much to ask of you.' He picked the paper up from the nightstand and handed it to her.

Her smile, as she slipped the paper into her pocket, made the task ahead of them seem bearable. 'Of course not. Why don't I make some tea and we can find out what's on there together?'

Adam pulled on his jeans and a sweatshirt, then went through to the sitting room and switched on a lamp. She appeared from the kitchen, two steaming mugs in her hands, each with the tag from a herbal tea company draped over the side. In her bright, flowing robe, with her hair tumbling loose around her shoulders, she looked like some ethereal pre-Raphaelite beauty.

She put the cups on the coffee table with a clatter and plonked herself down next to him on the sofa, producing the paper from her pocket. 'Let's see, then, shall we? I'm afraid it's not that much. I wrote it down phonetically because I didn't understand what you were saying. I did think of recording you on my phone, but…' she shrugged '…I couldn't do that.'

He was grateful for that. It was going to be difficult enough to hear what she'd written down on that paper and Adam was not sure that he could listen to his own disjointed ravings. She'd taken that burden and kept it for herself.

'Thank you, Jen.' He tried to emphasise the words so that they might contain some measure of the gratitude he felt, and craned over her shoulder to look at the paper.

She'd been writing in the dark, and some of the lines of text veered off course, overlapping each other, but they were clear enough. He concentrated on the words, trying to sound them in his head but the noise was back, taking away his ability to concentrate.

'Perhaps it would be easier if I read it aloud.' She ran her finger along the first line, reading slowly and carefully.

'*Espera* means wait.'

'Right.' She paused. 'You mean it makes sense?'

'I know what it means. I've no idea why I said it.' Somewhere at the back of his mind there seemed to be an echo of something, but when he reached for it, it disappeared.

'What does it mean?'

'Wait, wait, wait. There's no need for that.'

She searched his face. 'And you don't remember saying anything like that? Or who you might have said it to?'

'No. Is there anything else?'

'You shouted the word *sangre* quite a few times. Does that mean blood?'

Adam nodded. That didn't get them any further either. He already knew that there had been blood. 'Yes. That's good, though. It's something.' He tried to sound convincing.

'Okay, well, what about this? *Detras de mi.*' She studied the paper carefully. 'I'm not sure whether that's with an *i* or an *e*.'

'It's *mi*, with an i. It means me. Get behind me.' A small glimmer of hope ignited in his brain. Perhaps, after all, he'd tried to protect Elena. But it was only hope. No recognition, no memories. Nothing but wishful thinking.

She'd reached for a pad that was lying on the coffee table and torn a sheet from it. 'Here. Write it all down, before we forget.' She handed him a pen and Adam obe-

diently wrote down the phrases, in Spanish and English.
'Now, what about this?' She ran her finger across her sheet
again, silently mouthing the sounds.

Adam craned over, following her finger. 'Don't bother
with that. I'm…er…making my feelings very plain at this
point.'

'Oh.' Her finger stopped suddenly. 'Good for you. I hope
you gave them what for.' She tapped the paper in front of
him. 'Write that down as well.'

'But it doesn't mean anything.'

'No, but it's what you said. It might jog your memory
later on.'

She had a point. Adam wrote the words down, omit-
ting the English version. There wasn't an exact translation
anyway. 'Is that everything?'

'Pretty much.' She surveyed the sheet in front of him.
'You shouted *lepra* a couple of times, but I guess you were
just getting mixed up in your dream. Seeing Hector the
other day at work.'

Adam put his head in his hands, straining to remember.
There was something, right on the edge of his conscious-
ness, that he just couldn't reach. 'I guess so. I don't know,
Jen.'

'Okay. Okay, relax. Stop trying.' Her hands were on his
wrists, pulling them away from his face. 'Just take deep
breaths and try and clear your mind. I'll be back in one
minute.' She sprang to her feet, almost running from the
room, and Adam heard her climbing the steps outside, up
to her own balcony. She was back almost immediately,
carrying one of the large artist's pads that she used for
sketching.

'Let's try this.' She put the pad down in front of him
and took his hands, putting them palm down onto a clean

page. 'Now spread your fingers…that's right. Feel the texture.' The thick paper felt silky smooth under his touch.

'This isn't going to work, Jen.'

'Maybe not. You've tried pretty much everything else.'

'In other words, just shut up and get on with it.'

'Exactly. Can you feel the paper?'

Adam closed his eyes. 'Yeah. I feel it.'

'Okay, now just let your mind drift. Let the paper take on a shape, any shape. Don't try to control it, just let it happen.'

Adam wasn't buying this. But she'd stuck with him this far and he appreciated that. He took a deep breath, feeling his shoulders loosen as he exhaled. The paper was cool, textured under his fingers. He did as Jenna told him, concentrating on its feel under each one of his fingers in turn. Then he waited. For what seemed like an eternity.

Suddenly an image shot into his head. 'A gun butt. No…a rifle.' He could feel beads of cold sweat forming on his brow.

'Good. That's fine. What else?' He could feel her hands on his shoulders, keeping him from harm.

'Someone's arm… Light and shade… *La lepra*.' He almost whispered the words.

'Are you sure?'

'Positive.' Adam's eyes snapped open. He could see the arm in his mind's eye now, clear and detailed. The skin wasn't that of a young man. It was an older man, gnarled and twisted with disease. 'It's not Hector, it's someone else. I've got it now. I can see it.'

'Good, that's great.' Her face was shining with success.

Adam looked down at the sheet in front of him, the outline of his hands still faintly visible from where the absorbent paper had soaked up the sweat from his fingers. 'I felt it, Jen.'

She shrugged. 'You were drawing it in your mind's eye. My grandfather taught me how to draw and he showed me how to do it. Putting your hands on the paper seems to help.' She focussed on the pad. 'It's not actually there. Obviously.'

'But it works.' The image was clear in his head now.

'Well, not for me. I think it's a load of hocus pocus, but Gramps swore by it.' She grinned at him, wayward and entirely entrancing. 'I expect it's just the relaxing thing, thinking about something else.' She ripped the top sheet off the pad, exposing a fresh leaf. 'Now, tell me what this hand you remember looked like.'

It took them an hour, Adam carefully describing the remembered images and Jenna transcribing them on to paper. When they'd finished he was exhausted. She laid the sheets of drawing paper and his written page on the coffee table in front of them. 'It's not enough, is it?'

He put his hand over hers, trying to give the consolation that he didn't feel. 'But it's a start, eh? It shows that the memories are there, at least some of them.'

'If only…' Her voice was laden with disappointment. She had to see the ambiguity of the disjointed phrases. Had his rapid invective been after Elena had been shot or had he argued with the bandits and prompted her shooting? *Get behind me*—the words of a hero trying to protect someone or the words of a coward as he ran away?

'It's a start.' He squeezed her hand. 'Thank you.' There was nothing more to do now but to go back to bed and try and get some sleep. And if he craved a few more minutes of her company before that happened, he knew that it was pointless. He would always want more time with her, however much he took.

'Do you need me to stay?'

'No.' He didn't want Jenna to see any more of this than

she already had. 'But can I take you out for breakfast in the morning?'

'I'd like that.' She sprang to her feet and Adam followed her into the bedroom. Head high, and without so much as a glance at the rumpled sheets on the bed, she slipped through the billowing muslin curtains. Then, closing the French doors behind her, she was gone, like a wraith in the night.

Jenna had woken early, and had not been able to turn over in bed and sleep again. Instead she'd showered and dressed, wondering whether Adam was going to make good on his promise. Maybe she'd just pop downstairs, see if he was awake.

She crept gingerly down the fire-escape steps and peered through the window. His bedroom was empty, the duvet and pillows straightened and neat. He must be up, but she could hardly tap on his bedroom door now that daylight was flooding through the windows.

Tiptoeing back up the steps, she walked through her flat and out of the front door. If she was going to go downstairs, she'd use the proper route. Halfway down, she caught sight of him, leaning in the open doorway to his flat, arms folded and a smile on his face.

'You're up.' Jenna tried to sound surprised.

'Yep. And I'm starving. Are you ready for breakfast?'

He'd remembered. And he was waiting for her. The bone-wrenching sadness of the last week dissolved, like a morning mist under the heat of the sun. 'Ready when you are.'

He didn't reply but pulled the door closed behind him with a smile. She wanted to run to him, but she didn't. Instead she took his arm when he offered it, hanging on tight.

Adam didn't mention last night's dream as they strolled to the small café on the high road and Jenna let the matter lie. If he wanted to talk about it, he would, and there was no sense in pushing it. Finding an empty table, they ordered coffee and two full English breakfasts. Jenna was hungry too. Perhaps not for food, but she felt hungry for life again, and a good breakfast seemed the place to start.

'So it was your grandfather who taught you to draw?' Adam was tackling his breakfast with verve.

'Yes. He was a painter.'

'Really?' Adam's fork was suddenly still, poised between his plate and his mouth. 'Do you have any of his paintings in your flat?'

He knew as well as she did that she didn't. It wasn't that she didn't love them, but Gramps's paintings could be unsettling at times. A little too much truth. 'They're quite big.'

He nodded. 'That's a shame.' He waited for a moment, giving her a chance to elaborate, and then put the fork into his mouth.

'I do have some. In storage.' Suddenly Jenna wanted him to see the pictures, if only to show him that she wasn't completely alone in the world. Her grandparents had never deserted her.

'Yes?' There was a glimmer of interest in his face. More than just a glimmer.

'I have them at the house.' Jenna returned her attention to the plate in front of her. A man like Adam, who believed in one fixed version of the truth about himself, would be challenged by Gramps's view of the world, the many truths that showed so clearly in his paintings. If he did want to see them, he was going to have to ask.

'Do you ever show them to anyone?' He was nosing at

the bait and Jenna almost held her breath, waiting to see if he'd bite.

'Of course I do, I'm very proud of them.'

He bit. With a grin that told her he knew that he'd been snared. 'May I see them?'

'Yes, of course. After breakfast?'

'I'd like that.'

'Wait till you've seen them. They can be challenging.'

'More than I can take?' His gaze met hers and suddenly this wasn't about paintings anymore. It was about two people, struggling to find a way to connect without tearing each other apart.

'I wouldn't ask any more than that, Adam.'

'No. Nor I you.' He slid his hand across the table towards hers and the deal was sealed in the moment that their fingers touched.

'Friends, then?' Jenna smiled at him.

'Always.' He tapped the edge of her plate with the tip of his fork. 'And since we are friends, maybe I can enquire whether you're going to eat your bacon. Shame to let it go to waste…'

'I'm saving it for last.' Jenna coiled her arm protectively around her plate and caught the waiter's eye. 'George, will you bring some more bacon, please?'

'And toast.' Adam's lips twitched into a satisfied grin. Jenna was not sure now which one of them had snared the other. 'I assume you're saving your toast for last, too.'

'As it happens, I am.' She picked the coffee pot up and tilted it towards his cup. 'But you can have the rest of the coffee if you want it.'

He nodded, and Jenna refilled his cup. Suddenly she didn't care who'd snared who, or what the consequences might be. This happiness was far too good to waste.

* * *

Adam had been expecting a dark, cluttered loft space, much the same as his own. Instead, Jenna led him past her front door and up a set of winding stairs, unlocking a door at the top and leading him into a large attic room. Odd angles and a sloping ceiling that followed the shape of the roof. High beams and white-painted walls. Light bursting in through the large dormer windows, flooding the space.

'What do you think?' She twirled around, showing off the space. 'This used to be my grandfather's studio, and now I use it.'

He saw that. The clutter of paints and canvasses. Photographs pinned up on the walls, some old and faded and some more recent. The whole space was alive with light and colour, bearing both the stamp of the man who had created it and Jenna's lighter hand.

She was leafing through a set of canvasses, stacked and wrapped in a shaded corner for safekeeping. 'Help me with this, will you?'

He helped her slide the one she wanted out from the stack, and watched while she removed the wrappings. 'So is this a self-portrait?'

'No, he never painted himself. It's of Laura, my sister. He painted it just after she died and I sat with him and helped him.' She gave a little shrug. 'With some of the brushstrokes.'

Adam could see it all. A man helping his granddaughter come to terms with her loss through the thing that connected them both. The thought made him smile.

She stood, the canvas propped against her legs, its back towards him. 'Everything's here in this painting, Adam. You just have to choose how to see it.'

His heart seemed to beat a little faster. 'May I see it, then?'

The painting was stunning. Powerful, intimate and quite

breathtaking. A young woman, painted in fine and loving detail, standing on a beach. She was blond, blue-eyed and blooming with promise. Serene, despite the rage and grief in the harsh brushstrokes of the sea, to her left. Adam stared, dumbstruck.

'Do you like it?' She was nervous, her fingers fluttering across the edges of the canvas.

'*Like* isn't the word that springs to mind. It's magnificent.' He stepped back to get a better view, and as he did so, the seemingly anarchic shapes of the waves formed into the suggestion of a gaunt face.

'You see what I mean?'

Adam stared at the painting. He saw. 'He was a brave man.' The stubborn refusal to turn away from tragedy, to face it and own it, reminded him of someone. 'Was he a redhead, too?'

She laughed. 'Not when I knew him. He was when he was younger. Grandma said she fell in love with his hot-headedness.'

Even with Jenna in the room, Adam still couldn't quite tear his eyes from the painting. 'She was very beautiful. Your grandfather painted kindness, too.'

'Yes, she was. She was one of those people who seem to be good at everything. Out of the two of us, she was the pretty one as well.' The small quirk of her lips told Adam that he had hit a sore spot.

'You think so?'

'That's what everyone used to say.'

'Everyone? What did your grandfather say?' Adam took a chance and trusted the man who had painted that astonishing portrait.

She shrugged. 'Well, Gramps never did go along with what everyone else said. Artistic temperament, you know.'

'I see clear-sightedness in this painting.' A lot of things

were beginning to make sense to Adam. The second-best child who'd lost her sister and been abandoned by her parents. He reckoned that was about enough hurt to make anyone diffident about accepting praise.

She stood, biting her lip for a moment, as if she was wrestling with an insoluble brain-teaser. Then she tossed it aside in frustration. 'I just wanted you to see it. That's all.'

'Thank you. I'm honoured that you shared this with me.' Her ears began to go pink, and she propped the painting against the wall, sitting on the stool by the easel.

'I'm glad you like it. It means a lot to me.'

'Did your grandfather ever paint you?'

She rubbed her palms together, uneasily. 'Yes, he did.'

'Are you going to show me?'

'It's… It's…'

'It's what? Not very good?'

She rose to the bait magnificently, tossing her head and stalking over to the stack of paintings. Adam noticed that she knew which one to select straight away, and that this one was loosely bound, as if it had often been taken out of its wrappings.

'He painted this when I was twenty. It was pretty much his last painting.'

She twisted the canvas abruptly round for him to see, and the force of it nearly knocked him off his feet. Jenna sat on a high stool, dressed in jeans and baseball boots, her hands planted on her knees in a posture of quiet assurance. A rainbow-coloured shawl hung over her right shoulder, contrasting vibrantly with her plain white shirt.

'Wow! That's…' He was unable to find the words just yet. It wasn't that this was a beautifully executed portrait of a gorgeous woman. Jenna's grandfather had somehow captured her essence, the fascinating contrast between beauty and vulnerability, practicality and her more artistic nature.

The real thing quirked her lips downwards. 'Gramps always was an old softie. He's done me a few favours.'

Adam bent to examine the portrait more carefully. Behind Jenna was the organised clutter of the attic studio, with one addition that was conspicuously absent from the room he was now in. A mirror, right behind her, the back of her head and shoulders reflected in it. Hair swept up in a complex arrangement of shining curls, even redder than the original. Bare shoulders, crossed by the dark green straps of what was obviously an evening dress.

'What's that?' The high back of the stool had something slung carelessly around the support, half-obscured by her shoulder.

She didn't reply and he looked again, and couldn't keep the grin from his face when he made it out. It was a coronet. Her grandfather had painted her as she was, but also how she seemed to him. 'An ordinary woman, who's also a princess.'

Jenna nodded. 'It's one of his little jokes. He used to call me princess sometimes.'

'It's beautiful.' Adam peered at the bottom right-hand side of the picture, wondering if his suspicions were right. There was a small signature there. 'Your grandfather was Alex Weston?' The man who'd painted many beautiful women in the 1960s and 1970s, then disappeared from the limelight to paint the ordinary, lending everyday things a little magic with his brush.

'Yes. Are you impressed?'

'Not by the name. But the kind of man who can paint something with so much love in it must have been quite extraordinary.'

He could see from her eyes that he'd given the right answer. The one she wanted to hear from him. 'That's a nice thing to say.' She grinned. 'I don't talk about Gramps's painting all that much because people get all excited about him being famous.'

'And that's not the most important thing about him.'

'No. Not by a long chalk.' The approval in her eyes told Adam that he'd passed some sort of test.

'Jenna, will you do something?'

'What's that?'

'Will you bring this painting downstairs? Put it in your sitting room somewhere so that you can look at it. Listen to your grandfather when he tells you what he thinks of you.'

She looked at him as if there was some catch to what he was saying. 'I'll think about it.'

'Do that. It's a beautiful painting and shouldn't be hidden away up here. Even if it does have one flaw.'

'What?' She twisted round to examine the painting, ready to spring to her grandfather's defence.

'I'm banking on your grandfather having been the first to say it. It doesn't do you justice.'

The flare in her eyes told Adam that he was right. She'd obviously just about reached the limit of what she was willing to admit to, though.

'Don't you try and wheedle your way around me with compliments.'

'I'm not. Not just yet, anyway.' She'd leant the painting against the wall, next to the one of Laura, and Adam caught her arm, spinning her round and imprisoning her in a loose embrace. Seized by a sudden awkwardness, he propelled her out of the door and closed it firmly behind them.

'Not while Gramps is watching, eh?' She was grinning up at him, snuggling close.

'Some things he doesn't need to see.' Adam ran his fingers over the filmy material of her collar. Soft, like an inferior copy of her skin.

'I doubt he'd mind.'

'Minding and seeing are two different things. Are you coming downstairs with me, or do I have to throw you over my shoulder?' She caught her breath in delighted shock at the abruptness of his demand and he silenced her with a kiss. Enough with words. He'd show her how beautiful she was if it killed him. And if the last time he'd had her in his bed was anything to go by, it might just do that.

CHAPTER TEN

JENNA had made her decision. And in the five days since she and Adam had been back together, she'd not regretted it once. Colleague, lover, friend—he did all of them better than anyone she'd ever known before. But now the time they had left was dwindling fast. Five days, not counting today. Saturday, Sunday, Monday, Tuesday, Wednesday. Actually, only half of Wednesday, because he had an evening flight and Jenna had already decided not to go to the airport with him. Airports made her cry.

Adam was officially not working today, but Jenna knew that he was in the hospital somewhere. Finishing off. Saying goodbye. He had already sent her a text to meet him in the canteen at lunchtime, and today she told Brenda that she would be taking her full hour's break. A and E wasn't busy, and just the once wouldn't hurt.

He wasn't alone. Two blond heads, sitting opposite him at the table, and next to him an older man, Julie's father, who jumped to his feet when he saw Jenna, motioning her to sit next to Adam, while he shifted across to sit with his daughters.

'Ah, thank goodness.' Adam gave her a beseeching look. 'I'm dying here and Terry's giving me no support.'

Julie's father laughed. 'I learned a long time ago that I'm

no match for two teenagers once they get started. Anyway, what's so bad about having a blog? I think it's a good idea.'

'Yeah, see,' Julie crowed, turning to Jenna. 'Emma and I will set it up for him, since he doesn't know how, and he can write all about the places he goes and the jungle and stuff. Then we'll know what he's up to.'

'Sounds like a plan.' Jenna wasn't sure what kind of plan. The thought that it might be possible to keep up with Adam's activities filled her with a mixture of dread and delight.

'See, Jenna thinks it's a good idea,' Emma chimed in. 'We can give it a name, can't we, Jules?'

'Yeah. Dr Danger Defies… Defies what, Em?'

Emma's brow creased in thought. 'Dunno. Dr Danger Defies Deadly something.'

'Ducks.' Jenna giggled and Adam's head sank into his hands.

There was a chorus of 'No's' from around the table and she feigned surprise.

'Ducks can be quite vicious at times.'

'You don't get ducks in the jungle.' Julie admonished her.

'You don't get broadband in the jungle either.' Adam was putting up a creditable fight.

Julie rolled her eyes. 'Well, you write it down in a note-book and take some pictures and then update your blog later. They must have broadband somewhere in South America.'

'Yeah. Quite a lot of places actually. But I'm not having you call it Dr Danger does anything. If I'm going to write a blog, it'll be under my own name. That's final.'

Julie and Emma exchanged glances. Jenna recognised that trick. Suggest something outrageous and then accept a compromise. Which was generally the thing you wanted in the first place.

'Okay.' Julie couldn't keep the smirk out of her voice. 'Not a bad tag line, though. Dr Danger Does Anything.'

'No. Adam Sinclair. It's that or nothing.' Adam seemed to have reached his sticking point. 'And don't expect me to update it more than once a week.'

'That's okay. We don't have time to comment more than once a week.' Emma was grinning, too. 'Anyway, Julie can't type at the moment, so I'll have to do it for both of us.'

'No way.' Adam turned to Julie. 'I know your fingers are stiff, but the burn therapist told you to keep them moving gently, didn't she? You can type just a couple of words, slowly, to let me know how you're doing.'

Busted. He'd just given himself away, to Jenna if not to Julie and Emma. He'd been playing them at their own game. Giving them something to do together, keeping in touch with them. Letting them both know that he wanted to hear how they were doing. She shot Adam a grin. 'Yes. I'll look in as well and put some comments on, so I'd better see yours there as well, Julie. And Emma's.'

'You will.' Julie's voice had a note of confidence in it. She was so different now from the pain-racked, terrified teenager that Jenna had seen a month ago in A and E. So much care, from so many people, and this was what could be achieved. 'I might even do a blog of my own.'

They'd said their goodbyes. Terry had shaken Adam's hand as if he could work it loose from his arm and take it home with him as a memento, and had given Jenna a hug and a kiss. Jenna had hugged Julie and Emma, promising to see them both soon, and Adam had kissed each of them on the cheek.

'Are you crying?' He sat back down and offered her a paper napkin.

'No.'

'Right. I wouldn't have blamed you if you were. Seeing them both like this. You usually see the start of the process, not the end.'

She'd been thinking about that. How she so seldom got to follow through with her patients. It had been such a pleasure to see Julie and Emma today, maybe not quite whole again, but well on the road to it. 'Do you think they'll be okay, Adam?'

He blew out a breath. 'Difficult to say. They've got exams, boys, careers, marriages, children, the property market and social networking to contend with. Bit of a tall order.'

'Stop it. You know what I mean.'

'Yeah, they'll be okay. Julie's got the best medical care, they've got good family support and counselling help.'

'Yes, I heard you'd pushed the counselling through. And Terry told me about your offer, too. That was good of you.'

Adam shrugged as if it was nothing. 'It may not come to that. Julie might not need any follow-up surgery, and if she does, she might not need me to do it. But she can always come to me, even if she just needs someone to talk to.'

'That's the most important thing right now. That she knows she has someone she trusts, who'll be there if she needs it. It's giving her the confidence to look forward to the future now.'

'Yeah. Hope so.' His lips twisted and for a moment he seemed to feel what Jenna was feeling. About his future and hers. Then the moment was gone, and he grinned. 'So what do you think of my foray into the world of cyber-space, then?'

'I think you're a manipulative, two-timing rat.'

The grin broadened. 'Well, thank you, you do say the nicest things. I've been thinking of doing a blog for ages.' He leaned across the table towards her. 'So are you going to join in then? Send me a few comments. You can be Dr Delicious. I quite like the sound of Dr Danger and Dr Delicious.'

'You'll be Dr Decapitated if you're not careful.' Jenna did too, but she'd decapitate herself rather than admit it. 'It would serve you right if I decided to send Julie and Emma a few sketches of you to put on there.'

He paled slightly. 'Which one? Not the one you did last night, Jen… Why do you always have to wait until I'm asleep, anyway?'

'Because you won't stay still for long enough when you're awake. Actually, I was thinking of the cartoons.'

'Oh, yeah, they're great.' He was grinning again. 'Just right.'

Adam wanted to make the most of these last few days they had together. He'd made his decision to go, and nothing was going to sway him from that. It might not be easy, but it was the right thing to do. Jenna needed a man who could commit, someone who would take care of her. He was unable to do either.

They were both adults, though, knew the score and had decided to take a taste of what life was ultimately going to deny them. Just a few days. And the more he could make her smile in those few days, the better.

His campaign started in earnest that evening. He'd taken her to see a film in a small independent cinema, where armchairs replaced rows of seats, and drinks were served in the auditorium before the beginning of the film. Then on to a South American restaurant, run by friends of his and home late.

'You, sweetheart, are the prettiest card sharp I've ever met.'

She laughed, dumping the bag of coins on the coffee table. Two pounds fifty-seven in pennies. 'And you are the worst I've ever met. You're so easy to read.'

'For you maybe.' Sometimes he wished that he didn't feel so transparent under her gaze. 'So what am I thinking right now?' He pulled her into his arms and kissed her, savouring the faint taste of tequila on her lips.

'You're wondering if you can distract me enough to get your hands on my bag of pennies. And the answer is that you can't.'

'Not even close. That tequila tastes nice.'

She giggled. 'It was. I've never had tequila before.'

'Well, that was the good stuff. You don't just throw it down for a buzz, you sip it slowly, like brandy. Leave the salt and lemons in the kitchen cupboard.'

She nodded. 'Pity you were driving. Was that a bottle of it I saw you put in the car?'

'Yeah. Thought I'd give it to Rob. He can crack it open when the baby's born.'

'Good idea. I might pop over there and give him a hand with that.' She twisted her lips in an expression of sudden regret, and it was Adam's turn to know what she was thinking. Unless the baby came in the next four days, he wouldn't be there. He hated it too, but there was no point in dwelling on it.

'So, now that you've cleaned me out of small change…' He grinned down at her, endeavouring to make her smile again. 'Don't suppose there's much chance of winning it back, is there?'

'Not a great deal. You could try.' She looped one finger inside his shirt, and the room swam slightly before his eyes. Those moments of anticipation, when he knew exactly where they were headed. Without breaking the kiss, he backed her through the door and down the hallway towards the bedroom.

He woke in the middle of the night. A warm haze was spreading through his body, moving from his chest to his groin and then fluttering up to his chest again. He felt as if he were being bathed in sunlight, sharp sensations of pleasure pulsing through his body, and he moved drowsily in time with them.

His eyes snapped open. Jenna had just climbed on top of him, astride his hips, her skin pale against his. He loved that. The way her skin seemed almost to shimmer in the half-light, contrasting with the darker tones of his own.

'Hey, you.'

'Mmm. Is this my wake-up call?'

'Yes.' She smiled mischievously. 'You like it?'

The answer to that one was obvious. Adam stretched languidly beneath her, settling his hands onto her hips. 'I love the view.'

She laughed quietly. She was the same woman he'd first made love with two weeks ago, but she'd changed, too. Then his compliments had been received awkwardly, as if she hadn't quite believed them. But he had kept them coming and slowly she had begun to accept them. Now she was revelling in them.

He reached over and flipped the bedside lamp on, laughing as she blinked. 'You are so beautiful. Your skin's like porcelain, did you know that?'

She grinned at him. 'What else?'

'Flame-haired.'

'Mmm. You deserve something for all these nice things you're saying about me.' She reached over to the bedside cabinet and tore at a foil packet. Lifting herself up onto her knees, she rolled the condom down in place, taking the opportunity to caress him at the same time.

'That feels…so much better when you do it, honey.' Adam was fighting for control. Battling not to sink into incoherence. He didn't want her to just know how he felt about her. He wanted her to hear it from his own lips.

Carefully, she sank back onto him, taking him inside her as she went. He felt his body begin to tremble and his hands tighten on her waist. Dipping towards him, she whispered against his cheek 'This is all for you, sweetheart.'

'Oh, really?' He canted his hips, gripping hers to control her movements, and she gasped, colour rising in her cheeks. Again, and she arched her back, throwing her head back. Magnificent. Alluring. He told her so, in as many words as he could summon. He told her that he loved the way her eyes caught the light. The way she'd been so ready for him, and that they seemed to fit together so well.

The balance tipped again, and she rocked backwards, twisting her hips as she went, and his eyes snapped upwards in their sockets, quite of their own accord. There were no words for this, none that he could think of anyway. His body shuddered beneath hers, and he gave himself over to the waves of pure sensation that ebbed and flowed along with her movements.

Finally he could stand it no more. It took just one movement and he had twisted her over onto her back. She gave a delighted squeal, and Adam realised that this was what she had wanted all along.

She saved the best for last, her body blossoming under his like living flame, her muscles tightening around him, till he couldn't hold on any longer. He thought he called her name, but he wasn't sure. Maybe it was just that it was the only thing in his head at the moment. And then he almost passed out from sheer, head-spinning, heart-grabbing pleasure.

'Jen.' Somehow he'd managed to collapse beside her, rather than right on top of her. 'Jenna, honey.'

'Mmm. So nice. You are *so* nice.' Her voice was small, choked with emotion, and he pulled her into the curve of his body, holding her tight until she began to drift off to sleep in his arms.

When she woke, light was filtering through the curtains. Jenna lay on her back in his arms, staring at the ceiling, wondering whether it would be considered kidnap to lock him in here all weekend.

Mind you, perhaps he'd be the one to lock *her* in. Or perhaps they'd just have done with any dispute in the matter and lock each other in. She shifted a little so she could see his face. Long lashes, closed over those beautiful eyes, a slight smile curving his lips, as if his dreams were good ones.

A noise from the sitting room caught her attention and his eyes fluttered open. 'It's only my phone.' Jenna didn't move. 'Whoever it is can leave a message.'

'No, they can't. I want you all to myself today.'

'Oh, do you?' She loved the early mornings. Lying next to him, talking lazily. 'Oh, who on earth is it?' The sound of her mobile drifted through from the hallway.

He rolled away from her. 'Better get it. It might be urgent.'

'Well, it can wait.' She lay on her back, arms folded.

'You'll only be wondering if you don't find out who it is.'

He was right. She climbed out of bed and padded

through to the hallway, just in time to hear her mobile stop ringing. One missed call.

'Who was it?'

'Rob. What does he want at this hour?' Jenna sat back down on the bed. 'Suppose I'd better call back, just in case it's anything. Cassie's very close to her due date now.'

Before she could dial, Adam's phone started to ring and he grabbed it from the bedside table. 'It's okay, he's calling me now.' He punched the Answer key and spoke into the phone. 'What is it, mate? It's seven o'clock in the morning.'

She could hear Rob's voice on the other end of the line, talking fast. Suddenly Adam sat up. 'Okay... Sure, text me the address. Jenna? I imagine she's in bed at this time in the morning and didn't answer her phone... No, don't worry, I can track her down.'

'What is it?'

Adam ran his hand through his hair. 'There's a demolition site, just around the corner?'

'Yes, I know it.'

'Apparently someone got in there overnight. There's been a collapse and there are casualties. The fire department is digging them out now, and it would help if there was a doctor on the scene, but the shift in A and E already have their hands full.'

There was no question that he was going to go. Or that she'd go, too. He was into his jeans in a moment, picking up the rest of his clothes and heading for the front door. 'I'll just go and get changed. If you've got a heavy jacket and boots, put them on. It's going to be rough work down there.'

They went on foot, Jenna taking him at a run along a back alley that led almost directly to the scene. A police cordon was already blocking the road, and she flashed her hospital tags at the constable who was standing by the fluttering strip of yellow and black plastic stretched across the road.

'Doctors. Let us through.'

The young constable looked relieved, then shot a glance up the road. 'Where's the ambulance?'

'It probably won't be here for a few minutes. I live just around the corner. Will you direct the ambulance crew through to us as soon as they arrive?'

'Right you are.' The constable lifted the tape, and Adam ducked under it, motioning her through.

He was ahead of her, jogging down the road to where a fire engine was parked outside a wooden hoarding, which sheltered the site from view. Adam made for what looked like the senior man there and was already talking rapidly to him when Jenna caught up.

'Parker, Fire and Rescue. I've called for backup, but the whole building's unstable and we can't use any heavy lifting gear. My men are having to move the rubble by hand. Any sign of the ambulance yet?'

'Not yet. How many in there?'

'Three, we think. Can't tell just yet.'

Another man, florid and rotund, who looked as if he had just rolled out of bed, marched up to them. 'This is my site. What the hell's going on?'

Parker rounded on him. 'No, it's *my* site now. Stay back there, where I told you.' He turned back to Adam. 'No point going in there just yet. It's just more weight and the floor's already unstable. My men will let you know when they've reached the casualties.'

'These two can't go in.' The florid man spoke up again. 'Listen, I'm the site manager, and my insurance doesn't cover this. It's one thing for the fire department to go tramping in there, but health and safety regulations state quite clearly—'

'We're doctors. We can help your men.' Jenna spoke calmly, trying to defuse the situation.

'I don't care if you're bloody Mother Theresa. You as much as cut your finger in there and I'm liable.' The man was waving his arm, practically shouting in her face.

'You heard what the lady said.' Adam's voice was as cold as steel. Ten times more threatening, and the site manager took a step back.

'They're not my men. Bloody scavengers, after what they could get.' The man's voice tailed off and he turned, walking away to lean against a dark blue Mercedes parked next to the fire truck. Jenna turned and caught a glimpse of Adam's face. She wasn't surprised the site manager had backed off. That glare was enough to face down a basilisk.

'What was that all about?' Adam turned off the glare and looked questioningly at Parker.

'Oh, Mr High and Mighty Site Manager was the first down here. Apparently some of the neighbours heard something going on and called the number on the hoarding. There were some men inside, looking for architectural salvage. Happens quite a lot in these old buildings, it's worth a fair bit. I wouldn't be surprised if he was in on it as there's no sign of a forced entry.'

'And he called you?' Jenna was trying to work out why the site manager had called the fire service.

'Yes. Covering his own back, afraid of any passersby being injured by anything. It was us who called for an ambulance.' Parker's face showed exactly what he thought of that. 'I'll make sure my report makes that very clear.' His eyes flipped to the end of the street. 'Ah, here they are.'

An ambulance was making its way down the road, lights still flashing, and Parker swung into action. 'Right, I'll just go and get them up to speed. You two, find some hard hats, they're in the back of the truck. I'll take you in there but it's at your own risk, understand.'

Jenna nodded. 'Understood.' She wanted to take Adam's hand, but she couldn't do that here. Instead she turned quickly, finding that he was standing right behind her, and was too late to stop herself bumping into him.

'Okay.' His hand on her arm reassured her. 'I'll go in, and you can take the casualties as they come out.' He gave her arm a squeeze and made his way over to the fire truck.

'Correction. We both go in.' She muttered the words at him as he climbed up into the cabin. He might be able to intimidate the site manager, but he didn't scare her.

'No, Jen.' He didn't even look at her.

'You can't stop me.'

'I can ask you.' He'd turned to face her now.

'Yes, and I can tell you to go and boil your head. Is someone going to die just because you're too pig-headed to let me go in there and save them?'

He pressed his lips together. 'I'll speak to Parker, make sure that there's someone in there who's responsible for your safety. You stick with him and do as he says. Right?'

Jenna's heart sank. Adam still couldn't trust himself enough to be the one to look after her. And he was the only person she wanted, the only one she needed. She took the yellow hard hat that he passed down from the cabin and dumped it on her head, finding that it was too big and needed some adjustment.

'Right, Jenna? Do we have a deal?' He wasn't going to let her get away without a reply.

'Yes. Deal. We have a deal.'

CHAPTER ELEVEN

It was hot, heavy work, and Jenna's thick jacket and boots were only making it worse. But she kept them on, sweating under the morning sun, which was just beginning to break into the filthy space that was still filled with choking dust.

They were inside the shell of a building. Two floors above them, the retaining walls were still standing, but the roof was off and the floors had collapsed through. On the far side of the ground floor the fire crew worked, steady and untiring, on a pile of rubble, which had obviously come from an internal wall.

The first man had been uncovered and she and Adam were let in close to do their work. Almost before he was strapped firmly to a gurney and carried out to the waiting ambulance, there was a second. And then a third. As Adam knelt beside him, the fire crew kept working, clearing the last of the rubble, to make sure that there was no one else.

'He's dead, Adam.' Jenna was standing behind him, but it was obvious the man was dead. Massive cranial destruction, his chest a mess of bloody pulp.

'Yeah.' Adam had still examined the body, as if there was some hope that it was possible to rebuild a man who had been shattered almost beyond recognition. He turned, and caught the ever-present Parker's eye. 'I'm pronouncing this man dead. Radio it in.'

There would be another ambulance here in a moment and they could be diverted to tend to the living. Even though the man was dead beyond any doubt or question, the fire crew would have been bound to wait for the paramedics and keep working as if he were alive, unless he was pronounced dead by a doctor.

Parker nodded and got on his radio. 'We'll check the rest, make sure there's no one else, and then get out of here. I don't like the look of this floor.' He turned to Jenna. 'You might want to wait outside.'

The words stung but it was a purely operational judgement. Adam was stronger than she was, and could help the fire crew dig. She was just an extra one-hundred-and-twenty-five pounds' worth of stress on the floor, which wasn't strictly necessary at the moment.

'Go.' Adam's voice brooked no argument. 'I'll stay and help them check the rest of the area, and I'll be with you in a moment.'

Parker was sending all but one of the rest of the fire crew out as well. Three men were needed and two of them would be Adam and himself. Jenna hesitated and then nodded, walking over to fetch the medical bag that had been dumped in the far corner of the space.

There was a grinding sound and the floor juddered sickeningly beneath her feet. 'Freeze!' Parker's voice was quiet but unmistakeably an order. Jenna froze. Looking around, she saw Parker and Adam over by the rubble and another member of the fire crew by the exit door, all caught in suspended animation. The floor seemed to have tipped and was suddenly at an angle.

'Easy. Stay still.' Adam's eyes were fixed on hers. Not letting her go. As if somehow his gaze was a lifeline that would reel her in, save her from whatever danger it was that Parker had seen.

There was a sudden crack, and noise and dust choked her senses. She saw Adam's face, a snapshot of agony, and then she was falling.

Adam watched in horror as the floor tilted, seemingly in slow motion, and seemed to buckle under Jenna's feet as she shifted the heavy medical bag. She was still now, in response to Parker's order, her eyes fixed on his face. In the silence, the rumble of traffic in the distance seemed suddenly to grow into a deafening din.

The floor was shaking, as if in response to some over-whelming force, and the sound of a train on the railway line behind the site reached his ears. All of his nerves were screaming at him to run to her, but he knew that would only increase the weight on the floor where she was stand-ing. He forced himself to keep his voice steady and quiet, and hoped that she wouldn't move.

She didn't move but the floor did. There was a deaf-ening crack and Jenna disappeared from view through a gaping hole in the floor. Adam felt Parker's hand on his arm, holding him back, but he shook himself free.

'Stay back. I'll go.' Parker rapped out the quiet order.

Like hell he would. Adam heard Parker's muttered curse behind him as he slid across the floor and reached the edge of the hole. She was down there, curled up, knees almost to her chin, her arms protectively over her head. Good girl. She wasn't moving, but Adam could hear her whimpering quietly, in fear, pain or both.

'Behind you. Watch out.' Parker's urgent voice made Adam look around. Some of the debris on the floor was beginning to slide towards the steeper incline at the rim of the hole. A pane of glass leant carefully up against one wall fell and shattered, scattering shards across the floor.

Afraid that if he called out to her she might move her head out of the protective cradle of her arms, Adam quickly let himself down through the hole, jumping the final few feet and throwing himself towards her.

'Get away from the hole.' Adam could hear Parker's voice, rising above the sound of sliding debris above his head. There was no time to assess her injuries. He had to move her now, before they were crushed together beneath a pile of masonry. He picked her up and she screamed, fingers grappling for a hold around his neck.

It was pain, not fear. Adam had heard both before, and she was in pain. He prayed that it wasn't her spine. Running for the back wall of the space, he put her down against it as gently as he could and threw himself over her.

There was a moment of silence, broken only by the groaning of overstressed timbers and the ominous rumble of something moving above them. He cradled her head against his chest, talking to her in the hope that she could hear him. 'Jenna. It's okay, honey. You're okay.' It wasn't medical opinion, just agonised hope. She had to be okay.

She moved under him, and his heart almost burst. 'Adam.' She was conscious, airway clear. And it was his name that she called.

'Okay. It's all going to be okay. Just hang in there.' The roar of falling masonry blocked everything else out as rubble crashed down, bringing half of the ceiling along with it. Something hit his back, then again, a blow that took his breath away, but he didn't care. If fate was going to dictate that only one of them made it out of here alive, all he could do was make sure it was her.

'Adam. I'm okay, it's just my leg.' She was squirming under him, crying his name, but he held her fast, preventing her from moving from the shelter of his body. The stream of debris slowed to a shower of dust.

'Status. Adam, your status.' Parker's low, urgent call reached his ears.

'She's hurt. Can't tell how badly yet.' The words seared through him as he called.

'And you?'

'Fine.' Adam looked around quickly, his eyes becoming accustomed to the gloom. They were in a large basement room, one side of which was completely full of collapsed brickwork. What was left of the ceiling over their heads was groaning, and little streams of dust were trickling downwards. He needed to get her out of here before the whole thing came down on them.

'Okay. Can you get out of that room, towards the back of the building? It's more stable there.'

Adam scanned the walls. 'Yes, there's a door. I don't know where it leads.'

'Find out. Now, before any more of this comes down.'

Adam got to his feet, feeling his back pull as he did so. Bending to gather her up in his arms, he heard her groan in pain. 'Sorry, honey. Just hang in there a little longer.'

'Do it, Adam. I'm okay.' She clung to him, nestling into his shoulder, and he gasped for air. She wasn't okay, but she was trusting him to take care of her. He would do anything, everything to do just that.

He nudged the door open with his foot, turning sideways to get her through it. The room beyond was smaller, darker, but the ceiling seemed undamaged. It had obviously served as some kind of stockroom as there were racks on the walls and an old desk and chair, with an area of carpeting at the far end. Adam carried her through, laying her carefully down on the floor.

'That's better. Thanks.' Her voice was steadier now,

none of the slurring associated with concussion. She tried to move and he quieted her.

'Stay still, Jen. Please, just for a minute.' He found her hand and clasped it. 'I'm going to call up to Parker.'

He moved quickly over to the door, feeling for his phone in his pocket and flipping it open, checking it was undamaged and that he had a signal. Calling the number out, he heard Parker repeating it back to him.

'Got it.'

'Give me five minutes. I need to see how she is. I'm putting my mobile on to vibrate.' Adam didn't want the shrill tones of his phone dislodging anything else.

'Right you are. I'm going around the back to see if there's a way down to you, but I'll leave a man up here. Call up if you need anything.'

'Thanks.' Adam moved back into the gloom, to where Jenna was lying on the floor, still. He knelt down beside her and took her hand. 'Okay, honey. You know the drill.'

'Yes. Airway clear.' She managed a laugh. 'Clear enough to ask you what the hell you're doing down here.'

He chuckled, unzipping her jacket and slipping his hands inside. 'I'm a sucker for women covered in grime. Didn't I tell you?'

'Not that I remember. But I'll keep it in mind.' Her sharp intake of breath told him that he'd found a sore spot and he stopped, investigating carefully.

'Maybe a cracked rib. Deep breath.'

She obediently took the breath. 'It's okay. I think I hit my side when I fell. Probably just bruised.' One hand moved to her wrist and she felt for her pulse.

'Will you stop that? That's my job. Did you hit your head?'

'No. And my pulse is steady.'

Adam checked anyway. Her heart was beating more

strongly and steadily than his was. He ran his hands over her hips, pressing gently. 'Any pain in your hips and back?'

'No. My ankle hurts.'

'Okay, first things first.' He checked her chest and back thoroughly, feeling for any signs of injury. 'Can you taste any blood in your mouth?'

'No. Just dust.' He felt her hand on his arm. 'It's just my ankle, Adam. I'm okay apart from that.'

He chuckled into the gloom. 'Stop self-diagnosing.'

'I'm not. I'm telling you my symptoms. My ankle hurts.' He could hear the pain in her voice now and she shifted, feeling for the pocket of her jacket. 'Here. Will you take a look at it for me?' She pressed something into his hand.

'Where did you get this?' It was a small torch.

'I keep it in my bag for when I come home late at night. I slipped it in my pocket when I got dressed this morning, thought it might come in handy.'

Adam grinned into the darkness. 'Good thought.' He flipped the torch on, directing the beam away from her face. It was powerful, even if it was small. Adam wondered how long the batteries would last. Setting it down on the floor, he turned to her. Her face was covered in grime and streaked with tears. 'Hey, there, beautiful.'

'Hey, yourself.' Her voice was laced with pain now that the adrenaline in her system had spiked and dropped. She nodded down towards her feet. 'Right ankle.'

'Okay, lie still. Let's take a look.' Adam took his jacket off, folding it into a makeshift pillow, and carefully cut the laces of her boot, opening it as wide as he could. 'You know the next line, don't you?'

'Yes. This may hurt a little, but I'll be as quick as I can.' He cut through as much of the boot as he could, and then carefully pulled it off.

It would have been better if she'd screamed, cursed

him, anything. But Adam couldn't block out the whimper of agony as he carefully laid her foot down on his folded jacket and swiftly cut her sock away to expose her ankle.

'How does it look?' She was sitting up now, speaking between gritted teeth, and he turned, wrapping his arms around her, holding her tight, as he rubbed her back gently.

'I think it's broken. I…I'm sorry, Jen. It must have hurt like hell when I picked you up.'

She snuffled into his chest. 'Don't be such a wuss. If you hadn't then I wouldn't be feeling anything right now.'

She was right but that didn't make him feel any better. She couldn't have moved fast enough to get out of the way of the pile of masonry that had come through the hole in the ceiling. But all the same he'd handled her roughly and she hadn't complained once. He pressed her to his chest. 'You're going to be just fine, Jen.'

'I know. I'm glad you're here. Even if I am angry with you for coming after me like that, landing yourself in this situation.'

He hadn't even thought about that. As far as he was concerned, the best place for him was by her side. It was the only place, and instinct had dictated that before reasoning had confirmed it. He bent and brushed a brief kiss across her lips. She tasted of brick dust and strawberries.

'No place I'd rather be.' It wasn't just some meaningless pleasantry, it was a binding vow. He'd stay with her, come hell or high water, until she was out of there. And he'd keep her safe with the last breath in his body. It wasn't a matter of choice or decision, that was just how things were.

He was holding her tightly, his heart beating fast against her cheek. She could almost, almost but not quite, block out the pain in her leg when she was in his arms. No, scratch that. It hurt. It was just more bearable when he was holding her.

She half felt, half heard his phone, vibrating in his pocket. He pulled it out, keeping her supported against his body with his free hand. Someone was on the other end, speaking quickly, and Adam listened, giving only short acknowledgements to let the other person know he'd heard and understood.

'She's okay. Probable broken ankle, but apart from that she's good.' Jenna felt his arm tighten around her. 'Can you get some medical supplies down to us? Good.' He reeled off a list of what he wanted, and Jenna's heart sank. It sounded as if they were going to be down here for a while, if he needed all that.

'Okay, thanks.' Adam paused. 'If you hear how the two casualties are, will you let me know? Yeah, thanks. Wait a minute, will you?' He let the phone drop from his ear. 'Jen, do you have your phone on you?'

'Yes.' He loosened his grip on her slightly, just enough to allow her to feel in her pocket. 'It's here.'

'Okay, check if it's working and how much battery time you've got left.'

She thumbed a key and the display lit up. 'Yeah, I've got three bars on reception and it's practically fully charged.' She dialled the speaking clock and listened carefully. 'Yes, it's fine.'

'Good.' He recited her number slowly into his phone. 'My battery's low, so if you can't get me, call Jenna.' He nodded into the phone and grinned. 'Thanks, Parker. Much appreciated.' He snapped the phone closed and wound his other arm around her shoulders. 'Okay. We're good.'

'What did he say?' It hadn't sounded all that good.

'They can't get to us from where you fell, the floor's far too unstable for them to work on. But they know where we are, and the structure above us looks much more stable. There's a staircase at the back of the building and they're coming that way, but it's full of rubble from the demolition and clearing it might take a while.'

'How long?'

'I don't know. It won't be five minutes, but it won't be all day. Somewhere in between. I'm sorry, Jen.'

'Don't be.' Jenna took a breath, trying to steady her nerves. 'We'll just sit tight and wait, yes?'

'Yeah. And meanwhile, there are some things on their way to make you more comfortable.'

It took fifteen minutes for the bag to come down to them. Adam had made her as comfortable as he could, carefully elevating the leg and propping it up on a wooden box, his jacket still folded under it. The basement was cool, and when he laid her down flat she began to shiver so he held her, supporting her body against his. He rubbed her back, massaged her neck, the tops of her legs and even the palms of her hands. It was unconventional, but it seemed to work. With the tension gone from her body, and warm and safe in his arms, the pain receded a little.

Finally, Adam's phone rang. He answered it, listened for a moment and then turned to her. 'I'll be one minute.'

She couldn't bear for him to go out there. It wasn't safe. Jenna clung to him, imploring him silently to stay.

'One minute, I promise. Count it off.' He laid the phone down on the floor and took her by the shoulders. 'Parker's up there, keeping an eye on things.'

She didn't care that the line was open, and that whoever was on the other end could probably hear her. 'No, Adam. I don't need anything in that bag, not as much as I need you in one piece and here with me.'

He brushed a kiss against her lips. 'It's okay. Trust me, Jen. I'll be back.' Adam felt for the torch, switched it back on and picked up the phone. 'Sixty. Fifty-nine...count with me.'

'Fifty-eight. Fifty-seven.' He rose and quickly made his way towards the door, pushing it open and looking upwards. Then he disappeared.

'Forty. Thirty-nine.' She was beginning to cry, straining her ears for the sound of anything that might mean that he was in trouble out there.

'Nineteen. Eighteen.' He appeared in the doorway, a large bag in one hand, and a bench mattress from an ambulance, rolled around red blankets and a pillow. Depositing them on the floor next to her, he lifted his phone to his ear and spoke into it.

'All right. Thanks, Parker... Yeah, okay, I understand. Don't rush it, we're okay to sit tight.' He cut the line, and stuffed the phone back into his pocket.

'What did he say?'

'It'll be at least a couple of hours, more likely three before they can get to us. There's a lot of rubble between them and us.'

'You told him not to take any risks with the men, though, didn't you? We can wait.'

'I told him. Now, let's get you sorted.'

He unrolled the mattress, sliding it carefully under her, and Jenna relaxed back onto it. Unzipping the bag, he rummaged around inside and brought out a lantern torch, switching it on and bathing the whole room with light. A bottle of water followed and he used a little to sluice the worst of the grime from his hands then washed them with cleansing gel. Pulling out a cardboard box, he took out a blister pack containing a syringe.

'Oh, no, you don't.' Anything that touched the searing pain in her leg was going to make her feel drowsy. Which would mean he couldn't leave her alone.

'Jen, are you seriously going to tell me that your leg doesn't hurt you?' He stopped what he was doing and knelt beside her.

'No. But I need to keep my wits about me.'

The look of hurt on his face was palpable, slamming against her senses, making her forget for a moment about the pain in her leg. 'You trust me so little.' It was the resignation in his voice that hurt most.

'I trust you so much I know you'd never leave me alone if you'd just given me a shot of morphine.' She jutted her chin aggressively. It was the only way to get through the frustration of him continually questioning himself.

He caught on, and something like hope sparked in his eyes. Jenna could have cried at the cruelty of it all. 'I won't leave you with a broken ankle. I wouldn't leave you with a broken fingernail. That's non-negotiable.'

'But…but suppose…' Jenna was casting around in her mind to find some scenario that might mean he'd have to leave her behind. That he could get out of here before she could, while she waited for the fire crew.

'Suppose nothing. I'm not going anywhere and that's final. And since I'm stuck here with you, I'd rather you were comfortable and not biting my head off because you're in pain. What do you say?'

Warmth flooded through her. Like the heat from the injection he was about to give her, but far more potent. 'Okay. How good are you with finding a vein, then?'

He shrugged cheerfully, rolling up the sleeve of her jacket. 'Guess you're about to find out. Taking any other medication?'

'You know I'm not.'

'Previous contra-indications? Asthma, Kidney…?'

'No! Just give me the pain control, will you?'

'That's more like it.' He put on a pair of gloves, snapping them theatrically, swabbed her arm and slid the needle in first time. 'How's that?'

'Not bad.' Warmth was beginning to spread along her arm.

'I thought that was pretty near perfect myself.' He disposed of the syringe and sat next to her on the floor, holding her hand while the morphine kicked in. 'Feeling better?'

'Yes. Thanks.' She knew now what it felt like when that smile spread across a patient's face. The relief when pain receded into the background was pleasure in itself. Something like what she felt when she was with Adam.

The object of her rose-tinted speculations was busying himself, carefully cutting the leg of her jeans to the knee, powdering her ankle and carefully slipping an inflatable splint over her foot. 'Can you feel that?' He was gently tapping her toes.

'Hmm? Yes.' She smiled at Adam. 'Thoughtful of them to put powder in the bag.'

He chuckled. 'Yeah.' He propped a cushion gently behind her head. 'Comfortable?'

'Yes, comfortable. Come here.'

CHAPTER TWELVE

SHE was beginning to drift slightly. Not so much that she couldn't still think for herself, he'd made sure to give her a low dose so that he could give her more if needed. But the pain receptors in her brain were zoning away from her ankle, which was just what he wanted them to do. If he couldn't get her out of this basement, the least he could do was to help her concentrate on something else.

He gave her some water and used some of the antiseptic wipes to clean her face and hands. He was probably using more of their limited supply than was strictly sensible, but it seemed to give her comfort that even now they were a long way from doing just what was strictly necessary. He stretched out on the carpet next to her, arranging the blanket over her body.

'I don't need that, I'm too hot. Fold it up and put it underneath you.' He felt her hands and foot and she was warm enough. He slid the blanket away from her, and folded it up.

'Better?' His own back was aching now, but that didn't matter. It didn't matter that he could still feel a stickiness right where the top of his jeans met his spine. The bleeding had stopped now, and he wouldn't show her that he was hurt. And he wouldn't leave her alone, take the surgical tape that was in the bag, and apply it out of her sight. There was time enough for that later.

'Yes.' She looked up at him. 'Thanks, Adam.'

'My pleasure.' He picked up the water bottle. 'You want a little more to drink?'

She made him drink first, and he took a couple of sips from the bottle, grateful for the moisture in his throat. She drank a little, screwing the top back on to the bottle. 'How much longer do you reckon?'

He looked at his watch. 'A couple of hours at least. If Parker hasn't called me by then, I'll give him a ring, see what's up.'

She nodded and he rolled onto his back, shifting the folded blanket underneath his head. That was better. His back didn't hurt as much now. Casually he pulled one knee up slightly to stretch it a little and as the arch of his back touched the floor, he winced.

'What?' She was suddenly alert.

'Nothing.'

'I distinctly heard a sharp intake of breath.'

'I thought I felt a moth on my face.'

'Crap.' She was up on one elbow, now. 'What was it, or do I have to strip you to find out?'

He grinned up at the ceiling. Even here, even now, the thought didn't seem like a bad one.

'Adam, do you want me to come after you? I will, you know.'

'You can't. I'm faster than you at the moment.'

'I'll still try.' A small sound escaped her throat as she twisted round, trying to catch hold of his arm.

'Stop it.'

She ignored him. Pulling herself up into a sitting position, she leaned farther over, and he caught her arms before she collapsed onto his chest. 'Stop it, Jen. Since when

did the meaning of immobilise become so hard to understand?' Her face was contorted with determination and
pain. 'Okay, okay.' He guided her back onto the mattress
and turned, wincing as he pulled his sweater and shirt up
over his head.

'Adam. For goodness' sake, why didn't you tell me?'

He sighed. 'It didn't feel too bad up till now. It just
caught me when I lay on my back.' It was true. He'd been
so concerned for her that he hadn't even realised he was
in pain.

'I'm not surprised, you've got glass in there.' She had
picked up the lantern and was shining it onto his back.
'Go and get the bag, will you? And do you have a pair of
tweezers in your penknife?'

'Yeah.' He passed her his penknife and rose to fetch the
bag. He sat back down, his back to her, while she rummaged inside it, bringing out gloves, sterile wipes and
water. 'Ow! Go easy there.'

'Serves you right. Keep still, will you?'

'Fine bedside manner you've got. Remind me never to
be carted into Casualty when you're on shift. Ow, Jenna!'

'Be quiet.' They both knew that she was being as gentle as she could, but it felt good to let off a little steam.
He felt a trickle of water on his back, and shadows swung
back and forth on the wall in front of him as she tilted the
torch, making sure there were no shards of glass left in
the wound.

'Okay, that's it. When exactly did you think you were
going to do something about this?'

'Later. I can't see the small of my back, I'm not double-
jointed.'

She giggled. 'That's not what you said—'

'Enough!' It was bad enough being here like this, her

laughter echoing in his ears, her fingers on his skin. 'Be a bit professional, can't you?'

He felt her lips brush his spine. 'A minute ago you were complaining about my bedside manner.'

'Well, you're supposed to put your patients at ease, not attack them and then make a pass at them.'

She huffed a short breath. 'I resign, then. Consider me officially no longer your doctor and pass me the surgical tape, please. I'll just put some gauze on it and leave it open so they can wash it out properly later on.'

He chuckled. 'You can't resign. I'm sacking you.' He dropped the tape into her hand, and felt her fingers on his back again. 'Gross misconduct.'

'Watch it. You want misconduct, I'll give you misconduct.' She ran her fingers down his spine, making him shiver with pleasure. 'Hold it, don't turn around yet.'

He felt her thumb higher on his back and winced. He hadn't even felt that cut until now. She washed and dressed it, and tapped his shoulder. 'You can turn around now. And give me your shirt.'

He turned, and saw her eyes, bright with humour, scanning his body candidly. 'Cut it out.' He grinned at her, making no move to pull his shirt back on.

'A girl can look, can't she?'

'She can do whatever she likes.' He leaned in slightly, and she pulled him the rest of the way. The kiss was nothing to do with the memories of their nights together and everything to do with reassurance, a solemn promise that he would care for her and keep her from harm. For the time being, anyway.

She was the first to break the spell. Catching up his shirt, she held it up to the light, examining it carefully. 'I just want to make sure there's no glass in here.'

'Careful. Don't cut your fingers.' He couldn't keep his eyes off her.

'It's okay. Look, there's just a tiny bit there, can you get it out?'

Adam reached for the tweezers and disposed of the piece of glass, caught in the threads of his shirt. Taking it from her, he pulled it back over his head. 'I guess we'd better switch the light off. Conserve the battery.'

She caught his hand. 'Okay. Just keep hold of me, eh?'

'Don't want you running out on me in the dark.' He flipped the torch off and lay down next to her, his head resting on the soft folds of the blanket. 'Now that the lights are out, do you want a story?'

'Mmm. That would be nice.'

'Okay. Are you sitting comfortably?'

'Yes.'

'Then I'll begin. Once upon a time, in a land far away, where hummingbirds will feed from your hand...' The sound of bumps and falling debris reached his ears, but Adam didn't stop. He told her stories about his work, his patients, the communities he'd visited. The smile in her voice when she commented kept him talking, trying to weave a spell that would banish her fears and some of her pain.

'So what happened to the goat?'

'Oh, the goat was all right. Goats are very resilient creatures, they take most things in their stride.'

'And the bride's mother?'

He shrugged, one hand finding her cheek so that he could brush the backs of his fingers against it. 'She got over it. The groom's uncle promised to rebuild her veranda and when we went back the following year, everyone had forgotten about it. I helped deliver the couple's first child.'

'That's nice. So everything worked out, then?' She

turned her head so that her lips came into brief contact with his fingers.

'Yeah. Everything worked out.' They lay in silence for a while, holding hands, until a buzz from his pocket roused Adam.

It was Parker, and he had good news. Adam snapped his phone closed and reached for the torch. 'Cover your eyes a moment, I'm just going to switch the light back on. They're almost through.'

He was blinded for a moment and then began to make out her face, shining with happiness. 'Go and see, Adam.'

'No. Parker said we should wait here. He doesn't want to worry that we're on the other side when they push through the last of the rubble.' He sat up, stretching his limbs. 'Just be patient. It won't be much longer.'

It seemed to be longer than the time they'd spent in the darkness, talking together, but in reality it was just a few minutes. The sound of footsteps echoed along the corridor, and two grimy, burly figures appeared in the doorway.

'Hi, guys.' Jenna propped herself up on one elbow and gave them a smile of pure joy. 'Good to see you.'

It wasn't that she was sorry to be rescued, but Jenna was still aware of having lost something. Those few hours, when the only person she'd had in the world had been Adam. And she had been the only one in his world. It was almost an intrusion when two of the fire crew appeared in the doorway.

Adam jumped to his feet, striding over to them and shaking their hands. There was a brief exchange of words over the shortwave radio, and then the two came to squat down next to Jenna.

'Comfortable, then?' One of them enquired cheerily.

'Yes, thanks. Thought I'd sit it out while you did all the work.' Jenna joked off the pain in her leg.

'Wise lady.' The fireman was looking at her leg. 'Now, we just need to decide how best to get you out of here.' He looked up at Adam. 'A stretcher's out of the question, and it'll take a while to get things clear enough to get a chair down here. I think our best bet is to carry her.'

Adam nodded. Jenna knew that time was everything. More time, more risk, to both her and Adam and the fire crew. 'Yes, let's get out of here, guys.'

She felt for Adam's hand. She wanted him to take her out of here but she couldn't ask. He was tired and hurt, he would be better leaving it to one of the firemen.

'I'll take her.' There was no mistaking the possessiveness in his voice.

A brief querying glance between the two firemen was quickly suppressed as she reached for Adam, winding her arms around his neck. He'd come down here to get her. It was his right to take her out, if he wanted to, and the fact that he did warmed her.

'Okay, mate. Fair enough.' The fireman backed off. He knew what Adam had done, too. 'Let's be quick about it, though.'

Adam slipped his arms under her back and legs. 'Okay, you know the next line, don't you?'

She grinned at him. 'This is going to hurt a little, but I'll be as quick as I can.'

'You've got it. Hang in there, honey, we're nearly there.'

The morphine was beginning to wear off a little, and her ankle hurt much more than a little when Adam lifted her. Jenna hung on to him, squeezing her eyes shut, trying not to cry as he carefully carried her through twists and turns and then climbed a staircase, following the firemen's quickly worded directions. She heard the noise of the street and felt the breeze on her face and opened her eyes.

Parker was there, grinning at her and motioning Adam towards the ambulance stretcher that stood ready. Adam had kept his promise. He'd said they'd get out together and they had. Tears started to well up again and she buried her head in the crook of his shoulder, hanging on to him as gentle hands laid her down on the stretcher.

'Hey, Jen. Trying us out to see what the ride's like?' It was Joel, with Andy by his side, grinning.

She tried to reply, make a joke back at him, but the words wouldn't come. Only tears, and she covered her face, ashamed at her sudden loss of control, there in front of everyone.

She felt Adam's hand on her shoulder, squeezing gently. 'Brave lady, this one. Took a fifteen-foot fall, a broken ankle and being shut away with me in the dark for a couple of hours without a single complaint.'

Parker laughed. 'Ted, do you hear that?' Jenna took her hands away from her face in time to see him gesture towards one of the crew. 'He tripped over a hose and broke his arm last year and bawled like a baby.'

A ripple of laughter surged around the men, and Adam produced a medical wipe from his pocket, handing it to her. Jenna blew her nose and managed a smile.

'Nice job.' Parker took her hand and gave it a shake. 'I heard about the two men who were taken to hospital and they're going to be okay. One of them was touch and go for a while, and the guy I spoke to at the hospital said that if you hadn't given him medical attention on site, he wouldn't have made it.'

At least they'd managed to achieve something by being there. Jenna only had the chance to squeeze Parker's hand

and mouth a silent 'Thank you' before she was on the move, being lifted into the ambulance.

Adam climbed in behind her as Joel secured the stretcher securely in place. 'You'll be staying a couple of minutes?'

'Yep. Just to get everything sorted. Are you coming with us?'

Adam nodded. 'Don't go without me.' He turned to Jenna. 'Something I have to do first.' He gestured back towards the fire crew, who were drifting away to form a group around the back of the fire truck. 'I'll be right back.'

'Go. Tell them thanks from me, too.'

'Of course.' Adam flashed her a grin as he ducked back out of the ambulance and hurried over to the group of men. Jenna saw him shake each man's hand, and the small group turned in her direction, their thumbs-up signals telling Jenna that Adam had done as she'd asked.

'Lie down, will you?' Joel was grinning at her. 'Just pretend you're the patient for a minute.'

'Wait.' Jenna batted him away and watched as Adam hurried back.

'Can you do anything with this one? We've got a struggler on our hands.' Joel turned to Adam.

'Nope.' Adam was grinning broadly. 'You might have to sedate her.'

Jenna lay back on the trolley. It was narrow but soft and comfortable and now that Adam was there there was no need to keep straining to sit up. Her whole body ached, and she began to wonder how many bruises she had. It felt like one very big one at the moment.

'Okay. Just relax.' Joel was in medic mode and she felt him clip the pulse monitor on to her finger. 'Has she had any pain relief?'

Adam leant over, unpinning the note that he'd written

and secured to the front of her jacket. 'Here. Time and dosage.' In case anything had happened to him, then they'd know immediately what drugs she'd had and when.

Joel nodded. 'Okay. Jen, how much pain have you got? One to ten.'

'Three and a bit.'

'Yeah, looks like a big bit. You're very pale. Do you want something more?'

'Yes. Thanks.' She relaxed back into the small pillow and closed her eyes. She let them get on with it, feeling the cool swab on her arm and the prick of a needle. Adam's fingers brushed hers and then closed firmly around them. Good. Everything was good.

CHAPTER THIRTEEN

EACH bump in the road jarred Adam's aching limbs, but he didn't let go of her hand, even when it seemed that she was sleeping. He knew she wasn't. The way she gripped him, her fingers wound around his tightly, told him so.

She was safe. It had been the only thing he could think about in that basement. How to keep her safe. How to get her out of there. And he'd done it. Not without a great deal of help, but he'd been the one she had clung to and he hadn't let her down. Adam's limbs shook at the thought.

Joel tried to get him to submit to a cursory examination and backed off when Adam refused. He was obviously good at what he did and knew when to insist and when to leave it be. All Adam wanted to do was to stay with Jenna, keep the promise he'd made, the one that was his only reason for being at the moment.

She stirred as they lifted her down from the ambulance and he had to let go of her hand. 'Still here. We won't both fit through those doors together.'

'Hmm. Okay.' As soon as they were out of the ambulance and through the doors to A and E he caught up and took her hand in his again. Joel waved him over to a nearby chair and he shook his head, receiving a slight shrug in return.

'All right, what have we here, then?' Rob's voice penetrated his consciousness, and Adam breathed a sigh of relief. Jenna was going to be seen right away.

'Rob.' She opened her eyes and smiled up at him. 'Don't you have anything better to do?'

'Not at the moment. Thought I'd come and see what kind of dog's dinner Adam's managed to make of your ankle.' Rob grinned at Adam as he helped wheel the trolley over to a cubicle.

'I'm not jumping the queue.' Jenna's lips were pressed together.

'Quite right. You aren't. We've got a couple of minor cuts and someone who's been gummed by a toothless poodle out there. Do the math.' Rob grinned down at her. 'Okay, what have we got?' He turned to Adam. 'Want to sit down, old man?'

In other words get out of the way. Adam eased himself into the chair beside Jenna's trolley, one hand resting on the rail at the side. Anything to keep some kind of contact with her. He watched as Rob gingerly felt along Jenna's arms and legs and he jumped as she winced.

'Please…' His lips formed the words but they were no more than a whisper. How many times had he heard that from people as he had examined his patients? Please don't hurt her. He knew that Rob was doing what he had to do, but watching him do this was almost more than he could bear.

'Look.' Rob turned on him. 'You're filthy. I don't want you near my patient until you've cleaned up. Go and take a shower.' Rob felt in his pocket. 'Here are the keys to my locker.'

Rob was right. He was more than qualified to do whatever Jenna needed. He flipped his gaze to Jenna and she turned her beautiful blue eyes on him. 'Go on. I'll be here when you get back.'

* * *

When Adam returned to the cubicle, wearing a clean T-shirt from Rob's locker, she was propped up on the bed, watching as Rob examined her ankle. Her face was pale, but she managed a smile when she saw him.

'Hey, there. Okay?'

'That's my line, isn't it?'

'Oh, and can't a girl enquire? Don't hog it all to yourself.'

Adam grinned at the flash of defiant humour. Jenna winced as Rob gently probed her ankle and Adam almost turned on him in rage. He knew Rob was only doing his job, but did he have to hurt her?

He forced himself to perch on the edge of the seat by the bed and reached for her hand. If that was the role he was consigned to then he'd better get on with it. Someone had cleaned her hands and face, but she still had a smudge of grime over her eyebrow.

'They've missed a bit.' He took a wipe from the box by the bed and gestured towards her brow. 'Close your eyes.'

He'd said that last night, and the brief twist of her mouth before she obeyed him told Adam that she remembered it, too. Carefully, he cleaned the dirt from her face, brushing her hair back from her forehead.

'Can I have something to drink?' She was asking him, not Rob, but Adam gritted his teeth and turned towards Rob.

'Yeah, just some water.' Rob resumed his inspection of Jenna's leg and Adam hurried to fetch some water from the cooler.

She sipped the water slowly, nestling in the crook of his arm as he supported her back. Rob turned, seemingly satisfied with his examination.

'Right, Jenna. It appears that through a miracle of modern guesswork Adam has correctly diagnosed the fact that you have a broken ankle and a number of rather nasty bruises.' He pointed to her eye. 'Looks as if you'll have a shiner in the morning.'

She grinned at him. 'Yeah, I reckoned as much. Thanks, Rob.'

'My pleasure.' Rob rounded on Adam. 'Next...'

Jenna giggled. 'I sneaked on you, Adam. Better show him those cuts.'

'They're okay.'

Rob rolled his eyes. 'So which speech do you want? The one about doctors thinking that they're different from every other mortal on the planet because they don't need medical treatment, or the one about untended cuts? I'll set Brenda on you if you're not careful and she's been taking tae kwon do classes.'

'She's quite good at it. You'll be flat on your face in an arm lock before you know what's hit you.' Jenna's eyes were twinkling and a little of the colour had returned to her face. 'She's not on duty today, though, is she, Rob?'

'On her way in. I called her just before you two arrived.' Rob grimaced at Adam. 'So which is it, then? My healing hands or a well-placed smack on the jaw from Brenda?'

Adam sat down quickly on the stool that Rob had indicated, keeping his eyes on Jenna. 'Have you ordered the X-rays yet? What about pain relief?'

Adam could feel Rob probing his back, and he suddenly ripped off the dressing that Adam had hastily applied after he'd got out of the shower. 'Never thought of that. Might not be a bad idea. What do you say, Jen?'

'Dunno.' Jenna's gaze was on him, a little bleary, but right now her eyes were the most beautiful things in the world. She patted his hand reassuringly. 'It's all done. They'll be along in a minute to take us over there.'

'I'll have a snap of your ribs while they're at it.' Rob's voice brooked no argument. 'Breathe.'

Adam complied, wincing when he felt Rob's fingers around his rib cage. 'Yeah. Sorry, mate.'

Rob snorted. 'Don't sweat it. You should have seen me when Ellie and Daisy were born.'

'We were contemplating giving the midwife a break and sedating him.' Jenna was smiling, holding his hand. Making jokes. She was okay. 'Doctors are always the worst. We know all the things that can happen.' She gave a little nod to emphasise the point.

All the things that could have happened. If he hadn't been able to move Jenna out of the way of the crushing debris falling towards her through that hole in the floor. If she'd been badly hurt when she'd fallen. If she'd died, like Elena. Adam took a deep breath. It hadn't happened, and that was all there was to it.

'Hey.' She was tapping her finger on his hand, the way she did when the rage took him. It was okay. She didn't need to. He'd been angry, fearful, all those things, but that was different. Normal and under control. The blind rage that paralysed him and took away his very being when it hit had not surfaced.

'It's okay.' He nodded to her, a silent acknowledgement that he was still there. Still caught in her enchanting blue eyes.

'Keep still, will you?' Rob seemed to be pretty much done with him now. 'I'll tape those cuts, but they look fine. How Jenna managed to get all the glass out by torchlight and with a broken ankle and a dose of morphine in her system I'll never know.'

'She's good.' Adam saw the warmth bloom in her eyes at his words.

'Few of us have a right to be that good.' Rob was tap-ing and dressing the wound and when he'd finished, he slapped Adam on the shoulder. 'Done.'

Adam turned and gave him a nod. 'Cheers. Thanks for everything, Rob.'

'No problem.' Rob folded his arms, looking back and forth between Adam and Jenna. He was obviously still in professional mode. 'I'm thinking of discharging you both, only I don't want Jenna on her own tonight. She needs someone to keep an eye on her.'

'That's okay. I'll be there.' Adam tried to make it sound as if he was volunteering for the duty on medical grounds, and saw Jenna nodding quietly out of the corner of his eye.

'Fair enough. Assuming that the X-rays don't show up anything unexpected, we'll put a temporary cast on Jen's leg and then you can both go.' A tone sounded from Rob's pocket and he stripped off his surgical gloves and pulled his phone out. 'That's Brenda. She's here now and she's checked on the wait for the X-rays and it'll be another half-hour.'

'That's okay. May I have some more water, please?' Jenna looked at Rob imploringly and he nodded.

'Sure. Brenda's got you some fresh clothes and I think she's planning on helping you clean up a bit.' Jenna's look of relief was enough to make Adam want to kiss Brenda. On the cheek.

'That would be lovely.' A tear ran down her cheek and Adam resisted the urge to wipe it away. Kiss her as he did so.

Rob's gaze held his for just one second too long. Long enough to tell Adam that he knew full well what the score was and that for the sake of appearances he had to leave now. 'Good. In that case we'll make ourselves scarce while Brenda sorts you out.' He grinned at Adam. 'Come on. I'll buy you a cup of coffee.'

* * *

Jenna relaxed back into the sofa cushions. It was so good to be home, not being rattled around on a trolley or bumped along in Brenda's car. Home. Safe. There was one more thing she wanted and he was hovering in the doorway to the sitting room.

'Would you like some tea? Or something to eat?'

She shook her head. 'No, thanks. Why don't you come and sit down?'

He grinned. 'Okay. Whatever you want.'

What she really wanted was a good long soak in a hot bath. It wasn't a good idea as the heat would only make her ankle swell even more, and she was meant to be trying to bring the swelling down. And it was definitely out of the question with Adam there. He might have seen—kissed—every part of her body already, but she didn't want him to see the bruises. 'I think I just want to sit here for a while.'

He walked over and sat down next to her. 'You'll be stiff tomorrow.'

'I'm stiff already. It doesn't matter, it's nothing.'

He hesitated. 'I can help with that.'

Jenna chuckled. 'Yes, I know, but I'm not sure that I'm up to that right now.' Worse luck.

His whole body tensed. 'I meant… Sorry, I wasn't…'

'It's okay.' She laid her hand on his and he almost flinched. 'I know you didn't. So what did you mean?'

'I learned from a village midwife that you don't always need drugs for pain.' He grinned. 'Although they do help. Do you want to let me try a little therapeutic massage?'

'That sounds fantastic.'

He'd carried her into the bedroom and laid her on the bed, making sure she was comfortable. He started with the palms of her hands, working up her arms and then sitting her up, letting her rest her body against his, while he worked on her shoulders and back.

His fingers were sure and steady. He'd done this before with the intent to arouse, but now his whole purpose was to calm her screaming muscles. And Adam always seemed to get exactly the reaction he wanted from her body.

'Better now?' He had managed to massage her back and legs without removing her T-shirt and sweat pants, and now he'd covered her with a throw.

'Much. Tell the midwife thanks. She does good massage.'

He chuckled. 'Okay, well, just lie still for a little while and keep warm. It'll help you relax and heal.'

'Mmm. Think I will. You go and…do something…' The sentence trailed into drowsy relaxation.

When her eyes flickered open again, it was almost dark. Adam had switched a lamp on in the corner of the room, and he was sprawled in the armchair next to it. Jenna closed her eyes again. Everything was fine.

'I saw you.' His voice was relaxed, the smile running through it like a thread of gold. 'Hungry?'

Jenna opened her eyes again. 'I could eat a horse.'

He chuckled. 'Good. What do you fancy? An omelette?'

'Sounds wonderful. Thanks.' She caught his hand as he went to turn, pulling him back. 'Adam?'

'Yes. You okay, Jen?'

'I just want to know that you're okay. Are you?' He grinned and went to laugh the question off, and Jenna tugged at his hand. 'Really okay, Adam?'

He sat down next to her on the bed. 'Yes. I am. Rob made sure of that, didn't he? After you set him on me.' He twitched at the bottom of his T-shirt. 'You want to check…?'

'That's not what I mean.'

His brow furrowed. 'No, I guess it's not, is it?' He took

her hand between his and clasped it on his lap. 'I…I think we made it through.'

'We did. We did the best we could for those two men. And afterwards…' She felt tears prick at the corners of her eyes. That happened every time she thought about the terror of suddenly falling into a void. 'I know what you did, Adam. You risked your own life to come after me, and you never left me. I might not have made it if you hadn't moved me away from that pile of stuff that was about to come down on my head.'

She was trembling, two large tears rolling down her cheeks. 'Shh, honey. It's okay.' His hand brushed her cheek, its touch soothing. 'Anyone would have—'

'No, they wouldn't. You might not see that you had a choice, but that's because you're wired that way. If I'd been down there alone, I don't know whether I'd have made it out. You were the one who brought me out, Adam.'

The light that ignited in his eyes told Jenna how much that meant to him. 'Hey…' He wiped at her cheek with his thumb. 'Don't cry, Jen. Please.' He reached for a tissue from the box at the side of the bed and handed it to her. 'Actually, perhaps you should. You've been such a trouper so far. You might like to relax your guard a little now it's all over.'

'And it's good to cry, eh?' Jenna mustered a grin.

''Course it is. It ought to be mandatory after a day like today.' Suddenly he was awkward again. The man whose strength had carried her through reduced to hopeless incompetence in the face of a few tears.

'I don't much feel like it anymore. Maybe later. You can join me if you want.'

Adam laughed. 'Don't start without me. In the meantime, I'll go and get us something to eat.' He got to his feet, hesitating at the doorway, not seeming to want to take the risk of turning to look at her. 'Thanks, Jen. For trusting me.'

Then he was gone.

By the time Jenna made it through to the kitchen, he had laid a place for her at the table. Knife, fork, napkin and a rose from the climber that wound its way up the trellis behind the fire-escape steps.

'Smells good.' She made her way carefully over to the cooker and craned to see the contents of the pan in front of him.

'Go and sit down. Be ready in a minute.' He nudged her gently away. 'Go on. This is the crucial moment and I need to concentrate.'

'Oh. Don't I get to see it, then?'

'No. A guy has to retain some secrets.' Jenna made her way back to the kitchen table and he chuckled, never taking his eyes from the pan. 'You sound like the crocodile in *Peter Pan*.'

'The crocodile ticks. And it's not me squeaking, it's the crutches.'

'All the same, you won't be creeping up on anyone any time soon.' Adam bent and opened the oven, pulling out a pan and tumbling some chips onto the two plates he had waiting on the counter. Then he divided the omelette, sliding half onto each plate, and carried the plates to the table.

'Eat. Before it gets cold.'

She didn't need to be told. They ate in silence, Jenna almost wolfing her food she was so hungry now. When she'd cleared her plate, he picked it up, putting it into the sink and switching the kettle on for tea.

'Jen, I've been thinking.' He was clearly considering his words carefully and she nodded him on. 'Don't say yes or

no now, but think about it. I can delay going back to the
States for a few weeks. Until you're feeling better.'

She stared at him. 'But you're needed there.'

'Nothing I can't postpone for a couple of weeks.'

Jenna couldn't believe that she was even considering
saying no. 'I'm not sure that's such a good idea, Adam.'

'Will you think about it? You might feel different tomorrow.'

She might well feel differently tomorrow, but that wasn't
going to change the way things were. They'd been through
this before, and nothing was different.

'No, Adam. I think that we should stick to the plan.
Please don't talk about this any more.' She was going to
cry if he did.

Concern flashed in his eyes. 'No. I'm sorry. It's been
a tough day for both of us.' He summoned up a grin from
somewhere and got to his feet. 'Want a cup of tea?'

'Yes, thanks.' She caught his arm. 'Why don't we go
and make ourselves comfortable in the sitting room and
you can show me the notes that your colleague in America
sent you?'

'Eh?' He sat back down again, opposite her.

'I want to know what you'll be doing there.' If she was
going to lose him, it would be good to know that there was
some purpose to it other than their mutual unwillingness
to even try for something more than they already had. And
to remind him of that purpose, too.

His eyes searched her face. Then understanding flooded
into them, and he nodded. 'I have pictures as well. You
want to see?'

'Yes. That would be even better.' Knowing their faces,
knowing their names. How could she keep him here a moment longer than planned if she could see their faces?

'I'll make the tea then go and get my laptop.'

CHAPTER FOURTEEN

'So the freezer is all stocked up.'

'Adam, there's enough in there to feed an army for a month. And if I need anything I can just order it on the internet and get it delivered.'

'Good. And where's that call button?'

'In the drawer. I don't need it when you're here, do I?'

'Yes, but you should get used to carrying it around. It's just for a few weeks, until you're a little steadier on your feet.'

'I'll carry it around.' Jenna pulled herself off the sofa and swung herself over to the dresser, opening the drawer and taking out the emergency call button that Adam had obtained. 'Honestly, I feel as if I'm eighty-five, wearing this thing. If I need anything I've always got my mobile.'

'Your mobile's where?'

'Over there.'

'Exactly. You're on your own in the house and you're unsteady on your feet. You could fall and be lying here as dead as a doornail for days before anyone found you.'

'No, I couldn't. Not with about a hundred people calling me every day. Anyway, if I were dead I wouldn't be able to press the button, would I?'

'Just work with me here, Jen.'

'Okay. I have my button. It's around my neck.' Jenna dropped the button down the front of her top. 'Happy now?'

He rolled his eyes. 'You have no idea.'

Somehow they were getting through this. By an almost superhuman effort they had managed to neither refer to nor to try and put off the parting that was getting closer by the hour. And now it was measured in minutes, rather than hours.

Adam was standing by the window, watching for something. Jenna knew what that something was. It was a car. The one that Rob drove, which would take him off to the airport and away from her.

He was wasting time. Precious minutes when something that might make sense of all of this might have been said. Something that would make them both feel better about this parting.

There was no point in thinking that way. If they hadn't come up with anything before now, an extra couple of minutes wasn't going to make any difference. Nothing was going to make this any better. It was just a matter of facing up to it and getting through it without making a fool of herself. 'What time's your flight?'

'Eight-thirty. There's plenty of time.'

'Are you all packed?'

'Pretty much.'

'Why don't you go and finish off now? Before Rob comes.' Perhaps it would be better for him to be downstairs when Rob arrived so she didn't have to see him wrenched away from her.

He turned and looked at her, reproach in his face, as if she had stolen his most prized possession. These last few moments alone. 'There's time.' He walked over to the sofa, bending down on his heels in front of her. 'There's something I wanted to say, Jenna.'

Jenna suddenly didn't want to hear it. She was coping with this—just—but if he managed to put all the things that she saw in his tawny eyes into words, she'd be devastated. 'Me, too. But maybe it's better left unsaid.'

He seemed to be debating the point with himself. 'You think so?'

'I think we know, don't we?'

'Yeah.' He dropped his gaze from hers and rose quickly. At that moment the doorbell sounded. A small cry that might have been exasperation and might have been anguish escaped his lips and he turned without a word to go and answer the door.

There was the sound of voices on the stairs and the commotion told Jenna that Rob had brought the children with him as well as Cassie. She wiped away her tears and summoned up a smile.

Ellie was first to appear, running into the sitting room ahead of the adults and flinging herself on the sofa next to Jenna. 'Dad says I mustn't touch you because you're hurt.' The child's eyes were on the cast on her foot.

'Oh, not so hurt I can't give you a hug. Hugs from you always make me feel better.' Jenna reached for Ellie and took her in her arms. The small body next to hers made her want to cry again and she bit her lip, hard.

'What did I say, Ellie?' Rob's voice boomed from the doorway.

'It's all right, Dad, I'm making Jenna feel better.' Ellie squeezed tight, as if she had the power to chase all of Jenna's hurts away.

'Well, just be a bit gentle, please.' Rob crossed the room and bent to brush a kiss on Jenna's cheek then reached for his phone, flipping it open and listening into the earpiece. 'Apparently you're in some distress.'

'What?' What had Adam been saying to him?

Rob shrugged and snapped his phone shut. 'I just got a recorded message from that emergency button of yours.'

'Oh.' Jenna shifted Ellie from her lap and found the button. 'Sorry. Must have set it off when I gave Ellie a hug.' She shot Adam an apologetic look. 'I suppose it'll be ringing everyone else on the list now.'

'No, that's okay. I accepted the message so it'll stop now. It only goes on to call the other numbers if I don't press three to say I've got the call and that I'm dealing with it.'

'So you'll know every time she hugs someone.' Adam's tone was jocular, but there was a trace of harshness there, too.

'Looks like it.' Rob grinned. 'Just make sure to take it off if you go on any hot dates.'

Cassie appeared in the doorway, shooting Rob a look that would have stopped a charging rhinoceros in its tracks. 'I don't think there's any danger of that.' She slipped her hand into the crook of Adam's arm and he looked down at her, the look of hurt anger slipping from his face. Jenna sent her a silent thank-you.

'Come on, now, Adam, give a pregnant woman your arm over to the sofa.' Cassie was blooming, heavily pregnant and, as always, the peacemaker who soothed ruffled feathers without even trying. 'I was wondering whether I might stay here with you, Jen, put my feet up for a while. We were going to take the children to see the planes at the airport, but it's too hot for me today.'

Jenna grinned. She was obviously part of Cassie's master plan. 'Yes, of course. It'll be nice to have some company.'

'Right, then.' Rob clapped his hands together, obviously eager to get going. 'Come along, mate, you never know what the traffic's going to be like.'

Cassie and Jenna sat side by side in the suddenly quiet house. Both had their feet propped up in front of them, and Jenna stared at the four sets of bare toes, trying not to cry.

Cassie blew her nose, loudly. 'I hate goodbyes.' She handed Jenna a handkerchief from the seemingly inexhaustible supply in her handbag.

If Cassie could cry, then Jenna could venture a few tears. It was almost a relief to allow herself to wipe her eyes and blow her nose. 'Me, too.'

'That's why I can never look.'

Cassie was a good friend. She had told Adam that she wouldn't watch him leave, waited for him to bend for a goodbye kiss and then resolutely clapped her hand over her eyes. When he'd brushed his lips across Jenna's cheek, he'd whispered to her to do the same. 'Close your eyes.' She'd felt Cassie's arm around her as the sounds of his footsteps had faded along the hallway and her front door had closed quietly behind him.

'Don't look back, eh?'

Cassie shrugged. 'You could put it that way. Or you could say that you'll look forward to the next time you see someone.'

There wasn't going to be a next time. She'd had her time with Adam and Jenna knew that he wouldn't be back. 'I prefer "don't look back".'

Jenna pressed her lips together. A cool calm settled around her heart, and she recognised the feeling. It was the same calm that had consumed her when Laura had died, when it had become clear that her parents weren't coming back, and when Joe had left. The calm that told her she *would* survive, come what may.

'Fancy a cup of tea?' Cassie dropped her feet down onto the floor.

'Stay there. I'll make it.' Jenna slid to the edge of the sofa and got to her feet. 'I'm getting a bit tired of being looked after.'

They sipped their tea and talked a little and then watched a film together, an old weepie. Cassie cried, and Jenna stared impassively at the screen. Who cared? It didn't really matter if two people met, fell in love and then had to part. There were more important things in life.

'Aren't you due soon?' Cassie had been trying to get comfortable on the sofa and had obviously failed miserably.

'Another two weeks. Ellie and Daisy were both late, so I reckon it'll probably be three.'

'Perhaps it'll be sooner. They get earlier each time.'

Cassie rolled her eyes. 'Well, I hope so. I've got…' She tailed off, clapping her hand over her mouth. 'Jenna, I'm sorry.'

'What's the matter, Cass?' Something in her friend's tone told her that there was something.

'My water's just broke.' Cassie moaned in embarrassment. 'Oh, dear, Jen, your sofa.'

Jenna was on her feet more quickly than she'd thought possible. 'Forget the sofa. Are you sure?'

'Oh, yes.' Cassie's hand went to her side and she gasped for breath. 'Jen, I'm so sorry.'

'Hey, there.' She gave Cassie a bright smile. 'Just concentrate on the baby. Stay there for a moment and I'll get you a towel.'

Jenna pulled some clean towels from the cupboard and

fetched her stethoscope from the bottom of the wardrobe. When she got back, Cassie was trying to stand.

'All right, just sit back here.' She got Cassie comfortable and reached for her stethoscope, which had fallen onto the floor. 'Contractions?'

'Yes.' Cassie caught her breath again. 'I thought it was just backache at first. Then I thought it was a Higgs-Boson.'

'Braxton-Hicks. How long for?'

'Couple of hours. Maybe longer. They're getting stronger, Jen.' Cassie's eyes were wide with panic.

'Okay, okay. No problem. I've delivered babies before and even if it comes now, everything's going to be all right. Just relax.' Now was not the time for the truth. Jenna had seen a baby being delivered. She knew what was supposed to happen. She propped a cushion behind Cassie's head and started to pray.

'Thank goodness.' Cassie's hand found hers and gripped tight. 'Rob hasn't, you know.'

'Well, just as well this happened when you were with me. Now, do you have your prenatal stuff?'

'In my handbag. Listen, don't go pressing that emergency button of yours, Rob's going to have kittens. And he's got the kids with him in the car.'

'It's okay. This is not an emergency, you're having a baby. We've both done this before.' Jenna grinned encouragingly and Cassie smiled back. 'Good. Just hold on there and let me call the hospital.' Jenna found the number in Cassie's handbag and hobbled over to the phone.

CHAPTER FIFTEEN

JENNA held the baby in her arms, Rob's arm steadying her at the side of the font. One month old. She made her promises, solemnly and carefully. To keep James from harm. To care for him if there was ever a time when his parents couldn't. She knew just how much of a responsibility that was, and she took it seriously. James would always have a home with her, any time he needed it.

Ignoring the tall figure standing on the other side of the font, she concentrated on the words of the christening ceremony. Rob took the baby from her and he began to whimper fretfully.

'They say it's good luck if the baby cries.' Adam caught up with her as she planted her crutches on the stone steps leading out of the church. 'Want a hand?' He held out his arm towards her.

Jenna ignored it and made it down the steps on her own. 'So you made it back? Rob and Cassie didn't think you would.' Outside in the sunlight he looked almost dazzling. He wore a lightweight off-white suit with a crisp white shirt, open at the neck, which contrasted with his tan. His long, sun-bleached hair was slicked back, making him look even more striking. The last month had obviously been kind to him. Kinder than it had to her.

'Only just. I'm straight off the plane. My bags are in Rob's car. I hear you delivered our new godchild.'

Our child. The two words suddenly leapt out of the sentence and collided with each other. Jenna swallowed hard. 'Well, I did the sitting-down bits. The paramedic arrived just in time and did the running around. Cassie did all the work.'

'I heard you did a fantastic job.' His eyes searched her face and Jenna tried hard not to flinch under the scrutiny. 'I pulled out all the stops to get here, Jen. This is important.'

'Yes.' She tore herself away from his gaze. 'I've just seen my lift. I'll see you back at the house.' Jenna hobbled away from him, aware that he was following her retreat with his eyes, but she was determined not to turn around.

Jenna had offered her garden for the christening party, and Rob and Cassie had accepted, descending on her with an army of helpers who insisted that she didn't lift a finger. Which was just as well, because it was taking all her time and energy to avoid Adam.

He almost caught her in the garden by the drinks table, but she gave him the slip and found Cassie in her bedroom, feeding the baby. Pleading tiredness, she stayed upstairs while Cassie went back down so that James could be passed around the guests one final time.

Okay, so it was rude. But Cassie would smooth things over, she always did. And Jenna couldn't bear to go downstairs, say hello to Adam, hear about all the great things he'd been doing in the last month, and then watch him go again. Finally, the sound of crockery being washed and stacked in the empty downstairs flat subsided, and Cassie walked into Jenna's bedroom, not bothering to knock, and sat down on the bed.

'You can come out now.'

Was she that transparent? 'Sorry, Cass. I just didn't want…'

'I know. It's okay, everyone understood. You were tired and needed to lie down.' Cassie grinned at her.

'You're a star, you know that?'

'I do my best. And you're the one who's the star, letting us have the run of your place for the party. I don't think everyone would have fitted in our garden.'

'It's a pleasure. Glad to help, you know that.'

'Thanks.' Cassie leaned forward and kissed her cheek. 'Well, Rob's stacking the kids away in the car, so we'll be off. Anything we can do for you before we go?'

'No, I'm fine. Go home and put your feet up.' The silence in the house pressed down on her like a heavy load. A heavy load that wasn't going to be lifted any time soon.

'Still missing him?' Cassie didn't move.

'No. Well, maybe a bit.'

'You should talk to him.'

Jenna shrugged. 'There isn't much point, is there? Look at him, Cass. He looks…' He looked like a new man. Adam still, but without the cares that had dogged him so stubbornly. 'He'll be going back soon.'

'Okay.' Cassie gave up surprisingly easily. Maybe she was tired, too. It had been a long day. 'Rob'll be round tomorrow to pick you up for lunch.'

That silence again. Cassie's footsteps had echoed down the stairs and Jenna had heard the front door close. She took a deep breath. Don't mope. Get up, put your happy face on, even though there's no one here to see it.

She drew back the curtains and smoothed her hands over her dress, looking at herself in the mirror. She liked this dress. White, flowing, with pale embroidery all over the bodice. The thought that she was glad that she'd been wearing something nice when Adam saw her filtered through her defences, and she slammed it back.

Suddenly she couldn't bear to wear the dress anymore. She slipped out of it, almost tearing it as she hopped on one foot and rolled backwards onto the bed. Slipping into the sweat pants that she'd already decided to burn the minute she got rid of this cast, a T-shirt and a cardigan, she made her way out onto the balcony.

Looking down, she saw a figure sitting on the fire-escape steps, his long tawny hair bright in the evening sun. His elbows were resting on his knees, and he was obviously waiting for someone. And that someone could only be her.

'Adam.' She couldn't bring herself to say anything else. She wanted to turn, go back into the house, slam the balcony door closed and wait till he went away. But she couldn't.

He looked up, his direct gaze just as unsettling as it had ever been. When he caught sight of her, he smiled. 'Jen.'

'What are you doing here? I thought that Cass and Rob had left.'

'They have. I didn't go with them.' He stood up, his eyes never leaving her. 'I came here to talk to you.'

She shook her head. 'You came for James's christening.' She didn't want to hear any lies from him. He'd never lied to her before and now was no time to start.

'I was coming anyway. For you.'

Jenna's knees wobbled and she hung on to her crutches. 'Don't say that, Adam.'

He shrugged. 'Okay. But it's the truth.' He was still looking up at her. 'Can I talk to you, Jen? Please.'

'I'll come down.' Jenna grasped the handrail of the balcony firmly, hanging on tight while she walked down the steps. Even her good leg felt as if it couldn't bear her weight.

He ran up the steps towards her. 'Let me help you.'

'I'm okay, thanks.' The thought of his touch was the last straw, and she swayed dangerously, before strong hands fastened themselves around her waist.

'Here, you'll fall. Don't make me have to patch you up again.' He kept tight hold of her arm, guiding her down until she was on the patio. Jenna sank down onto the steps.

'Thank you. Thank you for coming down. For hearing what I've got to say.'

She forced a smile. 'I haven't heard it yet. Anyway, if I hadn't, you'd have still been there tomorrow morning, wouldn't you?' She knew him well enough for that.

'And the day after. May I sit with you?'

Those silly little things that he had used to do so naturally, and that he was asking her permission to do now. Touching her, sitting next to her. It was as if everything that they had once had was now lost. Something twisted, deep down in her stomach. This was worse than losing him the first time.

'Of course.'

He sat next to her, one arm on the step behind her, his body not touching hers. 'Jen, I won't take much of your time. Just a few minutes, and then I'll go.'

'That's fine, Adam. Take as much time as you want.' Yet another lie. Since when had so many lies stood between them?

He took a moment, as if he were flipping through a set of mental notes, reminding himself where he wanted to begin. 'It ripped my heart out to leave you, Jen. I did it because I thought it was the right thing to do. I couldn't see past my own fears and I knew that I couldn't give you what you needed.' Jenna opened her mouth to speak, but he held up his hand. 'Hear me out. Please.'

The anguish in his voice stopped her short. 'Okay. Go on.'

'When I went back to Florida, I did everything I could to try and remember, hanging on to the hope that I might still be someone who could care for you. I went to a hypnotherapist, pulled the medical and crime reports from that day and studied every word of them.'

'And you know now what happened?' He must do. There was nothing else that could explain the way he stood taller now, as if a heavy load had been lifted from his shoulders.

'No. I realised that even though I want to know what happened, it wouldn't change anything. I'd still be second-guessing myself, indulging in what-ifs. But time and time again I kept coming back to one thing. That I trust and respect you. And that if you could find it in your heart to trust me, the way you did in that basement, I'd better start living up to that.'

Trust. Respect. Two very fine words. Jenna swallowed down her disappointment. 'That's good, Adam. It's great.'

He seemed to sense her lack of enthusiasm. 'What I'm trying to say to you, Jen, is that I can change. I have changed. Not by delving around in the past, looking for things that might not be there. But by loving you. Being loved by you, and wanting to be the man who deserves that love.'

'No.' The word whispered in her throat. She could hardly comprehend, let alone believe, what he was saying to her.

'Yes, Jen.' He took hold of her hand and hung on to it possessively. 'I know that I abandoned you. And after everything that's happened, that was the worst thing I could have done to you. But I do love you. I can't offer you my past, but everything that I am now, everything I will be is yours. And I might not have any right to ask this, but I want you to forgive me.'

She pulled her hand away from his. 'No.' Jenna could

feel the tears rising in her throat. 'No, you can't mean that.' She didn't know what to do with this sudden confession of his. Didn't know how to respond, when no one else had said anything like that to her before.

'I mean it.' He reached into the open neck of his shirt and pulled out a chain, which had something dangling from it. 'I know that you probably can't trust me now, but I want to show you something.'

Jenna focussed through her tears. It was a ring. Sparkling in the evening sunlight.

'This is yours, Jen, whenever you want to take it. Until then, I'll keep it safe for you as a sign of my intentions.'

She reached out and touched it. It was beautiful. Its fire seemed to burn her fingers, and she snatched them away. 'I…I don't know what to say, Adam. This is…unexpected.'

'I know. I'm not asking for your answer now.' His lips twisted in regret. 'In fact, I don't want to hear your answer yet. I'll warn you in advance that I'm aiming for a *yes* and nothing much else is going to do.'

She grinned at him. It was one of the things she loved about Adam. So charming, but underneath it all he was as solid as a rock. 'What's that engraved on the inside?' He'd gone to put the ring away, sliding it back inside his shirt, but she wanted to look at it a while longer. Fix it in her mind, so she could believe.

His face lit up. He knew they'd taken that first step. He held the ring steady so she could see properly. 'It says *"True North"*. You see the diamond?'

It was hardly possible to miss it. It wasn't exactly small. 'Yes.' Jenna stared at the ring.

'Well, I looked at hundreds of rings, trying to decide which one was good enough. Then I saw this one, and it reminded me of something, back at the observatory. The Pole Star. The one star that's guided men for centuries, helped them find their way. You're my true north, Jen, my only direction from now on.'

A tear rolled down her cheek. 'You'll always find your way back, wherever you are.' He'd come a long way in the last month. But maybe he hadn't travelled quite as far as she had hoped.

'No.' He shook his head. 'I never want to leave you.'

'But your work?' That was always going to come between them. Always going to take him away.

'That's important to me. But there are lots of ways that I can do what I do, and travelling's just one of them. I can stay in Florida, or here, and specialise in major cases.' He hesitated and took a breath. 'Or, if you want to, you can travel with me.'

She could see how hard that was for him to say. But it was the only thing left that she still wanted from him. 'You mean…go with you…to South America?'

'Wherever the work takes us, if that's what you want. I can't tell you that I'll never be concerned for your safety, or that I won't do everything I can to protect you, but I won't clip your wings.' He raised a trembling hand to her cheek, brushing away her tears.

'It's easy to say, Adam.' She couldn't believe he meant it. Didn't dare.

'I know. That's what I mean about true north. Any time I need reminding of the right course to take, I'll know where to go.' His lips curved in a smile. 'To someone who's more than capable of telling me I'm an idiot and giving me a good shake.'

She nudged his shoulder with hers. 'You're an idiot.'

'See?' He raised trembling fingers to her cheek, tilting her face towards his. 'I won't let you down, Jen.'

'I know. I need… This is all so sudden, Adam. I need to slow down.'

'Take your time, honey, I'll wait.'

It was his final, precious gift. He knew that she needed a little time, and he wasn't going to push her until she'd come around to the idea that there was someone in this world who would never leave her. That *he* would never leave her.

'Want to come inside? You can wait there, if you like.'

They were in Cornwall. Just for a few days, before Jenna was due to go back to the hospital to have X-rays and to get rid of the cast on her leg. The last week had been magical. Adam had never left her side. He had repeated his promises to her, as many times as she had wanted to hear them, and slowly the wounds that she had hidden for so long had begun to heal.

'Would you like to go down to the beach? There's a full moon tonight.' Their hotel was just a short walk from the sheltered, sandy cove that was almost deserted after the sun went down.

'Yes. I'd like that.' Maybe that would be the place.

He strolled with her along the gently sloping cliff path, and carried her down the steps and to the water's edge. The moon was large and low, tipping the dark waves with silver.

She hung on to his waist, not for support but just because she wanted him close. His arm around her shoulders, keeping her warm in the night breeze. This was the place.

'When you get that cast off your leg, and it's a bit stronger, I'll teach you how to surf, if you like.' His eyes were on the sea.

'I'd like that. Might come in handy, living in Florida.' The words sounded so right. So full of promise.

'What did you say?' He turned slowly, as if unable to believe his ears.

'That I'd have a go at surfing.'

'No, you didn't. You said it would come in handy, living in Florida.'

'Did I?' Jenna assumed a look of exaggerated innocence.

'I heard you quite plainly. Florida, you said. Living in Florida.'

'Hmm. Suppose I must have done, then.'

He twisted round, falling to one knee in front of her, holding on to her waist to steady her. 'Here.' He pulled her down onto his knee. 'I don't want you falling over, right in the middle of this.'

He had a point. Her legs were already shaking. Her fingers too as she reached around his neck and unclasped the chain, putting the ring into his palm. She'd seen it many times now, but it was still as beautiful as when she'd first laid eyes on it.

'Jenna, this isn't a request, I'm going to insist on it. You *are* going to marry me.'

She could feel his heartbeat. So strong. So true. And right now it was racing, as if it couldn't wait for everything the future held.

'Yes, Adam. I am going to marry you.'

He slipped the ring on to her finger and it looked just as she had imagined it would there. 'Where's the North Star?' She tilted her head towards the night sky.

'Right here, honey.' He kissed her, and suddenly the course ahead was clear. 'True North.'

* * * * *

MILLS & BOON

THE HEART OF ROMANCE

A ROMANCE FOR EVERY KIND OF READER

MODERN

Prepare to be swept off your feet by sophisticated, sexy and seductive heroes, in some of the world's most glamourous and romantic locations, where power and passion collide.
8 stories per month.

HISTORICAL

Escape with historical heroes from time gone by. Whether your passion is for wicked Regency Rakes, muscled Vikings or rugged Highlanders, awaken the romance of the past.
6 stories per month.

MEDICAL

Set your pulse racing with dedicated, delectable doctors in the high-pressure world of medicine, where emotions run high and passion, comfort and love are the best medicine.
6 stories per month.

Celebrate true love with tender stories of heartfelt romance, from the rush of falling in love to the joy a new baby can bring, and a focus on the emotional heart of a relationship.
8 stories per month.

Indulge in secrets and scandal, intense drama and plenty of sizzling hot action with powerful and passionate heroes who have it all: wealth, status, good looks…everything but the right woman.
6 stories per month.

HEROES

Experience all the excitement of a gripping thriller, with an intense romance at its heart. Resourceful, true-to-life women and strong, fearless men face danger and desire - a killer combination!
8 stories per month.

DARE

Sensual love stories featuring smart, sassy heroines you'd want as a best friend, and compelling intense heroes who are worthy of them.
4 stories per month.

To see which titles are coming soon, please visit

millsandboon.co.uk/nextmonth

JOIN US ON SOCIAL MEDIA!

Stay up to date with our latest releases, author news and gossip, special offers and discounts, and all the behind-the-scenes action from Mills & Boon...

 millsandboon

 millsandboonuk

 millsandboon

It might just be true love...

MILLS & BOON
MODERN
Power and Passion

Prepare to be swept off your feet by sophisticated, sexy and seductive heroes, in some of the world's most glamourous and romantic locations, where power and passion collide.

MILLS & BOON
True Love
Romance from the Heart

Celebrate true love with tender stories of
heartfelt romance, from the rush of falling
in love to the joy a new baby can bring,
and a focus on the emotional
heart of a relationship.